"SIR, [...] CHALLEN[...]

"Since you will not engage me in our bed, my lady, I suppose engaging me in the tiltyard is a reasonable alternative." Pagan held her gaze and slid his sword from its sheath with suggestive languor.

Deirdre swallowed hard. The man was incorrigible. Even on the field of battle, he attempted to seduce her. And God help her, 'twas having some effect. His eyes burned into hers with the smoldering promise of pleasure. And his mouth, set in that self-assured grin . . . she remembered too well how it felt upon hers, warm and sweet and demanding.

Nay! She wouldn't think of that. She had to fight him.

Moreover, this time she had to win.

Please turn to the back of this book for a preview of Sarah McKerrigan's next novel, *Captive Heart*.

Lady Danger

Sarah McKerrigan

WARNER
FOREVER

NEW YORK   BOSTON

Cover design by Diane Luger
Book design by Giorgetta Bell McRee

Warner Books

Time Warner Book Group
1271 Avenue of the Americas
New York, NY 10020
Visit our Web site at www.twbookmark.com

Printed in the United States of America

First Printing: April 2006

10 9 8 7 6 5 4 3 2 1

For all damsels in shining armor,
but especially my kick-ass daughter,
Brynna,
who thrives on challenge and always prevails.

With special thanks to
Melanie, Helen, and Lori,
who believed.

Acknowledgments

A hearty thank you to . . .

Gail Adams, Debi Allen, "America," Kathy Baker,
Carolyn Burns Bass, Dick Campbell, Dylan Campbell,
Richard Campbell, Carol Carter, Jane Chung,
Cherie Claire, Lynette Gubler-McKinley, Susan Hancy,
Josh Holloway, Karen Kay, Jill Lorg,
Meghan McKinney, Lauren Royal, Michelle Squyars,
Linda Stearns, Maura Szigethy, Betty and Earl Talken,
Shirley Talken, Michelle Thorne, Uma Thurman,
Charles and Nancy Williams, Michelle Yarned,
and everyone who plays "Diablo"

Lady Danger

Chapter 1

The Borders
Summer 1136

So. Where is the *third* wench?" Sir Pagan murmured casually, feeling *far* from casual as he and Colin du Lac hunkered behind the concealing cloud of heather, spying upon two splendid maids bathing in the pond below.

Colin almost strangled on his incredulity. "God's breath, you greedy sot," he hissed. "Is it not enough you have your choice of the pair of beauties yonder? Most men would give their sword arm to—"

Both men froze as the blonde woman, gloriously drenched in sunlight, sluiced water up over a creamy shoulder, rising above the waves enough to bare a pair of perfect breasts.

The blood drained from Pagan's face and rushed to his loins, making them ache fiercely. Lord, he should have swived that lusty harlot in the last town before he came to negotiate such matters. This was as foolish as shopping for provender with a full purse and an empty gut.

But somehow he managed an indifferent grunt, despite

the overwhelming desire disrupting his thoughts and transfiguring his body. "A man never purchases a blade, Colin," he said hoarsely, "without inspecting all the swords in the shop."

"Ha! A man never runs his thumb along the edge of a sword presented him by the *King*."

Colin had a point. Who was Sir Pagan Cameliard to question a gift from King David? Besides, 'twas not a weapon he chose. 'Twas but a wife. "Pah." He swatted an irritating sprig of heather out of his face. "One woman is much the same as another, I suppose," he grumbled. "'Tis no matter which of them I claim."

Colin snorted in derision. "So say you *now*," he whispered, fixing a lustful gaze upon the bathers, "now that you've laid eyes on the bountiful selection." A low whistle shivered from between his lips as the more buxom of the two maids dove beneath the glittering waves, giving them a glimpse of bare, sleek, enticing buttocks. "Lucky bastard."

Pagan *did* consider himself lucky.

When King David first offered him a Scots holding and a wife to go with it, he'd half expected to find a crumbling keep with a withered old crone in the tower. One glance at the imposing walls of Rivenloch eased his fears on the first count. And to his astonishment, the prospective brides before him, delectable pastries the King had placed upon his platter, were truly the most appetizing he'd seen in a long while, perchance *ever*.

Still, the idea of marriage unnerved Pagan like a cat rubbed tail to whiskers.

"God's eyes, I can't decide which I'd rather swive," Colin mused, "that beauty with the sun-bleached locks

or the curvy one with the wild tresses and enormous . . ."
He released a shuddering sigh.

"Neither," Pagan muttered.

"Both," Colin decided.

Deirdre of Rivenloch tossed her long blonde hair over one shoulder. She could feel the intruders' eyes upon her, had felt them for some time.

'Twas not that either sister cared if they were caught at their bath. They suffered from neither modesty nor shame. How could one be ashamed or proud of having what *every* woman possessed? If a stray lad happened to look upon them with misplaced lust, 'twas no more than folly on his part.

Deirdre ran her fingers through her wet tresses and cast another surreptitious glance up the hill, toward the thick heather and drooping willows. The eyes trained upon her now were likely just that, belonging to a couple of curious youths who'd never seen a naked maid before. But she didn't dare mention their presence to Helena, for her impetuous sister would likely draw her sword first and ask their business afterward. Nay, Deirdre would deal with their mischief by herself, and later.

For now she had a grave matter to discuss with Helena. And not much time.

"You delayed Miriel?" she asked, running a palm full of sheep tallow soap along her forearm.

"I hid her *sais*," Helena confided, "then told her I saw that stable lad skulking about her chamber earlier."

Deirdre nodded. That would keep their youngest sister busy for a while. Miriel allowed no one to touch her precious weapons.

"Listen, Deir," Helena warned, "I won't let Miriel sacrifice herself. I don't care what Father says. She's too young to wed. Too young and too . . ." She sighed in exasperation.

"I know."

What they both left unspoken was the fact that their youngest sister wasn't forged of the same metal they were. Deirdre and Helena were their father's daughters. His Viking blood pumped through their veins. Tall and strong, they possessed wills of iron and skills to match. Known throughout the Borders as the Warrior Maids of Rivenloch, they'd taken to the sword like a babe to the breast. Their father had raised them to be fighters, to fear no man.

Miriel, however, to the Lord's dismay, had proved as delicate and docile as their long-departed mother. Whatever warrior spirit might have been nurtured in her had been quelled by Lady Edwina, who'd begged that Miriel be spared what she termed the perversion of the other two sisters.

After their mother died, Miriel had tried to please their father in her own way, amassing an impressive collection of exotic weapons from traveling merchants, but she'd developed neither the desire nor the strength to wield them. She'd become, in short, the meek, mild, obedient daughter their mother desired. And so Deirdre and Helena had protected Miriel all her life from her own helplessness and their father's disappointment.

Now 'twas up to them to save her from an undesirable marriage.

Deirdre passed her sister the lump of soap. "Trust me, I have no intention of leading the lamb to slaughter."

The spark of battle flared in Helena's eyes. "We'll challenge this Norman bridegroom then?"

Deirdre frowned. She knew that not every conflict was best resolved on the battlefield, even if her sister did not. She shook her head.

Helena cursed under her breath and gave the water a disappointed slap. "Why not?"

"To defy the Norman is to defy the King."

Hel arched a brow in challenge. "And?"

Deirdre's frown deepened. One day Helena's audaciousness would be her undoing. "'Tis *treason*, Hel."

Helena puffed out an irritated breath and scrubbed at her arm. "'Tis hardly treason when we've been betrayed by our own King. This meddler is a Norman, Deirdre . . . a *Norman*." She sneered the word as if 'twas a disease. "Pah! I've heard they're so soft they can't grow a proper beard. And some say they bathe even their *hounds* in lavender." She shuddered with distaste.

Deirdre had to agree with her sister's frustration, if not her claims. Forsooth, she'd been just as outraged upon learning that King David had handed over Rivenloch's stewardship, not to a Scot, but to one of his Norman allies. Aye, the man was reported to be a fierce warrior, but certainly he knew naught of Scotland.

What complicated matters was that their father had launched no protest. But then the Lord of Rivenloch hadn't been right in his mind for months now. Deirdre frequently found him conversing with the air, addressing their dead mother, and he was ever losing his way in the keep. He seemed to live in some idyllic time in the past, where his rule was unquestioned and his lands secure.

But with the crown resting uneasily on Stephen's head, greedy English barons had begun to wreak havoc along the Borders, seizing what lands they could in the ensuing chaos.

So for the past year the sisters had hidden their father's infirmity as best they could, to prevent the perception of Rivenloch as an easy target. Deirdre had served as steward of the holding and captain of the guard, with Helena as second in command, and Miriel had overseen the household and the accounts.

They'd managed adequately. But Deirdre was wise enough to know such subterfuge couldn't last forever. Mayhap 'twas the reason for this sudden appointment by the King. Mayhap rumors of their father's debility had spread.

Deirdre had thought long on the matter and finally came to grips with the truth. While Rivenloch's knights were brave and capable, they hadn't fought a real battle since before she was born. Now, land-hungry warmongers threatened the Borders. Only a fortnight ago, a rogue English baron had brazenly attacked the Scots keep at Mirkloan, not fifty miles distant. Indeed, it might serve Rivenloch well to have the counsel of a warrior seasoned in combat, someone who could advise her in her command.

But the missive that had arrived last week bearing King David's seal, the one Deirdre had shared only with Helena, also commanded the hand of one of the Rivenloch daughters in marriage to the steward. Clearly, the King intended a more permanent position for the Norman knight.

The news had hit her like a mace in the belly. With the responsibility of managing the castle, the furthest thing from any of the sisters' minds had been marriage. That the King would wed one of them to a *foreigner* was inconceivable. Did David doubt Rivenloch's loyalty? Deirdre could only pray this compulsory marriage was his attempt to keep the holding at least half in her clan's hands.

She wanted to believe that, needed to believe it. Otherwise, she might be tempted to sweep up her own blade and join her hotheaded sister in a Norman massacre.

Helena had ducked under the water, cooling her wrath. Now she sprang up suddenly, sputtering and shaking her head like a hound, spraying drops everywhere. "I know! What if we waylay this Norman bridegroom in the wood?" she said eagerly. "Catch him off guard. Slice him to ribbons. Blame his death on The Shadow?"

For a moment, Deirdre could only stare mutely at her bloodthirsty little sister, whom she feared might be serious. "You'd slay a man unawares and accuse a common thief of his murder?" She scowled and grabbed the soap back. "Father named you rightly, Hel, for 'tis surely where you're bound. Nay," she decided, "no one is going to be killed. One of us will marry him."

"Why should we have to?" Hel said with a pout. "Is it not loathsome enough we must surrender our keep to the whoreson?"

Deirdre clutched her sister's arm, demanding her gaze. "We will surrender naught. Besides, you know if one of *us* doesn't wed him, Miriel will offer herself up, whether we will it or nay. And Father *will* let her do it. We can't allow that to happen."

Helena bit out a resigned curse, then muttered, "Stupid Norman. He doesn't even have a proper name. Who would christen a child Pagan?"

Deirdre didn't bother to remind her sister that *she* answered to the name of Hel. Even Deirdre had to agree, however, that Pagan was not a name that conjured up visions of responsible leadership. Or honor. Or mercy. Forsooth, it sounded like the name of a barbaric savage.

Helena sighed heavily, then nodded and took the soap again. "'Twill be me then. I will wed this son of a whelp."

But Deirdre could see by the murderous gleam in Hel's eyes that if she had her way, her new husband would not last out the wedding night. And while Deirdre might not mourn the demise of the uninvited Norman, she had no wish to see her sister drawn and quartered by the King for his murder. "Nay," she said. "'Tis *my* burden. I'll marry him."

"Don't be a fool," Hel shot back. "I'm more expendable than you. Besides," she said with a scheming grin, rubbing the sheep tallow soap back and forth between her hands, "while I lull the bastard into complacency, you can marshal forces for a surprise attack. We'll win Rivenloch back from him, Deirdre."

"Are you mad?" Deirdre flicked water at her reckless sister. She had little patience for Helena's blind bravado. Sometimes Hel boasted like a Highlander, thinking all England could be conquered with but a dozen brawny Scots. "'Tis *King David's* will to marry off this Norman to one of us. What will you do when *his* army comes?"

Hel silently pondered her words.

"Nay," Deirdre said before Hel could come up with another rash plan. "*I* will wed the bast—Norman," she corrected.

Helena sulked for a moment, then tried another tactic, asking slyly, "What if he prefers me? After all, I have more of what a man favors." She rose from the water, posturing provocatively to lend proof to her words. "I'm younger. My legs are more shapely. My breasts are bigger."

"Your mouth is bigger," Deirdre countered, unaffected by Hel's attempt at goading her. "No man likes a woman with a shrewish tongue."

Hel frowned. Then her eyes lit up again. "All right then. I'll fight you for him."

"Fight me?"

"The winner weds the Norman."

Deirdre bit her lip, seriously considering the challenge. Her odds of besting Hel were good, since she fought with far more control than her quick-tempered sister. And Deirdre was impatient enough with Hel's foolishness to take her up on her offer at once and see the matter settled. Almost.

But there were still the spies on the hill to deal with. And unless she was mistaken, Miriel was hastening across the meadow toward them.

"Hist!" Deirdre hissed. "Miriel comes. We will speak no more of this." Deirdre squeezed the water from her hair. "The Normans should arrive in a day or two. I'll make my decision by nightfall. In the meantime, keep Miriel here. I have something to attend to."

"The men on the hill?"

Deirdre blinked. "You know?"

Hel lifted a sardonic brow. "How could I not? The sound of their drool hitting the sod would wake the dead. You're sure you don't need assistance?"

"There cannot be more than two or three."

"Two. And they're highly distracted."

"Good. Keep them that way."

*   *   *

"God be praised," Colin said under his breath. "Here comes the third." He nodded toward the delicate, dark-haired figure scampering across the grassy field sloping down toward the pond, disrobing as she came. "Lord, she's a pretty one, sweet and small, like a succulent little cherry."

Pagan had suspected the last sister might be missing a limb or several teeth or most of her wits. But though she looked frail and less imposing than her curvaceous sisters, she, too, possessed a body to shame a goddess. He could only shake his head in wonder.

"Sweet Mary, Pagan," Colin said with a sigh as the third maid jumped into the pond, and they began splashing about like disporting sirens. "Whose arse did you kiss? The King's himself?"

Pagan frowned, bending a stem of heather between his fingers. What *had* he done to deserve his pick of these beauties? Aye, he'd served David in battle several times, but he'd met the King in Scotland only once, at Moray. David had seemed to like him well enough, and Pagan *had* saved a number of the King's men from walking into a rebel ambush that day. But surely 'twas no more than any commander would have done. 'Twas an enigma.

"Something's amiss."

"Aye, something's amiss," Colin agreed, at last tearing his attention away from the three maids to focus on Pagan. "You've lost your wits."

"Have I? Or am I right to suspect there may be a serpent in this garden?"

Colin's eyes narrowed wickedly. "The only *serpent* is the one writhing beneath your sword belt, Pagan."

"Tell me again, what exactly did Boniface say?"

Pagan never rode onto a field of combat blind. 'Twas what had kept him alive through a score of campaigns. Two days earlier he'd sent Boniface, his trusted squire, in the guise of a jongleur, to learn what he could about Rivenloch. Forsooth, 'twas Boniface who had alerted them to the daughters' intention to bathe in the pond this morn.

Colin rubbed thoughtfully at his chin, recounting what the squire had reported. "He said the lord's wits are addled. He has a weakness for dice, wagers high, and loses often. And, oh, aye," he suddenly seemed to remember. "He said the old man keeps no steward. He apparently intends to pass the castle on to his eldest daughter."

"His *daughter*?" This was news to Pagan.

Colin shrugged. "They're Scots," he said, as if that would explain it all.

Pagan furrowed his brow in thought. "With Stephen claiming the English throne, King David needs strong forces to command the Border lands," he mused, "not *wenches*."

Colin snapped his fingers. "Well, that's it, then. Who better to command Rivenloch than the illustrious Sir Pagan? 'Tis known far and wide that the Cameliard knights have no peer." Colin turned, eager to get back to his spying.

In the pond below, the voluptuous wench playfully shook her head, spattering her giggling sister and moving her naked torso in a manner that made Pagan instantly aroused. Beside him, Colin groaned, whether in bliss or pain, he wasn't sure.

Suddenly realizing the significance of that groan, Pagan cuffed him on the shoulder.

"What's that for?" Colin hissed.

"That's for leering at my bride."

"Which one's your bride?"

They both returned their gazes to the pool.

Pagan would be forever appalled at the momentary lapse of his warrior instincts then. By the time he heard the soft footfall behind him 'twas too late to do anything about it. Colin never heard it at all. He was too busy feasting his eyes. "Wait. I see only two now. Where's the blonde?"

Behind him, a feminine voice said distinctly, "Here."

Chapter 2

Pagan didn't dare turn to look. Her blade pressed firmly against a pulsing vein in his throat. Beside him, Colin sputtered in surprise and toppled backward to stare up at her. If Pagan hadn't been furious with himself for letting down his guard, he might have laughed at the sight.

"Are you lads not a bit old to be spying upon maids at their bath?" Her voice was throaty and mocking. "I thought to find beardless boys up here, not men full grown."

The clever wench must have skirted round the base of the hill, climbed up, then descended behind them. Humiliation burned Pagan's ears, and 'twas only made worse by the fact that instead of coming to his aid, Colin half-reclined upon his elbows with an awestruck expression that told him the blonde was even more beautiful at this proximity. He wondered if she was still naked.

"You're not from here," she guessed. "What are you doing on these lands?"

Pagan refused to answer. He owed the woman no explanation. "These lands" would soon belong to him.

But Colin, the traitor, was easily charmed out of his silence. "We meant no offense, my lady," he said when he'd gathered his wits, "I assure you." He grinned, making his emerald eyes dance in a way that never failed to beguile the wenches. "You see, we're friends of Boniface . . . the jongleur."

While Colin kept her entertained, Pagan took advantage of the distraction to slip his hand slowly down his side and along his calf. If he could retrieve the dagger from his boot . . .

Colin raised his brows in feigned innocence and chattered on. "An innkeeper told us he'd passed this way. We only wished to meet up with him. We never meant to intrude upon—"

The sword point suddenly dug into the flesh of Pagan's neck, in violent contrast to the lilting sound of the woman's voice, which poured over him like heather honey. "That had better be an itch you're reaching for."

He clenched his fist. Damn! He was a warrior, a commander of knights. To be held at sword's point by a *maid* . . . God's wounds, 'twas humiliating. And doubtless Colin would never let him hear the end of it. "What do you want?" he growled.

"What do I want?" she mused. "Hmm. What *do* I want? I think . . ." She swung the sword down to slap Pagan's thighs irreverently with the flat of the blade. But before he could react, she had it back at his throat. "Your trews."

Choked laughter came from Colin's quarter.

She chuckled softly in return. "*Yours* as well."

Colin's smile froze upon his face. "Me? You want me to take off my . . . trews?"

"Aye."

Pagan's ire rose. "Halfwit!" he snapped at Colin, who actually looked to be enjoying this exchange. "Seize her sword. Bloody hell, she's only a woman, a bit of a thing. Are you going to cower there like a—"

Colin laughed. "She's not a bit of a thing at all, are you, lass? Besides, if the lady wants my braies, I'll be glad to oblige." Colin stood, dropped his sword belt, stepped out of his boots, and began loosening the ties of his hose. "After all, 'tis only fair. I had a peek at *her* best parts."

Colin's enthusiasm as he stripped off his hose and braies only fueled Pagan's anger. But to both of their surprise, when at last Colin stood brazenly before her, his staff stretching his long tunic out like the center pole on a pavilion, the woman seemed indifferent to his manly display.

With her free hand, she scooped up his discarded sword belt and heaved it down the hill, where it tangled in a clump of thistles. "Now you," she said, prodding Pagan with the point of her sword.

Pagan thought not. Colin might consent to playing the lady's pet, grinning there like a fool in naught but his tunic, but Pagan was not about to concede anything to a woman.

"Nay," he said.

"Come now," she urged. "'Tis fitting payment for your spying."

"'Tis no crime to spy upon that which is so wantonly displayed," he chided. She'd already wounded his knightly pride. He wasn't about to let her win a battle of wills as well.

Her voice gained a hard edge. "Take off your trews. Now."

"Nay," he said just as stonily.

Though the blade never moved from his neck, the woman shifted behind him, bending down to whisper in his ear. "You are dangerously arrogant, sirrah." Her warm breath sent a shiver through him, and the scent of her freshly washed skin was perilously distracting. But he refused to acknowledge her.

At his silence, she circled around to the front of him, crouching until she was directly in his line of vision. He had no choice but to look at her. What he saw made his heart stagger and his mouth go dry.

Thank God, she was no longer naked, else lust would have crushed all the will from him. Even so, his rage melted instantly, and 'twas difficult for him to form thoughts, much less words.

She was as beautiful as a dewy summer morn. Her hair, drying now into wavy tendrils, seemed painted with sunshine, and her eyes shone as clear and blue as the sky. Her skin was so golden, it looked like it would be warm to the touch, and her lips were a pale pink that Pagan longed to make rosier with kisses. He lowered his eyes to the sweet hollow betwixt her breasts. A silver Thor's hammer hung from a chain there, in harsh contrast to her delicate flesh.

Her voice was soft now. "Is it truly worth your life?" There was a curious flutter in her eyes, as if she didn't quite believe he would refuse her demands.

He swallowed hard. If she'd thought to disarm him with her beauty, 'twas a commendable ploy. And it worked to some extent. But as he continued to gaze upon her gentle, lovely, feminine face, he realized a significant truth, glimpsed a chink in her armor. For all her boldness and brash words, she was a woman. And a woman's heart was tender, compassionate.

The blade menacing his throat was but her plaything. She would never use it on him. She was no more dangerous than a kitten.

"You will not slay me," he breathed, challenging her gaze.

A frown flickered across her brow. "You would not be the first."

Pagan didn't believe her for an instant.

Colin, troubled by the serious turn of the exchange, broke in with a chuckle. "Peace, friends. We need not let this become so grave a matter. Come, take off your braies like a good lad, eh, Pagan?"

At his words, faint alarm streaked across the maid's features like lightning, vanishing again so quickly that Pagan wondered if he'd imagined it.

She drew herself to her feet then, towering before him like a conqueror. Colin was right. She was *hardly* a bit of a thing. Forsooth, she must stand nigh as tall as he. And her voice was as commanding as her height. "Your trews, sirrah. Now."

Pagan narrowed his eyes at her hips, which were encircled by a knight's heavy, iron-buckled leather sword belt, yet draped in a damsel's soft blue kirtle.

"Nay," he challenged.

A long silence grew between them, charging the air like a growing current before a storm.

And then lightning struck.

'Twas so unexpected and so swift that at first Pagan didn't feel it.

"Holy Mother!" Colin gasped.

A sharp sting burned across Pagan's chest.

'Twas impossible. Unfathomable.

Stunned, he lifted his fingers to the place. They came back bloody.

The wench had cut him. The sweet-faced, soft-voiced, azure-eyed wench had sliced his flesh.

Before he could gather his wits to launch a counterattack, she whipped the blade back up to his throat, and he was forced to crouch there like a wounded animal while blood from the shallow cut seeped into his sliced tunic.

He'd been wrong about her. Utterly wrong. No remorse softened her cool stare. No pity. No mercy. She might well kill him without blinking an eye.

Never had he seen such strength of will in a woman. And only in the most ruthless warriors had he glimpsed such icy resolve. It both impressed and infuriated him. Huddling there, helpless, glaring at her in silent rage, he couldn't decide which he felt for her, admiration or hatred.

"Sweet Mary," Colin said hoarsely to the woman, "do you know what you've done?"

Her stare never wavered. "I gave him fair warning."

"Oh, lady," Colin said, shaking his head, "you've baited the bear now."

"'Tis but a scratch," she told him, narrowing her gaze upon Pagan and adding, "to remind him who wields the sword here."

"But, my lady," Colin pressed, "do you know who—"

"Let it be," Pagan interrupted, staring back at her and

allowing a subtle, wicked smile to lift one corner of his mouth. "I'll do as the lady wills."

For now, he thought. But in a few days, nay, by *morn*, he would claim Rivenloch for his own. He'd chosen his bride now. Come the morrow, he'd marry the third sister—the small, delicate, biddable-looking one, the one who appeared as if she wouldn't hurt a flea. As for *this* wench, he'd lock her up for her impertinence. He couldn't wait to see the ice of her composure crack when he informed her she'd be spending the next month in Rivenloch's dungeon.

Deirdre's heart pounded fiercely, but she willed her bones not to tremble. The slightest quiver in her gaze could prove deadly. She'd come this far, and now, knowing who she faced, she dared not back down, lest the Norman presume she was the kind of woman he could intimidate.

Still, she wished she'd dealt with his defiance more diplomatically. Responding with such a blow was unworthy of her; this kind of violent reaction more suited quick-tempered Helena. It shamed Deirdre to admit she'd been startled from reason. But hearing the name Pagan attached to the man she'd thought but a harmless, mischievous knave had come as a shock. And enduring the steadfast scrutiny of those smoldering eyes—so fearless, so insolent, so bold—had utterly unnerved her. In alarm, she'd lashed out at him.

She'd expected to dispense with the spies quickly and easily. On first approach, she'd correctly guessed that the grinning black-haired varlet was benign, and so she'd trained her sword upon the other, more dangerous-looking man. But she'd underestimated the full extent of his cunning. And though she'd rather die than admit it to anyone, when she'd finally glimpsed Pagan's face, she'd been more than a little shaken by the fact that he was the most handsome man she'd ever beheld. Forsooth, she'd expected the coming Norman steward to be far more . . . stewardly. And far less young, far less magnificent.

Even now, 'twas difficult to look upon him, standing before her but a sword's length away, without noting the gray-green allure of his eyes, the rich tousle of his tawny curls, the strong angle of his jaw, the curving mouth that seemed to beckon . . . intriguing her . . . enticing her . . . inviting her to . . .

She jerked her gaze back to his eyes. Lord, what was she thinking? It didn't matter that he was handsome. This was her foe. This was the Norman bastard who'd come to claim her castle and her lands. A hot shiver coursed uninvited through her body as she remembered what else he'd come to claim.

She forced her brows into a frigid scowl. Had he discerned her distraction? The wavering of her resolve? Forsooth, a subtle light altered his gaze. It might well be amusement. Or satisfaction. Neither boded well.

She steeled herself as he pulled off his boots, unbuckled his belt, and began tugging at the points of his hose, all with deliberate leisure. Bloody hell, her palms were sweating. The haft of the sword was slippery in her hand. If she wasn't careful, 'twould slide out of her grasp.

"Make haste," she muttered.

His eyelids dipped with suggestive insolence as he removed his hose. "Patience, my lady," he murmured.

She longed to strike him again, but fought the urge. He mustn't learn how he provoked her or she'd hold no sway over him. Ever.

Still, against her will, her gaze kept flitting to where his fingers now deftly loosened the laces of his trews. His knuckles were battle-scarred, but his hands moved with a sure grace and dexterity that made her knees go strangely weak.

Then, without ceremony and before she could brace herself, he hauled his trews down.

She gulped. 'Twasn't as if she hadn't seen scores of naked men before. Spending half her days in the armory, 'twas inevitable. But even the glance she gave his briefly exposed nether parts rattled her, for though he seemed generously endowed, he *clearly* was not moved by her beauty, as other men invariably were. Which meant she had one less weapon in her arsenal.

Bloody hell.

His eyes sparkled dangerously, like sunlight on a raging sea. "Now what?" he asked softly, holding his braies aloft. "Do you wish to see if they fit you?"

If he thought to insult her, he failed. From the time Deirdre had wielded her first sword and worn her first chain mail, she'd suffered ridicule from men and women alike. She was hardened by years of insults, which she'd learned to answer, at first with a blade and later with indifference.

She reached out to drag his discarded sword belt closer, then cast it into the briers as well.

"Come, my lady," said his companion, tossing his hose and trews to the ground at her feet. "Forgive my friend. He is slow of wit and quick of tongue. You've taken our weapons. You have our braies. You've won the day. I pray you, let us depart in peace."

Despite the fact that she had indeed won the day, bested them both, and wrought vengeance by condemn-

ing them to a humiliating afternoon of wandering about
the countryside in naught but their tunics, Deirdre
couldn't get over the sense that somehow she was the
pawn in their encounter.

The Norman still stared at her with those soul-searing
eyes, and it didn't matter that she held him at sword
point, that he stood bare-legged before her, that he was
marked by the slash of her blade. There was the look of
victory about him, and she knew she'd never faced a
more formidable foe.

Lord, what would happen when he discovered who
she was? What was in store for Rivenloch when this
brute came to claim his rightful place in the great
hall . . .

And in her bed?

Quickly, before a shiver of foreboding could betray
her, she snatched away Pagan's trews and those of his
companion with her free hand, slinging them over her
shoulder. Then she gave the men a curt nod and hastened
up the rocky rise to the crest of the hill.

She was halfway there when Pagan called out.

"Did you forget something, damsel?"

Always on guard, she wheeled with her sword at the
ready. Too late. Something whistled past her ear and
lodged with a thunk in the tree beside her. The dagger
from his boot.

She gasped. The blade had missed her by mere inches.
But when she locked eyes with Pagan, standing there in
scornful defiance, she knew at once he'd meant to miss
her. Which was even more menacing.

His message was clear. He could have killed her. He
simply chose not to.

Her nostrils flaring, she sheathed her sword and

strode away with as much calm as she could feign, silently cursing the Norman all the way home.

"What the bloody hell just happened?" Colin demanded when the lass had disappeared over the rise.

Pagan still bristled from Colin's betrayal. "We've lost our braies, no thanks to you."

"Our braies? Pagan, you've lost your mind." Colin tromped off down the hill toward the patch of thistles where their weapons lay. "You know, if you wanted to choose a bride by process of elimination, you could have told me. You needn't kill the other two. I'd be glad to take one of them off your hands."

Pagan slogged after him. "I wasn't going to kill her."

"Nay?" Colin cursed as a thistle pierced his bare foot.

"Nay." Pagan narrowed his eyes. "I have much worse planned for that one."

"Don't tell me," Colin said, hopping about on one foot as he yanked a thorn from the other. "You're going to marry her."

"Now *you've* lost your mind." Pagan couldn't deny that the thought of bedding the wench was devilishly tempting. Forsooth, her beauty had naturally aroused him, despite his determination not to show it. But there was something else. Where most wenches made him feel superior—stronger, smarter, cleverer—this one challenged his dominance. For the first time in his life, he had felt on an even footing with a maid, physically and mentally, and the idea of lying side by side with such a woman . . .

But in one instant, with the cruel slash of her sword, she'd shown the cold nature of her heart.

"Nay," he told Colin bitterly. "I'm going to put her in chains. Break her spirit. Teach her obedience."

"Aye, as I said," Colin said with a shrug, "you're going to marry her then."

"I'm going to marry the runt of the litter," he declared, though the thought brought him little joy. "She'll no doubt prove a dutiful wife, grateful and compliant, only too happy to do my bidding. And the frail thing doesn't look as if she could *lift* a sword, much less come at me with one."

Chapter 3

"AGAIN!" Deirdre raised her weapon and bid her sister attack once more.

Hel charged forward with a wild grin, and their blades clashed in a flurry of sparks.

The violence was cathartic, empowering after Deirdre's unsettling morning encounter. She'd not spoken to her sisters of her meeting with the Normans, nor did she intend to. She preferred to bear that knowledge alone. At least Helena and Miriel would spend their last hours as the stewards of Rivenloch in blissful ignorance.

Hel's shield clanged suddenly against Deirdre's, jarring her bones. Deirdre pushed off, returning with a horizontal slash from her sword that would have cut anyone else in half. But Hel was fast. She leaped backwards with a yelp, then dove into a roll, tumbling forward to come up beneath Deirdre's blade.

"Aha!" she cried, her sword point at Deirdre's chin, her eyes alight with victory.

But even the joy in her sister's face, which was dusted

with the fine silt of the practice field, didn't lessen the impending doom that weighed heavily on Deirdre's mind.

He was coming. Mayhap not tonight. Mayhap not even on the morrow. But anon. He was coming for her.

Deirdre had known the instant she'd locked eyes with Pagan that she *must* be the daughter to wed him. Miriel could not, for she would disappear beneath the man's overbearing shadow. Hel could not, for one of them would be dead by the end of their wedding night, and she feared now it might not be the Norman.

Nay, Deirdre must sacrifice herself.

'Twould be a hellish marriage, she was sure, but she'd endure it. For Miriel. For Helena. For Rivenloch.

Hel interrupted her thoughts, patting Deirdre's cheek with one gauntleted palm. "Work on your speed, sluggard," she taunted. "We ought to at least make this Norman bastard give chase for a bride."

Hel's words echoed through her soul like discordant bells. There would be no giving chase. Not with Pagan. He would come and claim her. Simply. Swiftly. Irrefutably.

His image, as indelibly engraved upon her mind as the designs on her dagger, assailed her again—his proud stance, his mocking smile, his derisive gaze—and her pulse began spiraling faster.

God's blood, what ailed her? She wasn't some frail maid who cowered in the face of danger. She was Deirdre of Rivenloch. She had routed thieves and tamed beasts and slain outlaws. She'd not let one devil-eyed Norman daunt her.

Rage heated her cheeks. She shoved Hel's sword aside with her shield. "Again!"

Sparks exploded as their blades clashed once more. Hel spun and leaped, twirling her sword as if 'twere a plaything, but Deirdre's shield was always there to answer. While Hel tired herself with her antics, Deirdre powerfully met her blows with her own blade, knocking Hel back with her superior strength and a raw determination that left no room for defeat.

Forsooth, 'twas not her sister she sought to conquer, but rather the demons that beleaguered her thoughts.

That, she thought, striking diagonally downward, *is for spying upon me like a stable lad. And that* . . . She thrust forward, missing Hel by inches . . . *is for mocking me with your dagger.* She deflected Hel's blade as it came at her head. *And this* . . . She advanced relentlessly, slashing left and right in rapid succession, until Hel was backed up against the fence of the lists. *This is for leering at me with those unyielding, knavish, violating, breathtaking eyes* . . .

"Deirdre! Helena!" Miriel scolded from the tiltyard gate, startling Deirdre from her thoughts. Her little sister lifted up her skirts to pick her way across the pitted field. Deirdre and Hel paused in their fighting long enough to see that, scurrying deferentially behind her, as usual, was Sung Li. Miriel had collected the ancient handmaiden years ago, along with several other sharp-toothed weapons from the Orient.

Hel used the distraction to slip underneath Deirdre's guard and past her, smacking Deirdre's backside with the flat of her blade. Deirdre turned and lunged forward, but Hel skipped out of range with a whoop of glee.

"What are you two doing?" Miriel demanded, her hands on her hips. Behind her, the maid mimicked her posture.

Accustomed to Miriel's disapproval, Deirdre and Hel ignored her. Deirdre charged, swiping at Hel's knees. Hel neatly jumped over the blade and returned with a swing that, had she not ducked, would have taken off Deirdre's head.

Miriel gave a disgusted growl. "Why did you bother bathing? Now you're both filthy!" she complained. "'Twas a waste of good soap."

The servant clucked her tongue.

Hel rolled back, then arched and sprang to her feet again, ready for battle. Deirdre scrambled up, tossing her braid over her shoulder.

"Prithee cease, sisters," Miriel pleaded.

Deirdre blocked Hel's next swing and yelled over her shoulder. "Go back in, Miriel. You'll dirty your skirts."

"But Father bid me come fetch you to supper."

"Supper?" Deirdre swung twice, then spared a quick glance at the sun. *'Twas* low in the sky. Time had flown on swift wings this day.

"Aye," Miriel said. "It grows late."

"Just one more bout," Hel insisted, tossing the sword to her left hand to deflect Deirdre's thrust. "Don't fret. We'll come anon."

"But Father says you're to come *now*. The new steward has arrived. He's been here for nigh an hour, and you're not even dressed proper—"

Pagan was here? Already? Miriel's words startled Deirdre, and that instant of inattention cost her a tiny slash across the cheek from Hel's blade. She flinched, sucking a quick breath between her teeth.

Miriel gasped.

"Oh, Deirdre!" Hel lowered her sword at once. "Sorry."

Deirdre shook her head. 'Twas hardly the first scratch the sisters had dealt each other. "My fault."

"Maybe we *should* go in," Hel said, exchanging a conspiratorial nod with Deirdre. "Don't wait on supper, Miriel. We'll clean up and come anon."

Miriel perused them doubtfully, likely wondering if they'd ever scrub clean. "Hurry then," she bade them. "Sir Pagan seems most anxious to meet you." She scurried off, her maid in tow.

"Most anxious," Hel muttered when Miriel had gone. "No doubt, the rutting bastard." She pulled off her gauntlets. "Shall we go then, before the old goat starts mounting the hounds?"

But Deirdre was too distracted to appreciate Hel's sarcasm. Dread filled her veins. The hour of reckoning had arrived.

The man had certainly wasted no time, she thought. She'd hoped to have a day or two for his wrath to cool. For when he discovered just who she was . . .

But Deirdre refused to yield to maidenly fears. She was a warrior, after all. "Aye, the hour is late," she croaked, sheathing her sword and wiping the blood from her cheek with the back of her gambeson sleeve. She straightened with a sniff and squared her shoulders. 'Twas time to confront the devil who would shortly be her husband.

"'Tis settled then," the harried scribe muttered.

Pagan watched as the man swept the hastily scrawled document from the table before the old lord could spill his supper on it, blowing on the wax seal to harden the mark of Rivenloch. No doubt the servant was peeved at being inconvenienced in this manner. But Lord Gellir had insisted the papers be drawn up at once, despite the fact that everyone was in the midst of a meal.

The lord smiled vaguely, dismissing the scribe from the noisy great hall with a wave of his bony hand, then returned his attention to the roast coney in the trencher before him.

Pagan picked at his own supper. He could not help but pity the old Lord of Rivenloch. He'd surely been a formidable warrior in his day, for his great two-handed sword hung upon the wall above a dozen shields of conquered knights. He was large of bone and broad of shoulder, with fingers long enough to singlehandedly choke a man. What few strands remained of his hair were light, and his eyes were a startling blue, marking him as the son of Viking stock. But time had worn him down like a river wears rock, softening his frame and unfortunately softening his mind as well.

'Twas painfully clear now that the King had handed Rivenloch over to Pagan not so much as a gift, but as a duty. For in the hands of a witless lord with three daughters and a company of knights grown rusty with peace, Rivenloch would surely fall to the English. And that would be a tragedy. The castle was magnificent, its location enviable.

At Pagan's request, when they'd first arrived, the youngest daughter and her wizened, white-braided servant had shown the two of them about the holding.

He realized there were changes he'd need to make. Some of the outbuildings were rotted and in need of repair. There wasn't enough storage. And the curtain walls surrounding the keep and its generous yard could stand to be fortified.

But those walls enclosed everything one needed to

survive in the wilds of Scotland. A sturdy stone chapel stood in the midst of the courtyard, flanked by a well. A large orchard supplied apples, wardens, walnuts, plums, and cherries, and the pottage garden grew thick with vegetables. Various workshops abutted the curtain wall, as did two kitchen sheds and an armory. Behind the keep were housed the hounds, horses, and hawks. And at the farthest end, running the width of the wall walk was an extensive tiltyard. The keep itself, from the tops of its four towers with their cunningly placed windows to the depths of the spare, but well-secured cellars, was a castle to make any man proud. A prize, he supposed, worth the price of marriage.

"Aye, 'tis all settled," the lord repeated, giving Pagan a distracted grin as he fondly patted his youngest daughter on the head.

The poor maid had gone as pale as milk, but Pagan couldn't summon up a smile of reassurance for her. He was suddenly burdened with a sickly heaviness that robbed him of his appetite.

"You'll not regret your decision," Colin said gently to the damsel, trying to ease her fears with a friendly word and a wink. "Though many a maid will be melancholy to learn Sir Pagan Cameliard's heart has finally been won."

The lass swallowed hard and lowered her dewy gaze to the mazer of ale before her, which she hadn't touched.

"To your health!" her father cried, startling the poor girl and raising his cup so briskly that ale sloshed over the rim and onto the white linen tablecloth.

The castle folk, seated at trestle tables about the great hall and unaware of the cause of the lord's outcry, nonetheless cheered him in halfhearted answer.

Pagan dutifully lifted his cup, though his heart, too,

was not in the toast. Why he was malcontent, he didn't know. After all, didn't he have what he wanted? The Lord of Rivenloch had welcomed him gladly, and his chosen bride seemed submissive and sweet.

Yet he was hesitant to claim her. The fact that Pagan had practically come to usurp Lord Gellir's holding seemed enough of a slap in the old man's face. But to appropriate one of his daughters as well . . .

In the end, Pagan had decided to do the noble thing, to let their father choose which of the maids he wished to relinquish in marriage.

Then, to his astonishment, before the lord could make that decision, before the other two dawdling sisters had even bothered to make an appearance at supper, the youngest had quietly, meekly, offered herself.

Pagan was no fool. He could tell instantly by the tremor in her voice that she'd tendered herself not out of desire for him, but as some sort of honorable sacrifice. 'Twas tragic, and yet there was naught to do but accept her offer. To do otherwise would not only give insult, but belittle her grand gesture.

Her father naturally approved the union. For the lord, the youngest daughter was obviously the most dispensable. 'Twas the same in Norman households. The first-born son was trained to rule, the second to fight, but the third could only hope for a place in the church or a profitable marriage. Certainly, marriage to Pagan would be profitable for her.

Still, 'twas not happily that Pagan gazed at the somber lass who was afraid to meet his eyes, nor the dull-witted lord with a foam of ale above his lip, nor the company of Scots about him that eyed him with a combination of awe and mistrust.

Only Colin seemed at ease among the castle folk. But then he always seemed at ease. The beguiling varlet could strike up a conversation as readily with a titled lady as a milkmaid and have either dining from his fingers by the end of the evening.

Pagan seldom wanted for a woman's affections either. But his appeal had always been his strength and prowess and well-favored looks, never his charm.

This time, however, these reliable attributes failed to diminish the terror filling the eyes of . . . what was her name? He scowled. Bloody hell, if he wanted to diminish the damsel's terror, he'd better remember her name.

"Here now," Colin chided, elbowing him in the ribs. "Do not frown, Pagan. You'll frighten Miriel."

Miriel. That was it. Ever since he'd matched wits with the tall blonde this morn, his mind had been as muddled as a lovesick cow's.

"Forsooth," Colin continued, "he's a gentle soul, my lady. For all his dark looks, he is renowned for his love of the harp and his sweet way with small creatures and babes."

Pagan's scowl deepened. What nonsense was Colin spouting now? The only use he had for small creatures was to eat them, and as for the harp . . .

"Pah! You're late!" Lord Gellir barked abruptly.

Pagan looked up from his roast coney. God's eyes, 'twas about time. Walking with measured leisure across the rushes toward the high table, their faces proud and lovely, were Miriel's sisters. If they were this late to supper when *he* was lord, he decided, he'd let them go hungry.

Pagan thought he'd etched the blonde's face upon his mind, but he saw that his memory did her an injustice.

She wasn't only beautiful. She was breathtaking. Stately and elegant in a kirtle of sky-blue silk, she glided across the flagstones with the sure grace of a cat. Her sister followed, dressed in pale saffron, looking warily about, as if, given the right provocation, she might suddenly leap atop one of the tables.

Even Colin's chatter dwindled off as the magnificent sisters made their way across the hall.

Unbidden, Pagan's pulse quickened, and he felt the wound the blonde had dealt him throb beneath his tunic.

For hours, he'd imagined the look of utter shock on her face when she discovered his identity. Relished the thought of her mortification when she realized she'd attacked her future lord.

But his thirst for her humiliation was not to be quenched. Her countenance as she calmly met his gaze was as cool as ice. Not only did she seem unsurprised by his presence, but she looked utterly unashamed. The brazen wench! Had she known all along who he was? If so, then her actions had been cold and calculated. The witch had provoked him deliberately.

As she neared, her eyes glittering like icy stars, the anticipation of delicious vengeance hastened his heart. All afternoon, while his cut seeped and the breezes taunted his bare legs, he'd envisioned taming the wayward wench. He'd thought of locking her up with naught but bread and water. He'd imagined putting her in the stocks in naught but her shift. He'd pondered cutting off an inch of her precious golden locks every day until she yielded to him. And now that his revenge was close enough to taste, 'twas only natural he should savor it like rare Spanish wine.

But somehow, as he watched her draw closer, her unbound hair shimmering in the candlelight, her bosom pressing gently against the low neckline of her kirtle, her lips full and ripe and rosy, thoughts of these punishments took on a distinctly sensual air. He was abruptly assailed by visions of her nibbling bread from his fingers as she knelt chained in the tower. He imagined her in those stocks, shivering in her shift as the wind whipped it to sinful transparency against her lithe curves. He saw his hands delving into her silken sunlit tresses as he drew that knife to slice them from her, inch by tortuous inch.

Curse his errant thoughts, they were heating his blood. Damn! There was only one thing worse than being subjugated by a woman with a weapon, he decided, and that was being subjugated by one's own lust for her.

"My eldest daughters," Lord Gellir said by way of introduction, gesturing to them with a leg bone from his coney carcass.

Pagan briefly met the blonde's gaze and gave her a careful nod. She apparently didn't intend to disclose their earlier meeting. Then neither would he. But he noted that since he'd seen her last, she'd earned a tiny scratch along her cheekbone. He wondered where she'd gotten it.

"Sorry, Father," the second sister said, taking a seat next to Merewyn . . . Mildryth . . . Margaret . . .

By the Saints, why couldn't he remember his bride's name?

"We were in the lists," she added, turning a challenging glare upon Colin and him.

"Ah," the lord said, munching on a scrap of meat. "Who won?"

"Helena won, Father," the blonde beauty replied, slipping

onto the bench between her sisters. "Of course, I *let* her win."

"Let me?" Helena flared. "The hell you did. I—"

"Helena!" the youngest sister softly intervened. "We have . . . guests."

"Oh," Helena said, letting her gaze travel derisively up and down the pair of them as if she were sizing up warhorses for combat. "Aye."

"This is Sir Colin du Lac," Pagan's bride politely continued, "and this . . ." She didn't exactly shudder, but he could feel her distaste as she introduced him. "This is Sir Pagan Cameliard. Sir Colin, Sir Pagan, these are my sisters, Lady Helena and Lady Deirdre of Rivenloch."

Deirdre. Ah. From the Thor's hammer hanging about her throat, he'd expected her name to be of Viking origin— something ugly like Grimhilde or Gullveig. He lowered his gaze. The piece still nestled there upon the sweet, supple flesh of her . . .

Colin found his voice first. "'Tis a pleasure to meet you."

Helena smirked with false courtesy, then shook out her napkin and draped it over her lap. She elbowed her sister and grumbled, "You know I'm your better, Deir. *Let* me win indeed."

"Win?" Colin snapped up the bait. "Win what, my ladies?"

Helena turned to him then with her full attention, as if she'd been waiting for just this chance to shock him, and said distinctly, "Our sword fight."

"Your sword fight?" Colin asked with a dubious smile. He doubtless thought "sword fight" was a Scots game of some sort. Pagan suspected otherwise.

Helena shot Colin a sly smirk. Pagan frowned, caring

for neither her cunning or her cockiness. They were traits he'd have to guard against in the future. At least Deirdre, for all the ice in her veins, seemed honest and forthright.

Helena turned to face her father then, though she blatantly spoke for Colin's benefit. "You should have seen it, Father. Deirdre came at me and would have lopped my head from my shoulders. But I threw aside her attack, jabbed left and thrust right, then ducked under, rolled forward, pinned her against the fence and set my blade at her throat."

For the first time in his life, Colin was left speechless. But Pagan, his suspicions all but confirmed, looked to Deirdre. Her smile was one of smug reassurance. Oh, aye. 'Twas true. The lasses were both accomplished swordswomen.

And now, by the queer prickling at the back of his neck, he began to understand why the King had offered him, Sir Pagan Cameliard, captain of the Cameliard Knights, the most highly respected Norman fighting force, this particular dish of sweetmeats. They were laced with a poison no man but the strongest could survive. Only the most clever, the most capable, the most competent commander of men could ever hope to tame these warrior wenches.

Chapter 4

"YOU'VE NEVER HEARD OF THE WARRIOR Maids of Rivenloch?" Helena asked around a mouthful of boiled neeps.

One corner of Pagan's lip lifted in a sardonic smile. "Word of your exploits has not reached the greater world as yet," he drawled.

Deirdre raised her cup in a subtle salute. His barb had been well placed.

Helena, however, took exception at the insult. "Well, we've never heard of the Knights of Cameliard either."

Colin seemed genuinely surprised. "Nay?"

Pagan arched a brow. "Rivenloch *is* rather . . . remote."

Deirdre saw Helena's fist tighten around her knife and placed a restraining hand on her sister's forearm.

Forsooth, she had to admire the Norman. He was quick-witted and cleverer than most. Indeed, she was beginning to wonder if the fighting force he boasted of even existed. 'Twas likely just this pair of them sojourning across the land, calling themselves the "Knights of Cameliard" and inventing tales of daring exploits.

She let her gaze drift over Pagan's curious attire. The man was apparently as resourceful as he was witty. He'd used what could have turned into a humiliating episode to his advantage. He and his companion had found a pair of plaids somewhere, draped them over one shoulder and pinned them at the hip, in the Scots style, not only disguising their lack of trews, but endearing themselves to the people of Rivenloch by dressing like them.

At least, Deirdre reflected, she'd be wedding a man with brains.

As Helena continued torturing their guests, trying to shock and horrify them with gruesome tales of her past battles, Deirdre sipped at her ale, studying the man who would soon be her husband.

He *was* incredibly well-favored. His hair, the color of gold-dusted chestnuts, spilled rampantly over his ears, down his neck, upon his brow. His sun-darkened skin seemed to glow in the firelight. The bones of his face were strong and broad, his stubbled jaw scarred faintly along its edge by what might have been a blade. His eyes, focused intently now on Helena, reminded her of Highland woods in the mist, gray and green and deceptive. A woman might lose her way in those woods, she reminded herself, tearing her gaze away to peruse the ale in her cup.

"He dresses all in black," Hel was telling Colin du Lac, serving herself a second roast coney. "People call him The Shadow. He hides in the trees, waiting for victims, and no one has been able to . . ."

Deirdre let her gaze drift back to Sir Pagan Cameliard. As he listened to Hel's tale of the local outlaw, likely as amused by her healthy appetite as by her story, he lazily ran his middle finger around the rim of his cup. Deirdre found herself spellbound by the movement. His hands looked brutal and heavy, marred by scars and calluses, yet capable of such subtle gestures . . .

Her heart fluttered inexplicably, and she laced her fingers around her own cup to still their trembling.

As Hel droned on about the mysterious thief who lived in the forest, she saw Pagan's mouth shift almost imperceptibly. What had been a grim line of disapproval now softened until the corners curved slightly upward.

Deirdre raised her eyes in surprise. God's wounds, the man was staring at her. And smiling. A secret, knowing smile full of dire promise and palpable threat.

She glanced away, clenching her silver cup so tightly that she felt the soft metal yield. She might have to marry the man, but she'd never let him believe he had any manner of control over her.

Nor would she ever reveal that she found the idea of wedding him to be anything less than completely loathsome.

Nay, she had to seize the reins now, before he took them in his own hands and bore her away to some dark lair to wreak his revenge.

She took a deep, steadying breath, set her cup upon the table, and interrupted Hel's graphic discourse, which was turning Miriel as white as her napkin.

"So, Father," she said without preamble, "have you had the marriage documents drawn up?"

He nodded. "Oh, aye," he said around the wad of neeps in his mouth, "drawn up, settled, and signed."

Deirdre exchanged a frown with Hel. "Settled?"

"Signed?" Hel asked, nearly choking on a bite of meat.

"Aye," he told them happily. "No need to worry, Edwina. I've called the priest, and we'll have the wedding come morn."

Deirdre winced as he called her by their mother's name. "Morn? But we've not been consulted, Father. Which of us—"

"*I've* agreed to wed him," Miriel said in a rush.

For a full three heartbeats, Deirdre and Hel could only stare at their little sister.

"What?" Deirdre finally managed in a whisper of disbelief. "But Miriel . . . There must be some mis—"

Hel slammed her fist on the table, rattling the dishes. "Nay!" She rounded on Pagan. "Curse you, Norman. Could you not wait to meet all three of us? Did you have to choose so hastily?"

Miriel set her fingertips lightly upon Hel's forearm. "Helena, do not be angry with him. 'Twas not his choice," she said softly. "'Twas *mine*."

Another silence ensued as Miriel's words sank in.

"*Your* choice," Hel finally echoed in amazement.

Deirdre said nothing. She felt suddenly ill, as if her world had been spun awry. One look at Miriel's wide blue eyes and her quivering lips told her the truth. Her little sister had sacrificed herself before Deirdre ever had the chance.

Hel whipped around to their father and hissed, "How could you let her do this?"

"Helena!" Deirdre snapped at her ill-mannered sister. As irresponsible as the old man had been of late, he was still their lord. He deserved their respect. Deirdre spoke to him as evenly as she could. "The troth has been signed and sealed then?"

"Oh, aye, all taken care of," her father cheerfully replied, oblivious to their distress. "We'll have the wedding in the morn."

She turned a grim gaze upon Hel, whose eyes smoldered like coals, and told her, "Then what's done is done."

A ponderous silence filled the air then, relieved only by the soft clatter of cups and knives and the busy chatter of the common folk at the lower tables. They supped on, ignorant of the drama taking place among the nobles, all but Sung Li, who, Deirdre noted, watched the proceedings from a distance with an almost eery intensity.

Hel continued to hold her tongue, as did Deirdre. Pagan had obviously approved the match. 'Twas to his benefit, after all, to wed Miriel, a young lass who would never contest his authority.

But Deirdre didn't intend to let that happen. Though she kept up a serene mien, inwardly her thoughts churned as furiously as a milkmaid late to rise. By supper's end, she had a plan.

"By th' Sain's, I'll no' stan' fer it," Helena slurred, lending irony to her words by sliding off the edge of Deirdre's pallet and landing with a thump on the rush-covered planks of her bedchamber.

Deirdre rescued Hel's half-empty cup of wine before it could spill, then grabbed her sister under the arms and hauled her upright again onto the bed.

Hel swayed for a moment, then continued her ranting. "We mus' do somethin', Deir. We mus' take care o' those mis'rable sons o' . . . sons o' . . ."

"Sons of Normans?" Deirdre prompted, refilling Hel's cup.

"Aye," Hel sneered, angrily snatching the cup and downing another generous gulp. She wiped her mouth with the back of her sleeve, and Deirdre's eyes widened as the long silk tippet swept perilously close to the flame of the tall candle beside her bed.

Deirdre lifted her own still-full cup. "Aye, here's to the Warrior Maids of Rivenloch. May we always triumph."

Hel nodded, her chin quivering with pride as she banged her cup against Deirdre's. They drank together, but while Helena drained her cup, Deirdre took only a small sip. She needed her wits about her this night.

Hel's eyes rolled drunkenly, and her empty cup dropped onto the pallet. Deirdre hoped her sister might swoon into slumber then and there. Then again, Hel could drink most men into the rushes. After a moment, she sighed and started muttering again, inventing vile new names for the Normans.

Deirdre glanced out her chamber window. The full moon was yet framed within the stone sill, but it moved steadily upward. She had to hurry Helena along. There wasn't much time.

She retrieved and filled Hel's cup once more. "Let's drink to Miriel."

"Poor Miriel," Hel wailed. "I tell ye, Deir, if that bloody knave ever lays a han' on her, I swear . . . I swear . . ."

"Aye, let us swear to it then. If he touches her . . ." She raised her cup.

"We'll kill 'im," Hel snarled. She gulped down a

generous swallow, then slammed the cup on the chest at the foot of the bed.

Deirdre paused, then took a thoughtful sip. Pagan would never touch Miriel. Deirdre wouldn't give him the chance.

"Ooh," Hel exclaimed, pressing a hand betwixt her legs, likely in dire need of a chamber pot. "I better go." She giggled and pushed herself up off the pallet, swayed for a moment until she could get her bearings, and slogged toward the door. "G'night. An' don' forget, Deirdre. You swore. You swore."

The last Deirdre saw of Helena, she was swaggering and staggering along the hall to her own chamber, where she would hopefully find her chamber pot in time. With any luck, after that she'd fall upon her pallet in a stupor and doze away half the morn.

Now Deirdre had to take care of her littlest sister.

Separating Miriel from her meddlesome servant would be difficult. The strange little maid followed her everywhere, like a duckling scurrying after its mother.

But there was no time to waste. Deirdre gathered up the small satchel of supplies from her chamber and started toward Miriel's room. As much as it grated against her sense of honor, Deirdre supposed she would have to deceive her little sister. Forsooth, 'twas for her own good.

Standing before the door with her hand raised, Deirdre hesitated. Was she doing the right thing? Mayhap Miriel *would* be content with Pagan for a husband. Mayhap her very sweetness would bring out the decency in him. Mayhap she would grow to cherish him, and he would bow to her gentle nature.

Then she remembered the wicked smile Pagan had

flashed her at supper, the one full of knowing menace. Nay, the man was too clever, too conniving to even comprehend that kind of innocence. If he was allowed to marry Miriel, he'd crush her heart as carelessly as a moth in his fist.

Resolute, she knocked upon the door.

Miriel was not yet dressed for bed, but, as predictable as the sun's setting, Sung Li was laying out the linen dressing gown that she always insisted Miriel wear to bed. Deirdre could see by the modest old woman's wrinkled pout that she was displeased at the intrusion.

"Deirdre, come in." Miriel opened the door wider to allow her entrance.

Deirdre was tempted to simply grab her sister and run. 'Twas so much more direct and honest than all this trickery. But Sung Li, for all her obsequiousness, could, when she had a mind to, make a commotion louder than a coop of hens threatened by a fox, and the last thing Deirdre needed was a flock of servants descending upon them.

"I bring a message from your . . . from Sir Pagan," Deirdre lied. "He . . ." *Demands your presence*? Nay, that sounded too harsh. "Requests your company."

"Now?" Miriel's brow creased in puzzlement.

Deirdre could feel Sung Li's mistrustful gaze upon her. She'd never been very good at lying. She nodded. "I'm to take you to him."

Miriel swallowed visibly, obviously reluctant, reinforcing Deirdre's determination to carry out her plan. The poor child was truly afraid of the steward. 'Twas a noble service Deirdre did her.

Deirdre gave her sister a smile of reassurance. "'Tis all right. He means you no harm. Mayhap he only wishes to know you a little better before you wed."

Miriel nodded. Then Deirdre hazarded a glance toward Sung Li, half expecting the woman to launch into a scolding protest. But the servant was curiously silent, lowering her eyes and running a withered hand fondly over the fabric of Miriel's dressing gown.

"Sung Li," Miriel called, "are you coming?"

Before Deirdre could intervene, the servant shook her head. "Too busy. Too busy. Too much to do for wedding. You go."

'Twas a rare instance when Sung Li let Miriel go anywhere unaccompanied. Deirdre narrowed her eyes at the curious maid. Perchance the old woman was wise enough to recognize that Miriel's allegiance now belonged to her bridegroom. With any luck, she'd not question Miriel's failure to return to her bedchamber this night.

All the way up the stairs, Miriel rattled on nervously, making Deirdre's task all the easier, for she took no notice of where Deirdre was taking her. When they arrived at the tower door, Deirdre, her heart sinking at what she was about to do, pulled out the iron key and unlocked it. Only then did Miriel frown in dawning confusion.

"He wanted to meet me *here*?"

Without a reply, Deirdre nudged her gently but firmly into the empty tower room with its pair of narrow windows.

"But where is he?" Miriel asked. "Where is Pa—"

Before guilt could set in and melt her resolve, Deirdre tossed the satchel into the room and began to close the door between them.

"Deirdre?"

The bewilderment in Miriel's eyes caught at Deirdre's heart. But she couldn't afford mercy, not now.

"Deirdre? Nay!"

The slam of the oak door cut off her scream. But the thick wood did little to muffle Miriel's pounding, so like a panicked heartbeat. Deirdre fought back overpowering remorse as she fumbled with the key until the bolt clicked into place.

For a moment, she could only stare at the locked door and try to turn a deaf ear to the dull thuds. She wished she'd had the time to reassure poor Miriel, to show her the comforts she'd left in the satchel—a cloak, a chamber pot, provender enough for two days—and to tell her she'd release her after the deed was done. But her little sister wouldn't understand. And now she'd believe that Deirdre had betrayed her.

Sick at heart, Deirdre trudged back down the steps, trying to console herself as the hammering diminished. Surely 'twas for the best. Though Miriel might not come to realize it for days or weeks or years, Deirdre had saved her sister this night. Mayhap from the Devil himself.

Chapter 5

Pagan was dreaming of women—beautiful, naked women bathing in a pond, smiling and inviting him to join them. He smiled in return, shedding his clothes, wading into the warm waves. One of the wenches caressed his shoulder, and he turned to find a tall goddess with soft blue eyes and long golden hair, sighing and opening her sweet mouth for . . .

A heavy blow to the belly suddenly folded him in half, wrenching him instantly from dreamy sunlight to stark midnight. He groaned in pain and instinctively seized his sword, at the ready beside him.

It took a moment to get his bearings. He knew he'd been sleeping on a pallet in one of Rivenloch's bedchambers, but in the dim light of the banked fire, he couldn't see what grappled and gasped upon him like a fallen horse. And hampered by its weight, he could neither strike nor dislodge the thrashing burden. The strong smell of wine suddenly assailed his nostrils.

"I told you, Pagan!" Colin's voice emerged from the

foot of the bed as he struggled to contain whatever beast twisted atop Pagan's lap. "I didn't trust her from the moment I laid eyes on her."

Her? Pagan heard a muffled scream of feminine fury as Colin finally hauled the intruder off of him, taking the fur coverlet along.

"Let's see what mischief you're up to, eh, my sotted lass?" Colin said between his teeth, his voice tight with strain. "Stir the fire, would you, Pagan?"

Pagan, shaking the cobwebs from his head, staggered toward the hearth—naked, sword in hand—and jabbed the coals to life.

The sight before him would have been comical had the circumstances been less serious. Colin clung tenaciously to what appeared to be a great, furry, writhing, kicking, pummeling she-beast. He'd stifled her screams of rage with a wad of the coverlet, but that didn't smother the fire of pure hatred emanating from her eyes.

"Tsk, tsk, tsk," Colin scolded companionably, though it took much of his strength to keep her contained. "You've been a naughty lass, haven't you? What's that in your hand?"

By the blossoming light, Pagan saw 'twas Helena, the lord's middle daughter, drunk as an alewife. As Colin had suspected, her sudden quiet at the supper table after the marriage announcement had seemed strangely portentous, like calm air before a violent squall. Fortunately, Colin, expecting foul play, had insisted on quartering in Pagan's chambers for the night.

"Come on," Colin coaxed the maid, applying pressure to her forearm, growing more serious. "I don't want to break your wrist. Let it go, lass."

After a long moment, her brow creased sharply in pain, she cried out, and something clattered to the floor.

Colin whispered a curse.

A dagger gleamed golden in the firelight. Jesu! The she-devil had meant to stab him.

At her venomous glower, Colin's good humor vanished entirely. "You bloodthirsty little fool," he muttered. "Would you murder the King's man?" He gave her a punishing shake. "'Tis treason! Christ's bones! You'd hang for that. You *should* hang for that."

Her struggling diminished as the possibility of execution slowly sank into her besotted brain.

Pagan knew, of course, that Colin's growl was much worse than his bite. Executing the sister of the bride, the daughter of the old lord, was a certain way to insure a Scots uprising.

Still, 'twould be folly to let the woman believe she could commit such a monstrous crime and walk away unscathed. 'Twas better to put the fear of God into her.

Colin must have read his thoughts. He let out a weighted sigh and bluffed. "I'll see to it," he told Pagan sternly.

Helena squealed in protest and bucked against Colin's confining arms, but he had a firm grip on her now and didn't look likely to relinquish her any time soon.

Pagan nodded. "But not tonight. Best keep her confined until my marriage is completed. Afterwards, you may deal with her as you see fit."

"'Twill be my pleasure," he sneered. "What about the other one?"

He knew Colin meant Deirdre. It stood to reason if one sister had plans to murder him, so might the other.

"Can you handle *her*?" Colin asked, looking as if he

could barely handle *his* captive as she heaved hard against his hold.

"She's nothing like her sister," he said, narrowing scornful eyes upon Helena. "If Deirdre comes to kill me, 'twill not be as I sleep. She'll look me in the eye to do it."

Colin turned his attention to his struggling quarry. "Now, little Hel-fire, what shall I do with you?"

She stiffened.

"Steal you away, mayhap," he considered, "where no one can hear you scream. Break you of your wild ways at the crack of a whip. Keep you on a short leash to make sure you suffer from no more lapses in judgment."

She twisted in his arms, and he chuckled grimly. "Ah, lass, if you knew what all that squirming was doing to my nether parts . . ."

That stopped her.

Meanwhile, Pagan's thoughts raced ahead. "Lock her in one of the cellars below the keep." Despite Colin's sinister threats, Pagan trusted his man to handle the shrewish maid with wisdom and patience. Colin would be watchful in her presence, and she'd be safe in his care. "If anyone asks her whereabouts at the wedding, we'll tell them she's . . . suffering from the aftereffects of too much wine."

But there was one detail troubling Pagan, one thing he needed to clarify before Colin whisked the damsel away. Helena had meant to slay him, aye, but Pagan had seen enough of the Rivenloch loyalty now to recognize her motive. She was trying to protect Miriel.

"Heed me well," he told her softly. "You needn't fear for your sister. I'm a man of honor, a knight sworn to protect your sex. I've never hurt a woman in my life. I give you my oath no harm will come to her, nor will I force myself upon her in any way."

Whether she believed him or not, he couldn't tell. But at least he'd given her his word of honor.

He dismissed her with a nod, then Colin swept up his reluctant prize, coverlet and all, and stole from the chamber to the hall and down the stairs.

Pagan stared into the glowing hearth, where the coals were already drifting back to ashen slumber. But he knew he'd sleep no more this night.

In the morn he'd be married. Absolutely, completely, irrevocably married. And though 'twas to the maid of his choosing, a lovely treasure with gentle curves and soft dark hair and wide blue eyes, 'twas not Miriel's face he imagined when he thought of his marriage bed.

He tossed his sword onto the pallet, and the movement pulled at the bandage over his chest. Aye, he thought, like the scar that would forever mar his body, Deirdre of Rivenloch had engraved her mark upon his soul.

Deirdre gazed out her window at the dreary gray clouds of dawn, slung low in the sky with their heavy burden of summer rain. 'Twas fitting weather, she thought, for such a miserable event. Even the heavens would mourn this day.

She shivered despite the heavy brown cloak she wore over her plain, sky-colored kirtle. 'Twas hardly the bright raiment of a bride, but this was no joyful event. Besides, she didn't intend to remove her cloak at all.

She watched as the castle folk gathered in the courtyard below, some of them scattering petals upon the steps of Rivenloch's small stone chapel. 'Twas nearly time. She took a deep breath of moist air and murmured a prayer that her sisters would forgive her.

She'd only done what *had* to be done, she reminded herself. 'Twas better that she live with the guilt of having deceived them than forever regret her lack of intervention. 'Twas for the best. In another hour, the ceremony would be over, and she'd have a lifetime to make amends for her perfidy.

She only prayed she could pull off this deception. Deirdre stood a half a foot taller than Miriel, and her shoulders were far broader. She'd need to stoop to make herself appear small. Hopefully the bulky cloak would help mask her size.

She doubted her father would know the difference. By the Saints, half the time he called Deirdre by his wife's name and thought Miriel was a maidservant. 'Twould be a miracle if he even remembered there was to be a wedding today.

Indeed, 'twas a blessing the marriage had been called for in such haste and at so early an hour. The chaos of wedding preparations would excuse a lot of things—the lateness of Miriel's sisters, the bride's lack of a proper wedding gown, Pagan's failure to notice he was marrying the wrong sister. But Deirdre meant to add one final note of credibility to her deceit—Sung Li. She cracked her knuckles. 'Twould be easy enough to secure the tiny old woman's cooperation.

But she'd have to hurry. No doubt the maidservant would shortly be flapping around the keep like an indignant mother hen, demanding to know what had become of her chick.

When Deirdre snatched open the door to Miriel's chamber, she expected to find Sung Li circling the room in a panic. But the old woman stood calmly beside the pallet, hands clasped, staring stoically ahead, as if she'd been waiting for Deirdre. "What have you done with Miriel?"

Wary of the old woman's strangely quiet mood, Deirdre told her, "She's safe." She closed the door, then advanced purposefully on the puny maid till she towered over her in menace. "And she'll stay safe as long as you do exactly as I say."

Undaunted, Sung Li crossed her arms and clucked her tongue. "If we stand here talking, you will be late for the wedding."

Deirdre bristled at the maid's impertinence. "Listen, I'm going to marry the Norman, and you're coming with me. You're going to make everyone believe I am Miriel. And if you breathe a word otherwise to anyone, I swear I'll rip your arms off and beat you with them."

The tiny maidservant turned her head slowly and looked her up and down, and Deirdre would have sworn there was amusement in her eyes. "You could not."

Deirdre's brows shot up.

"You hurry now," Sung Li urged. "The real Miriel would not be late."

Deirdre peered down at the wizened old crone with dawning comprehension. Of course. The clever woman meant to help her. Sung Li didn't want Miriel to suffer this unwanted marriage any more than Deirdre did.

The maid threw back her shoulders and thrust out her pointy chin. "And she goes nowhere without me."

A look of collusion passed between them, and Deirdre gave her a nod of approval. Then she took a deep breath and stepped toward the door, toward her destiny.

In time, her family would forgive her, she knew. And

they would eventually accept that Deirdre had acted in their best interests.

But Pagan . . . She had no idea how he would react. His wrath might explode upon her. Or he might shrug it all off as inconsequential. He might punish her with a lifetime of misery. Or he might treat her with indifference. 'Twas not knowing that made Deirdre's heart falter as she pulled the hood closer about her face, cracked open the outer door, and prepared to meet her unwitting bridegroom.

The sky rumbled with thunder as if to announce her arrival and her mood, and a torrent suddenly descended from the heavens, drenching her with fat drops that pitted the sod and peppered the pale stone of Rivenloch. Deirdre allowed herself a secret smile of approval. The storm was welcome. If witnesses were forced to squint through the driving rain, 'twould make her deception all the easier. No one would question why the bride concealed her face within the hood of her sodden cloak.

"Small steps," Sung Li reminded her.

Deirdre peered through the folds of wool and forced herself to walk to the chapel in a hundred strides instead of fifty.

Pagan had already arrived. He and Colin stood just below the upper stair of the small sanctuary, speaking to the priest. He'd never bothered to change his clothing. Mayhap, she thought scornfully, he was but some penniless knight-errant who possessed no other garments. Indeed, he seemed to have brought no belongings at all with him. 'Twas little wonder he was in a hurry to wed. He was doubtless already drooling over the dowry.

She could see by the upraised knee he planted on the top step that his legs were thick with muscle. She faltered in her step, imagining those strong legs wrapped around her this night, trapping her, demanding her surrender.

Clenching her jaw to steel her resolve, she continued forward, forcing herself to mimic Miriel's stride.

As she neared, Pagan's head was the first to swing around, almost as if he'd sensed her approach. She withdrew into her hood like a startled turtle, spying upon him through the narrow gap. Christ's bones, the sight of his face stole the breath from her. Everything about the man exuded confidence. He stood with bold command, bareheaded, as if he were impervious to the weather, and the rain drenching his dark amber locks only made him look more savage.

One by one, the people of Rivenloch turned toward her, smiling in encouragement and blinking against the rain, though they doubtless wished this whole business over with so they could return to their warm fires. Her father stood beside Pagan with her dowry, the bag of silver coins Miriel had carefully counted out the night before. His face was a mask of blank contentment, and he glanced up at the sky as if he wondered from whence the drops came.

There was one awful moment when Deirdre feared her trickery had been discovered, when Pagan's eyes narrowed, and it seemed as if his gaze burned through her cloak and into her deceiving heart. But she ducked her head, as would any shy bride. Sung Li covered for her, patting her hand in reassurance, and the moment passed. When at last he extended his hand to help her up the steps, there was naught but the gentlest of welcoming smiles upon his lips.

Custom dictated that the first part of the vows be spoken outside the chapel. The bad weather ensured a brief ceremony, which suited Deirdre. The sooner she was done with this duplicity, the better. Still, she scarcely heard the priest's words, her blood was rushing so loudly in her ears. She was careful to bend her knees so as not to seem too tall, and she spoke in a meek whisper. When the priest asked for her hand, she gave him but the tips of her sword-callused fingers and kept her head humbly inclined as was Miriel's habit.

Fortunately, there had been no time for Pagan to have a proper ring made, and so he slipped his own crest ring upon her finger, which fit loosely around her knuckle.

And then everyone was crowded inside the chapel, standing shoulder to shoulder for the sanctification of the marriage. Prayer after prayer was said as Deirdre and Pagan knelt before the altar, and with each, she felt more and more guilty. Deccit was uncomfortable enough, but to speak such falsehoods in the house of the Lord . . .

Despite the priest's thoroughness, Deirdre thought she'd never heard such a brief Mass. Before she could completely brace herself for the unveiling, the ceremony was coming to a close. The holy father blessed their union, gave them a jovial smile, and enjoined them to share a lover's kiss.

Deirdre held her breath. 'Twas not as if she'd never been kissed. But most men unwise enough to dare such a trespass had earned from her a blackened eye or a bruised jaw.

God's teeth, never had she desired her sword more. How gratifying if she could uncloak, unsheathe, and meet her husband with a naked blade while he reeled in shock.

But she'd wisely forborne her weapon. She'd known

this moment would come, known she must confront it bravely. Straightening to her full height, she turned and faced Pagan.

He lifted both hands to her hood and slowly peeled the wet cloth back. As her face was revealed, everyone gasped in astonishment, including the holy father. But as they murmured in stunned speculation, to Deirdre's chagrin, Pagan's features curiously betrayed not a hint of surprise. Instead, one corner of his mouth curved up in that knowing smile she was beginning to detest, and he curled his finger under her chin, lifting it for his kiss.

Her first absurd instinct was to seek an avenue of escape. A hard jab to the stomach, followed by a blow to the back of the head would do it. Or a knee to the groin, then a clout on the ear. She squeezed her eyes shut against the overwhelming urge to fight. He'd known, she realized. The devil had known of her trickery all along. And yet he'd said naught.

Perchance it didn't matter to him. As long as Rivenloch was his, 'twas of no consequence which of the sisters he wed.

"Afraid?" His taunt was a whisper, so low even the priest could not have heard it, and yet 'twas laced with a subtle challenge she had to answer.

She forced her eyes open again and faced him squarely. Nay, she was not afraid. Though 'twas disconcerting to have to look *up* into a man's face. Deirdre was accustomed to intimidating men with her size.

This man she'd never intimidate. His gaze was steady, unflinching, despite eyes whose color shifted like the storm clouds boiling across the sky, from gray to green to silver. His eyes dipped to her mouth, and she suddenly found it difficult to breathe.

Lightning flashed through the stained glass windows, reflected in his viridescent gaze, and raindrops from his drenched locks fell upon his dark lashes and streaked down his cheek like tears as he drew closer.

The instant their lips touched, thunder cracked the air. But Deirdre, swept away in a torrent of unfamiliar sensations, scarcely noticed. His mouth was wet with rain, but warm, and his kiss was unexpectedly tender. His scent, an intriguing blend of woodruff and smoke and spice, enveloped her, flirting with her nostrils like an elusive memory.

'Twas not so dreadful, she thought. His kiss was pleasant, his touch gentle. His manner was kind and courteous, and she sensed he'd not force himself upon her. Aye, she could endure a loveless marriage to such a man.

Or so she thought. Until he deepened the kiss.

The fingers under her chin spread to clasp her jaw, tilting her head for his pleasure, while his other hand slipped around her back to draw her closer. She raised her hands defensively, and they contacted the unyielding barrier of his chest. He teased at her lips with his tongue, and she opened her mouth in shock at the sensation, pushing at him with ineffectual fists. And then his tongue was inside her mouth, tasting her, devouring her, and though some small voice inside her warned that she should fight him, she found resistance impossible. Her head swam in a sensual deluge of rain and fire, and her body stirred as if some mysterious woman inside was awakened from a long slumber.

He groaned then, a soft sound that reverberated in her own mouth, and a current like lightning snaked through her, quickening her heart and leaving her skin aflame.

His hand moved to cup her buttocks, and he hauled her up against him, against that part of him that bulged now with obvious lust, pressing deliberately against her woman's mound. As if to claim her. As if to boast of that claim.

'Twas that realization that gave Deirdre the strength to fight her way to the surface of desire's drowning river and come up for a breath of pristine air. She wrenched her mouth from his and pushed against his chest with all her might. To no avail.

Heedless of the witnesses around them, furious with her own slip of control, she drew back her fist, intent on knocking that amorous, self-satisfied smile off of his face.

But he caught her fist, his great fingers somehow enveloping the whole of her hand, and he clucked his tongue. Then he murmured, "'Tis my right now . . . wife."

Chapter 6

DEIRDRE BIT BACK A SCREAM OF FURY. She would have stomped on Pagan's foot or kneed him in the groin to gain release, but in the next instant, he secured her under his arm. And before she could squirm away, he turned them as one to face the cheering congregation.

"Smile, bride," he said under his breath, waving at the crowd. "This is supposed to be a happy moment."

"I am far from happy," she bit out.

"You will smile," he commanded between grinning teeth, "or I'll finish what I started and swive you here and now on the altar."

She stiffened. "You wouldn't dare."

He continued smiling. "Curious. That was *my* thought yesterday when you threatened me with your sword." When he looked down at her, promise smoldered in his eyes. "*I* wagered wrong. And you? Care to wager on *my* threats?"

She frowned. 'Twas not that she believed him. Surely a God-fearing knight would never commit such an act of desecration. But the raw lust in his gaze was undeniable, and a sliver of doubt made her heart flutter. She tore her glance away and forced a tight smile to her lips.

After all, she reasoned, 'twas not as if she smiled for *him*. 'Twas for her clan, to assure them she was still in power, still the lady of the keep.

"Give me your hand," he whispered.

"I think not," she said, waving to the crowd.

He leaned closer. "Give me your hand . . . now."

She ignored him. He might be able to coerce her into putting on a false show of cheer, but . . .

He slipped his hand surreptitiously beneath her cloak, resting his palm on her back, between the blades of her shoulders. Then his hand slid slowly down, tracing the laces of her surcoat along her spine. Not two yards in front of the priest, and while Deirdre nodded and smiled at the onlookers, the shameless cur let his hand stray farther until it settled upon her buttock. Then he gave it a squeeze.

Snapping her head around with an overly brilliant smile, she thrust her hand out for his.

He took her hand in his with a knowing grin and placed a smug kiss upon her knuckles. Then he started forward.

Livid with frustration, she ground her teeth and endured the long walk through the crowd, her hand trapped within his like a mouse in a falcon's talons.

But the moment they were out, she swiftly closed the chapel door behind them against Colin and Sung Li and anyone else who would follow, then tore her hand from his and turned on him. "Heed me well, sirrah," she said betwixt her teeth. "I am not a dog, to be leashed and led

about at your pleasure. Nor think to beat me into submission, for I refuse to whimper at your feet."

He stared at her as the rain dripped from his hair onto
his surcoat, unmoving, silent, his face unreadable.
Deirdre thought for a moment she had effectively
stunned him, as oft occurred with men who underestimated her self-assurance. She was wrong.

In the next instant, he grabbed a fistful of the bodice
of her surcoat and yanked her forward until they were
nose to nose. "Now *you* heed *me*, my sweet." He spoke
softly, and a smile played about his lips, but his words
and the dangerous twinkle in his eyes were as menacing
as the distant thunder. "I am your husband, your lord,
and your master. You agreed to that when you decided to
take your sister's place. 'Tis within my rights to do anything with you, or *to* you, I please."

He winked, then released her suddenly, and she staggered back, mortified.

Never had a man seized her so brazenly. Men either
cowered in her presence or worshiped at her feet. But
this man, he laid hands on her as if he . . . owned her.

Sweet Jesu, what had she done? Marrying the Norman had seemed the right thing to do, the *only* thing to
do. But now she realized she didn't even *know* the man
she'd taken to husband. He seemed a monster, a devil.
And God help her, she'd sworn obeisance to him.
Bloody hell, what insidious form of slavery was marriage?

The congregation spilled out the door then, Colin and
Sung Li and the rest, with Lord Gellir at the fore, grinning hugely. Deirdre glimpsed an opportunity for reprieve from her wretched bridegroom. Rushing toward
her father, she linked her arm through his, then shot

Pagan a scathing smile, as if to say, *here* is my lord and master.

Her victory didn't last long. Pagan was a formidable opponent.

"If I may, my lord?" he said with a slight bow to her father. "I believe it ensures good luck for the bridegroom to carry the bride over the threshold."

"Nay!" Deirdre blurted out. Then, at the crowd's murmurs of surprise, she softened her tone. "Nay, good husband, I could not ask you to carry me through all this mud and mire." She clung tighter to her father.

"Dear heart," he said smoothly, drawing near to run a finger fondly down the bridge of her nose, "What is mud and mire? You I would carry through . . . flood and fire."

She resented his condescending gesture almost as much as the soft ahhs of all the womenfolk in the crowd who appreciated his couplet and believed his mawkish declaration. But when her father disengaged his arm and nudged her toward him, there was naught she could do.

With a wicked twist of a smile, Pagan scooped her from the steps and hefted her into his arms.

She held herself rigid, determined to make his task as difficult as possible.

She hoped she was heavy.

She hoped he would slip in the mud.

She hoped the heavens would open up and pour down buckets of rain.

But none of it happened. He carried her as if she were made of goosedown. His footing was as sure as an ox's. And to her irritation, the rain stopped momentarily, and the sun chose that moment to break through the clouds, casting a vivid rainbow across the sky.

"'Tis a sign, my lady," someone said. "Your marriage must be truly blessed."

Deirdre stared bleakly across the courtyard. Blessed? Never in her life had she felt more cursed.

Pagan took a deep sobering breath, filling his nostrils with the rain-pure air, as he carried his new-made wife across the soggy ground. Deirdre smelled of damp wool and earth and anger, but 'twas a scent that nonetheless aroused him. Her body felt strong and willful in his arms, like spirited prey, but that, too, filled his veins with thrilling heat. Forsooth, he feared the fierce throbbing betwixt his legs, undisguised by his usual braies, lent conspicuous evidence to his lust.

By the Rood, what was wrong with him? He'd dreaded this moment half the night and all morn, dreaded the thought of the wedding feast with Miriel by his side, where the clan would doubtless taunt the subjugated groom and his unwilling bride, dreaded even the marriage bed, where he knew he'd face a virgin's fears and tears and regret.

But the instant he'd seen the figure mincing toward him across the wet sward, bundled heavily enough for a hailstorm, he'd suspected foul play. And when his eye caught the soft glint of a silver Thor's hammer beneath her cloak, he knew who had come to be his bride. Then, to his chagrin, his apprehension dissolved away like butter on warm bread, and his heart began to pound with the exhilaration of battle.

If she thought her deception would embarrass him, she was wrong. He'd never claimed to perceive a difference between one sister and the next. Nor did it matter. If she thought 'twould invalidate the marriage contract, she was wrong there, too. He was pledged to marry "a daughter of Rivenloch," no more, no less. And if she thought that once she revealed herself, he'd refuse her hand, she was very, very wrong.

And so all through the ceremony, he'd been distracted by delicious visions of his lusty retaliation. For now, through her own devices, Deirdre would be his.

In every way.

For aye.

His loins tightened as he imagined her whimpering for mercy while he seduced her, imprisoning her hands in one fist and stripping away her garments; envisioned the sweet horror in her eyes as he whispered lurid eventualities in her ear; foresaw her hungry anticipation as he let his fingers roam over her gentle curves, stroking, tormenting, invading . . .

Sweet Jesu! Mayhap he misjudged his command of his own wits. His heart beat far too forcefully. His breath came too shallow. His body ached with yearning. He wanted Deirdre . . . now.

As soon as they crossed the threshold of the great hall, Pagan glanced toward the steps leading up to her bedchamber, weighing the moral consequences of foregoing the feast to bear her hence and claim his husbandly rights at once.

'Twas Colin who saved him from his unruly passions.

"Pagan!" he barked jovially, clapping him twice on the shoulder, hard enough to jar him from death. "Let your bride go and make herself ready for the feast. Come have a cup with me by the fire, and we'll toast your marriage."

That idea apparently appealed to everyone. They cheered and began milling into the great hall, and

Deirdre struggled to be free of him. But Pagan hesitated, unwilling to let her out of his arms or his sight.

"She'll cause no trouble," Colin murmured in assurance, then raised his brows at Deirdre. "You'll cause no trouble, will you, lass? After all, 'twill be but you and Pagan in the bedchamber this night. You and Pagan. Alone."

Again, she astonished Pagan. Instead of shuddering in fear, she gave Colin a grim smile. "Then he had better watch his back."

Colin chuckled in surprise. "Well said! But methinks you are too wise for that sort of sabotage. Surely you know that slaying your husband will only call the King's wrath upon your clan."

"I would not slay him," she said. "I would only maim him."

Pagan could easily guess upon which part of him she intended to inflict damage. "Mayhap you're right, Colin," he considered, nodding thoughtfully. "I should not be alone with her. Methinks the *both* of us should share her bed this night."

That sufficiently startled her from her dire threats. She glanced back and forth between them in disbelief.

Colin delightedly agreed. "Oh, aye, 'twould be my privilege, my lord," he said, raking his gaze lasciviously along her body.

"What! Nay!" she cried, unsure whether they were serious. "You would not," she said, searching both men's eyes for the truth.

Colin shrugged. "I do not see where you've left me any choice. You've made threats on my lord's life. I am honor bound to protect him."

Her exasperation was most amusing. "I'll not slay him. I swear it."

"Nor maim him?" Colin asked.

Suspecting now that they but provoked her, she gave him a grudging sigh. "Nor maim him."

"Very well." Colin took two cups of ale from a passing maidservant, giving the lass an appreciative perusal that made her giggle. "Then I shall find somewhere else to sleep this night." He nodded farewell and followed the blushing wench toward the hearth.

Reluctantly, Pagan let Deirdre slip from him. But before she could escape, he caught her by the arm. "Do not think to run away, wife, or . . ."

Pagan had heard of brides taking their own lives rather than facing the terrors of the marriage bed.

"Run away?" She drew herself up proudly. "This is *my* castle, sirrah. And I am no coward."

Her words gave Pagan curious relief.

"Besides," she fired boldly as a parting shot, "*someone* has to teach you how to steward a castle."

She turned her back on him before he could glower at the insult. Instead, he shook his head and sighed, watching her hips twitch provocatively as she climbed the stairs, trailed by Miriel's handmaiden. Devil's ballocks, but this new wife of his was going to be a handful. And yet, he had to admit he'd rather be wed to a willful wench full of fire than a shrinking shadow of a maid.

Deirdre felt Pagan's heated gaze follow her all the way up the steps, and for once, the attention unsettled her. Her face flushed hot, and she would have tripped on the last stair, but Sung Li, following close behind, caught her.

"He who fears to fall, falls hardest." The little maid, stronger than she looked, helped her regain her balance.

Deirdre frowned at her cryptic remark. Most of the time she didn't understand Sung Li even when she *wasn't* speaking Chinese. Still, the woman had been of great help today, and Deirdre owed her a debt of gratitude.

"Here." She dug in the small purse hanging from her belt, withdrew the tower key along with a piece of silver, and pressed them into the maid's palm. "Miriel is in the south tower. Free her. Make her understand."

Sung Li's lips thinned. She kept the key, but returned the coin. "My loyalty is not for purchase." Then with a proud snap of her chin, she turned and swaggered off.

Deirdre couldn't enter her chamber quickly enough. Once safely inside, she slammed the door and leaned back against it, taking solace in the solid barrier between her and her new bridegroom.

Lord, she felt as edgy as a lone mouse in a barn full of hungry cats.

Deirdre was accustomed to having the upper hand. For years she had daunted men with her imposing stature and her noble status as a lord's daughter. Her clansmen followed her orders without question. And strangers quickly learned to treat her with the proper respect.

This Norman afforded her no deference whatsoever. Not as a noble heir. Not as the steward of Rivenloch. Not even as a woman. How would she ever retain control of her castle, of her lands, of her people, if she could not control this one man?

She hung up her cloak, then crossed to lean against the shutter of the window. The blustery rain had returned, and she shivered, but not because of the cold.

Resting her brow upon her hands, she gazed out over the misty knolls and rain-studded trees of Rivenloch, frustrated.

She was Pagan's captive. From the moment the priest declared them man and wife, he had subtly enslaved her in one way or another, snagging his fingers in her hair for their kiss, imprisoning her hand as they walked the length of the chapel, encircling her body with fierce ownership as he carried her to the keep. And tonight, he would claim her in the ultimate act of possession.

She swallowed thickly. 'Twas not that she was truly afraid. She'd caught enough servants swiving to know 'twas merely a disgusting display of thrashing and moaning, over in a few moments. And yet she sensed from the way her heart pounded as Pagan kissed her, the way the blood rose in her cheeks, the way her head swam in confusion, that coupling with him would be somehow dangerous.

Still, how could she avoid it? She'd sworn not to harm him, though forsooth that had never been her intent. She supposed she could plead illness or fatigue, but deception came uneasily to her. Besides, 'twould only delay the inevitable. Even if she drugged his wine every night . . .

Through the window, a distant flicker of light from the far hills distracted her. She narrowed her eyes. What was that? Another flicker. She lifted her head and studied the source of the reflection, a gap between two pines on the hilltop. There 'twas again, a quick glint where a slim beam of sunlight caught on something.

Suddenly the flashes increased, and Deirdre's heart flipped against her ribs. Knights. Four, five, six, maybe more, cresting the rise. Their helms sparkled in the patch of sun. As she watched with breathless intensity, a pennant fluttered past, no larger than a tiny moth, too small to identify.

"Ballocks," she cursed under her breath.

Seven, eight, nine . . .

She clenched her fist against the shutter. They had turned now and were coming straight down the hill.

God's blood! It must be the English. They'd come for Rivenloch.

Chapter 7

THERE WAS NO TIME TO WASTE.

The guards manning the parapets had spotted the knights now, and they began to pass the message of invasion along the wall.

Her heart pounding like the hooves of a warhorse, Deirdre slammed and bolted the shutter. She eyed her chest of armor. Later. Later she would arm herself. First she had to prepare the keep for battle.

She'd never done it before. She'd never had to. But because of the recent attacks in the Borders, she'd gone over the scenario a hundred times in her head, and the men-at-arms had been drilled in defensive maneuvers by Helena until they could do them in their sleep.

Helena! Christ's bones! What if she was still drunk?

There was no time to rouse her. The castle walls had to be fortified first. She'd send someone to fetch Helena when the keep was out of danger.

Her pulse doubling, she raced out the door, picked up

her skirts, and flew down the stairs to the great hall, where the wedding revels had already begun.

"Clansmen!" she cried, her voice strong despite the urgent thrumming in her veins. "Give ear!"

The room gradually silenced.

"An army is approaching Rivenloch," she announced. At their gasps, she raised her hand for quiet. "There is no need for panic. You've been trained for this. You all know what to do."

To her satisfaction, though they chattered worriedly amongst themselves, the castle folk began to walk purposefully toward whatever task they'd been assigned in the event of an attack.

But Pagan suddenly stepped in front of her, blocking her view with his imposing chest. "Wait!" he barked over his shoulder.

To Deirdre's consternation, they did.

"How big is this army?" he asked her.

She clenched her jaw. "I know not," she muttered impatiently. "They were mounted knights. A dozen . . . maybe more." Bending past his broad shoulder, she yelled, "You, lad! Quick! Gather the livestock within the walls!" She tried to sidle past Pagan, but he blocked her way again.

"From what direction?" he asked.

"Would you move?" she growled. "You, you, and you!" she commanded, pointing at her best archers. "Man the battlements!"

Over his shoulder, he shouted, "Fire only at my command!"

Deirdre almost choked on her outrage. "*Your* co— This is *my* castle, sirrah! Do not think to—"

"From what direction do they come?" he asked again.

"The south," she hissed. "How dare you usurp my authority! I've defended this keep for years. You've been here but one day. I will not have you countermand my orders!" To prove her point, she issued another command. "Angus! When the beasts are in, drop the portcullis!" At least, she thought, the wedding had served one useful purpose—the castle folk were already safely congregated within the walls.

"Is it the English?" Pagan asked.

She tried to push past the brute, but he was as unmovable as a deep-rooted oak.

He seized her by the shoulders then and held her still, though in truth he pinned her more with his fierce gaze than his hands. "Is it. The. English?" he asked, as if he were speaking to a halfwit.

"Aye." She bit out the word, not caring a whit whether the invaders were English or not, only wanting the meddling Norman to get out of her way. "Aye, 'tis the English."

"You're certain?"

Now her patience was at an end. This was the reason one didn't send a Norman to defend a Scot's holding. If Pagan had spent any time in the Borders at all, he'd know that Highlanders, their only other enemy, fought afoot in sheepskins, not mounted and in armor. She shrugged off his hands. "If you do not remove yourself this instant, I swear by all that's holy—"

"How many battles have your men fought, milady?"

"What? I have no time for your chin-wagging, sirrah! Let me—" She tried to heave him out of her path again, to no avail. If only she'd brought a dagger to prod him . . .

"Answer me."

She made daggers of her eyes instead. "My men train in the tiltyard every—"

"How many *real* battles have they fought?"

The question gave her pause. She compressed her lips, reluctant to answer. "'Tis no matter." She wanted to lie, tell him they'd fought in dozens of wars, but she could not.

"How many?"

"None, but—"

"And how many times have you been under siege?"

"Never," she admitted. "But my people have been well trained. They know what to—"

"I've commanded armies in a dozen battles," he boasted. "And I once survived a siege of half a year. *I* know what to do."

Why she should believe him, she didn't know. She still suspected he was but a landless knight-errant. Yet the cool confidence in his eyes, as cocksure and annoying and superior as it may be, was also reassuring. Pagan would not let Rivenloch fall.

But what she told him was also true. He'd been there but one day. She knew the castle, knew the land, knew the people. She could better manage them.

Before she could explain, Colin skipped up, clearing his throat. "Did you, my lady," he asked, lifting his brows nonchalantly, "happen to glimpse the banner of that army?"

"'Twas too distant."

He nodded. "Mm."

"Why?"

He scratched his chin. "I climbed the parapets to take a look. Something about the colors seemed . . . vaguely familiar." He exchanged a curious look with Pagan.

But Deirdre had no patience for Colin's musings. There would be time to discover exactly who the knights were later, *after* the keep was secure.

Between Colin and the hearth, she spotted an idle maidservant. "You! Fetch Lady Helena! She's in her chamber. Tell her—"

"Nay!" Colin cried. "Nay. I'll . . . I'll do it. I'm certain the maid has more important duties. Besides," he said, clasping his hands together with a clap, "'twill make me feel useful."

"Then tell her 'tis urgent," she bade him. "Tell her the men-at-arms await her orders."

Colin gaped. "*She* commands the men-at-arms?"

Deirdre let out an agitated sigh. "Are you going to help or not?"

Without a word, Colin sketched an elaborate bow and started across the great hall.

"Wait!" she yelled. "Where are you going? Her chamber is not that way."

He looked confused for a moment, then stuttered, "I . . . I'm just going to the cellar to . . . to fetch her breakfast. Can't command men-at-arms on an empty stomach."

She frowned, then returned her attention to Pagan. He was gazing at her strangely now, as if he weighed her worth or divined her future.

"Your archers," he said, "they're experienced? They won't fire prematurely?"

"Nay," she assured him smugly. "They'll only fire at *my* command." To her satisfaction, this time he didn't argue the point.

*　　*　　*

Pagan hoped she was right. After all, 'twould be unfortunate if a Rivenloch archer shot one of his knights.

He supposed he should enlighten her, tell her that Colin had recognized the approaching army as the knights of Cameliard. But 'twould be useful to know, and he was curious to see, how well she commanded the keep and how organized Rivenloch's defenses were. Of course, if it had been a *real* assault, he never would have let her take charge. He would have sent her or dragged her, if need be, to join the rest of the women and children of Rivenloch in the innermost chambers of the keep for safety.

He turned to observe the mass of people scrambling to and fro across the great hall. Each seemed to know his purpose, and none was panicking. But in the midst of the orderly chaos, the Lord of Rivenloch stood dazed, as if he were set adrift in the sea of clansmen.

Turning back to Deirdre, he said, "Your father is confused. Go to him. Make certain he's safe. I'll gather the men-at-arms while Colin is fetching your sister."

She visibly bristled at his tone of command. 'Twas clear his willful bride craved the upper hand. He couldn't decide if that trait was aggravating or entertaining. His thoughts strayed to the marriage bed they'd share this night, and he wondered if she'd insist upon the upper hand there, too. 'Twas an intriguing possibility.

Deirdre's frown melted as she observed her father, and Pagan glimpsed the weight of responsibility settle upon her shoulders. No doubt 'twas burdensome, caring for a feeble parent. Pagan didn't know. His parents had died suddenly of the murrain years ago. "Very well," she conceded. "Do so."

He watched as she made her way to the lord, guiding

him with loving care up the steps to his chamber. She was an enigma, this new bride of his, as rough as an alewife one moment, as gentle as a nun the next.

Pagan squared his shoulders and headed toward the armory, where the knights would be donning chain mail and taking up sword and pike, bow and mace. 'Twas time to see what manner of fighting force Rivenloch boasted.

As soon as Deirdre made certain her father was comfortable, residing in his chamber with a squire for company, her heart began its rapid patter once again. Aye, 'twas one less thing to worry about, but there were a hundred others. As much as it stuck in her craw to say it, she was almost glad of Pagan's aid. At least he had experience in warfare, something not one of her men could claim. What troubled her most, however, was the fact that Rivenloch's walls had never been tested. Of course, Helena made it her duty to maintain the defenses, to look for weaknesses and inspect for damage. But no firebrand or battering ram or sapper's spade had ever attempted to broach the walls. As far as anyone truly knew, the stones might crumble with the tap of a broomstick.

Deirdre gave her head a shake, dismissing the thought. There were too many other worries at the moment.

She snagged a squire in the passageway to help her don her armor. The sooner she was protected enough to mount the battlements, the sooner she could see what manner of men she was up against and how best to defend the keep.

While the squire tied the points on her gambeson and helped her into her mail chausses and hauberk, Deirdre opened the shutter the tiniest crack and peered out at the arriving army. They were still distant figures, but 'twas clear now there were at least a score of mounted knights and, behind them, several afoot. There were also a number of heavy-laden carts. Deirdre imagined they were filled with arms, provender, and materials for building pavilions, should they decide to lay siege.

As the squire slipped her tunic over her chain mail, the wind picked up the corner of the invaders' far-off pennant, and she glimpsed the coat-of-arms, some beast of argent upon a sable field. As Colin had mentioned, something about the design seemed familiar to her, too.

"Ian, look at that pennant," she bade the squire. "Where have you seen it before?"

He squinted into the distance, chewing upon his lip. "Was that not upon the tunic of that jongleur, the one who played at supper but two—"

"Bloody hell." Realization slowly dawned. "Bloody hell!"

She glanced down at her wedding ring. A pale unicorn upon a black field. By the Rood, these men were Pagan's own knights!

"That son of a . . ." She slammed the shutter.

So he wasn't a mere knight-errant after all. He commanded his own army. He must have sent Boniface the jongleur as a spy, then ordered his knights to follow in the event Pagan's suit was refused. 'Twas a brilliant strategy. But that didn't diminish Deirdre's anger with him now for his deception. Why had he not revealed their identity? Did he hope to make a fool of her?

'Twould be a snowy day in hell before he'd do that. She might be inexperienced, but she was well prepared. And she had more wits than he imagined. Did he wish to humiliate her, put her in her place? Then she'd show him that two could play at that game.

Pagan tried not to look disappointed as he reviewed the ranks of Scots soldiers. Though they were admirably disciplined and seemed to be brave of heart, they were the most motley bunch of knights he'd ever seen assembled. They might well be Scotland's finest, but they weren't fit to polish the sabatons of the Knights of Cameliard. Six of them claimed to be trained as horsemen, and while their armor was intact, it looked to date from the last century. A dozen more were men-at-arms whose arms were sadly lacking, limited to but one or two weapons apiece. The three archers, already dispatched to patrol the parapets, appeared to be the *only* adept bowmen at Rivenloch. And the rest of the odd company—white-bearded old men, skinny-armed lads, and one tiny lass he smacked on the bottom and sent on her way—looked barely fit to defend a honeycomb from ants, much less protect a prize like Rivenloch.

'Twas indeed a good thing the King had sent Pagan to be Rivenloch's steward. With the worthy Knights of Cameliard living among them, these simple Scots could go back to whatever 'twas they did in their daily life— farming or fishing or frolicking with their sheep—while his men defended the keep.

Still, Pagan knew better than to insult them. A captain had to be diplomatic, to inspire his men, even if they were outnumbered ten to one. He had to give them hope, even when there was none.

"Who is the best horseman here?" he asked.

There was no argument. One of the armored men stepped forward.

"And the best swordsman?"

This time there was an awkward shuffling. Finally one man asked, "For power or speed?"

"Both."

"For power, 'twould be Will here," he said, pointing a thumb at the man with the broadest girth. "For speed—"

"That would be Helena," a feminine voice chimed in.

Pagan glanced up to see what woman came uninvited into the armory. 'Twas Deirdre, but a Deirdre transformed. No longer the lovely, silk-gowned goddess he'd married, she was a warrior clad head to toe in chain mail and armed with a broadsword.

While he gaped in surprise, she swept past him and addressed the man who'd volunteered himself as the best horseman. "Are the chargers being saddled?"

"Aye, my lady."

"Your blades are sharp?" she asked Will.

"Aye."

Utterly shocked, Pagan found his diplomacy deserted him. "What the bloody hell do you think you're doing?"

She ignored him. "Helena has not yet arrived?" she asked the men-at-arms. They shook their heads, and she wheeled to face him in accusation. "What is keeping your man?"

Pagan was not about to be questioned, especially not by a woman who mocked the very essence of chivalry with her presence in the armory. "You have my permission to see what is keeping him," he said with a sweep of his arm, "and leave me to my command."

"You've served your purpose," she countered. "I'll take over now."

"Forsooth?" he said, arching a brow. "And will you ride into battle with your men as well?"

"If it comes to that."

Over my rotting corpse, he thought, but he held his tongue. If there had been a true threat, he would have stripped the armor from her and given it to some more likely lad, one who might slay a foe or two before he fell. His wife he would lock in the cellar with her sister, if need be. But since 'twas only a drill, he decided to see just how far she would go before her feminine nature got the better of her and she ran, weeping and wailing in fear, to hide behind more capable warriors.

Meanwhile, he needed to be certain no overeager Scot loosed a premature arrow, for retaliation from the knights of Cameliard would be swift and complete. And tragic.

"I'm going to climb the parapets," he told her, "to see what we're up against."

Though she took visual note of his lack of protective armor, she said naught of it. She doubtless hoped he'd get shot, saving her the nuisance of an unwanted husband.

He took one final glance at her as he exited the armory. 'Twas strange to admit, but he found Deirdre alluring, armor and all. There was something about the close fit of her chausses, the way the chain mail draped over her breasts and the blade hung upon her hip, that was curiously seductive.

By the time he mounted the curtain wall, his men had drawn close enough for anyone to see 'twas not an army, but an entourage of families. Aye, his knights were armored and armed, but only as a precaution. Behind them, ladies rode palfreys, and maidservants slogged through the mud while children scampered about with tireless energy. Men-at-arms and squires brought up the rear, guarding half a dozen carts of furnishings, provender, and arms.

Pagan decided to make conversation with the archer at the foremost tower. "They don't look very threatening, do they?"

"Nay, my lord."

"More like travelers than an army."

The archer sniffed and kept his bow at the ready, poised between two merlons of the wall walk. He was obviously not about to be dissuaded from his loyalty to his lady, regardless of his own opinion about the strangers. Forsooth, 'twas an admirable quality.

Pagan sauntered over to the second archer, positioned to the right. "Methinks they are friend, not foe, to approach the castle so openly."

"Begging your pardon, my lord," the man murmured, his eyes trained on the company, his fingers wrapped loosely about his bowstring where an arrow was already nocked. "I'd rather not converse while I've got something in my sights."

Pagan nodded. This man, too, was well disciplined. As ill-equipped and inexperienced as they were, he had to admit these Scots seemed to know what they were doing.

He backed away and approached the third archer, a young lad whose upper lip was beaded with sweat and whose arms trembled as he tried to steady his bow against the merlon. This was the one Pagan would have to watch.

"Easy, lad," Pagan whispered.

"Sweet Mary!" the lad cried, startled so much that he almost fired the arrow on the spot.

His heart leaping into his throat, Pagan clasped his

hand over the lad's to prevent an accident. "Easy. You don't want to shoot one of those children, do you?"

The lad shook his head.

"Have you never fired a bow before?" he asked.

"Aye. I'm the best hunter in the clan, can fell a buck at fifty yards. But—" The lad gulped.

"You've never shot a man."

The boy bit his lip.

Pagan dared not release his grip on the bow. "I have. Would you like me to take your station?"

"Nay," the lad said vehemently. "Nay. I've been entrusted with this post, and I'll not abandon it." He seemed to gather strength from his own words.

Pagan had to admire the lad's courage and sense of duty, though he'd be far more comfortable if the boy had handed him the weapon. "Very well." Reluctantly, carefully, he loosened his hold. "But take care you do not fire until you are ordered to do s—"

"Prepare to fire!" came a shout from behind him.

Chapter 8

PAGAN'S HEART SLAMMED AGAINST HIS RIBS. "Nay!" he roared.

Deirdre, in all her armored glory, stood with her sword drawn and raised, ready to give the order to shoot. As one, the archers nocked their arrows and took aim.

"Wait! Wait!" he said, willing his voice to remain calm, but taking huge strides toward her. "Hold your fire."

"Must you countermand all my orders, sirrah?" she snapped, her blade still lifted. "Or is that the way *Norman* soldiers fight?"

Pagan could barely draw breath as he watched the archers' arrows train upon his people. "Can you not see?" he asked. He made a grab for her sword, but she drew it back out of his reach. "They're not soldiers. They're innocent women and . . . and children and—"

"That one with the battleaxe," she said, nodding at the knights and raising her sword a fraction, "he is no innocent. What do you say? Should we take him out first?"

"Nay!" Pagan's eyes grew wide. God's blood, Sir Rauve d'Honore was one of his best knights.

"What about that man with the standard?" she considered. "They say there is naught more crushing than to have the coat-of-arms fall."

"Nay." The standard-bearer, Lyon, was but a lad with a wife of two years and a babe. "By God's grace, you do not even know who these people are."

"I know they're upon my land," she said coolly.

"They may mean you no harm."

"I'm unwilling to take that risk," she said decisively, lifting her blade again.

"Wait!" This time he successfully caught her wrist and brought her up close. He gazed upon her beautiful face, her smooth brow, her flushed cheeks, her determined mouth. Then he frowned. Something lurked in those cool blue eyes, something devious, something dangerous, some spark of mischief.

"Mayhap I should have the archers aim for that pretty redhead in the blue cloak," she murmured pensively, the shadow of a smile playing about her lips. "Shooting a woman would certainly cause a stir in their ranks."

Then he saw the truth. The damned wench was bluffing.

He narrowed his eyes. "You know," he accused.

One corner of her lip curved up. "Oh, aye."

The breath went out of him then, but he did not release her wrist. "And how long have you known?"

"Almost as long as you."

"Colin." The traitor must have told her. He was ever siding with the fairer sex.

"Nay." She wiggled her ring finger.

"Ah." Clever wench. Clever and infuriating. "Well, my cunning lady, will you call off your archers now?"

"That depends."

Why the woman believed she had the upper hand, he couldn't imagine. Her men might fire the first shot, but if they did, the Knights of Cameliard would turn Rivenloch into a bloody massacre within moments.

"Depends upon what?" he asked.

"Upon your reason in neglecting to tell me your men were coming."

'Twas a fair enough question. "Call off your archers, and I'll tell you."

"Let go of me, and I will."

The two of them stood at an impasse, he with her blade at bay, she with her archers poised to fire. One of them had to cede. Pagan let go of her wrist. She lowered her sword.

"Archers, rest," she ordered. They lowered their bows. "Well?"

"I wanted to see how battle ready your men were," he admitted openly.

"And?"

"They need much more training and practice. Their numbers are pitiful, and their arms are in sad repair."

She bristled. "I'll have you know—"

"But," he continued, "they are organized and well ordered. And they have discipline and heart, things which cannot be gained by aught but fierce loyalty."

His amendment seemed to smooth Deirdre's ruffled feathers. A curious warmth flowed through his veins to see how proud she was of her bedraggled and unseasoned clansmen. Forsooth, 'twas a shame she was a woman. He imagined she'd make a fine second in command.

"Well, now that you've measured *my* people's worth," she said with a trace of irritation, "how long will *yours* be staying?"

He scowled. Did she not realize? The King hadn't sent him solely to claim a bride. Pagan had come to claim a castle. His knights and their families came with him. "Rivenloch will be their home now."

Her eyes widened. "What?" She crossed to the rim of the wall walk and stared down at the approaching horde. "All of them? There are too many. Rivenloch cannot possibly sustain—"

"Do not fret. I've skilled huntsmen, cooks, and an alewife or two in the ranks. I've already planned to have the castle enlarged, add a cellar, double the kitchens, increase the size of the stables . . ."

Something he said infuriated Deirdre, though he couldn't imagine what. After all, he offered to improve the castle. But she let out an exasperated sigh and turned on her heel, marching down the steps as if she stomped them into submission.

He watched her go, belatedly deciding he'd better follow her. He'd not have her open the gates of Rivenloch, only to greet his people in full armor.

Deirdre stiffly raised her mazer and drained the last of her honey mead. All around her, strangers ate and laughed and jested . . . and infiltrated the ranks of Rivenloch, like sly foxes in a dovecot.

"Deirdre," Miriel whispered beside her.

"What?" she snapped. Miriel's face fell, and Deirdre was instantly contrite. "Sorry."

"The stores of wine are running low," she said under her breath.

Deirdre clenched her teeth and muttered, "Then let them drink pond water."

Miriel sighed, speaking softly so that Pagan, seated on Deirdre's other side, wouldn't hear. "Oh, Deirdre, you should have let me marry him. Then you wouldn't be so miserable."

"Nay, *nay*." She clasped her little sister's hand. "Do not even think of it." She forced a smile of false cheer to her face and gave Miriel's hand a reassuring pat. "'Tis only that I'm . . . overwhelmed."

Miriel winced in apology. "And here I've come to trouble you about the wine. 'Tis no matter. On the morrow, I'll send a lad to the monastery for more. Meanwhile . . ." She pensively tapped her pointed chin. "I'll fetch the . . . heather hippocras from the cellar."

"The what?"

But Miriel only gave her a wink and a sweet grin and left to perform a small miracle.

Deirdre couldn't help but smile back. Miriel was brilliant and inventive when it came to rationing provender and sparing coin. But though she might have solved the wine quandary, Deirdre pitied the poor cook, who faced the impossible task of stretching a single roast boar into food for well over a hundred.

By Deirdre's count, the company consisted of no less than two dozen mounted knights, a considerable number. As much as she hated to admit it, she was impressed. The King had wed her to no worthless adventurer after all. Pagan was the captain of a sizable fighting force. But accompanying that sizable retinue were wives and children, as well as a score of squires, servants, and hounds.

And now the poor hall and stables of Rivenloch were packed as tightly as a barrel of herring.

"Do not trouble yourself," Pagan murmured beside her, as if he'd read her thoughts. "Rivenloch's stores will be well replenished. I'll send my men to hunt on the morrow, and the older lads can fish in the loch."

"They may be too drunk by then to stand," Deirdre grumbled.

Damn the meddling Norman. Rivenloch was *her* responsibility. What did he know about the crofters or the land or the loch? He'd probably never even spent a winter in Scotland.

She glanced down at the trencher she was expected to share with her new husband. He'd hardly touched a bite, and his cup of mead was yet half full. 'Twas apparent that Pagan, at least, was doing his part not to deplete Rivenloch's resources.

The same could not be said of his knights. One of them, Sir Rauve d'Honore, obviously drunk, tottered to his feet and raised his cup. "A salute to Lord Pagan's prize," he slurred, "the most beautiful bride in Scotland."

Cheers went up around her, but Deirdre sighed at the shallow flattery. By the Saints, what did beauty matter? Besides, 'twas nonsense. She wasn't nearly as pretty as Miriel, and Helena had a far more voluptuous—

Helena.

She frowned. Where *was* Helena? And where was Pagan's man? He'd gone to fetch her hours ago. She started to push up from the bench, but Pagan caught her arm, a silent question in his glance.

She chose to overlook his possessive grip. "Where is my sister?"

"Miriel?"

"Helena."

He released her. "She's fine. Sit down."

Something guilty in his eyes made her heart trip with mistrust. "What's happened? Where is she?"

"She's with Colin. Sit *down*."

"And where is Colin?" Deirdre demanded a little too loudly, startling the diners beside her.

"Aye, Colin," someone echoed from a lower table. "Where *is* Colin?"

"God's blood, where's the varlet gone?"

Anon all of Pagan's knights were asking after the man.

"Colin?" Pagan smiled for their benefit. "Ah . . . Colin has gone to . . . to fetch more ale from the cellar."

The knights cheered and drank, if possible, even more heartily.

Deirdre scowled. Pagan wasn't any better at lying than she was. And the knave was holding her fast again, as if she were a charger inclined to bolt. She clenched her fists and her teeth, finally taking a seat. "Damn you, where *is* she?"

"The last time I saw her, sometime after midnight," Pagan muttered, "she was so sotted, she could hardly crawl."

Deirdre felt her face go hot with guilt.

Noting her high color, Pagan leaned close and murmured, "What's this, wife? Your blush betrays you." His grip tightened on her arm. "Do you know something about her devilry of last eve?"

Deirdre refused to look at him. Devilry? Dear God, what had her impulsive sister done now?

Pagan cursed softly, his breath harsh against her cheek. "Bloody hell, did you send her?"

Deirdre's thoughts were whirring by too fast to answer. "Did you send her to kill me?" he bit out.

She flinched. Kill him? Sweet Jesu!

Pagan's fingers dug painfully into her arm. "You *did* send her." He hissed against her hair now. To anyone else, 'twould appear he whispered naught but lover's promises into her ear. "You sneaking shrew. And I credited you with more honor."

That shook her from her woolgathering. She faced him squarely. "I swear I didn't send her anywhere. But tell me. You've not hurt her, have you?" Her eyes narrowed, half in dread, half in threat. "Have you?"

He seemed insulted by her question, though he let go of her abruptly, as if suddenly aware of his own strength. "Nay. 'Tis not the way of a Norman knight to attack God's weaker creatures."

Weaker creatures? Now *he* insulted *her*, but she was too relieved to take him to task for it. "What have you done with her?"

"She's safe enough for the moment."

"Do not harm her," she charged him. "I'll see to her chastisement myself."

"Forsooth? And what chastisement will you administer to your sister for murder and treason? Will you slap her naughty wrist?"

Deirdre colored. She was beginning to hate Pagan's sharp wit. Mostly because, in this instance, 'twas deserved.

Pagan lifted his cup and sipped at his mead.

"I'll make a bargain with you," Deirdre said. "Here is the truth of it. 'Twas my fault. I suspected Helena might do something . . . impulsive to halt the wedding. So I plied her with drink, enough, I'd hoped, to keep her drowsing, to prevent just this sort of . . . mishap."

He gave a mirthless chuckle. Apparently, he considered Hel's attack far more than a mishap.

Deirdre straightened and looked him in the eye. "Punish me. Punish me in her stead."

'Twould be best. She was stronger than Helena. She could endure pain without a word. Hel would only earn herself a harsher penance by spitting curses at him.

"You would pay for her sins?" he asked softly.

"She's my sister. You know she meant no treason. She only thought to save Miriel from—"

"From having to wed me." His voice was flat. "But *you* managed to save her instead." There was a sharply sardonic edge to his words as he lifted his mazer of mead. "I applaud your noble sacrifice." He finished off the cup all at once, then let out a long sigh. "You know, at home, beautiful wenches used to fall all over themselves for my favors. I come to Rivenloch, and everyone thinks me a demon." He shook his head. "What is it? Have I grown horns?"

Deirdre hated to admit it, but even with horns, he'd be the most handsome man she'd ever seen. Instead, she explained, "You are Norman."

He lifted a brow. "You *do* know 'tis Normans who are your allies against the English, do you not?"

"We're not at war with England."

"Not yet, but now you have naught to fear. The knights you see here," he said, gesturing to the men around him, "are the best warriors in the land. As soon as they train your men in the finer points of warfare—"

"Train my men?" Deirdre said, affronted. "My men need no training from your . . . your—"

"Lord Pagan!" someone shouted. "What promises do you whisper in your bride's ear to make her blush so?"

"He doubtless boasts of the length of his broadsword!" someone else cried.

"Why waste words, my lord?" another taunted.

"Aye, show the lass what steel 'tis made of!"

Suddenly the great hall was filled with the clamor of cups banging on tables and chants of "Pagan! Pagan! Pagan!"

Deirdre felt suddenly smothered. Sweet Saints, was that her father joining them in their lusty cries? She again had an overpowering desire to draw her sword in answer to the barbaric noise. But Pagan, mayhap sensing her unease, placed one placating hand upon her shoulder and stood, raising the other to quiet his men.

"Come, you'll frighten my bride," he said. "Let the women take her above and make her ready. I'll stay and have one last drink with you."

Before Deirdre could protest, a dozen Rivenloch and Norman maids surrounded her. In a flurry of giggles, they hoisted her atop their shoulders to carry her up the winding stairs to her chamber.

'Twas foolishness, she thought as they tied back the bedhangings, then undressed her and scattered rose petals across the linens of her bed, dabbed lavender oil at her throat and lit the candles someone had placed all around the chamber. 'Twas a silly waste of labor and ceremony and candles. Pagan had said it himself—he was accustomed to beautiful women begging for his favors. What use had he for a towering warrior wench like Deirdre?

Yet her pulse raced absurdly as she let the women guide her to the pallet, almost as if in anticipation. They tucked her in, releasing her braid and arranging the blonde waves artfully over her bosom, but she refused to let them take the Thor's hammer from around her neck.

The din of men approaching, drunk and loud and raucous, sent the maids into gales of nervous laughter, and their inane excitement shot a frisson of dread up her spine. A sudden banging upon the door made her jump, and she frowned at her own lack of nerve.

'Twas ridiculous! She wasn't some fainthearted craven to cringe in terror. With a defiant toss of her head, she threw off the coverlet and sat up proudly to face the invading horde.

She was prepared for a string of bawdy jests. She was prepared for crude gestures and lewd leers and mindless, drunken raving when they flung open the door.

She was not prepared for sudden silence.

Chapter 9

PAGAN'S JAW DROPPED. Unbidden, his gaze coursed over the lush contours of his bride's body, following the graceful waves of firelit hair that swept past her wide, yet fine-boned shoulders, only partially covering her elegant breasts, and leaving bare her flat stomach with its inviting navel.

He could draw no air into his lungs.

He'd known Deirdre was beautiful. He'd glimpsed her naked from afar as she bathed. And he'd seen her dressed in both soft, flowing silk and body-hugging chain mail. But he'd not expected the perfection before him now. And he'd never guessed how much knowing that she belonged to him would enhance her beauty.

Another woman might have gasped and shielded herself. But Deirdre made no move to hide from him, and her self-assurance aroused him tremendously. Blood surged suddenly in his loins, shaking him to the core.

Then he realized that his men, shoving each other behind him for a peek, were struck dumb as well, that they, too, felt the effects of Deirdre's unabashed beauty. His lust swiftly took a possessive turn then, and he wanted them gone. All of them. Now.

But even through his own blinding desire, when he met Deirdre's bold gaze, he detected the subtle hint of fear in her eyes. Like cornered quarry, it seemed she put on a brave face and stood her ground when she likely wished instead to retreat into some safe warren.

And that courage made him feel something else, something wholly unfamiliar to him. 'Twas a kind of admiration and ownership, a strange respect, but also a desire to protect her.

Somehow he found his voice. Somehow he found the patience to resist commanding them all to get the bloody hell back down the stairs and away from his bride.

"People of . . ." He *thought* he'd found his voice. That telltale squeak, he feared, gave away the rattled state of his composure. The men crowding the doorway let out their breath in a collective chuckle of relief.

He started again. "People of Rivenloch, Knights of Cameliard, I thank you for bearing witness to our holy union." He glanced at Deirdre. Though she kept up a serene mien, her hands were balled into fists upon her lap. He felt a powerful urge to unclench them for her. "However *this* union only God shall witness."

As was customary, the men sent up a loud and drunken protest, but they soon dutifully retreated from the doorway. The women, too, abandoned Deirdre with whispered wishes of good fortune.

Only Sir Rauve was sotted enough to yell, "We'll come for the bloody linens on the morrow, lad. Don't disappoint us!"

The others joined in with merry threats, but Pagan

closed the door on them. He took a deep breath and turned to face his wife.

She hadn't moved from her spot. Sitting in the midst of her fur-covered bed, lit by a host of ivory candles, she looked like a saint about to be martyred. Her eyes shone with courage, her belly rose and fell with each shallow breath, and her fingers clenched tightly in the bed-clothes. He felt almost sorry for her.

Until she spoke.

"Touch me, and 'twill be *your* blood upon the linens."

Her words extinguished his lust like a bucket of cold water. If Deirdre was akin to a frightened beast, then she was decidedly the kind with claws. And he'd already endured one of her painful scratches. He'd not do so again.

He needed a moment to think, to best consider how to approach this dangerous animal.

While she kept a wary gaze upon him, he perused the chamber. 'Twas furnished in a manner ill befitting a lady, aside from the rose petals scattered upon the bed and the fresh rushes strewn with heather that covered the floor. There were no perfumes, no ribbons, no trinkets upon the single table that stood at one side of the bed, only a quill, a few pieces of parchment, and a vial of ink. A heavy oak chest dominated one wall, and a second chest of pine sat beneath one of the two shuttered windows. A worn chair squatted beside the hearth, where a modest fire burned steadily. A hook on one wall held her cloak, and beneath it nestled a pair of pale leather slippers. Blue velvet bed hangings softened the square frame of the bed, but lent little femininity to the room. No painted garlands decked the plain plaster walls, and instead of tapestries, there hung a pair of shields, a mace, a flail, a battleaxe, and half a dozen swords and daggers. 'Twas the unadorned chamber of a warrior.

Like her chamber, he thought, Deirdre was straight-forward, forthright. She displayed her weapons for all to see, made no pretenses about what she was, and wasted no space on frivolity. He, too, must be equally blunt with her.

He approached the bed, unbuckling his belt with purposeful leisure. Then he wrapped the leather round his fist and though he let his hand drop to his side, she gave it a fleeting glance, clearly wondering what he intended. He let her wonder. 'Twas best to keep one's adversary guessing.

He towered over the bed, looking down his nose at her. "Perchance you did not hear me the first time, wench. Mayhap you will hear me better now. You are my wife. You wedded me of your own free will. You wear my ring, and your lips sealed our troth." He saw her hands fidget restlessly in the linens. "I will not be denied that which is my right."

He was going to go on, to tell her that despite that right, he'd made a vow to her sister, and indeed, 'twas in keeping with his honor as a knight, not to take Deirdre against her will. Despite the lust raging inside him, he would willingly rein it in if she refused him.

But she never gave him the chance to say a word.

As fleet as a fox on the hunt, she reached beneath the bolster on her bed and whipped out a dagger.

Thank God, she didn't lunge for him. If she had, he would've swung his fist instinctively, breaking her hand and lodging her knife in the far wall. Fortunately, she only brandished the weapon before her, her gaze an unspoken threat as chilling as the silver steel of the blade.

Stunned though he was by her violent response, he quickly schooled his movements to casual unconcern, as if she wielded but a feather, and carefully unwrapped and rewrapped the leather around his fist.

"I seem to remember that earlier in the great hall, you proposed a barter—your sister's penance for your own."

She was silent, but he noticed an uncertain flicker in her eyes.

"Yet you look most unwilling to endure that penance now." He let his gaze drop briefly to the gleaming blade. "Forsooth, you seem very unlike the humble maid who bargained with me before, who begged me to accept her sacrifice, who was willing to offer up her own body so her sister wouldn't have to suffer. Is this so? Do you wish to withdraw your offer? Shall I take the sin out of Helena's flesh?"

"Nay! Nay." A crease of confusion marred the smooth space between her brows, and her grip shifted upon the dagger. "But why would you seek to punish me here, now, in our marriage bed?"

He lifted a brow. "'Tis abundantly obvious you wish for naught *else* here." He glanced pointedly at her weapon.

Bit by slow bit, Deirdre lowered the dagger, but he could see the struggle in her eyes. How it frustrated her to succumb to him. Yet in the end, she'd bound herself by her own words, and so at last, she conceded.

But he wasn't a man to be twice stung. He held out his hand for her dagger. Reluctantly, she flipped the blade in her hand and surrendered it, hilt first.

"I trust you have no others within reach," he said.

She shook her head.

He took the dagger, and with a quick flick of his wrist,

sent it sailing across the room. It lodged with a thunk in the oak chest.

From the corner of his eye, he saw her flinch, not much, but enough to let him know she'd not fully let down her guard. She stole a glance at the belt wrapped round his hand, and he knew she expected him to use his fists on her.

Colin would have laughed to imagine such a thing. Pagan had never beat a man in his life. He'd never needed to. His dark looks alone could send servants scrambling to do his bidding and make soldiers tremble in their tracks. But Deirdre didn't know that. And mayhap 'twas best to keep her in doubt.

Despite her gruesome expectations, still she neither quailed nor lost her dignity, but only offered him this blunt advice: "Do as you will. But take care, sirrah, not to lose your temper and forget your strength. 'Twill do you little good to have a dead wife."

Faced with her bluntness and astonishing courage, Pagan could not keep up his pretense of menace. She was uncommonly valiant, this new bride of his, and his heart swelled with a curious pride. And again, as preposterous as it seemed, he considered what a fine soldier she'd make.

But when his gaze slipped down to the place where her golden tresses had parted now to reveal the delicate, rosy crest of her breast, all thoughts of battle vanished like ashes in the wind. He slowly unwrapped the leather belt and set it upon the bedside table.

Nay, he had a different kind of punishment in mind, a penance he'd first imagined while bandaging the cut she'd dealt him with her sword, and later perfected in the chapel, pressing warm lips to hers in primal possession.

The only suffering she'd endure in this chamber would stem from her own passions.

"Oh, my lady, 'tis not death I dole out this night," he told her cryptically, "but life."

While she looked at him in mistrust, he unpinned the plaid from across his shoulder and tossed it onto the chair. He noticed that her knuckles were white where she gripped the coverlet, and he frowned.

"You fear me," he prodded.

"Nay," she said. "I dislike you."

"Liar."

She glared past him. "Make no game of this. Have done with it. Do your worst."

"You will not struggle?"

She shook her head once.

"Nor scream for help?"

"I do not scream."

The ghost of a smile touched Pagan's lips. *He* could make her scream. "Nor cower in fear?"

"I told you. I'm not afraid."

"And yet you strangle the poor coverlet with your fists."

She immediately released the fabric.

He planted one boot upon the end of her bed to untie the laces, and he chuckled as she swiftly averted her eyes. Still unaccustomed to his lack of braies, he found some aspects of the revealing Scots attire entertaining.

Once his boots dropped to the floor, he pulled his tunic over his head and loosened the laces of the long linen shirt beneath. As he did so, Deirdre stole peeks at him, glances she thought he couldn't detect, and this pleased him immensely. She was not so numb with fear that she couldn't indulge her own curiosity about the man she'd wed, which was good. Deciding to keep her curious, he left his shirt on and dragged a tall candle stand close to the bed. He wanted light—warm and illuminating—for what he planned.

Deirdre wished he'd get on with it. Sweet Saints! What did the man intend? 'Twas pure torture to be braced for suffering and yet ignorant of its nature. Pain she could tolerate, but this anticipation would drive her mad.

Worst of all, it grated against her grain to willingly endure such abuse. She was accustomed to fighting, not yielding. 'Twould take all her strength of will to resist *resisting*.

Now he'd stripped to his shirt and brought a candle near. Dear God! What perversion was this? Did he plan to torture her with hot wax? Or was the candlelight so he could better admire the bruises he inflicted? Sweet Mary, she wished she hadn't surrendered her dagger.

"Your hands are clenched again," he murmured, bending near.

This time she couldn't release them. Every nerve was stretched as tightly as a drawn bowstring. Even her voice, despite her bold words, was colored with tension.

"Whatever vile thing you intend," she croaked, "be done with it. You keep me from my obligations."

He laughed wholeheartedly then, and though the sound was pleasant, it made her ears bristle.

"Your only obligation tonight is to me," he said.

Lord, she hated how his eyes twinkled, the way his lip curved up in that smug grin as he stood at her bedside. She shut her eyes tightly against the sight and braced herself for the first blow.

Almost instantly, his palm caught her cheek, but 'twas

not with a cuff. Instead, his thumb caressed the corner of her mouth, and he brushed a fingertip over her earlobe. "Open your eyes," he bid her. "I would have you know who is making you feel this."

Christ's bones, he *was* debauched. She forced her eyes open, gaining strength from the determination that she'd give him no satisfaction. 'Twould be over soon, after all, and she need only remind herself that 'twas for her sister's sake she endured this hell.

He slipped his hand from her cheek. "I think . . . aye." Then he made his way to the foot of the bed. "I shall begin with your feet."

Despite her determination to remain calm, images of a dozen horrible tortures invaded her thoughts. Would he pummel her soles? Break her toes? Hold a candle to the bottoms of . . .

He slowly tugged the coverlet down. Never had she felt so naked, so vulnerable.

"Lie back," he said.

It took every ounce of self-command to comply. She compressed her lips, hoping 'twould be enough to stop her cries.

His hand cupped her heel, and he lifted it slightly. "Beautiful," he said, stroking the bridge with his other hand.

His palm was warm upon her icy skin, his caress almost soothing. "But so cold," he murmured, enclosing her foot between his hands.

She held her breath, waiting for him to squeeze her bones till they cracked or to give her ankle a violent twist. But he did neither.

Instead, he pressed his thumbs into her arch and moved them upward, spreading them as he reached the pad of her foot. A strange frisson of warmth sizzled up her leg. He repeated the motion, this time brushing the undersides of her toes.

"Breathe," he said softly. "I'm not going to hurt you."

She wasn't so naive as to believe him, and she half hoped she'd faint for lack of air.

He stopped massaging her foot. "Deirdre, breathe. I mean you no harm. I swear it. Upon my honor as a knight."

Mayhap he did tell the truth. A trusted knight of the King would not take his vows of chivalry lightly. She let out a ragged breath and sucked in a new one.

But what about Helena's penance? Didn't he say Deirdre might ransom her own flesh for that?

As if he read her thoughts, he murmured, "I intend to have my way with you this eve, as any man with a new bride. And you, dear wife, have vowed not to resist. As penances go, I'd wager this will be far worse for you than any amount of beating."

Emotions coursed through her so rapidly she scarcely had time to feel them. Relief. Wonder. Dismay. Shock. Humiliation. Rage.

Curse the Norman bastard! He was right. It appalled her to admit it, but he was right. To endure his caress, his tenderness, his seduction, without protest—'twould be sheer agony. Naught was more important to her than control—over her castle, over her body, over her emotions. Pagan's overtures threatened that control. And yet she'd given him her oath to allow them. Damn him, he'd trapped her in the shackles of her own promise.

When she glanced at Pagan, she saw that self-satisfied grin again, the knowing look in his eyes, and she longed to clout the expression from his face once and for all. But she'd given her word not to fight him.

Still, there were more ways than one to confound his victory. She might be bested, but she'd not make conquest easy for him. If she could be stoic under pain, then by the Saints, she could be stoic under pleasure.

"In time, you may come to welcome my touch."

Never, she thought, ignoring him to train her eyes upon the ceiling, determined to think of something, *anything* other than this ordeal. Mentally, she began to recite the alphabet.

Pagan reached for her again, his hands tenderly surrounding the inlet of her ankle. *A* for ankle.

She clenched her teeth against the sensation. *B* for bastard, she thought. And beast. And . . .

Bliss.

For somehow, despite his . . . *C* for calluses, his hands were incredibly gentle as they eased the tiny muscles between the sensitive pads of her toes.

She lost her focus for a moment, then frowned to get it back. *D* for damn him. Devil. Demon.

Desire.

Nay, not desire.

E for escape and evade and elude.

F for . . . for . . .

"Don't fight me, Deirdre. Don't fight your own pleasure." His deft fingers seemed to knead the very will from her.

Fight.

Flounder.

Fail.

Her eyelids dipped as he moved to her other foot and began working his wizardry on it as well.

G . . . She could think of naught. She could not think at all. No one had ever touched her like this, in a way that sent waves of warmth up the entire length of her leg.

His hands moved up her calf then, squeezing the sore muscles there. But the slight pain was soothing, as if his touch served to heal her.

"Does that hurt?" he asked.

She scowled. Nay. 'Twas . . . heavenly, *H*. But she'd not tell him that.

'Twas amazing how he could gauge the exact amount of strength to use, enough to send sparks of current along her skin, yet not enough to inflict hurt.

When he finished her calves, he worked his way to her thighs, pressing the heels of his hands slowly up the long muscles until they seemed to melt under his steady pressure. Again and again, he stroked upward, and though his touch left her limp, 'twas also strangely energizing.

Only when he ceased did she realize her eyes had been half-closed. She opened them wide.

He caught one of her hands then, and she started to pull it back defensively.

"Do not resist me," he reminded her.

She reluctantly let him take it again, centering her stare once more on the ceiling. Where was she? *G*? *H*? *I* . . . *I* . . .

Aye. Somehow his fingertips managed to delve into the crevices between her knuckles, into pockets of strain she didn't know she possessed.

"You display your emotions here, your tension," he told her. "Your fists betray you."

'Twas nonsense, she thought. She'd had years of practice at concealing her emotions.

But when he pressed into the meat of her hand betwixt the thumb and first finger, she sucked in a quick breath as pain shot up her arm. He lightened his touch, circling the area gently until the ache subsided.

"You see?"

She didn't want to see. As he slowly worked his way up her arms and across her shoulders, she sensed he was doing more than merely loosening her muscles. He was weakening her armor. And as glorious as it felt, as pleasurable as his touch was, she dared not let him crumble her defenses, dared not let him rob her of her control. She was a Scot, she reminded herself, tough and strong and hardy, not some spoiled Norman with a perfumed horse.

Steeling herself against the divine sensation as his fingers pressed along the stiff cords of her shoulders, she bit out, "Are you almost finished?"

Chapter 10

PAGAN PAUSED IN HIS LABORS. Any other man might have been wounded by her tart question. Finished?

But he knew better than to believe her attempts at deception. Women loved his caresses. They moaned at his strength and sighed over his gentle touch. Deirdre could not help but enjoy what he was doing.

But then she was unlike any other woman he'd known. Deirdre was a warrior. A combatant. 'Twas doubtful any man had ever presumed to lay a hand on her, tender or otherwise. To have to succumb to such handling, no matter how pleasurable, probably sent her into a defensive panic.

Almost finished?

"Nay," he assured her, determined that patience would win out the day. "I've only begun."

Of course, that patience meant that he'd have to curb his own mounting desires, not an easy task, given the eager ache in his loins. Forsooth, he was astounded by the depth of his desire. Not since his first coupling had he felt so perilously close to losing control. The mere sight of his bride had roused him as surely as a rooster to sunrise. Touching her silken flesh had heated that passion till it simmered in his veins. And now, hovering close to her lithe, ripe, perfect body, a body that rightfully belonged to him alone, for aye . . . Sweet God, 'twas enough to make him mad with craving.

But if her will was strong, his was stronger. He was a seasoned lover. She was a novice. If he could last the distance, he'd win the day.

He wove his fingers through her hair, cupping the back of her head, turning it so she was forced to look at him. The truth resided in her eyes. The smoke of desire veiled her gaze, no matter how her speech denied it, and the knowledge that he'd made her feel that emotion sent a tide of raw, unadulterated pride through his body.

"Kiss me," he whispered.

"N—"

To her credit, she didn't finish the word, but panic flared nonetheless in her eyes. She knew her vulnerabilities. She'd enjoyed their last kiss. And he threatened to make her enjoy the next.

Lowering his gaze to her mouth, he moved in slowly, close enough to feel her breath upon his face like moth's wings. "Kiss me."

She was unresponsive at first, but he'd already tasted the fruit of her lips in the chapel. He knew her capacity for passion.

It didn't take long. Slanting his mouth over hers and coaxing her with his tongue, he parted her lips to access the delicious recesses within. He held her still for his gentle intrusion, making languid thrusts of his tongue to mimic the mating to come. But though she yielded readily enough to him, relaxing her jaw, closing her eyes, moaning softly in her throat, still a part of her resisted him. Her fists pressed against his shoulders as she tried in vain to escape.

Calmly, carefully, without stopping their kiss, he clasped one of her wrists and drew her arm up until it rested on the bolster above her head. While she mewled in half-protest, he dragged the other arm up to join it, securing them both beneath one hand. She might have sworn not to resist, but for what he was about to do, she couldn't be held accountable for her instinct to escape.

With his free hand, he smoothed her fretful brow and caressed her velvety cheek. He clasped her narrow throat, feeling the increase in her pulse beneath his thumb and finger, and let his hand drift downward, pausing over the silver Thor's hammer. Her chest rose and fell more rapidly now as she sensed his intent.

Reluctantly, he withdrew his lips and nudged her face to the side to whisper in her ear. "You know you want this. You know you crave my touch. Your flesh longs for the brush of my hand."

She gasped, and while he breathed softly against her ear, he traced her collarbone, then let his palm course over the swell of one breast, circling her tender nipple with his middle finger. It stiffened at once in response, fueling his own lust, and he stole a glance at the perfect bud, golden pink in the candlelight. Sweet Mary, was there anything as seductive as the silhouette of a woman's aroused nipple? Aye, he thought—the knowledge 'twas *he* who had caused it.

Try as she might, Deirdre couldn't will her body not to respond. Pagan's warm breath and dire promises wound their way into the secret hollow of her ear, sending a shudder of simultaneous horror and delight through her. As his hand grazed her bosom, she arched reflexively, all but thrusting her breast into his palm. And when he caught her sensitive nipple gently between his fingers, sending a jolt of heat through her, it took every ounce of self-control not to make a sound.

"Oh, aye, my lady," he murmured against her cheek, "see how you answer to my touch?"

Nay, she wanted to scream, but 'twould have been a lie. And when his hand strayed to her other breast, she could barely breathe with the anticipation of that contact.

But he stopped short.

"Look," he whispered.

She squeezed her eyes shut and shook her head. 'Twas humiliation enough that her body thwarted her. She didn't want to see how his hand covered her breast as if 'twas his possession.

"Watch," he coaxed.

He needn't remind her she'd given her word not to resist him. She was honorable enough to remind herself. But to pry open her eyes and watch her own body's betrayal 'twas the hardest thing she'd ever done, and her face flushed hot with shame.

His fingers looked enormous and dark and rough against her pale skin. 'Twas a miracle he didn't maul her with his great paws. But as she watched by the flickering light, his thumb circled her nipple as tenderly as a wet nurse coaxing a babe to suckle, and with one light flick, he brought it to life.

She gasped, and for one terrifying instant, their eyes met. Then Deirdre buried her head against her shoulder, too incensed and mortified to look at him.

"Aye, sweetheart, you see what I can do to you," he rasped out. "Now feel what you've done to me." He pressed close against her until the linen of his shirt draped her thigh. Through the linen, she felt the searing length of his cock, full and hard and menacing.

Instinctively, she tried to wrest loose from his hold on her wrists, but his grip was firm.

"Admit it. You are helpless against desire."

His words piqued her ire. No one called Deirdre helpless. 'Twas her own honor that held her here, not desire.

As if to test that resolve, he said, "You fight me. Do you wish to withdraw your offer? Is the price too steep for your sister's freedom?"

She turned her most withering glare upon him then, a look that sent most men scurrying for cover. "Never."

A strange, almost pitying smile graced his features then, and he eased forward until he reclined on the pallet beside her, throwing an anchoring leg over hers. The linen felt perilously thin between them, and she could feel the well-muscled contours of his chest and thighs and . . . and that obscene dagger with which he wished to impale her.

But not yet. Apparently he had other depravities in mind first. He drew a finger slowly down the center of her throat, into the hollow where her pulse throbbed, then lower, between her breasts. But this time he didn't stop there. Turning his hand, he continued down her belly, dipping briefly into her navel, then past, till his fingers grazed the place where her woman's hair began.

He nuzzled at her ear again. "There is an ache betwixt your thighs, is there not?"

"Nay," she lied.

"Oh, aye, 'tis there," he assured her, his fingers teasing along the edge of her curls.

She silently cursed him for knowing what he did to her.

Then he nudged her head, angling his own to capture her mouth. This time his kiss was sweet and tender, like that first kiss in the chapel, and despite her determination to remain impassive, she found herself answering him.

But like a hunter luring a stag, as he wooed her with light kisses, his hand stole stealthily over her woman's mound. 'Twas not till his fingers boldly spread her nether lips that she realized how much he'd dared. But he was ready for her rebellion. He caught her shocked gasp between his lips, and his other hand tightened on her bound wrists.

His heavy leg held her immobile while he continued his perversions, stroking and squeezing and circling the place between her thighs until she thought she'd scream into his plundering mouth. And then he touched her where she most wished he would not, for it made her body arch upward of its own will, out of control.

"There," he murmured against her mouth. "Aye, there."

Once he found it, he wouldn't leave it be. While her body writhed in bittersweet torment, he stroked her again and again, sliding wet, warm fingertips along the sleek folds of her most secret place.

"And here," he breathed, slipping a thick finger partially inside her while his thumb danced expertly over the center of her need.

As she squirmed beneath his ministrations, a sheer mist seemed to gather about her, a soft cloud of nameless, growing pleasure that obscured her vision and thoughts and resistance. Suddenly she felt no struggle, no memory, no will of her own. There was only this point, this feeling, increasing, evolving, focusing. All else receded into a vague haze.

"Aye, my lady. That's it. Aye."

His voice pierced the fog just enough to make her remember. But now 'twas too late. She'd stepped into his snare. She was beyond help. To her horror, she could resist no longer. As if some devil wind picked her up and cast her through the air, she was flung to a heavenly plateau where she could do naught but hold on for dear life and cry out in amazement.

Wave after wave of ecstasy buffeted her, robbing her of her senses and her control. She trembled with the power of it, thrashing so violently upon the bed that she feared she might lurch free of the very world.

A surge of primitive need coursed through Pagan's veins as he watched Deirdre arch and shudder in the throes of her release, her fists clenched within his, her face contorted with wondrous agony. God, he wanted her now! While she writhed in climax. While she screamed in pleasure. Before she finished and drifted back to earth.

'Twas excruciating to wait.

But wait he would. He was a man of his word. So he languished in unspent lust while she lay panting in the aftermath of her ordeal.

At long last, he nuzzled her throat and wheezed, "You didn't resist. You kept your word. I honor you for that." Sweat beaded his brow as he spoke the words he must. "Now I must keep mine." He reached up to tuck a damp curl behind her ear. "I vowed to your sister I wouldn't take you against your will." He rested the backs of his knuckles alongside her neck, where her pulse raced. "If truly in your heart, you do not wish this union, speak the words now. For I warn you, my lady, naught else will douse the flames of my desire."

Deirdre was mortified. Completely mortified. And embarrassed. And ashamed. And appalled. And a million other shades of humiliation she'd never before endured. Aye, she'd been bested in the past, on the field of battle, but not in her own chamber and never by her own machinations. Against her most formidable foe, her own body had utterly betrayed her. She'd completely lost control.

The worst of it was she still, *still* felt a fierce, inexplicable, unrequited hunger for the conniving brute who called himself her husband. Her cursed loins *still* quivered with need. Her breasts craved his touch. And her lips felt absurdly naked, deprived of his kiss.

Even as she lay loathing him, her flesh burned for want of his caress.

But she could not yield to that longing. Deirdre of Rivenloch *never* yielded. 'Twas a lesson learned hard from long days in the tiltyard. Pagan had relinquished his sword and held his hand out to her to put an end to this combat, offering his own surrender. By God, she would seize it.

Her heart pounded harder than an armorer's hammer. But she rallied the courage to stare into his desire-glazed eyes, to say what her body wished she would not. "Know this, sirrah." Her voice cracked. "I do not resist, because I have given my word. But I will not lie willingly with you this night or any other."

His lids grew flat, and it seemed as if chips of ice slowly crystallized in his eyes. But his wintry glare was deceptive, for in his jaw, a muscle tightened and released, and behind the silvery thunderheads of his eyes, a violent summer storm brewed.

"As you wish," he snarled quietly.

He released her then and backed away. She should have been relieved. But she didn't trust the silent fury in his countenance. Carefully, she reached down for the linens and dragged them up to her chin, feeling uncomfortable with her own nakedness for the first time in her life.

He turned toward the fire, where red coals shimmered on the hearth, mirroring his dangerous mood. She saw by the rise and fall of his shoulders that he fought to gain control of his breathing. And mayhap his temper.

After a pregnant silence, he turned to face her again, his expression inscrutable. Then he reached down and pulled his linen shirt over his head.

For one awful instant, she thought he'd changed his mind and meant to break his vow, to force himself upon her. But 'twas resignation, not vengeance, that dulled his eyes.

And in the next moment, she found her gaze roaming involuntarily over the magnificent contours of his nude body. The golden glow from the candles accentuated each formidable muscle, and Deirdre saw he possessed a more powerful frame than any of Rivenloch's knights. His shoulders were broad, his arms thick, his chest massive. 'Twas little wonder he'd been able to subdue her so easily. And lower, before she hastily averted her eyes, she glimpsed his still aroused shaft emerging from its nest of dark hair.

Her skin grew warm, and the breath caught in her throat. Sweet Saints, he *was* the most handsome man she'd ever seen. Against her wishes, the prickling began again between her legs. Bloody hell! Despite reason, despite her good intentions, God help her, she was . . . moved by the sight of Pagan.

It could not be!

Mayhap he'd cast some enchantment upon her, binding the two of them. Or perchance 'twas but a temporary affliction that would fade with each passing moment. But in *this* moment, curse her weak soul, she wanted him again.

He cast the shirt brusquely aside. As if she were not there, he snatched the linens from off the bed. She drew her knees up defensively. And then he did the oddest thing. With a grunt and a violent tug, he tore the bandage from his chest, exposing and opening the wound she'd dealt him. Fresh blood seeped from the cut. With a casual sniff, he let it well up, then wiped across the wound with the bed linens.

Virgin's blood. Of course. 'Twould look as if they'd consummated their marriage. Deirdre felt a pang of guilt as she glanced at Pagan's reopened wound. 'Twas a chivalrous thing he did.

But he neither touched her nor spoke to her again. After he circled the chamber, forcefully blowing out all the candles, he climbed in beside her, hauled up the coverlet, and flounced over on his side, facing away from her.

She should have felt satisfied. She'd won their skirmish. Aye, her pride was badly wounded, for Pagan had turned her own body against her. But in the end, had she not prevailed? After all, she'd prevented him from consummating their marriage. She'd won the day.

Why then did she feel so uneasy?

Because, she realized, 'twas not *she* who had stopped him. Forsooth, though it pained her to confess it, she'd wanted him to continue. Nay, 'twas *he* who had called upon his honor, been true to his oath, and allowed her to withdraw. If not for his steadfast chivalry, she'd lie beneath his thrusting hips even now.

Damn! The reality was as bitter as rue wine. Though Pagan seemed arrogant and brutish and cruel, she had to face the truth. Her new husband was a man of unwavering honor.

Pagan punched the bolster to fit his aching head. Curse his spurs, for once he wished chivalry would look the other way. For God help him, he longed to seize his new bride, willing or not, and drive his aching cock deep into her velvety flesh.

'Twas not fair. She should be his. 'Twas his right to lay claim to her this night, body and soul. He'd rather have bitten his tongue than divulge that damned promise.

But he'd been so certain Deirdre would succumb to him. Women *always* surrendered to his seduction. He was bloody *good* at it.

Somehow the stubborn wench had managed to remain unmoved. 'Twas unimaginable.

He'd hoped that the sting of opening his wound would temper his lust. But his cock throbbed mercilessly, reminding him that he dared not even soothe the savage beast by delving betwixt another maid's thighs this eve. Not tonight. Nay, he was bridegroom to the lady of the keep, and 'twould not sit well with the people of Rivenloch should their new steward stray from the marriage bed on his wedding night.

On the morrow perchance, if Deirdre still wished to play her game of resistance, he'd seek out some toothsome Scots wench to warm his bed.

He frowned into the darkness, wondering if 'twas possible. He'd not seen a maiden here to compare to Deirdre. Not only was she beautiful, but she was full of life and wisdom and wit. Forsooth, though it rankled him to be thwarted in his lovemaking, he had to admire Deirdre for her force of will, even against her own desires. 'Twas uncommon in a woman, at least in the women with whom he was acquainted. If she ever decided to lie willingly with him, he was certain she would prove a wholly engaged lover. Aye, that would be a night of unrivaled ecstasy.

But that night was not *this* night. This night was going to be long and painful and empty and miserable.

Chapter 11

Hours later, Deirdre tossed irritably on the pallet, stealing back the coverlet Pagan had expropriated. 'Twas impossible to sleep with someone else taking up most of the bed. Especially when that someone else was so bloody . . . invasive.

He could have been far more invasive, she reminded herself. And though she didn't want to think about it, one night he *would* be. She wasn't so stupid as to believe 'twould never happen, that she could hold her husband at bay forever. After all, 'twas her duty to produce heirs for Rivenloch.

But for the moment, her bedchamber was just another arena of control for him, one where he could claim victory. Already she felt her dominance slipping as he intruded upon her stewardship, imposing his people upon her, ordering her servants about, planning changes to the keep. At least in her bed, she'd managed to keep the upper hand. So far.

Still, she wondered how long he'd endure her refusals. Worse, she wondered how long she could refuse.

Pagan's greediness with the coverlet wasn't the only thing that kept her awake. Curse her wayward mind, she couldn't stop thinking about his perfectly sculpted body, the careless fall of his hair, his sultry, smoldering gaze. She recalled in vivid detail how his hands felt on her skin, caressing, soothing, arousing, remembered how his lips had drained from her, in one kiss, all care. Even now, his sensual whispers echoed in her thoughts. All night long, she relived the intense sensations he'd introduced to her—his thumb coaxing her nipple, his warm tongue filling her mouth, his fingers dancing across her most private places. All night long, no matter how her mind balked at the appalling idea of surrender, her body ached with the keen hunger with which he'd left her. 'Twas torture of the worst kind.

For most of all, in making him cease, she wondered what further pleasure she'd missed.

The sky was not yet light when Deirdre decided she could lie abed no more. Though he didn't touch her, the heat from Pagan's sleeping body was a palpable thing that left her skin tingling most unnaturally, keeping her awake and as bristly as a cat in a windstorm. There was but one way she knew of to diffuse such a volatile current.

Quietly, she crept from the bed. She donned her undergarments in the dark and slipped her chain mail from her armor chest. She wiggled the embedded dagger free, and for an instant, weighing the blade in her hand, she considered how foolish Pagan was to leave it within her reach.

Venturing one last look at her slumbering bridegroom, who hadn't stirred a muscle and whom she suspected might sleep through a full-scale attack, Deirdre slipped out the door, past the invaders snoring in the great hall, and out to the tiltyard.

Dew darkened the hard-packed dust of the field. The dawn was just beginning to pale the indigo sky. Nothing stirred the air, not even birdsong. 'Twas the kind of morn Deirdre liked best, with naught to distract her from her exercises.

She pulled her hair back into a loose braid, then did a few practice stretches to loosen her muscles. Though she was loath to admit it, her muscles weren't as stiff as usual, probably owing to the work of Pagan's hands.

She'd chosen her favorite sword this morn, the one her father had made her when she was twelve. She'd scratched her name into the hilt to distinguish it from Helena's weapon, and she'd notched the crossguard for every skirmish won against her father until she'd run out of room.

Once she held the familiar weapon in hand, once she began to lunge and thrust, once her blood warmed with the heat of battle and her thoughts centered on naught but assault and defense, she forgot all about her sleepless night and her Norman husband and her demeaning surrender to him. She attacked and retreated, slashed forward and fell back, over and over, challenging invisible opponents.

By the time the cock began to crow, sweat was pouring down her face, and her lungs burned with exertion, but it felt good, *wonderful*. The feeling of power was intoxicating. Her blade sang through the air and caught the first rays of the rising sun as she whipped round, as comforted by the familiar motions as a priest by his prayers.

*   *   *

Pagan awoke with the sun. He was disappointed to find Deirdre gone, but he wasn't surprised. He himself oft left a woman's bed before morn. After all, promises made in the foolish heat of passion were best left to the dark recesses of midnight. But theirs had been no moonlight indiscretion, and Deirdre was no disporting maid he might use and toss into another man's bed. She was his wife, by God! She'd better get used to leisurely morns spent abed with her husband.

Still stinging from her cool dismissal of the past night, Pagan frowned as he glanced at the linens stained with blood, *his* blood. He'd made that sacrifice to protect her honor. And how had she returned the favor? By deserting him. What would happen now when his men paraded up the stairs to congratulate the bride and groom and fetch the sheets, only to find the groom alone? Jesu, he'd never hear the end of it.

He had to find Deirdre. Before they did.

He dressed quickly, wondering where she could have gone. Mayhap to visit her sister in the cellar. Or to the kitchens to break her fast. Or to chapel to pray. He smirked. She'd *need* to pray for the strength to hold out against his seduction.

He eyed the oak chest where he'd sunk her dagger. The knife was no longer there. He opened the lid. Inside were the braies Deirdre had stolen from Colin and him, which he reclaimed. The rest were a knight's things— helm, spurs, leather gloves for riding—but her chain mail was missing.

He shook his head. Unless he missed his guess, his warrior bride had donned light armor to spar.

By the time he crossed the courtyard, fully armed, a few servants had begun to stir. Plumes of vapor curled into the air where sunlight brushed the wet planks of the outbuildings. Hounds lifted their heads as he passed, sniffed the air, then dropped back into slumber. As he neared the tiltyard, a cloud of dust from the field heralded the presence of a lone fighter.

Deirdre.

He faded back into the shade of the stables to observe her unseen.

He'd been vexed with her. After all, she'd insulted him—abandoning him for pursuits that were apparently more entertaining for her. He'd come in heavy armor, half looking for a fight, expecting at the least to have to discipline her. But now, watching her from the shadows, he found his ire dissolving into utter fascination.

Sword play was not play to her after all. He could see that immediately. The force with which she threw herself into the exercise was genuine. She knew all the right stances, the right moves. Her father had obviously taught her well. Despite the fact that she was a woman, or mayhap because of it, her movements were quick and lithe and graceful. She made sword fighting look almost like a dance, spinning and dipping and leaping with amazing balance and precision.

Of course, 'twas unnatural. Combat was not a woman's prerogative. Deirdre might practice at weaponry, but women were not made for warfare.

Yet there was something intriguing, something extraordinary, something undeniably *right* about the way she moved, as if she was born to wield a sword.

And as she continued to battle unseen foes, he realized that watching her more than riveted him. God's blood, it aroused him.

The ladies he knew seldom exerted themselves beyond

tossing a falcon into the air or waving farewell to their husbands or reaching for another sweetmeat. 'Twas oft why he preferred common women in his bed. While noblewomen were willing enough partners, they seemed to imagine they were made of spun sugar, too frail for the more demanding rigors of lovemaking.

He could see Deirdre was no fragile flower. And it didn't take much imagination to envision the ardor she displayed on the field translated to . . .

"Are you going to stand there spying all day?"

He started. How Deirdre knew he was there, he couldn't imagine. He'd been absolutely silent. And she'd never glanced once in his direction.

Even now, as she spoke, she neither looked at him nor missed a beat of her practice.

"Or . . ." Her sword slashed left and right, making a great X in the air before she turned to face him. "Do you plan to challenge me?"

He laughed aloud in delight. Aye, he wanted to challenge her. Something about the confidence in her movements thrilled him. She was a tempting vixen, and he suspected she knew it.

There was a coy sparkle in her eyes. "You think I jest."

He drew in a breath of crisp air. Lord, she was lovely this morn. Messy tendrils of hair escaped her braid, framing her pink cheeks. Her bosom rose and fell with each fortifying breath. Sweet Mary, he thought with absurd envy, she looked as if she'd just been thoroughly swived.

*　　*　　*

Deirdre could hardly believe she was speaking to Pagan, much less baiting him. She thought she'd never be able to look him in the eye again for shame.

But something about donning chain mail and hefting her sword had restored her sense of power and control. And once she had that, she felt she could conquer anything, even disgrace.

She found it amusing that Pagan thought he'd stolen up on her. 'Twas nigh impossible for a man of his size to move unnoticed. Besides, Deirdre knew the sounds of Rivenloch—the birds, the hounds, the horses, the servants. She recognized unfamiliar noises instantly. The soft scrape of Pagan's sabatons had perked up her ears and quickened her pulse.

If ever there was a time and place to repay Pagan for his merciless conquest of the night past, 'twas here and now. This was an arena where she could best him, where she could rely on her body not to betray her, where she could repair her damaged pride.

"Afraid?" she asked, echoing his challenge of the day before.

Pagan pushed away from the wall into the sunlight and ambled lazily up to rest his crossed arms atop the gatepost in the wattle fence separating them. "Only that I may harm you."

For a moment, her courage stuttered. Lord, was he always so enormous, or did he just seem so because of his armor?

She forced a cocky grin. She dared not show her doubt. Half of victory was bravado. "You'll not get close enough to harm me."

"Do you plan to run then?"

"Pah! I never run."

He bent forward to rest his chin atop his crossed arms. "You ran quickly enough from my bed this morn."

"Well, if you were not such a layabed . . ."

A chuckle escaped him, and it occurred to her that their conversation was almost . . . flirtatious. "Layabed? Come, my lady, you must have risen well before the sun."

"And I suppose Normans lie abed till noon?"

"Aye." He gave her a sly smile, then straightened. "If we have willing women in our beds."

His soft suggestion brought swift heat to her cheeks, as if he'd whispered the words against her hair, the way he had last night. Lord, why must she think of that? If she was going to fight him, she needed to concentrate on the battle at hand.

"Sir, you veer from the subject. Do you accept my challenge or not?"

He unlatched the gate, swung it open, and entered the field. "Why not?" Dusting his hands together, he brushed past her, so close that she could smell the sleep upon him, and whispered, "Since you will not engage me in our bed, my lady, I suppose engaging me in the tilt-yard is a reasonable alternative." He held her gaze and slid his sword from its sheath with suggestive languor.

Deirdre swallowed hard. The man was incorrigible. Even on the field of battle, he attempted to seduce her. And God help her, 'twas having some effect. His eyes burned into hers with the smoldering promise of plea-sure. And his mouth, set in that self-assured grin . . . she remembered too well how it felt upon hers, warm and sweet and demanding.

Nay! She wouldn't think of that. She had to fight him. Moreover, this time she had to win.

With a preparatory slash of her sword through the air, she flexed her knees and readied for attack.

He perused her slowly from head to toe, then beckoned her with his fingers. "Come."

Everything happened so quickly, Deirdre hardly knew what befell her. In one moment, she was hacking forward at Pagan's right arm. But his blade grated along hers, foiling her blow. In the next instant, he seized her sword arm, spun her around backward, and hauled her back against his chest, holding her there like a lover cradling his sweetheart. She struggled against his unwelcome embrace, jabbing him with her elbows, but he only chuckled into her hair, easing her gently down onto her bottom.

"My apologies," he murmured with false regret.

Disoriented, she scrambled to her feet, tossing the hair out of her eyes. Apologies indeed. He wasn't sorry in the least. Licking her lips, she prepared for a second strike.

Already she could tell that Pagan was stronger than any of her men. Mayhap the Knights of Cameliard were an elite force after all. If so, besting him was going to be more of a challenge than she'd anticipated.

She feinted low, then swung her sword up and around toward his midsection. This time she surprised him. He dodged back, narrowly avoiding a gash across his belly. Her confidence bolstered, she pressed her attack, driving him back with a succession of quick jabs until she almost had him pinned against the wattle fence.

But as her blade swung round to force him back the last few feet, he brought up his own in a jarring cross block. The impact of steel on steel sent a shiver of pain up her arm. Her advantage lost, she stumbled out of range of his sword.

"Forgive me," he whispered, a wretched twinkle in his eye. "Again."

Deirdre shook off his mockery. She wouldn't give in to anger. She would *not*. Pagan might be big and strong and, aye, now she knew it, fast. But he wasn't infallible. Even the mighty could fall. And when they did, 'twas with a mighty crash.

This time when he slashed forward, she called upon a move she'd invented when she'd caught a man raiding sheep in Rivenloch's meadows. She took an unexpected step forward, ducking under his sword arm to pop up behind him. As he reeled in confusion, she quickly booted him in the hindquarters. His own forward momentum pitched him face-first into the dust.

While he lay stunned in the dirt, she bent down by his ear and whispered, "*My* apologies."

She danced out of the way then and allowed him to rise. The expression on his dust-rimmed face, a sort of bewildered irritation, was sweet reward indeed.

But her victory wasn't yet assured.

With a grim smile, he sliced viciously downward, the gesture more intimidation than intention. She skipped out of his reach, uncowed but alert.

For a long while, they circled each other, eyes locked. Finally, like two charging stags, they clashed together, their blades sparking and clanging and tangling in unbridled violence.

Every time she gained the upper hand, 'twas but a matter of moments before he won it back. Never had she fought so long and hard against an opponent, save Helena, without seizing the advantage.

At long last, breathless and desperate, Deirdre found her opportunity. When his sword drifted wide, she lunged forward with a mortal thrust, straight for his heart. But as quick as a whip, he dodged sideways, blocking it aside with such force that she whirled around backward, staggering into him. He caught her against his thigh with his free arm to keep her from falling.

"Are you finished yet?" he asked. To her consternation, Pagan wasn't even breathing hard.

"Nay." She struggled loose. "Unless you wish to yield."

"Yield?" He grinned. "A Cameliard knight does not yield."

"Then continue."

She rolled her shoulders back and braced her legs again. What was his weakness? she wondered. Where was the chink in his armor? Gripping her sword in both hands, she raised it overhead and came straight down as if to split him in two. Predictably, he raised his blade to block her. As he did, she leaned sideways at the waist and snapped her foot around to kick him in the belly.

He folded forward with a satisfying "oof." While he recovered, she lifted the tip of her sword up to his chin.

But he wasn't as incapacitated as she expected. With his free hand, he batted the flat of her blade down, then swept up his own sword, lightning quick, to rest across her throat.

"Interesting," he said, commenting on her unique move. "You're certain you don't wish to surrender? After all, I am still fresh. You've been sparring half the morn."

"I was but . . . warming up," she bragged, though they could both hear the breath wheezing in her chest.

Clucking his tongue, he covered her forehead with his hand and playfully pushed her back away from his blade.

Panting, she wiped the sweat from her face with the back of her hand and studied her opponent.

He was a fine fighter. There was no argument. He was strong and quick and clever. But she'd managed to surprise him twice already. With a few more tricks from the repertoire of the Warrior Maids of Rivenloch, he'd fall, dumbfounded, at her feet. She was sure of it.

Her resolve renewed, she exchanged a few benign blows with him, then, borrowing her sister's wily ruse, dove forward into a roll, planning to come up with her blade at his throat.

But to her surprise, Pagan, resisting the natural instinct to retreat from attack, instead stepped *toward* her. When she sprang to her feet, they collided. Her face smashed into his chest, and he clamped her sword arm beneath his own, trapping her so she could do no more than flail away uselessly at the air behind him.

She tried to wrest away, but his arm held her close.

"Now will you cede?" he asked silkily.

She tried to shout, "Never!" But the words came out muffled in the folds of his tabard. She jerked against him, stuck fast.

Still, there was more than one way to get free. She and Helena had invented scores of moves for just such situations as these, situations in which a woman's strength was no match for a man's and she must rely on adroitness and cunning.

With her next breath, she drove her right knee up toward his groin as hard as she could. Forsooth, he *was* caught off his guard, but at the last instant, he must have sensed her intent, for he twisted enough to ruin her aim.

Still, he swore as her mailed knee caught a portion of his unprotected ballocks.

She expected him to release her at once. But his hold upon her did not lessen in the least, and as he sagged forward, groaning in pain, he took her down with him.

"Let . . . me . . . go . . ." she bit out, pushing up against him and trying to free her trapped arm.

"Nay . . ." he panted, clutching her tighter.

'Twas time for more ingenuity. As she maintained pressure against his chest, she eased her left foot between his two, then swept it quickly sideways, catching the back of his right heel to trip him.

This time, he was too distracted to brace for the impact. His foot flew up, throwing him backward. Like a felled tree, he hit the ground with an earth-shaking thud.

Unfortunately, he took Deirdre with him.

He turned just enough as he landed to avoid crushing her sword arm with his shoulder. But still she could not free herself from Pagan, who clung to her as tenaciously as a tick to a hound. And now she lay splayed atop him like some wanton harlot.

Chapter 12

For a moment, as the dust rose around them, Pagan was silent, all the wind knocked from him. But as soon as he managed to rake in a ragged breath, Deirdre braced herself for his angry bellow.

It never came. What came instead was a low peal of laughter, so genuine and charming that it startled Deirdre half out of her battle mood.

"Clever lass," he coughed out with an approving grin. "Where did you learn that?"

The question took her aback. "I . . . my sister and I . . . made it up."

He gave her a dubious glare.

"We *did*." His doubt renewed her irritation, and she tried to wriggle free again. "We invent most of our own moves." Curse Pagan's powerful grip, she might as well have been wrestling a bear.

She could feel his assessing gaze upon her, as if he measured her honesty or her worth. When she dared meet his eyes, what she found there was more than judgment. There was a dangerous shine of pride or admiration or respect that she didn't expect. And as she tried to absorb that emotion, another crept in, one far more perilous.

He wanted her.

With a mighty heave, Pagan rolled them both over until she lay flat on her back in the dust and he stretched out atop her. 'Twas a humiliating position, indicating not only his dominance and her submission, but evocative, by the smoldering in his eyes, of the marriage bed and coupling.

He was heavy atop her, despite the bulk he held upon his elbows. While she fought to be free of this demeaning arrangement, she was ashamed to admit a part of her thrilled to feel his weight and his strength, to be intimate with him again. And that terrified her.

"Get off me," she whispered furiously, blushing like a nun at her bath.

"Nay."

"'Tis . . . shameful."

"No one is here to see."

"Yet."

He lowered his gaze to her mouth, staring as if he planned to devour her. "There is naught to be ashamed of. We are newly wed."

Deirdre and her sister had invented methods of escape from all sorts of predicaments. But not this one. She feared that her only defense was words. "I will not brook this, sirrah."

"Ah, but you *will* . . . wife," he said with quiet self-confidence.

She swallowed hard. He didn't intend to swive her here in the tiltyard, did he? Surely he was not so heathen as that. And there was still his promise. "Do you mean to break the vow you made my sister?"

One side of his mouth curved up in a crooked smile. "Hardly."

He might not mean to break his vow, but Deirdre knew he wanted to. Even through chain mail, she swore she could feel him hardening against her thigh.

"I only wish to speak with you," he continued dryly, "in a position where you cannot knock me to the ground or unman me with a swift kick."

Deirdre scowled, and, in the interest of extricating herself as quickly as possible, stopped struggling and dropped her weapon. "Speak."

He set his sword aside as well. "You have some skill."

The compliment surprised her, but she didn't want him to know that. "As do you."

He chuckled, and his stomach jostled hers with each soft laugh. "So I'm told." Apparently, there was not an ounce of humility in him. "How long have you trained?"

"My father says I was born with a sword in my hand," she told him proudly.

"Forsooth?" Laughter danced in his eyes. "And did you stab at your nursemaid then?"

She fixed him with a grim stare. "At twelve winters old, I cut the fingers from a fletcher who tried to swive my sister in the stables."

A frown flitted across his brow, and his smile faded. He was silent a long while, studying her thoughtfully, and she almost wished she hadn't told him about the fletcher. After all, the man was only the first of a long line of men who had met misfortune at the point of her sword.

At last he spoke. "Mayhap your father was wise in teaching you to fight."

Deirdre was again astonished. No one had ever said that before. Her mother, the servants, even some of her own knights, were of the opinion that the sisters should have never taken up weapons. 'Twas only by her father's bidding that their training had been permitted.

Perchance, Deirdre dared to hope, Pagan understood. Perchance he recognized the wisdom in allowing her to be well-prepared and battle-ready and self-reliant. Perchance there would be no struggle for the command of the army of Rivenloch after all.

In the next instant, however, her hopes were dashed.

"But now, my lady," Pagan said, his gaze at once magnanimous and patronizing, "you and your sister need not trouble your precious heads over such things. The Knights of Cameliard are here to protect you. You need never wear chain mail, never wield a sword, never suffer the scars of battle. From this day forward," he vowed, "I will be your champion."

Apparently, Pagan thought, smiling tenderly, Deirdre was too grateful for words, for she could do little more than stare at him and sputter. It would be a great relief to her not to rely upon that motley bunch she called the army of Rivenloch for defense. Now that he and his men had arrived, she could return to stitching surcoats and picking flowers and whatever else women did.

And now that he had her where he wanted her, soft and flustered and grateful, perchance she'd be amenable to a kiss . . .

"Deirdre!" someone suddenly called.

She stiffened beneath him. He lifted his head to peer

through a gap in the wattle fence. Bloody hell, 'twas Miriel, looking for her sister.

"Deirdre! Where are you?"

Panicked, Deirdre struggled to push him off of her.

"I know you're here, Deirdre," Miriel scolded, drawing near. "I heard swords. You can't . . . oh!"

Miriel's eyes went as round as quail eggs as she peeked over the fence.

But Pagan refused to jump up like an adulterer caught with his mistress. Deirdre was his wife. This was his tiltyard. And if he wanted to swive his wife in his tiltyard, 'twas his own affair.

Deirdre apparently did not concur. Her fingers had wormed their way under his chainse, and now she gave his bare flesh a hard pinch. With a grunt of pain, he reluctantly moved off of her. And with a glare of disapproval, he helped her to her feet.

Miriel stood frozen in her tracks, her jaw lax. Her strange servant scowled beside her.

"What is it?" Pagan snapped. It had better be important, or he would string the both of them up by their braids.

"Oh . . . oh . . ." Miriel gaped from one to the other, as if she didn't quite understand.

The maidservant stepped forward, planted her fists atop her narrow hips, and demanded, "What have you done with Helena?"

Pagan glowered at the old woman, unaccustomed to such effrontery from a servant.

Miriel seemed jolted from her paralysis. She placed a placating hand on the maidservant's arm. "I've looked everywhere," she explained to Pagan. "I can't find her. And I can't find your man, Colin, either."

"What?" Deirdre exploded. She turned on him. "Where are they? So help me, if he's harmed one hair on her head—"

"Wait!" Pagan said, forestalling their panic. "There is naught to fret about. Colin is a trusted friend. I told him to lock her in the cellar. He is doubtless tending to her there."

Almost before he spit the words out, Deirdre charged past the tiltyard gate. He dogged her steps all the way back to the keep, praying that Colin had indeed spent the night watching over Helena, that he'd done naught untoward or unwise.

But when they arrived at the cellar, his worst fears were confirmed.

'Twas damningly empty.

"Rauve and Adric, you take the east road," Pagan ordered as the stableboy led several saddled horses into the courtyard. "Reyner and Warin, go west. Deirdre, have your—"

"Ian," she interrupted, already a step ahead of him, "send Rivenloch men north and south. And Miriel, have all the servants check the keep again. Leave no stone unturned."

"Good," Pagan decided.

He'd never been so angry with Colin. The dallying knave had recklessly absconded with a noblewoman, calling Pagan's honor into question as well. Even now, the Rivenloch people looked at him with thinly disguised hostility. If Pagan could not safeguard the lord's daughter, how could he defend an entire keep?

Aye, the instant Colin came trotting back, smug from

his romantic escapade, Pagan intended to knock a few teeth out of the varlet's self-satisfied grin.

Deirdre would doubtless gloat over the lapse in Pagan's judgment. She deserved to. But for the moment, too worried about her sister, she neither chided nor condemned him.

Deirdre sounded the order, and the gates of Rivenloch swung open to allow passage for the first riders. But before the men could leave, Sir Adric spotted a monk approaching the castle, waving a rolled parchment in one hand. "My lord, a messenger."

"Wait." Pagan quickly mounted his own horse.

"Take me with you." Deirdre's words were more command than plea, but under the circumstances, he obliged her. He lowered his arm and let her pull herself up into the saddle behind him.

No sooner was she settled than he kicked the horse into a gallop out the gate to meet the monk.

The approaching steed almost frightened the tonsured young man out of his robes as it skidded to a halt in a cloud of dust.

"What have you there?" Pagan demanded.

"A m-missive, my lord."

"From whom?"

"I was t-told to deliver it to a woman named Deirdre."

Deirdre slipped easily from the saddle and reached for the parchment. "I'm Deirdre."

Pagan dismounted. He itched to snatch the missive away from her. After all, he could surely read much more quickly than a woman. But he waited impatiently while she perused its contents.

When her shoulders sank, he feared the worst. "What? What is it?"

She gave no reply, only let her hand drop, and he seized the parchment before it could fall from her fingers.

"Deirdre," he read aloud, "I have taken the Norman hos—" That couldn't be right. He read it again, slower. "I have taken the Norman hostage. I will not return him until the marriage is annulled. Helena."

For a moment, all he could do was stare in bewilderment at the childish scrawl.

"Shite," Deirdre muttered, startling the monk, who, deciding 'twas time to travel on, crossed himself and hied down the road.

Then the truth of Colin's predicament struck Pagan. At long last, the charming, sly, swell-headed varlet had met his match.

Laughter bubbled up from deep in Pagan's chest and shook his shoulders.

Deirdre scowled and snatched the parchment from him, rolling it up to rap him on the arm. " 'Tis not a matter for laughing."

"Oh, aye, 'tis," he said, chuckling. For Pagan, naught tasted sweeter than just deserts. "You do not know Colin."

"And you do not know Helena."

"She's a wench," he said with a dismissive shrug.

"Yet somehow she managed to singlehandedly take him hostage," she said pointedly.

He snorted. "She doubtless caught him off his guard." Forsooth, he was relieved to have the blame shifted from Colin. And under the circumstances, he was in no hurry to come riding to his man's rescue.

But something in Deirdre's grave manner took him

aback. He narrowed his gaze. "She isn't . . . daft . . . is she?"

"She's . . . impulsive."

"What do you mean, impulsive?"

"You should know. She tried to stab you."

"She was quite drunk."

"Aye," she admitted, "but she was also desperate to save Miriel."

"Which you've already done," he said sourly. The idea of the three sisters battling over the disgrace of becoming his bride still cut him to the quick.

"But she doesn't know that. She supposes you are wed to Miriel."

"Colin will tell her otherwise."

"Not if he's bound and gagged."

The image of Colin tied up lightened his mood again.

Deirdre wasn't so amused. "I think I know where she took him. There's an abandoned crofter's cottage about—"

"Let them be."

"What?"

"Let them be. If Colin let a woman get the best of him, I say the fool should find his own way free."

She frowned in surprise. "You're not concerned about your man?"

"Colin can look out for himself." A smile tugged at the corner of his lip. "Forsooth, I'd worry more about your sister in the company of such a honey-tongued knave."

A dangerous gleam came into Deirdre's eyes. "Trust me. Helena is well fortified against the seductions of men."

"Indeed?" He flashed her a sly grin. "Then I'm glad 'tis not a family trait."

He turned to march back to the keep, just in time to dodge the venomous glare she shot his way.

"So what shall we tell *them*?" he said, nodding to the castle folk gathered at the gates.

She thought for a moment. "We'll say she took him on a cattle raid."

"A cattle raid?"

"She goes on them all the time."

He raised a brow. "A kidnapper, a murderer, *and* a cattle thief?"

"She only steals back what's been taken from us."

He smirked and shook his head. Sweet Mary, Colin had his hands full. These Scots were strange creatures indeed.

Chapter 13

WHEN DEIRDRE RETURNED TO THE KEEP, she discovered that her father was having one of his bad days. She found him roaming the stairwells, weeping inconsolably, searching for his lost Edwina. His sorrow was almost too much to bear. Deirdre didn't have the heart to tell him that one of his daughters was gone now as well, dwelling in a hovel in the wood with a Norman. Not that he would have understood. Today he didn't even recognize Deirdre.

She knew she'd have to spend the day with him in his chamber, protecting him from the eyes and ears of gossiping servants. Offering him company and privacy was the least she could do to preserve his dignity. Ordinarily 'twas not too inconvenient. His bad days were infrequent enough that Helena and Miriel could manage the castle in her absence. But with Helena gone and Miriel overworked, cataloguing the assets of two households, there was no one to oversee Rivenloch's daily operations—assigning tasks, settling disputes, supervising labor, met-

ing out justice. 'Twas enough to make Deirdre curse the
Normans for their invasion and Helena for her impetuous escapade.

Seated by his bedchamber hearth, rocking in agita-
tion, her father began wailing for his missing wife.
Deirdre knelt by his side as he wept and took his hand in
hers, speaking in soothing syllables. Anon the feverfew
she had slipped into his wine would take effect. In sleep,
she prayed, he might find reprieve from his wretched
memories and the demons that haunted him.

Adjusting the coverlet over his lap, Deirdre reflected
upon her own marriage, her Norman husband.

Perchance 'twas best that she felt no great affection
for Pagan. She need only look at her father to be convinced that love was a cruel mistress—demanding and
jealous and enfeebling. Aye, her parents had enjoyed
happy times. She remembered the two of them singing
together and laughing like children, snuggling by the fire
and giving each other secret smiles at supper, kissing in
the stairwell and chasing through the meadow like frolicking harts. But ultimately, love had repaid them in misery. It had taken a warrior who'd once held his head high
in battle and reduced him to a sniveling old man. Nay,
Deirdre thought, 'twas good she didn't love her husband.

She stared into the flames, relishing the comforting
burn upon her face as tongues of fire licked at the chill
air. Eventually the lord's sobs subsided, and he drifted
off. Deirdre carefully disengaged her hands from his and
rose to add a log to the hearth.

The darkening sky outside reminded her that the day
would end in night, that night meant a return to her own
bedchamber. She wondered how fierce a battle Pagan
would wage there this eve.

Her defenses felt weak. She feared they'd not hold against him again. But she didn't dare give in, for if she surrendered, she would hold no sway over him . . . ever.

Deirdre was well aware that a woman might employ a man's passion to utterly master him. Lust was a potent force. It had been the downfall of men since the time of Samson. As long as Deirdre withheld her body from Pagan, she might exert control over many things. Reign over her own people. Amnesty for her sister. Command of the army.

But if he suspected how fragile her leverage was, how frail her hold was over her own desires . . . By the Rood, 'twould be her undoing.

Someone scratched at the door then and announced dinner, startling the lord from sleep.

"Deirdre?" Lord Gellir blinked at her, then eased himself up till he sat straight in his chair. Suddenly, he was transformed into her father of old, proud and strong, capable and wise. His eyes were clear, his gaze steady.

Deirdre's throat thickened with bittersweet affection.

"Deirdre," he said fondly, tousling her hair. "What are you doing watching me doze? Should you not be on the arm of your new husband?"

She gave him a shaky smile. At least he remembered some of what had passed. "Shall we go to dinner, Father?"

"Dinner. Aye."

He pushed up from the chair and stretched to his full height. An uninvited tear welled in Deirdre's eye as she glimpsed again the proud warrior he'd once been.

"And afterwards, a good game of dice," he said with a wink. "I have to win my coin back from those cheating Normans."

Deirdre hadn't the heart to scold him. Aye, he'd gambled away enormous sums. Seldom an evening passed when he didn't play at dice and lose. Thankfully, Miriel had long ago persuaded the men of Rivenloch to return their winnings to the household accounts. Now the only coin the lord lost was to strangers stopping in their travels. But with a house full of wagering Normans, new arrangements would have to be made.

Meanwhile, Deirdre intended to enjoy the company of her beloved father tonight . . . before he slipped back into madness.

Her plans for a pleasant meal were ruined. Apparently, while Deirdre was confined to her father's chamber, Pagan had taken it upon himself to wreak havoc with her household.

"You did what?" she demanded, nearly choking on a swallow of ale.

"Tore down the old mews," Pagan said, nibbling at one of the four dozen trout his Normans had caught in the loch.

To her consternation, her father nodded his approval. "Good. 'Twas nigh collapsing anyway."

She scowled. "And what did you do with the falcons?"

One corner of Pagan's mouth cocked upward. "You'll have to ask the cook."

Her jaw dropped.

Beside her, Miriel giggled. "He's jesting, Deirdre."

Deirdre did not find Pagan amusing in the least. She'd been absent but half a day, and he'd reordered everything in the castle, apparently now with her father's blessing.

"This trout is delicious, Ian," Pagan raved. "'Tis a pity I cannot send my men fishing *every* day."

Deirdre fumed. 'Twas just another example of Pagan's ignorance. "Don't even think of it. If you fish every day, you'll empty the loch. We'll have naught to eat come winter, and there will be no trout left to spawn."

"Aye," he agreed. "So Miriel has warned me."

Deirdre stuffed a neep into her mouth. She didn't care for the way Pagan insinuated himself into her household. Already he called the castle folk by name. Already he availed himself of Rivenloch's resources. And already he garnered the confidence of her father. This did not bode well.

"Pagan tells me he has brought a clever armorer with him," Lord Gellir told her.

"Josserand," Pagan supplied, finishing off his ale and motioning a maidservant for another.

"We *have* weapons," Deirdre stated.

"Not like these," her father said, his eyes shining.

"Toledo steel," Pagan said. "Light. Strong. Well balanced."

Despite the appealing sound of new weaponry, Deirdre felt her temper rising. "And do you intend to rebuild Rivenloch, stone by stone, as well?" she asked sardonically.

"Well, since you mention it . . ." Pagan began.

"Deirdre!" her father snapped. "Cease."

She colored. It had been months since her father had scolded her for anything. That he did so now, before this pack of strangers, particularly after she'd spent all day nursing his melancholy and preserving his dignity, was utterly humiliating.

Curiously, 'twas Pagan who intervened to soothe her bruised pride. "Forsooth, I wish to confer with your father about some alterations to the castle. I'd welcome his suggestions."

She was tempted to ask him why, since he didn't seem to need his permission for anything else.

Meanwhile, Lucy Campbell, one of Rivenloch's maidservants, sidled between them to refill Pagan's cup, blatantly displaying her enormous breasts. A jagged bolt of aggravation sizzled through Deirdre as surely as lightning drawn to water.

Eager for distraction, she turned to Miriel. "Did you get started on the accounts?"

"Started and finished," Miriel replied with a smile. "Sir Pagan's man, Benedict, had already recorded the Cameliard assets. 'Twas a simple matter to combine the two households."

Far simpler, Deirdre thought, than merging their peoples.

Chaos abounded, even here in the great hall. The rushes had apparently been changed *again*, even though Miriel had had servants lay fresh rushes only last month. The pennants decking the walls were rearranged to accommodate several banners the Cameliard knights had brought with them. A pair of Norman lads spoiled the hounds in the corner, feeding them morsels of venison. And now the kitchen boys brought out some unfamiliar dish to complete the meal, something . . . Norman.

Damn it all! This was *her* keep, *her* land. These were *her* servants. Pagan's interference felt like . . . an invasion. As intrusive as his presence in her bed.

But even as she put mental words to her thoughts, she realized how irrational they were. Forsooth, it didn't matter whose hands placed the stones of a castle wall, only that the keep was made stronger by it. She should be grateful for Pagan's aid.

But she wasn't. Between this new marriage, Helena's brash kidnapping, caring for her father all day, then emerging to find her world turned completely awry, Deirdre was too upset to feel thankful for anything.

She excused herself from supper, giving Pagan a meaningful glare that told him in no uncertain terms that he'd not get what he wanted from her this eve. Then she went off to bed.

Pagan swirled the dregs at the bottom of his cup and eyed the serving wench who poured Reyner's ale. She was a winsome lass with rosy cheeks and a plump bosom that swelled above her kirtle like rising loaves of pandemain. Her hair was dark, her eyes flirtatious, the pout of her lips alluring.

He tossed back his drink, wincing at the grit he'd forgotten at the bottom, and slammed the empty cup on the table.

The pretty wench approached him and refilled his ale for the seventh time, practically pressing the creamy flesh of her breast against his cheek. She giggled low and asked if there was aught else she might do for him.

He meant to tell her aye. He meant to whisper his lusty intentions in her ear until a blush rose in her cheeks. And then he meant to meet her in the pantry and serve *her* a draught from *his* stores.

But 'twas not to be. Every time he so much as considered fondling another wench, and this was the third tonight, Deirdre's image intruded upon his thoughts. 'Twas not guilt that stopped him. Guilt would have been easy to discount. After all, 'twas not *he* who refused to consummate this marriage. Nay, he had every right to swive whomever he chose. But he could not choose. Or rather, he *could* choose, and the one he chose every time was the sultry-eyed, blonde-haired wench who lay sleeping in his bed even now. Soft. Warm. And naked.

He let out a sigh and drank down the ale all at once. The maidservant giggled again and asked if he wanted more. He shook his head.

He eyed the steps to his bedchamber. He could go upstairs and claim her right now. 'Twas within his rights. No one would question him. Surely Deirdre didn't expect him to honor that promise to her sister now. Not when Helena had broken the law and kidnapped his man.

"Pagan, lad!" the Lord of Rivenloch called, jarring him from his scheming. "Come sit by me and share some of your luck!"

Pagan tried not to scowl at the interruption. After all, he reasoned, his threats were empty. He had no intention of forcing himself upon Deirdre, promise or no. For better or worse, he was, above all else, an honorable knight.

He might as well play at dice with her father. The old lord seemed to be fairly lucid this eve. Besides, he reasoned, 'twould keep him from thinking about the tempting, untouchable goddess slumbering upstairs.

The light of dawn nudged Deirdre awake on her second morn of marriage, wafting into the bedchamber like a lady's veil, softening the harsh features of the weapons on the walls and lending welcoming warmth to the room.

The peace was broken by an abrupt snort. Pagan. He snored on the pallet beside her, his face mashed into the bolster, his hair falling recklessly over one cheek. He'd come to bed very late, she seemed to recall, though he'd been careful not to disturb her.

Deirdre was not so careful. After all, 'twas morn. If Pagan wanted to be steward of this castle, he'd better learn to rise with the rooster. She flounced onto one side, then the other. She yawned loudly. She pummeled her bolster. She stole all the linens from him, then, blushing at what she'd revealed, covered him up again.

God's eyes! She wondered if the man might sleep through a battering ram at the door.

Very well, she thought, if he was too lazy to get up, she'd be only too happy to go about her usual activities without his interference.

Even the noise of chain mail being dragged from her oak chest didn't stir Pagan. She shook her head in disgust. What use was an illustrious, battle-seasoned Norman knight if the enemy could steal up on him at a full charge?

She collected her things and slipped out the door, resisting the urge to slam it as she left.

She had to wade through dozens of dozing Normans scattered in the great hall till she found a Rivenloch squire she could jostle awake to help arm the men. Her knights slept in the armory, and she roused five of them as well, the five who were not too drunk to stand. 'Twas obvious by their sullen glares that they were none too happy to be wakened at so early an hour. But she countered their complaints, telling them 'twas their own fault if they'd imbibed too much drink and caroused half the night away. 'Twas essential for the men of Rivenloch to be prepared for battle at all times, particularly since news of another English attack, this one at Cruichcairn, had reached them.

Soon she was sparring happily in the tiltyard, clashing blades with her men, inventing new maneuvers, crowing in victory as she cornered Malcolm against the fence.

In high spirits, she recklessly invited the lot of them to attack her at once. Of course, for the sake of courtesy, they advanced in turn. Not even the most capable warrior could effectively battle five at a time if they came from all sides. But 'twas nonetheless a challenge for her, and her arm soon ached from clang after jarring clang of steel. The action thrilled her to the bone, and the victory was exhilarating. For Deirdre, there was no diversion more thoroughly engaging than swordplay.

So lost in unbridled joy was she, forsooth, that she was late to notice the wretched brutes who came to interrupt her play and spoil her mood.

Bang, bang, bang, bang, bang!

Pagan grumbled and scrubbed at his eyes. Jesu! Who was pounding on the door? 'Twasn't until he sat up that he remembered where he was. Pale sunlight bathed the chamber, but he felt as if he hadn't slept a wink. He glanced at the bed beside him.

Gone again. Damn!

Bang, bang, bang, bang!

"Bloody hell!" he growled.

Bang, bang, bang!

"Just a . . ." He stripped the linen sheet from the bed in a wad and plodded toward the door.

Bang, bang . . .

Before another blow could land, he snatched open the door. "What!"

'Twas Miriel. And she almost fell into the room as her fist fell on empty air. Her shocked gaze coursed immediately down his naked body, and he quickly clutched the sheet over his most offensive parts.

"I . . . I . . ." She seemed to collect herself then and met his eyes. Her face took on a serious expression. "I think you'd better come."

The somber aspect of her eyes shook him. "What is it?"

"They won't listen to me. They won't listen to anyone."

"Who? Who won't—"

"Hurry!" She turned her back, obviously waiting for him to dress. "Hurry, or someone's bound to be killed!"

What the bloody hell was she talking about? He dared waste no time asking her. Instead, he wriggled into his long shirt, threw the plaid over his shoulder, and buckled on his sword. "Where?"

"The tiltyard," she said.

He catapulted past her and down the stairs, his heart in his mouth. He would have called his men to arms in the great hall, but curiously, none of them were there. All that remained were women and servants and children. Even the armory was empty.

He raced out into the courtyard and crossed the grassy expanse toward the fenced tiltyard. When he arrived, he could only stare in awe. What he saw was too incredible to comprehend.

Chapter 14

ABOUT A HALF DOZEN RIVENLOCH MEN in chain mail lay upon the ground as if dead, their shields discarded, their swords silent upon the sod. The Knights of Cameliard, most of them only half-dressed, none of them armed, stood in a rough semicircle upon the field. And against the fence, Sir Rauve and Sir Adric restrained a furious, spitting, wild-eyed Deirdre. She was dressed in full armor but for a helm. As she thrashed her braid loose and waved her sword rampantly, her eyes flashed with murderous intent.

Pagan couldn't begin to guess what had transpired. He couldn't even summon the words to ask.

Fortunately, Sir Rauve volunteered an explanation. "My lord," he bit out, his voice straining as he fought to contain his slippery captive, prying the sword from her grip and tossing it away. "We've rescued your bride."

Rescued? She couldn't have looked *less* like a grateful maiden in distress.

"Rescued!" Deirdre cried. "You stupid, overgrown f—"

Rauve diplomatically clapped his hand over her mouth before she could finish.

But Pagan was more concerned with the Scots knights strewn about the tiltyard. "Are they . . ."

"Oh, nay!" Rauve scoffed. "Just gave them a light tap, we did. Ballocks, we weren't even armed. They just—" He let out a sudden yowl and snatched back his hand. Deirdre not only had claws, Pagan noted, but teeth.

Sir Adric continued. "They were attacking her, my lord. Their own mistress." He shook his head in disbelief. "Five of them against one wench."

Deirdre wrenched against their grasp. "You imbeciles! Crack-brained fools!"

The men began to grumble amongst themselves. Clearly they expected not condemnation, but gratitude, from the object of their rescue.

Pagan held up a hand for silence. Everyone but Deirdre obeyed.

"Let me go, you halfwits!" she spat.

Pagan nodded to Rauve, and they released her.

Cursing under her breath, she tossed her head and shoved them aside to make her way to the fallen knights. Pagan would have let her pass then, but as she swept past him, she gave him a hateful glare, as if he were somehow to blame. Irked, he caught her arm.

"Unhand me, sirrah!" she snapped.

"Explain. What's this about?"

"You tell me. What kind of barbarians are you fostering, Norman?"

His head ached, and he'd had enough of her insults.

His grip tightened. "Do not disparage my knights, wench."

"Knights? How can they call themselves knights when they have wrought *this*?" She gestured toward the motionless Scots.

"Then tell me. What happened?"

"Your *knights* attacked mine," she snarled. "Viciously. And without provocation."

"What?" Rauve cried in disbelief. "'Tis not the way of it at all, my lord."

Adric added, "We saved her, my lord. We saved her from harm."

"Dolts!" she fired back. "I was never in danger. My men know perfectly well how—"

"Cease! All of you!" Pagan barked. He was starting to understand what had transpired, and already he saw the beginnings of his first major battle with his new bride. He blew out a forceful sigh. "You were sparring with them?"

She lifted her proud chin. "Of course I was sparring with them. Do you truly believe my own men would attack me?"

"Sparring?" Adric asked.

Rauve's jaw dropped. "What? Oh, nay, nay, my lord." He vehemently shook his head. "'Twas a full assault. They were on her five at a time. Heavily armed. Sharpened blades. Naught held back. 'Twas hardly sparring."

"Oh?" Deirdre sneered at him. "And what do *Normans* spar with? Willow twigs?"

Rauve spat into the dust. "I'll tell you what Normans do *not* spar with. We do not spar with wenches."

Deirdre's eyes narrowed then, and Pagan saw a dangerous gleam enter them. "Mayhap you'd like to try," she challenged.

"What the . . ." Rauve looked horrified, as if she'd suggested he swallow a live kitten.

Pagan had to stop the nonsense. "Listen! The next man to draw a sword will answer to me."

Rivenloch and Cameliard were allies now, after all, and by the King's order, 'twas up to Pagan to merge Scot and Norman forces into a cohesive army. He had no time for childish quarreling. Nor did he have the patience for a wife who wished to play dangerous games with men twice her size.

Besides, he still stung from Deirdre's rejection for the second night in a row. If the wench wanted a bit of . . . lunge and thrust . . . he'd be only too happy to oblige her in their chamber.

"Rauve, help these men off the field. Let them rest. We'll get a fresh start in the afternoon, training the Scots." He clucked his tongue, then muttered, "'Twill doubtless be a challenge to whip them into shape, considering that even fully armed, they couldn't defend themselves against half-dressed men."

Deirdre seldom lost her temper. 'Twas a point upon which she prided herself. Unlike Helena, she maintained control of her emotions, relying upon her head instead of her heart. But this morn, her restraint was sorely tested.

At Pagan's insult, she stooped down and retrieved her fallen sword with icy fury, then slowly turned and faced him, raising the blade. So the next to draw a sword would answer to Pagan? She'd do so gladly.

His men immediately froze, some of them swearing

softly in awe, reinforcing her suspicion that they were a bunch of cowards.

" 'The Scots' need no training from you, sirrah." She eyed his knights, who now stood in gape-mouthed anticipation. "Nor from your cowering men."

A tiny muscle ticked in Pagan's jaw, and for a long while he only stared at her, his expression unreadable. Her mouth curved up in a slow, scornful smile as she realized Pagan had not the courage to fight her in front of his men.

But just as she'd decided he was going to cede defeat, he surprised her by drawing his sword.

"Clear the field!" he ordered.

All around him, his men hastened to comply, some of them carrying the still unconscious men of Rivenloch between them.

'Twas a pity he'd dismissed them. She longed to prove, not only to Pagan, but to an audience of his knights, that the Scots were made of stern stuff.

All the while the Cameliard knights hurried to vacate the field, Pagan fixed a grim gaze upon her. She met him, stare for stare, as long as she could. But the unflinching courage and raw determination in his eyes were most unnerving. She resorted to distracting him with words.

"*My* knights would not flee in such fear," she said, glancing at his men, emptying the tiltyard. "They scuttle from the field like beetles from a fire."

"They likely fear for *you*, my lady," he said calmly.

She smirked. 'Twas a childish boast, one she'd expect from an unseasoned fighter. "Well, they need not. You and I know I'm quite handy with a blade, do we not, sirrah?"

His brow clouded. "Do not address me in that manner. You may say 'my lord' or call me by my given name. But you will not use that term of disrespect again."

"When you earn my respect, *sirrah*, then I will oblige you."

His sword whipped up to her throat with such speed that it whistled on the air, making her gasp involuntarily. God's eyes! She'd never seen a thing move so rapidly.

"You have much to learn about respect," he said. "'Tis not about who is faster or stronger or who has defeated more men in battle. 'Tis about honor."

Deirdre gulped in spite of herself. Her heart fluttered against her ribs. She still couldn't fathom how his sword had come to be at her throat so quickly.

"Now," he said, giving the field a quick perusal. "They're gone. Will you withdraw your challenge?"

She scowled at him. "Nay."

"I've dismissed all the witnesses," he said, "to spare you the shame of surrender."

"Surrender?" She didn't believe him for a moment. No one was that chivalrous. She narrowed her eyes, trying to guess his thoughts. He *had* ultimately prevailed over her yesterday, but she'd not been an easy conquest. "Nay, I think you're afraid of me. You're afraid to lose to a woman before your men."

To his credit, he didn't laugh at her, but a grimace of irony crossed his face. With a subtle shake of his head, he withdrew. "Fine. Do your worst."

He swished his blade through the air a couple of times before settling into a defensive stance.

"I'll wait while you don armor," she said.

He shook his head.

She frowned. "I won't have you report that our fight was unjust."

"Oh, I don't plan to report our fight at all, but . . ." He gave a slight nod of his head and murmured, "Thank you for the courtesy."

She sniffed. 'Twas no less than any knight would do.

With a nod, she planted her feet, raised her weapon, and began the shortest sword fight of her life.

Pagan was eager to put an end to this foolishness and even more eager to crawl back into bed for a few more hours of sleep.

Deirdre had to learn that a woman her size could never prevail against men like the Cameliard knights. She was determined, aye, relentlessly so, and she had a few cunning tricks at her disposal, but her enthusiasm far exceeded her skills and strength. Pagan had toyed with her in their first fight. 'Twas a matter of courtesy and custom to match an opponent's level in a friendly battle. Probably all of Deirdre's rivals did so, humoring her into a false self-confidence that could ultimately prove deadly.

He locked gazes with his beautiful, foolhardy bride. 'Twas an unpleasant task, but he had to disarm the lass before she hurt herself.

He didn't bother engaging her with his blade. Instead, he caught her sword arm at the wrist and, using his other hand, pried the weapon free with brute strength. Then he seized her by the front of her tabard, shoved her up against the wall of the stable, and pressed forward until he stood eye to eye with her.

He could see her pulse race in the throbbing vein at her neck. Her breathing was shallow and erratic, her mouth half open in shock. But contrary to his expectations, there wasn't an ounce of fear in her eyes. He couldn't say why, but somehow this pleased him.

He was close enough to feel the heat of battle coming off of her, close enough that her breath mingled with his, close enough that 'twas a temptation to bridge the tiny gap between them and prove his point with a triumphant kiss.

But he had to settle their arrangements here, once and for all.

"*Now* do you think I'm afraid of losing to you?"

She swallowed, still obviously shaken.

"Would you not agree," he said, "that I'm more than capable of protecting the keep?"

She frowned and chewed at her lip.

"And after the incident this morn, do you not trust that my men will guard you with their lives?"

After a long moment, she gave him a reluctant nod.

"Then let me do what I'm here to do," he told her. "I'm the best defense you have."

"You may be bigger," she murmured. "And stronger. And more seasoned. But I know this castle. I know this land. And I know my people. You cannot discount my experience. I know best how to command my knights."

Pagan knew he should argue with her, but he was beginning to feel like a hound slavering over a bone just out of its reach. His loins couldn't help but respond when Deirdre was so temptingly close and soft and seductive. The feel of her spirited body against his chest, the erotic glow of her skin, the cool fire of her eyes, the scent of leather and chain mail mingling incongruously with flowers, drove him half mad with desire.

"You know, my lady," he whispered, lowering his

gaze to her inviting lips, "I'd be more inclined to let you play at being a soldier, were you more inclined to play at being my wife."

She gasped. Her gaze hardened as she spoke between clenched teeth. "My affections are not for barter."

"Pity," he said, giving her a rueful smile. "You might find your affections are worth a great deal."

Her gaze lowered then to his mouth, and he could almost see her weighing his offer, reconsidering.

But he suddenly realized he didn't want Deirdre this way. He might have paid a woman for her favors in the past, but Deirdre was his wife. He wanted her to come to him of her own free will, not because he promised her a trinket or a trifle . . . or command of an army.

Before lust could get the best of him, he released her and backed away. "You fight admirably for a woman, Deirdre," he allowed, "but you *will* fight no more."

Deirdre replied with a strangled growl. Then she pushed him out of her way, retrieved her discarded sword, and shoved it into its sheath. For a moment, he thought she was going to speak. She furrowed her brow and narrowed her eyes, and her lips thinned in anger. But in the end, without a word, she wheeled and stalked off the field as angrily as a spurned harlot.

Pagan watched her go. She wrenched open the gate of the tiltyard and slammed it shut, rattling the wattle fence. By the Saints, she was far more complex than any woman he'd ever met. He hated to admit it, but she seemed to indeed have a true talent for battle. Aye, she was too light for genuine combat, but she had unique skills and a foxy mind. With a bit of training . . .

He patted his sword, safe in its sheath, unsoiled by

Deirdre's blood, and shuddered. Nay, he decided, the battlefield was no place for a woman.

He didn't care if she'd sparred with her countrymen from the time she was a babe, led armies, or slain dragons. 'Twas too dangerous a profession for a maid. Pagan had enough to worry about, trying to get the Rivenloch knights in shape for battle, without brooding over a lass who believed she was invincible. He'd seen warfare, seen what it did to the healthiest of flesh and the most indomitable spirit. There was naught that couldn't be destroyed by the slash of a blade. Nay, he'd not see Deirdre fall beneath the sword, she nor her sister.

A scream of rage built up in Deirdre's throat as she banged the gate behind her, a scream she feared might escape if she didn't kill something soon.

Fortunately, she was able to walk off her anger before anyone crossed her path. But the mere fact that she felt such fury meant she was losing control, which in turn made her more furious.

She had to regain command. Of her temper. Of her body. And of her castle. *You will fight no more* indeed! How dared he dictate to her what she would and would not do? Damn him! She needed no man's protection. 'Twas no matter that he was capable. And courageous. And heroic.

God's blood! What did he think she'd done before he arrived? How did he think they'd survived without him? Jesu, his arrogance was insufferable.

She should have told him so. But standing in such proximity to him, enthralled by the force of his gaze, consumed by the power of his desire, overwhelmed by the pure male essence of his body, she'd been unable to think properly.

Deirdre had reached the abandoned dovecot now, and she entered the dark hovel, eager to be far from the eyes of castle folk who might spread tales about her agitated state. The odor of mold and musty wood was strong, and though her eyes were not adjusted to see them, she heard mice skittering in the remote corners of the room. Closing the door behind her, she began pacing briskly back and forth through the rushes.

Damn the Norman! He was no less an invader than an Englishman would have been.

She kicked up a tuft of straw.

Pagan might claim to be doing her a service by being . . . what had he said yesterday? Her champion? But she could see through his deception. The fox meant to undermine her power.

She scuffed again at the dirt floor, making dust rise up in the slivers of sunlight made by the cracks in the walls. Lord, even in the cool of the dovecot, she felt unbearably warm. 'Twas likely the blood simmering in her veins, she thought.

She stopped pacing and sighed, trying to calm her mood. Rage would serve her ill. She needed to clear her head to consider her options. She pitched her rump against the wall and stared pensively at the straw between her feet.

If 'twere anyone else, she'd have simply challenged them to a melee, an even number of them against an even number of Rivenloch men. But sparring with Pagan had alerted her to his prowess, and watching a few of his men, unarmed and unprepared, take down her knights so easily had shaken her confidence.

Still, she had no intention of bowing to the Norman's wishes. This was her home. She was the lady of the keep. If she wished to take command of the knights or the armory or the whole damned castle, then by God, she'd do it.

She pounded her fist against the wall for emphasis, and suddenly a throng of doves exploded from the rotting perches in a flurry of cooing and feathers, stirring up the dust and flapping about Deirdre's head. She yelped in surprise, startling them further.

Bloody hell. The Normans had brought their doves with them. Not even the dovecot was safe from their invasion.

"Shh." She held her hands out, palms forward, as if by that gesture she could calm the birds and settle them onto their perches again. 'Twould have been easier to reattach a plucked flower. Or, she thought, to restore Rivenloch to what 'twas before the Normans came.

Her jaw resolute, Deirdre slipped carefully out the door so none of the flustered doves could escape. She was beginning to think 'twould have been wise to take Helena's suggestion at the first. The sisters should have waylaid the cursed Normans in the forest ere they arrived.

Chapter 15

"AGAIN!" DEIRDRE COMMANDED, closing her visor against the afternoon sun, bracing her feet wide, and raising her sword against Sir Reyner.

Sir Reyner lowered his shield. "My lady, I mean no disrespect, but—"

"Come." She slashed downward, sending up a cloud of dust as the tip of the blade furrowed the hard-packed ground of the list.

"My lady . . ."

"Have at me, coward!" She flexed her knees, tossed her head, and lifted the sword once more.

'Twas Pagan's loss, she thought, if he chose to make rounds of the castle with his builder, discussing changes in Rivenloch's fortification, rather than spend time training with his knights. And she'd be damned if she'd let his soldiers, *Rivenloch's* soldiers, grow lazy simply because he had better things to do.

Pagan's men were predictably hesitant to fight her at first. She was accustomed to that. Men feared they would hurt her. But she knew that once they engaged her, once she proved to be a worthy opponent, once she earned their respect, the Knights of Cameliard would learn to spar with her willingly, just as her own men did.

Meanwhile, she'd hold back nothing when she attacked them and give no quarter when they struck. With luck, she'd even dole out a scratch or two they could display to Pagan at supper.

Pagan thoughtfully walked the perimeter of the keep, nodding at the sketches, pleased with his builder's suggestions. The addition of an inner wall enclosing the keep would vastly improve the defenses of the castle. Grain might be kept within one of the six new towers of the wall, and cellars could be dug underneath for storage of provender—ale, cheese, dried fish, salted meat—for a hard winter or in the event of a siege.

Best of all, they could begin at once, and because the construction required no breaching of the outer wall, it could be done in complete safety. If the summer weather held, and if enough stone could be quarried, the building might be well underway before winter.

There was just one thing Pagan wanted to discuss with Sir Rauve, and that was the merits of digging a moat around the castle. 'Twould require extra fortification at the foot of the existing wall and the addition of a drawbridge. 'Twas considerable work, expensive, and Pagan was not entirely convinced of its usefulness.

Returning the drawings to the builder, he told him he'd have a decision by the morrow. Then he left to find Rauve.

As he neared the tiltyard, he heard the violent ring of steel on steel, the scuff of sabatons in the dirt, shouts of pain and rage and victory. He spotted Sir Rauve outside the field, leaning against the fence, watching the various battles with intense scrutiny. Forsooth, so focused was his man's attention that it took a third glance before Rauve realized who approached. Once he recognized Pagan, he pushed away from the fence and turned toward him. He looked uncomfortable, as if someone had put honey in his braies or told him that yet another black-haired whelp had been born to one of his mistresses.

"What is it?" Pagan asked with a chiding grin. "Have you got some Scots wench with child already?"

The big man only grunted, scowling and looking off absently across the field.

"What is it, Rauve?" Pagan said, keen to his man's dark moods. "Speak your mind."

Rauve spat into the dust and pounded a fist absently into his palm. "I'm not one to interfere. You know that." He sniffed, but wouldn't meet Pagan's eyes. "I know the Scots ways are . . . well, they're not the same as ours."

Pagan blinked.

Rauve struggled with the words. "I don't doubt her good intentions is what I'm trying to say, but . . ."

"Her?"

"Your wife." Rauve shifted his weight uneasily and began to speak more rapidly, as if preparing for the blow to come at the end of his speech. "She has determination. That much is true. And spirit? Well, what Scot hasn't that fierce kind of . . ."

"What is it, Rauve?" Pagan braced himself.

Rauve pressed his lips together, reluctant to say, then turned and nodded his head toward the tiltyard.

Sir Adric le Gris sparred out there, his knees bent, his shield held forward, his sword aloft but moving only infrequently, and then gingerly, as if he defended himself against a kitten's claws.

Then Pagan saw the kitten. She swung her blade around in both hands, slicing right and left, twirling, dodging, thrusting . . . His heart plummeted.

"Mother of God," he said under his breath, clapping a hand to the pommel of his sheathed sword and advancing.

But Rauve stopped him, placing his own body between Pagan and the tiltyard and ignoring Pagan's black looks. "'Tis no great matter to me whether she wields a sword or no. From what the men of Rivenloch say, she's done so since she was a child. But the knights fear for her safety, and—"

"Stand aside. You have cause to worry no more." To his amazement, he was trembling, and his voice came out like a feeble wind through a straw hovel.

Rauve was looking at him oddly, and Pagan knew he had to pull himself together before he confronted Deirdre. He swiftly closed down all his emotions save fury. Then, filching the heavy, studded mace that hung from Rauve's belt, he pushed past his man toward his target.

"Deirdre of Rivenloch!"

His bellow was loud enough to halt even the most distant bouts on the practice field. It startled Deirdre, though not as much as it did Sir Adric, who leaped into the air, all but dropping his sword and shield, as guilty as a mouse caught nibbling the Sabbath offering.

Pagan stalked across the field, the mace gripped firmly in his fist.

Adric fumbled his sword into its sheath. "Forgive me, my lord. I . . ."

Pagan ignored his man and marched straight up to Deirdre.

"Give me that sword." He hoped to God she couldn't hear the tremor in his voice. Sainted Mary, his voice served him well enough on the battlefield. Why was it shaking now?

Deirdre tossed down her shield. She removed her helm, and her hair spilled free like honey pouring forth from a comb. "Why should I—"

"Now!" he roared like a madman.

She compressed her lips and tightened her grip on the sword. But he reached forward, easily wresting it from her hand.

"What is the meaning of this?" she demanded. "You have no right to . . ."

But he wasn't listening. Angling Deirdre's sword with its point in the earth, he raised the mace high. Its studded head winked darkly in the sunlight. Then, with one powerful blow, he plunged the club downward. The refined steel was no match for the brutal mace, and the blade snapped with a brittle ring. The two pieces clattered to the ground like dry bones.

Deirdre felt as if a quintain had caught her hard in the stomach. For a moment, she couldn't breathe. Her sword. The sword her father had given her. The sword that bore her name, scratched in a childish scrawl upon the hilt. The sword she'd painstakingly notched for every victory. To her utter mortification, her eyes filled with tears as she gaped at the broken blade.

She bit her lip to stem the tide. Deirdre, the Warrior Maid of Rivenloch, didn't cry. Not from pain. Not from fear. And certainly not from something as insignificant as the breaking of a blade. She would not weep. She'd not give Pagan the satisfaction.

But to her horror, in the dreadful silence that ensued, a sob squeaked in her throat, and she knew she must flee at once, get out of their sight before she shamed herself in front of the knights.

She didn't trust herself to speak. Steeling her spine as best she could, she turned stiffly around. The knights moved aside as she made her dignified way to the gate and strode across the courtyard toward the keep. If she could maintain a pretense of composure and make it to her chamber, she could bar the door and cry her heart out into her pillow.

Later she'd deal with Pagan's treachery. Later she'd be able to think clearly enough to devise a fitting retribution. But for now, all she wanted was to make it to her chamber without falling to pieces.

Pagan watched her leave the field, then turned to find several pairs of sullen, judging Riveloch eyes boring into him. He glanced at the broken sword, winking up at him like a taunt, and cursed.

"She's a woman!" he yelled, loud enough for all to hear. "God's eyes! Would you risk the life of the lady of the keep? Do you not want heirs for Rivenloch?" He shook his head and raked his hand back through his hair, then fixed them all with a stern glare. "No one, *no one* will spar with her again. Do you understand?"

The Rivenloch men shuffled their feet and muttered grudging acceptance. He waved them back to their affairs with an annoyed flick of his hand. Then he trudged back to where Sir Rauve waited.

"She'll trouble you no more," he told his man, returning the mace.

Rauve grunted.

Pagan crossed his arms over his chest, over the spot where his heart felt strangely bereft. For some unfathomable reason, he suddenly needed to explain himself. "A wench truly has no place on the field of battle, Rauve," he murmured. "I care not what her father allowed. Her insistence on wielding her own weapon shows a lack of faith in my protection. 'Tis a man's duty to protect his wife, just as 'tis his duty to lay down the law for her."

Rauve's heavy black brows lifted almost imperceptibly.

Pagan tried to summon up a self-satisfied smile and failed. Damn it all, he thought, he *should* have felt satisfied. Mayhap he could talk himself into it. "'Tis my own fault. I should have made it clear for her earlier. A woman's place is in the keep," he continued with a frown. "Women are made for handling tapestries and . . . and seedlings . . . and babes, not weapons of war. She has . . . things to oversee . . . affairs to supervise."

"Aye." Rauve still looked skeptical.

"God's eyes! She has no business mingling with reckless knights who might unwittingly knock her senseless or . . . or slash her hauberk or lop off her . . ." He swayed as a too clear picture of Deirdre falling to her death hit him full force.

"My lord?" Rauve grasped him by the shoulder in concern.

Pagan looked at his man blankly. Who was he fooling? He wasn't looking to lay down the law for Deirdre. Even in the brief time he'd known her, he knew better. She was unlike any woman he'd ever met—strong-willed and smart and independent—and he respected those unique qualities. By the Saints, he *admired* them.

Nay, the truth was, he was terrified for her. When he'd beheld her battling Sir Adric le Gris, her shield bowing beneath his sword, his blade narrowly missing her leg, Pagan's breath had stopped. 'Twas different when *he* fought her. Then he was in control. But God help him, when he'd seen his beautiful wife fighting a man twice her size, risking her neck against his own seasoned knight, his heart had knifed so violently that he feared 'twould thrust through his chest.

Which could only mean one thing.

"Bloody hell," he muttered.

He was developing a weakness for his wife.

He shook his head, then took a deep breath before he started off toward the keep. If 'twas in his power to stop Deirdre from ever lifting a sword again, he would do so, if he had to break every blade in the armory.

"Deirdre."

Deirdre scrambled up from the bed, frantically wiping the despicable tears from her face, and stared at the bolted door. She wasn't about to open it.

"What do *you* want?" She tried to sneer, but the weepy hitch in her voice ruined the effect.

The latch rattled in reply as Pagan tried the door. Her heart thumped against her ribs. He jogged the latch harder, without success.

"Deirdre." His tone was calm and steady, but its hard edge made the bar across the door seem suddenly insubstantial. "Let me in."

"Nay."

A long quiet followed. Deirdre's pulse rushed in her ears.

"Open the door, Deirdre." His voice was softer this time, but even more dangerous.

"Nay."

There was no reply, no movement. No sound at all intruded from beyond the door. Deirdre listened breathlessly, but the silence lengthened until she was sure he'd given up, gone away.

And then the peace was split asunder.

The oak door exploded inward with the sound of a hundred lances cracking. Splinters flew everywhere. The iron bands twisted beneath the impact, and the leather hinges ripped from their fittings. What remained of the door sagged and slumped to the floor like a slain beast. And into the doorway, through the cloud of dust, her father's great war axe hanging from one fist, stepped Pagan, looking as ferocious as a Viking invader of old.

Chapter 16

PAGAN WAS INCENSED. Here he stood, like some barbarian plunderer with axe in hand, forced to break down the door of his own bedchamber—by his own wife! How dared Deirdre . . .

Deirdre.

She shrank back, glaring at him with wet-rimmed eyes, as defensive and edgy as a wounded wolf. He supposed the fact he'd come crashing in with a war axe didn't help matters.

"Leave me alone!" she cried.

Salty tracks stained her cheeks. Her eyes were red and swollen. And though she tried to disguise the hitching of her chest, a hiccough betrayed her. Bloody hell! His strong, fearless warrior wife had been crying.

His grip loosened on the axe. His shoulders dropped. The tension in his forehead relaxed. Nothing melted Pagan's rage faster than tears. Something about the soft, sweet lines of a woman's face transfigured by sorrow wrenched at his heart. And knowing he was the source of her grief . . .

Guilt washed over him. "Deirdre." He spoke with a gentleness that surprised even him. He carefully set the axe aside and stepped over the pile of debris between them.

Wild-eyed, she retreated, coming up against the edge of the bed. Before he could take a breath, she slipped her hand beneath the coverlet and withdrew a length of steel, a yard long and honed to a fine point. His eyes widened. Sweet Mary, did the lass have weapons stashed behind every tapestry?

"I'm sorry about your sword, but you gave me no choice."

"Sorry!" she snapped, lifting the sword to his throat. The tears in her eyes seemed to freeze into icicles. "My father gave me that sword, you bastard."

He winced as the point of the sword jabbed his chin and regretted discarding the axe so quickly. "Well," he said dryly, "you don't seem to be suffering from any shortage of blades."

"And yet you persist in thinking me unfit for battle."

He locked eyes with her. She had a point. "What is it you want?"

"I want my command back."

"Nay."

He saw her temper flare in the fiery depths of her eyes. But she controlled it like a flame burning in an enclosed lantern. "Do you know who I am?" She raised her chin proudly and looked down her nose at him. "I am Deirdre, Warrior Maid of Rivenloch. I have routed thieves, maimed robbers, and killed outlaws. I was born with a sword in my hand. You have no right to take my command from me."

"I have every right. I am your husband and steward of this castle, by command of the King."

She lowered her eyes to the tip of her sword, poised precariously against the vein in his neck. "You speak boldly for a man whose life hangs in the balance."

"You will not slay me. My death would incur the wrath of my men and start a blood battle between our people."

"Mayhap I shall only damage you."

He didn't believe her for a moment. She was fierce, aye, and fearless, and she had scratched him once with her blade. But she was no cold-blooded savage. He shrugged, as much as he could without driving the point of her sword into his throat. "'Twill be *you*, dear wife, waking up next to my mangled body each morn."

Deirdre had to admire Pagan's courage, marked in the even tone of his voice. 'Twould take but a twitch of her wrist to slit his throat. But he was right. She had no desire to injure him.

So they were at a standstill. And she had precious little leverage left. They stared at each other a long while, each sizing up the other.

Finally, after a long, weighted breath, Pagan spoke. "All right. I may live to rue this day, but I have a proposal for you."

"Go on."

He grimaced. "'Twould be easier to speak if I didn't have a blade at my throat."

Deirdre left her sword point where 'twas.

He sighed. "Very well. Know this, Deirdre. I will

never turn my knights over to your command. I've led them to victory too many times to hand them over to a lass with no battle experience." He glanced pointedly down at her blade. "No matter how many swords she owns. Furthermore, since we need to combine our forces, I cannot allow you to continue training the men of Rivenloch."

"What!" she said, poking him accidentally with the blade.

He grimaced. "Ah!"

"Sorry," she muttered.

He glared as if he didn't believe her. "An army cannot follow two leaders. You know that. I also think you're wise enough to know that pride should never get in the way of common sense. The simple truth is that I'm more experienced. I am the better commander."

A surge of indignation rose in her, and her fist tightened around the pommel of her sword. "How dare you assume that? How dare you assume that because I'm a Scot and a woman and a . . . a few inches shorter, I cannot manage an army as well as you? 'Tis an insult, sirrah."

"'Tis no insult," he said softly. "'Tis fact. And you know I'm right."

She scowled. Curse his Norman hide, she didn't *want* him to be right.

"You've never seen battle, have you?"

She compressed her lips.

"Have you?" he prodded.

"Nay," she admitted.

"Nor have most of your men."

She raised her chin proudly. "My father spent his youth soldiering about the Borders."

"That was long ago. There have been new weapons developed since then, new defenses, new strategies."

She smirked. "And I suppose you know all about them."

He gave her a wry smile. "I've done naught for the past seven years *but* command an army."

Damn him, she thought, chewing pensively at her lip. He *was* right. Sometimes her own infallible sense of logic, her grasp of reason, and her stubborn pragmatism were a frustration to her.

Still, Pagan offered her naught. He only told her what he intended to take away from her.

"What is your proposal then?" she asked bitterly. "That I crawl off somewhere and disappear, leave you to your command?"

"Nay." He frowned as her sword point jabbed him again. "Damn it, Deirdre. Will you not put away your blade?"

She moved it back a fraction of an inch. "Speak."

"My proposal is this. I've already ordered the men not to spar with you, and I'll not withdraw that order. But I will make an exception in exchange for something I want."

"Go on."

"I'll allow you to fight," he said. "But only with me."

"With you?"

"*Only* with me."

Deirdre was astonished. Given how arrogant he was about his own skills, why would Pagan want to waste his time with someone he considered an inferior fighter? On the other hand, if she sparred with him, she could learn his weaknesses, which might prove useful one day. "What is it you want in exchange?" She expected 'twould be appreciable. The immediate return of Colin perchance? A large sum of silver for his new construction? Full command of her father's household?

"One kiss each day."

She looked at him blankly. Mayhap she'd heard wrong. "One kiss."

"Aye," he said, completely serious. "One kiss each day. At the time and place of my choosing."

She smirked. He must be addled. One kiss was naught. She'd dreaded far more from the man who claimed her as wife. And the time and place of his choosing? Pah! What did it matter? He'd already kissed her in the chapel in full view of all Rivenloch. The stable? The kitchens? The great hall? 'Twas no matter to her.

But the skeptical part of her experienced a moment of doubt. Surely such a simple display of affection couldn't mean so much to him. "'Tis all?"

"Aye."

She narrowed her eyes. She might regret it later, but his offer was too tempting to ignore. "Done." She lowered her sword.

"Beginning tonight," he said.

"Beginning tonight."

Then he gave her a sly smile that sent a shiver of misgiving along her spine and made her wonder if she'd just stepped into the wolf's lair. "I will count the hours, my lady."

She silently wondered if he *could* count. Most men of war had more brawn than brains. Yet she'd already seen Pagan read. There was definitely more to him than muscles and girth.

With a flourish of farewell, he started toward the

doorway. Eyeing the wreckage, he said, "I'll send a man up to make repairs."

"Wait." She hated that Pagan had seen her weeping. "If you tell a soul that I was . . . that I . . ."

He sniffed. "Your secret is safe. On one condition." He picked up the axe and slung it over his shoulder, pinning her with a purposeful gaze. "Never. Never bar the door against me again."

Deirdre suspected Pagan was speaking of more than just the chamber door, the oak and iron and leather he'd demolished with a single blow. Nay, he meant the door to her *heart* as well.

She realized that he could shatter that as easily as the wood. Not that he'd have to. The residual hitch in her chest reminded her that for the second time, he'd witnessed her loss of control. Curse her frail feminine emotions, she'd probably given Pagan the *key* to the damned door.

By the time Pagan left and sent the carpenter up with planks and new leather hinges, Deirdre had changed out of her armor and into a soft brown kirtle, and her composure was restored. She left the workman to his toil and went to seek out Miriel. There were things to see to, she told herself, besides the castle's defenses. Something had to be done soon about Lord Gellir's wagering. According to Miriel, last night their father had suffered enormous losses to the Cameliard knights.

But when Deirdre confronted Miriel, she discovered that her sister, a paragon of efficiency, had already spoken to the men. Forsooth, Miriel volunteered that perchance Normans weren't quite as barbaric as Deirdre imagined, for the knights seemed chivalrous enough about the whole affair, returning their winnings with good-natured humor to restore the coffers, all but Lyon, who had wandered into the forest and been robbed by The Shadow. Still, Deirdre suspected their cooperation had more to do with Miriel's sweet nature and beautiful countenance than chivalry.

Eventually, despite her determination to keep busy with other things, Deirdre found herself drawn, out of curiosity, back to the tiltyard. She managed to avoid notice, standing in the shade of the kennels. From there, she watched as Pagan put her men through rigorous drills, tossing cloth bags of chain mail back and forth until they could barely lift their arms. Meanwhile, his knights took turns riding at the quintain, sending it spinning so hard, she thought 'twould fly off the post. After that, he lined all the knights up in a row and made them stand up straight, whacking them with the flat of his blade if they stooped so much as an inch. Then he had them practice lunges, not a few dozen, as Deirdre did to warm them up, but a hundred. In full armor.

She furrowed her brows in disapproval. Her men would hate Pagan by the end of the day, she was sure.

Pagan's next abuse was to challenge her knights to grapple with him, hand to hand. One by one they accepted his challenge, and one by one they were overthrown by his brute strength, tossed into the dust like discarded offal. Deirdre shook her head. By nightfall, Pagan's back would end up with a knife in it.

As she watched Pagan bowl over young Kenneth, the smallest of her knights, wrestling him to the ground as easily as a pup, her instincts took over.

She pushed off the wall of the kennel, intent on repairing his damage.

But before she'd even emerged from the shadows, she

froze in her tracks, stunned by the sight before her. Pagan, laughing in triumph, hopped to his feet. He helped the fallen Kenneth rise and ruffled the lad's hair. And to Deirdre's shock, Kenneth was grinning from ear to ear. Forsooth, *all* of her men were chuckling. Despite bloodied noses and blackened eyes, their faces were wreathed with tired smiles.

Where was their rage? Where was their shame? They'd just spent hours being battered, beaten, and bruised. They'd all been bested, soundly and single-handedly, by a Norman. Why were they not boiling with indignation?

She slumped back against the wall, bewildered. How had he done it? How had Pagan managed to mistreat them so callously and yet earn not only their respect, but their obvious adoration? That was what shone in Kenneth's eyes. The lad clearly adored Pagan. It seemed all the men did.

She sighed in wonder. Mayhap she'd never understand men. 'Twas as if by conquering their bodies, Pagan had somehow won their hearts.

She stared pensively at the ground, mulling that idea over in her mind. Then she glanced up at the handsome Norman with his broad shoulders and unruly hair, his sparkling eyes and flashing teeth. Perchance, she thought with a shudder, 'twas the same tactic he planned to use with her.

All evening, Deirdre felt as edgy as a mouse waiting for the cat to pounce, speculating upon when Pagan would claim his kiss. While he sat beside her at supper, joking with her men, she picked at her trencher, wondering if he might do it in this very public place.

But he didn't.

Nor did he approach her when Boniface strummed upon a lute and sang a bawdy lay about a man with three wives.

When her father started up a game of dice with Sir Warin, who gave Miriel a conspiratorial wink before he began wagering, Pagan made no move to draw her into his arms and claim his kiss then either.

He must have forgotten her, she decided. 'Twas entirely probable, given how attentive the maidservants were this eve, refilling his cup every time he took a sip and gushing over his impressive appetite. Their attentions likely made him go hard in his trews and soft in his head.

But when a Norman serving wench splashed ale onto Pagan's lap, then made a great show of wiping it up, Deirdre decided she'd had enough. She tossed her napkin onto the table and excused herself. Pagan might choose to act like an adulterous half-wit, but she had no intention of lingering about to witness his idiocy.

She stormed up the stairs, silently cursing men for rutting fools at every step. Never noticing she was being shadowed, she pushed her way in through her newly repaired chamber door. When she turned to slam the door shut, a broad hand caught it.

Pagan. She gasped in alarm.

He opened the door wider and entered the room. "Reflexes like a cat," he teased.

Her heart in her throat, she still managed to quip, "Lest you forget, cats have claws."

"Lest *you* forget," he said, securing the door behind him, "I know how to make cats purr."

A blush bloomed unbidden in her face.

"Did you forget our bargain?" he asked, advancing on her, lifting his hand to brush a stray lock of hair from her cheek.

She flinched in reflex.

He lifted her chin with his knuckle, studying her face. "You left in a rush."

"You seemed . . ." She pulled her chin away. "Distracted."

"Did I?" A glint of humor livened his eyes.

Despite her irritation with him, she felt her pulse pound as he gazed at her. All afternoon she'd braced herself for this moment, as if 'twas a pending joust. All afternoon she'd reminded herself 'twas but a kiss, after all. She could be stoic for one kiss. She'd simply think of something else—sword fighting or her horse or the loyal knights of Rivenloch—while he took his due.

She swallowed hard. Now they stood but a hand's width apart. His green eyes shone, calm and knowing and superior. One corner of his mouth curved up with sly intent. And now she remembered the power of his temptation. Or at least her body remembered. Her heart fluttered like a caged moth, her breath grew rapid, and blood warmed her cheeks.

Damn his eyes! She couldn't let him rattle her. She needed to be indifferent, dispassionate. She had to remember that this transaction was no more than a simple trade arrangement, no different than their marriage itself. But despite her best efforts, her voice came out on a broken whisper. "This is the place of your choosing? Our bedchamber?"

He only smiled that maddeningly devious smile and let his gaze roam over her body. Everywhere it lit, her skin tingled, as if longing for more than just his perusal.

Then he reached up to the neckline of her gown, and before she could protest, dragged it down over her shoulder and lower, baring one breast.

"This," he murmured, "is the place of my choosing."

Chapter 17

DEIRDRE'S EYES WIDENED, and her jaw fell open. The knave had tricked her. "Nay."

His eyes misted with desire. "Oh, aye," he purred.

She shook her head, incredulous. "Nay."

"You gave your word," he warned her.

She closed her mouth again. He was right, damn him. The varlet might have been devilishly clever, trapping her with a turn of phrase, but she'd been foolish enough to agree to his terms.

"One kiss," he whispered, reaching out to run his thumb audaciously, tantalizingly along the underside of her breast.

Her eyelids dipped as a wave of unwelcome desire washed over her.

"So soft," he sighed, stroking her bared flesh with the back of his knuckles. "So warm."

Against her wishes, her body responded, melting, tensing, aching. Her eyes drifted completely closed.

As he cupped her breast, hefting its weight in his

palm, he eased forward, grazing her cheek with his, and spoke softly against her ear. "So beautiful. Like a sweet . . . ripe . . . peach."

She caught her lip beneath her teeth as his words wound their way through her thoughts, drawing her in like a sorcerer's incantation.

With a hand at her back, he nudged her hips toward his, pressing the stone-hard manifestation of his lust against her belly.

"Feel how I hunger for you," he murmured.

His warm breath made the skin of her neck shiver, and as his fingertips danced lightly over the sensitive flesh of her breast, she felt her knees tremble beneath her.

"Shall I take my due now?" he breathed.

She shut her eyes tighter and bit out, "Aye."

But he was unsatisfied with her response. "You're afraid."

"Nay." But she refused to open her eyes. She didn't want to see the naked lust in his leer, the smug curve of his smile.

"Then look at me."

She drew in a deep breath and forced her eyes open.

And was astonished.

Pagan was not smiling. Nor was the glaze over his eyes as self-assured as she expected. Forsooth, he looked almost . . . helpless, as if he, too, was caught up in the current between them . . . against his will.

As she watched, she saw him swallow hard, saw a muscle in his jaw tense, as if he suffered under the utmost restraint. Then he muttered, as if to remind himself, "One kiss. No more."

He dipped his head, and she quivered as his hair swept over her shoulder, then lower, lower, until she felt the moist air from his mouth graze her skin. All the while her nipple tightened in anticipation, and she held her breath, dreading yet desiring what was to come. The tension was unbearable.

And then his mouth closed, hot and wet and tender, upon her. She dragged in a ragged breath at the sensation. His kiss was soft at first as his lips gently surrounded her, bathing her flesh with his tongue. She fought against the powerful pleasure, choking off the rapturous moan that rose in her throat. Then he increased the pressure, drawing her deeply between his lips. Sweet Mary, 'twas as if lightning streaked through her, setting her veins on fire. And even though his kiss centered on that one point, she felt echoes of ecstasy throughout her body, within her ears, at her other breast, between her legs.

He groaned low in his chest. 'Twas a sound of animal lust, aye, but also of adoration and yielding. 'Twas an erotic sound that drove her to the brink of surrender. She let her head fall back, reveling in the glorious torment, never realizing her fingers, of their own accord, crept forward to tangle in his hair.

Pagan felt as if he swirled in a storm-swollen river, utterly out of control, spinning recklessly away, further and further from shore. And yet he was neither capable nor desirous of swimming free.

'Twas not that he hadn't kissed bosoms before, of women far more buxom than Deirdre. Breasts were one of God's finest creations—soft and supple and delicious—and he worshiped them as much as any man. But never had that adoration had such an intense and dramatic effect upon him.

A moan was torn from his throat as he suffered an agony of his own making. God, he wanted her. With every fiber of his being. His tongue had never tasted anything so sweet, and he feasted upon her flesh like a starving man set before a king's table. His body shuddered with barely suppressed lust, and his cock throbbed insistently, demanding he bring it relief.

He'd thought his desire couldn't possibly increase, that his willpower was strained to the breaking point. But when he felt her hands move up to clasp his head to her bosom, holding him close, welcoming him, longing surged in him like a tide upon that river, hauling him past reason, past care.

God, he wanted her. Nay, *needed* her.

Damn his promise! Damn his honor! He must claim her. Now!

Deirdre whimpered once in sweet distress. The soft sound, so full of feminine yearning, was assurance that this time she'd not refuse him.

And yet even from the depths of desire, the cursed wench somehow managed to fight her own instincts with a stubbornness that defied nature.

"Nay!" she gasped, the word at obscene odds with her tightening embrace. "Cease!"

Disbelief and dismay and outrage warred within him. Cease? Surely she didn't mean that. She desired him. He *knew* she did. How then could she say him nay?

But when her fingers began to tug at his hair, pulling him away, 'twas clear she intended to frustrate him again. Her breast slipped free of his mouth, leaving his appetite whetted for a feast never to be served.

He staggered back a step, unable to do more than stare at her, his eyes half-lidded, his mouth open, his breath coming in great gulps. She, too, seemed dazed with desire, fumbling to pull her gown up over her shoulder again.

For a long moment, there was no sound in the room but the counterpoint of their haggard breathing.

When she finally spoke, her voice was rough and trembling. "I've paid your price. On the morrow then . . . in the tiltyard . . . at dawn?"

Pagan slowly closed his jaw until his teeth ground together. How dared Deirdre reduce this moment of shared passion to a mere bargain! Surely she realized 'twas much more than that. Was the wench heartless? Did ice run in her Norse veins?

Defying the urge to ram his fist through the wall in frustration, he snarled, "Aye."

She nodded curtly, then turned her back on him, making a show of folding back the coverlet, appearing to dismiss him as easily as a swatted fly.

He simmered with impotent rage, resisting the overwhelming desire to snag her arm, spin her around, and kiss her so fiercely on the mouth that her lips would burn for days. But he'd said it himself. One kiss. No more.

So he wheeled and stormed out into the hall, slamming the new door behind him so hard that he heard weapons from the bedchamber wall crash to the floor.

The first wench he laid eyes on he'd bed, he promised himself as he stomped down the stairs. His loins could only take so much frustration. Bloody hell! 'Twas unhealthy to dam the tide of lust this way.

As he entered the great hall, he glimpsed the serving maid from supper, weaving her way among the other servants who cleared away the trestle tables. She gave him a coy smile. He raised a brow and nodded toward the buttery. Her smile widened.

In his present state, 'twould take but a moment or two to alleviate his pain. Across the hall, Deirdre's father gathered men around him to play his nightly game of dice. Pagan would be discreet, and none would be the wiser.

He watched the wench slip past the buttery screens, waited a moment, then made his way toward the spot where she'd disappeared.

The buttery was dark and cool and smelled of ripe cheese. He would have preferred a more comfortable place for coupling, but his need was imminent.

Her soft giggle led him to the dimmest corner of the cell. He wasted no time, seizing her by the shoulders and placing a rough kiss upon her eager lips. While she wriggled closer, hiking her skirts up, he slipped a finger inside her low neckline, freeing one of her generous breasts. Slanting his mouth across hers, he mashed the soft flesh of her plump bosom in his palm. 'Twould be but another moment, he thought. Then he'd get the reward he deserved.

But even as he availed himself of her ripe and willing body, he realized she didn't send his heart hammering like Deirdre did. She didn't steal his breath away. No wave of desire swept him along. Her mouth was not nearly as sweet as Deirdre's. Even her mews of contentment seemed feigned and shallow in contrast to Deirdre's ragged gasps.

He tore away from her and felt his cock go limp. "Lucifer's balls," he muttered.

"What's wrong?" the maidservant whined.

"Go!" he barked. "Just go!"

Mumbling curses of disappointment and scorn, she scurried off.

When she was gone, he leaned forward against the wall and banged his head on the cold plaster in exasperation. Never had his body connived against him so pitilessly. 'Twas ludicrous. He was like an urchin who'd rather starve than eat anything less than lord's fare.

On the morrow, he vowed, he'd exhaust Deirdre in the tiltyard, work her till her limbs collapsed from fatigue. Maybe *then* she'd lack the will to resist him.

"Get up, you lazy wench! 'Tis past dawn." Pagan swatted Deirdre on the hindquarters, waking her with a jolt.

Even before her eyes opened, her hand thrust instinctively beneath her pillow for a weapon, coming up empty. "Where's my dagger?" she mumbled.

He banged open the shutters at the window, letting in the light of the rising sun. "You sleep with a Knight of Cameliard to guard you," he said, buckling on his sword belt. "You need no dagger."

She frowned, but was obviously too sleepy to argue. She sat up, her eyes only half-open, her hair an intriguing mess, her shoulders delectably bare.

But he forced his gaze away. He'd had a long night of watching his tempting wife slumber in self-satisfied repose while he lay mere inches away, fitful and frustrated, and he'd come to the conclusion that he only tortured himself with wanting her. 'Twas apparent from her behavior last eve that Deirdre wasn't likewise tormented. She might experience a measure of feminine longing, she might feel the stirrings of lust, but she still managed to refuse desire with all the resolve of a tonsured monk.

Very well, he decided. If Deirdre wished to deny her

womanhood, if she wanted to be treated like a man, if she wanted naught from him but a political alliance, then, damn the wench, he'd oblige her. He'd ignore his body's cravings. He'd forget she was his wife. In his eyes, she'd be no different than one of his knights. No matter how difficult that was to imagine.

"I'll be in the tiltyard," he said. "Don't be late. I have a full day."

Before he even opened the door to leave, Deirdre was out of bed and eagerly diving for her chest of armor. He didn't dare turn to look. He knew she was gloriously naked. If he looked, he'd never make it to the tiltyard.

He was still finishing his breakfast of a bannock and ale in the tiltyard, idly spinning the quintain with his hand, when Deirdre came hurrying toward the gate. How the wench managed to make chain mail appear feminine, he didn't know, but she looked as desirable as the goddess Athena, rushing breathlessly toward him.

The morning wore on as they engaged in a battery of military exercises. Pagan believed he'd never worked with a more dedicated soldier or a more voracious student. They sparred together for more than an hour, and he showed her no mercy, training her the same way he trained his squires. He had her lifting buckets of water to increase her arm strength. He showed her how to throw her body into her lunges to achieve more force. And he taught her a few shield defenses she didn't know.

But he learned from her, too. Deirdre possessed a speed and cunning he'd never seen in a man. She fought with uncanny instinct, and she showed him a couple of innovative tricks she'd perfected for overthrowing much larger opponents.

For a man accustomed to doing but one thing with a

woman, Pagan was surprised to find that he rather enjoyed Deirdre's company.

Eventually a small crowd gathered outside the fence, armored knights waiting to enter the field, watching the curious battle. But even though Deirdre's arms trembled and her legs kept crumpling beneath her, she refused to quit.

"Come!" she gasped out. "Have at me. Again."

He grinned and shook his head. The warrior wench was more focused than a priest in a room full of harlots. He doubted she'd even noticed they'd drawn an audience. "Once more, but this will be the last match."

From beyond her shoulder, Pagan glimpsed the men of Rivenloch, Deirdre's men, observing the fight with keen interest. For courtesy's sake, he wouldn't shame the lass by defeating her before her men. And yet he dared not be seen to fall beneath her blade himself, lest the men lose faith in him. Somehow he had to keep everyone's honor intact.

With a sly smile, he removed his helm, tossed it aside. Naturally, out of propriety, she did the same. His pulse quickened as he beheld her face, aglow with sweat and rosy-cheeked, her lips parted with deep-drawn breath, her belabored expression so reminiscent of desire. 'Twas impossible to imagine, looking upon her now, that she was anything but pure woman.

Steeling his resolve, he saluted and squared off against her.

They fought back and forth a long while, and Pagan was careful not to take the advantage. He knew Deirdre would eventually resort to one of her tricks. Even when he knew 'twas coming, he couldn't avoid falling prey to the wily foot she slipped behind his heel. He tripped and fell with a thud onto his back. Beyond the fence, he could hear the mixed responses of the men, the cheers of Rivenloch, the disgust of his own knights. He lay there, coughing in the dust, while Deirdre stood above him in triumph.

Then she made the mistake of reaching down to help him up.

With calculated purpose, he seized her wrist and pulled her down on top of him, snagged one hand in her hair and planted a big, wet, indiscreet kiss on her astonished mouth.

Everyone laughed then at the jest.

Pagan would have ended it there, released her and helped her back up to her feet. But after her initial shock, Deirdre, whether inflamed by battle or desire or an attempt to match his effrontery, answered his kiss with a passion as fast and fierce as her fighting. She cocked her head and pressed her parted lips hard against his, seeking with her tongue as if she hungered for whatever he harbored within his mouth.

'Twas no jest now. His blood, warm from battle, pumped into his loins in a molten rush. The crowd faded from his awareness as pure sensation overtook him.

Deirdre, too, seemed oblivious to the world. Groans born deep within her called to the beast inside him. A drop of her sweat rolled down onto his face as their joined mouths spoke a common language, the language of desire. And that desire, here on the hard ground of the tiltyard, raged nigh as violent as their battle.

The loud creak of the tiltyard gate brought Pagan back to his senses. He tore his mouth away from her. For an instant, he thought he glimpsed disappointment in her eyes.

Jesu, was it possible? *Was* she disappointed? Did she truly desire him? Sweet hope filled his heart.

Then she, too, heard the intruders, and gave a soft, startled cry. He released her, and she scrambled up, blushing fiery pink. Before he could whisper farewell, she quickly gathered her wits and her weapons and rushed from the field.

"Good match, sir!" someone called.

"Well met, my lord!" said another.

Pagan bounded to his feet and cast one last longing look toward his departing bride. 'Twas not mere lust he felt as he watched her, he realized. Nay, the feeling went deeper than that. By the Saints, he admired her. Before she was out of hearing, he announced, "If you knights had as much devotion to practice as my wife, no army would dare approach Rivenloch."

Fortunately she'd disappeared by the time Sir Benedict jested, "If you'd give *us* a little kiss, my lord, mayhap we'd be more agreeable to the long practice hours."

"Fifty lifts of the buckets, all of you," Pagan charged.

The men groaned.

"One hundred if you complain."

Chapter 18

DEIRDRE'S FINGERS FLUTTERED over her mouth as she hurried toward the keep. Her lips were still wet, still warm. God's blood! What had happened? One moment she'd been battling Pagan with all the ferocity of a charging boar, and the next, she'd found herself reacting to his kiss with the same fervor.

And now she overheard Pagan praising her to his men. To her consternation, a flush of pleasure rose in her cheeks.

'Twas absurd! She'd never needed a man to tell her she was a capable warrior. Besides, he was a knave who'd shamelessly tricked her into a kiss, curse his hide, a kiss that lingered pleasurably on her lips.

But while fighting him she'd realized something that she'd not acknowledged in their bedchamber, something she'd wanted to deny the invading Norman, something she could no longer withhold.

She respected Pagan.

As much as he infuriated her with his cocky swaggering and cruel seduction and merciless humiliations, she respected the lout.

He was a man of strength, an incomparable warrior, of course. But he was also a man of honor and fairness. Diplomatic and dedicated. A model of chivalry.

Curiously, she longed to impress him. To have such a man praise her publicly was a heady honor indeed.

To have such a man *love* her . . .

Nay! She'd not think of that. 'Twas but a kiss. And one stolen for the amusement of his men. Anyone who would mistake that for affection would be a fool. No matter how it made her head swim and her pulse race. Besides, a man so dedicated to warfare didn't have time for love. Lust, aye, but not love. It didn't matter that she'd glimpsed something suspiciously close to fondness in his gaze. Such emotions could be falsified.

'Twas enough that he afforded her some level of respect. With mutual respect, they might make a good marriage. Still, she considered, there were many men she respected. None had ever made her heart beat so recklessly.

'Twas a dangerous thing, this . . . fondness. She had lost control in the tiltyard, all because of a kiss. If she melted at the mere touch of his lips, how would she steel herself against more intimate contact? She must, of course, fight him at every turn. Though she'd ceded command of the army to Pagan, she'd not surrendered control of Rivenloch. Nor would she . . . ever.

As testament to that promise, Deirdre intended to devote the rest of the day to helping Miriel sort out the affairs of the household. With the addition of so many Normans to Rivenloch, there were still permanent quartering issues to address, provisions yet to purchase, and new servants to direct, in addition to the usual conflicts arising between the castle folk and crofters that needed solving.

But to Deirdre's exasperation, as she set about making changes and issuing commands, she discovered that Pagan had already sunk his claws deeply into the workings of Rivenloch. When she ordered a pair of Scots servants to beat the dust from the tapestries, they told her 'twas already done at Pagan's command. When she tried to set three Norman maids to mending surcoats, they complained that Pagan had directed them to launder the linens. The kitchen lads, who she meant to have scour pots, had been sent to the loch to fish. By Pagan.

The man seemed to countermand her every order. He reassigned servants on a whim, moved and removed the furnishings at will, and to her horror, had already torn down the very walls of some of the outbuildings. She thought she'd seen the worst of his interference as she stared at the demolished blacksmith shed, its rotted, splintered timbers lying on the sod like charred bones.

But naught could prepare her for the spectacle taking place in the courtyard as she rounded the corner of the west tower. A small crowd circled the castle's whipping post. She frowned. That post was seldom used. At Rivenloch, most disobedience was punished by assigning unpleasant chores to offenders or charging stiff fines of goods or coin.

Peering between the onlookers, Deirdre spied two young lads lashed to the post, face to face. Their shirts hung loose from their hips, baring their pale, scrawny backs, as yet unmarked. But they quivered with fear as a willow switch whipped through the air nearby like a hungry falcon swooping down to feed. Deirdre couldn't see the boys' faces, but her heart plummeted as she immediately recognized their flaming red hair.

Bloody hell.

Pagan whisked the switch once more through the air, preparing to mete out the first boy's punishment. But his hand was stayed by a feminine shriek.

"Nay!"

He sighed. 'Twas an unpleasant chore enough, he thought, chastising lads whose backs had probably never felt the rod before. 'Twas the reason he undertook the task himself rather than hand it over to some ham-fisted warrior like Sir Rauve d'Honore who might be overzealous in his blows. Now to have some frail-hearted maid interrupt his dispensation of justice . . .

"Stop!" she cried.

He turned toward the sound with a disapproving scowl, then cursed under his breath. 'Twas Deirdre, breaking through the startled crowd with all the wild-eyed fury of a rampaging Viking.

His fist tightened on the switch. Why did she have to appear now? Why did she have to challenge him at every turn?

"Get back!" he snapped.

"What the bloody hell do you think you're doing?" she bellowed.

Pagan could almost feel the hackles rise along his back.

"Wife!" he barked. "Out of the way."

The audacious wench ignored his warning. Hurtling forward, she flung her arms around the youngest boy, shielding him with her body.

"Nay," she bit out over her shoulder.

A lesser man would have let the first blow land upon her rebellious back to teach her a lesson about insubordination. But chivalry saved Deirdre from the full force of his temper. Instead, he whipped the willow switch through the air so it whistled past her, startling the lad, who began to whimper within her embrace.

"This is not your concern, damsel," he warned her. "I've rendered judgment upon these thieves. Now I undertake their punishment. If your stomach is too weak to endure the sight, then go inside and hide your eyes. Leave me to my task."

Pagan watched her back stiffen, bone by bone, as she straightened in unmitigated mutiny and snarled at him over her shoulder. "Never."

A hush fell, as chill and sudden as winter frost. For one weighted moment, no one dared speak or move.

Pagan, his forbearance stretched to its limit, finally cracked the silence. His words rang with icy menace. "There is room for three at the whipping post, my lady."

He took some perverse satisfaction at the soft gasp that sizzled through the crowd like a shock of lightning.

But that satisfaction was short-lived. While the castle folk believed his threat, 'twas clear that Deirdre did not. She turned until she faced him squarely, then lifted her chin and dared him, "Do your worst."

The onlookers gasped again, and Pagan narrowed his eyes. For one ignoble moment, as he studied her beautiful, willful features, he regretted not bedding her the very first moment he'd seen her. Surely laying claim to her body would have brought her to heel more quickly.

But as his gaze lingered upon her brave, vibrant, resolute face, he realized Deirdre wasn't just any wench to be bedded, tamed, and conquered. She was his wife. And she was an extraordinary woman. A woman accustomed to power and control. A woman unafraid to wield a blade. A woman who'd served as steward of Rivenloch. A woman deserving of his respect, deserving of her own opinions.

Ballocks.

Now he supposed he'd have to listen to those opinions.

But not in front of a bunch of gape-jawed onlookers with prattling tongues.

"Leave us!" he commanded. "All of you."

The crowd reluctantly dispersed, muttering as they scurried off, likely wondering if their new steward was about to beat his rebellious wife.

When they'd gone, Pagan returned his attention to Deirdre. She stood firm, her azure gaze as steady as a destrier's gait, but he glimpsed uncertainty in the clenching of her hands. She also apparently suspected he might use his fists.

Unable to hold onto his anger in the face of her fear, he shook his head in self-mockery. "Well, then, my lady, if 'tis not your weak stomach," he drawled, "what is your objection?"

Her fists unclenched in relief. "I know these lads. They are the sons of Lachanburn, to the north."

He sniffed. 'Twas not her stomach then. 'Twas her heart. But one couldn't afford to be dissuaded from upholding justice by one's heart. "'Tis no matter whose sons they are. They're thieves."

She creased her brow. "Thieves?"

He nodded.

"What is their crime?"

"They stole Rivenloch property."

"What property?"

He nodded toward the stables, where the pair of shaggy russet cows were tethered.

"That's all?" she asked.

He started. "What do you mean, that's all?"

"Just two cows?"

He frowned, annoyed. "Aye, two cows that might feed the castle all winter."

She only stared at him, as if struggling to find the right words. "Let the lads go," she finally said.

"What?"

"Let them go. We have the cattle back. Let them go."

This, he thought, was why one didn't heed the counsel of a woman. He sternly shook his head. "They must face the consequences of their actions or they will never learn."

"You don't understand."

"*You* do not understand. If you do not whip the dog that bites you, 'twill bite again."

"You've already frightened them enough. See how they quail?" She gestured to the boys, who had craned their necks around to watch the curious exchange.

"They quail now, but halfway home, they'll not remember their fear. A few welts will serve to remind them."

Deirdre blew out a hard breath. Damn the meddlesome Norman! If he'd just kept his nose out of castle affairs and left matters of the law in her hands, she wouldn't be standing here now, caught precariously between the sons of her foul-tempered neighbor and a bloodthirsty Norman's willow switch. And she wouldn't have to waste time now explaining Scots cattle raids to a man who probably flogged children for snatching tarts from the kitchen.

But curse his hide, she supposed Pagan *was* the steward of Rivenloch now, he *was* wielding the rod, and he *had* hesitated long enough to listen to her. Sooner or later, she'd have to teach him the Scots ways. She might as well begin now.

"They're not thieves," she said. "Not exactly."

"What do you mean, not exactly?" He tossed up his hands. "They were caught with their ropes about the cows' necks, leading the beasts over the hill."

She grimaced. "'Tis not that simple."

He rapped the willow switch impatiently against his thigh. "Then I suggest you explain quickly. Your delay of their whipping only increases the lads' torment."

She bit the corner of her lip. 'Twas difficult to explain to an outsider. "They took the cows as . . . retribution."

"Retribution."

"Aye."

"For?"

"For the two we stole last year."

"What!" he erupted.

She knew he wouldn't understand. "Will you . . . Just let them go. I'll explain it to you later."

"Nay. Explain it now."

"Look," she said. "If you keep them here, their father will . . . worry." Forsooth, their father would likely demand Pagan's head on a plate, but she'd not tell him that. "Lachanburn will send his men to search for them. If they discover we hold them behind Rivenloch's walls . . ."

But Pagan seemed fixated on the idea of cattle raiding. "You stole two of *their* cows?"

She sighed. "'Tis the Scots way. They steal our cattle. We steal theirs. 'Tis been so for generations."

Pagan blinked, as if she'd told him the world was made of ruayn cheese.

"Stealing cattle," she continued, "is a matter of . . . friendly rivalry for the lads of Rivenloch and Lachanburn."

He stared hard at her, doubtless wondering if the Scots were completely daft. "Unbelievable," he muttered.

"I insist you let them go."

He didn't answer her at once. 'Twas clear he both disbelieved and disapproved of her explanation. Moreover, he likely bristled at the idea of her insisting on anything.

At long last he seemed to come to a decision. With a dark scowl, he straightened to his full imposing height and tapped the willow rod against the palm of his left hand. He narrowed his eyes to green slits. "I've listened to you, damsel." Then he issued the grim order, "Now stand down."

Chapter 19

DEIRDRE'S HEART SANK AS HER IRE ROSE. She had no intention of moving aside. Not only did she owe the Lachanburn lads her protection, but she had no wish to face their father's wrath when he discovered his proud sons had been publicly whipped.

"I will not stand down," she told him firmly. "You'll just have to flog me as well."

Then, to her amazement, the corner of Pagan's lip slowly curled up into a sardonic grin. "You misunderstand, my lady. You've won their freedom." He dropped the willow switch to the ground. "Now stand down."

Deirdre blinked, confused.

Apparently, a few bold Rivenloch folk had remained near despite Pagan's orders, and they applauded now, much to his annoyance. He impatiently motioned her to move out of the way. Deirdre, stunned by her victory, staggered aside as he approached the whipping post, drawing his dagger.

"Heed me well, young pups," he said to them as he

cut their bonds. "'Tis only by the mercy of Lady Deirdre that you go free. Take care I do not catch you in the future, for I shall not be so merciful again." Freed from the post, the lads stood side by side, their thin frames and shock of orange curls making them look like twin candles topped by bright flame. Their eyes shone wide and solemn as they gazed at Pagan. He hiked their shirts back up over their narrow shoulders, and Deirdre heard him murmur, "Cover your heads next time. That red hair of yours can be seen a mile away." Then, swatting them on their rumps, he sent them scurrying out the gate.

He glanced over at her then with a gruff frown, and she realized that despite his irritable mien, he was no more dangerous than a hound barking with its tail all a-wag. Suddenly, she was surprised by a curious emotion she couldn't name, a sensation that warmed her heart and lightened her spirits. A powerful sensation that left her feeling perilously unguarded.

Muttering a hasty "thank you," she excused herself, retreating to the great hall. There she helped Miriel attend to supper preparations and tried to persuade herself 'twas not love she felt for her husband, for that would be foolish. Nay, 'twas simply appreciation of the fair-handed way he'd dealt with the Lachanburn lads and the joy of her own small triumph.

But when supper commenced, and Pagan arrived, dressed in his Norman braies and a pine-colored tunic that perfectly draped his magnificent frame and intensified the green depth of his eyes, her opinion was sorely challenged.

He caught her eye as he seated himself beside her, and she was startled by how richly verdant his gaze was tonight, like a Scots forest, beautiful and lush and vibrant. Bloody hell, he looked as handsome as Lucifer.

She braced herself with a swig of perry cider.

He was in fine spirits as he jested with his men, but Deirdre felt each warm chuckle like a brazen caress that threatened her composure. His knee contacted hers as they sat close upon the bench, and she noticed he seemed disinclined to move it. His fingers brushed hers familiarly as he cut the venison in the trencher they shared.

By the time she surrendered her napkin and excused herself to her bedchamber, pleading an aching head, she felt violated. Every inch of her skin prickled with current, like silk skirts in the north wind.

Mayhap with luck, she thought, scurrying hastily up the stairs, slamming the door, and casting off her surcoat, she'd be asleep by the time Pagan came to bed, deaf and blind to his allure.

But the knave must have followed at her heels. Scarcely had she hung up her clothes when he barged in at the door, making her jump like a child caught nibbling a tart.

He looked pleasantly surprised as his hungry eyes coursed slowly down her naked body. She held her breath, enduring his lusty gaze.

After an interminable silence, she finally asked, "Do you intend to close the door, or is it your wish to put me on display for all the servants?"

He grinned, easing the door shut. Then he lowered his brows in chiding accusation. "You sprinted up the stairs rather quickly for a maid with a . . . what was it? An aching head?"

She lifted her chin to answer, but could think of naught to say in her defense.

He smiled again, then leaned back against the door and began to remove his boots. "Dare I hope you're eager for my bed this eve?"

Her breasts tightened in the chill air. At least she hoped 'twas the chill air. As coolly as she could, she told him, "You may hope all you wish, but 'twill not make it so."

Unaffected by her jab, he tossed his boots toward the foot of the bed, then hauled his tunic and undershirt off at once. Deirdre's eyes were instantly drawn to the cut she'd given him. Twas healing well, which relieved her. Forsooth, the thin scar did naught to diminish the perfection of his body. His chest was smooth and taut, covered with thick muscle, and his shoulders were broad enough to pull an oxcart. God's eyes, even at this distance the sight of him made her knees weak.

She drew in a shaky breath. Then, with false imperturbability, she climbed under the coverlet into her pallet, taking the middle of the bed so he'd be unlikely to join her. "About the incident today . . ." she said, eager to talk of something, *anything*, other than the bristling tension between them.

"Incident?" He began untying the points of his braies.

She cleared her throat. "With the Lachanburn lads."

"Aye?"

"There will be . . . many things about Rivenloch you don't understand."

He chuckled. Lord, his smile was brilliant, dazzling. "You Scots *are* a different sort," he agreed.

"You cannot expect to change the ways of the people. You cannot bend the Scots to your will."

His grin turned devious. "Ah, my lady, I'd be content to bend just one Scot to my will." He sat down upon the edge of the bed, his weight drawing her toward him. "Perchance with a kiss?"

Her breath caught. So *that* was why he'd come charging up the steps after her. He still thought she owed him a kiss. But she knew better. She'd given him his due in the tiltyard. And thank God she had, for she doubted she could withstand another, not with the way her heart hammered as he regarded her with those knavish green eyes.

"Mayhap your memory is faulty," she said smugly. "You received your payment this morn."

He froze, his hands at the waist of his loosened braies. "That?" he said with a smirk. "That was no kiss."

"Oh, aye, 'twas."

"Nay." He glowered warily. "Nay. That quick peck? That did not count."

"Quick peck, my arse. It *did* count."

"How could you call that—"

"A kiss?"

"'Twas not a kiss!"

"Oh, it seemed very like a kiss. Your lips on mine? Aye, 'twas a kiss."

"Lucifer's ballocks!" He furrowed stormy brows at her. "'Twas stolen. The kiss you owe me is one given freely."

"That was not part of the bargain."

He shot to his feet, his eyes narrowed dangerously, and she saw his chest rise and fall deeply with each frustrated breath. But they both knew she was right. She owed him naught this eve.

Still, as he tied again the points of his braies, wrenching them so hard he ripped one loose, she realized the violence of which he was capable. As he shoved his arms back into his shirt with a low growl, she recognized the depth of his fury. And when he slammed the door behind him, rattling the weapons on the wall, she understood that there was a limit to his patience. One day, she feared, he'd take what was his, vow or not.

Pagan kicked the wall of the stable, startling his horse. The beast whickered once, then returned to contentedly munching oats. But Pagan's mood was not so easily pacified. He paced back and forth, kicking up bits of straw and dust and mouse droppings.

He was fed up with Deirdre's slippery wiles and empty enticements. He'd not fall victim to her guile again, have her tease him with her luscious body, only to repulse him when his loins throbbed with need. Pagan was no fool. Deirdre might feel the flutterings of desire, but at this snail's pace, she'd frustrate him long past the bounds of madness. He refused to spend another restless night beside his God-given wife, longing for what she wouldn't give him . . .

Yet.

Anon she'd succumb to him.

He knew it. He'd felt the smoldering in her body when he'd stolen that kiss. 'Twould not take much to kindle what was there into a fiercely burning fire. But in the meantime, her stubbornness and his honor kept them deadlocked in longing.

This seduction was turning into a war between the two of them. 'Twas clear Deirdre was determined to choose the field of battle and set the rules of engagement. But 'twas a deadly mistake to give her the upper hand. Nay, Pagan must seize the reins of this runaway warhorse of desire and steer it toward a domain where he was master.

Without her knowing.

But how would he accomplish that?

He stopped pacing and hunkered down to make a bed of straw in an empty corner of the stable. 'Twould be a chilly night. Forsooth, he'd been tempted to grab a milkmaid on his way to the stables to keep him warm. But he recalled what had happened the last time he'd tried to tryst with a servant. And so he resorted to burrowing into the straw for warmth while he considered his battle strategy.

The first key to combat was knowing one's enemy.

What did he know about Deirdre?

She seemed to respond most favorably in the tiltyard when he treated her like an equal—challenging her, spurring her on, expecting no less than her best. And ironically, once he began treating her like a man, she became even more enticing to him. He'd trained her hard this morn, thinking to expose her feminine weakness, and she'd astonished him by working harder than his own men.

Yet beneath her armor, Deirdre possessed the soft curves of a lady. Near her unbending spine beat the gentle heart of a maid. He'd glimpsed her tenderness when she'd sacrificed herself for her sister, when she'd cared for her father, when she'd intervened for the Lachanburn lads. Deirdre might think like a man, but she sensed things like a woman. She could be offended or impressed or hurt or pleased as easily as any female.

And therein lay his dilemma.

One moment he found himself clapping her affably on the back, and the next he longed to drag her into the nearest stairwell, tear off her gown, and ravish her.

How could a man fight a foe who was a constantly

changing target, whose tactics were as unpredictable as thistledown in the wind, who in one moment charged onto the field like a berserker, and in the next, blushed at the prospect of being caught in a kiss? How could one vanquish a foe that would not be forced or reasoned with or lured into surrender?

He asked himself those questions long into the night, while the moon cast a blind eye on the world below, and the stars tumbled across the sky like bright dice, divining the course of fate. Finally he slept, leaving his question for the reckoning of dreams.

With the revealing light of dawn, his answer came. He opened his eyes to find he was no longer alone. Miriel's strange maidservant, Sung Li, was staring down at him.

He sat up with a sharp gasp. Her expression was mildly amused, and her small hands were clasped before her in a gesture of patient waiting. How long she'd been standing there, watching him sleep, he didn't know, but the fact she'd come upon him unawares was highly unsettling.

"What is it?" he asked gruffly, scrubbing the straw from his hair.

She clucked her tongue. "You will never make sons for Rivenloch this way," she said bluntly, "sleeping with the horses."

Pagan's jaw came unhinged. "That is not your affair."

Undaunted, the woman continued, shaking her head. "You are a foolish, foolish man."

Pagan's temper rose. "Guard your tongue, wench, or I'll—"

"That is your mistake," she told him. "You are too much a warrior. Always you answer with threat."

Pagan's hands itched to throttle the rude servant. Of

course, now he could not, for 'twould make Sung Li un-equivocally right. He settled on a fierce scowl.

"Listen or do not listen," she said with a shrug. "It is up to you. But I have the answer you seek."

He got to his feet, towering over her so she'd not forget who was her master. "What answer?"

"There is only one way to claim her body," she said smugly.

Pagan was stunned by the old woman's perception. Did she possess some mystic window to his thoughts, or had he been talking in his sleep? He rubbed pensively at his stubbled cheek, then crossed his arms in challenge, sneering, "And how is that?"

Sung Li straightened to her unimpressive full height and wisely intoned, "First you must win her heart."

Pagan rolled his eyes. This was her counsel? "You've been listening to too many of Boniface's madrigals," he scoffed.

She ignored his scorn. "There is an ancient riddle in your land. Perchance you have heard it. The riddle is, What is it a woman desires most?"

Riddles. He loathed riddles. What a woman desired most? 'Twould depend upon the woman.

"Do you know the answer?" Sung Li prodded.

He scowled, biting out, "Flowers. Sweetmeats. Jewels. It could be anything."

Sung Li's black eyes twinkled. "Nay. Not anything." She looked about, as if to make sure the horses weren't listening, then confided, "Her *will*. What a woman desires most is her will."

Pagan narrowed his eyes. 'Twas a silly answer. Too simple. Too sweeping. Too vague.

And yet, upon reflection, he realized . . . Aye, it might be true.

He had tried to force Deirdre to *his* will. By seduction. By threat. By trickery. He'd never once considered bowing to *her* will. As a warrior, he'd been trained never to surrender, never compromise. But Deirdre, too, believed in victory at all costs. And thus was sired their deadlock.

If Pagan *let* Deirdre win, if he let her have her way . . .

He paced the small space of the stable stall.

'Twould not be easy. There were matters of castle defense and stewardship that he dared not surrender, for his experience was simply superior to hers. But if he conferred with her on other matters, as he had with the Lachanburn lads, if he listened to her and included her in his decisions, mayhap her heart would soften toward him.

And once her heart was receptive, discreet seduction would take care of the rest, as long as she believed 'twas *her* will.

"Sung Li, I believe I've misjudged—"

When he turned toward the maidservant, she'd vanished into the ether, as swiftly as shadow, without a sound, without a trace. He scratched his head. The woman was like some inscrutable wraith.

By the time Pagan emerged from the stables, brushing the straw from his braies and squinting against the sunlight, he smiled with new purpose. No matter how it went against everything bred into him as a man, how it countered all his basest instincts, when Deirdre appeared this morn like some shining Aurora, Pagan meant to steel himself against his natural lust and attempt to accommodate his wife's wishes.

If he succeeded, by tonight, they would share something far sweeter than fellowship. He knew exactly where he was going to place the kiss she owed him, and heaven help her when he stormed those gates.

Chapter 20

DEIRDRE COULDN'T MOVE.

'Twas not for lack of trying. Her body had somehow stiffened in the night, and even the warmth of dawn couldn't thaw her joints.

Pagan had never come to bed. 'Twas little surprise, given how angry he'd been. But if he thought he'd worm his way out of practicing with her today, he was mistaken.

Slowly, she rolled onto her side, but when she tried to lever up on one arm, sharp pain shot like lightning from her elbow to her shoulder.

"Ballocks," she gasped.

While she teetered on that shaky arm, she swung her legs gingerly over the edge of the bed. Lord, they ached as though a cart had run over them repeatedly. And now that she sat upright, every muscle in her body complained.

She'd overdone it. In her zeal to demonstrate what

strong stuff she was made of, she'd worked too hard sparring yesterday. Today she would suffer for it.

Grimacing and cursing, she managed to lift the heavy hauberk of mail over her head and let it shiver down over her shoulders. She didn't bother with the armor plate, simply cinching her swordbelt around her hips with trembling arms. She half-limped, half-dragged herself down the stairs as her legs quivered like newborn lambs. How she was going to hide her infirmity from Pagan, she didn't know. Every step was an agony.

She tried to walk as normally as possible as she neared the tiltyard, but a hedgepig could have easily outpaced her.

She heard Pagan before she saw him.

"You're late, my lady."

He reclined in the shadows, propped against the stable wall, his long legs stretched out casually before him and crossed at the ankles. He grinned, chewing on a piece of straw. She wondered if he'd slept in the stables.

As she walked stiffly toward him, he tilted his head, studying her with that infuriating smile. She frowned in chagrin. No doubt she resembled a stooped old crone hobbling along.

"Come, come!" he teased. "Don't dawdle. Do you not wish to spar?"

She clenched her teeth. "I do. And I'm not."

"I've seen ducks waddle faster."

"I'm . . . cold," she said, grasping at the first excuse she could. "It takes a while for my bones to thaw."

He spat out the straw and came to his feet, his eyes never leaving her. After a moment, he crossed his arms over his chest and clucked his tongue. "You're not cold," he guessed. "I'd wager you lifted one too many buckets yesterday."

"It doesn't matter. I can still fight."

His grin widened. "I suspect you could go missing both arms, wench, and still believe you could fight."

"Both arms and both legs."

His laughter startled her, ringing out as rich and warm as the golden sunlight. Apparently, his night in the stables had cooled his temper.

"If 'tis your will then . . . let's see what you have," he said, clapping her companionably on the shoulder.

She sucked a quick breath between her teeth as pain streaked down her arm. "Right."

To her amazement, he was merciful to her, considering what vengeance he could wreak while she was in such a helpless state. As they worked together in the tiltyard, he spent more time discussing techniques than employing them, guiding her through slow stretches rather than endurance-building exercises. She was grateful for his patience and his leniency, for when she attempted to wield her sword, she could scarcely lift it above her waist, rendering her blade about as deadly as a wet rope.

And while he occasionally chuckled at her lack of strength, 'twas never mean-spirited, even when her knees wobbled out of kilter and her shield sank pathetically lower and lower.

Deirdre had stumbled back into the wattle fence for the second time when he finally suggested, "Let's stop for the day."

Out of pride, she started to refuse. "I'm fine," she gasped. "I can—"

"You're fine. I'm weary. Quit for *my* sake."

She raised a dubious brow. He wasn't even breathing

heavily. Nonetheless, she nodded and eased back against a fencepost. "You're not weary."

He grinned, then leaned on the fence beside her, resting his forearms atop the gate and gazing off toward the keep. She glanced at his well-muscled hands, his wide shoulders, his corded neck. He'd hardly broken a sweat.

"Do you never tire?" she asked.

He chuckled, and Deirdre was struck again by the easy warmth in his laughter. "I conserve my strength. I suppose I've learned to choose my battles with care."

As he stared thoughtfully into the distance, Deirdre got the distinct impression that he spoke of more than just sparring. For a commander like Pagan, choosing battles was a way of life. Mayhap 'twas why he'd let go of his anger at her. Mayhap he'd decided 'twas not a battle worth fighting, that she was not worth his trouble.

She should have been relieved. After all, if he gave up the fight, if he no longer insisted upon consummating their marriage, 'twould be a perfect union, would it not? He might command Rivenloch's army by virtue of his greater skill, but as long as Deirdre withheld herself from him, he'd never have complete reign over her.

Why, then, was she left with a hollow place in her heart when his men began to arrive at the tiltyard and Pagan dismissed her with another casual pat on the shoulder?

She felt even emptier when, hours later, as she passed by the pantry with a midday havercake, she overheard two of the kitchen maids wagging their tongues.

"'Twon't be long now, a day or two at most," one of them gloated. "The lord never did go to his bedchamber last even."

"Well, he didn't go to *yours* either," the other quipped.

"Nay. But he met me in the buttery two nights past."

"And did he swive you in the buttery, or was he there for a piece of cheese?"

"You're a mean old trot, you are." She gave an offended sniff. "I had my skirts up around my waist for him."

"So he ran you through with his lance, did he?"

There was a pause. "Nay . . . not exactly."

The first maid snickered.

"But he *will*," she protested. "I'm sure of it. After all, he's a man, and he's getting naught from his wife." She lowered her voice to a whisper. "Forsooth, there's some who say the lady was born without . . . proper women's parts."

"Fie, Lucy! There's some who say you were born without a brain. Get on with you!"

Deirdre stole away then, but the women's words lingered as she slipped into the buttery to find herself a piece of cheese. She wasn't hurt by Lucy's gossip. She'd inured herself to such insults long ago. But the core of the conversation gave Deirdre pause as she perused the buttery shelves.

The fact that Pagan might stray hadn't occurred to her before.

She picked up a block of ripe cheese and sniffed at it, then put it back on the shelf.

Lucy was right. Pagan was a man. He had needs. And he certainly wouldn't let an unwilling wife keep him from satisfying those needs.

She chose a hunk of soft spermyse cheese and pulled out her eating dagger.

Forsooth, Pagan wouldn't be the first husband to stray in his affections.

She stabbed the cheese hard enough to kill it, then carved out a generous slice.

Deirdre was no innocent. Despite the censure of the church, she knew men felt free to swive whomever they willed, even other men's wives, as long as they weren't caught.

She testily shoved the cheese back onto the shelf and began spreading her portion over the havercake with the dagger. Then she frowned into the darkest corner of the buttery. Was that where Lucy had lifted her skirts? Was that the spot where Pagan had been tempted to break his marriage vows?

The havercake snapped in two.

With a curse, she jammed her knife back into its sheath. Then she stuffed the cheese and havercake mess into her mouth, biting down with a vengeance, and made her way out of the buttery, not wanting to spend another moment in Pagan's trysting place.

When she emerged in the great hall, her mouth full of food, she all but crashed into Pagan himself, sweaty, dusty, and breathless, obviously straight from the tilt-yard. God help her, when he perused her with those twinkling green eyes of his, even the knowledge that he was a faithless knave couldn't stop the fickle flutter of her heart.

"I've been looking for you," he said. Then, unable to overlook her bulging cheeks, he added with a smirk, "Hungry?"

She didn't dare try to reply. She would have spit havercake everywhere. Chagrined, she stared hard at the rush-covered floor and kept chewing, hoping to swallow the dry wad without choking.

"I need to discuss some improvements to Rivenloch's defenses with you," he divulged.

She glanced at him doubtfully.

"I'm considering building a moat."

"A moat?" she mumbled around the havercake. Surely he jested.

Suddenly he caught her hand.

"Come," he said, giving her little choice as he tugged her after him like one would a child. She might have resisted, but the boyish, spirited spark in his eyes as he lugged her across the great hall persuaded her to let him have his way. His enthusiasm was contagious, and soon the companionable grip of his rough, damp palm made her forget all about Lucy and the buttery.

With Deirdre in tow, he burst through the door of the keep and continued across the sunlit courtyard, past the chapel and the orchards and the workshops, where inquisitive castle folk stopped to stare, then out the front gates. In his eagerness, he'd forgotten her sore muscles, and Deirdre, wincing at every step, was hard pressed to keep up with him, despite her naturally long strides.

Several yards outside the gates, he stopped, then turned her to face the castle. "The barbican would be built here," he said, releasing her hand to draw an imaginary square, "with a drawbridge across."

She frowned, imagining it, wondering at his motives. Adding a moat to an existing castle was a strange undertaking. 'Twould be difficult, if not impossible.

"'Tis a lot of excavation," she told him.

"Aye."

"'Twould have to be wide enough to impede attackers."

"Aye, wide and deep."

She shook her head. "Digging that deeply near the wall might undermine the foundation."

He nodded pensively. "The builder tells me we'd have to reinforce the curtain wall."

She lifted her brows. Rivenloch's curtain wall ran a considerable distance around the keep. "'Tis an enormous feat."

He bobbed his head.

She frowned. "Even if 'twas possible, 'twould cost a king's ransom."

"'Tis no matter." His voice rang with fervent pride as he added, "No amount of coin is too great to protect our land."

She glanced sharply at him. The earnest shine of his eyes told her his sense of obligation was sincere. He truly meant to do all in his power to protect the keep. He might have come to Rivenloch as a usurper, but already he was charmed enough by the holding and the castle folk to speak of making monetary sacrifices for them.

Still, a moat seemed excessive. "We've never needed such defenses before."

"Forsooth, I'm not entirely convinced we need them now," he concurred.

"Have you talked with my father about this?"

"Nay. I thought to ask your counsel first."

"*My* counsel?" she asked dubiously, searching for signs of mockery in his face—an amused glimmer in his eyes, a wry twist of his lips—but there were none.

"If you think the idea unworthy," he gently confided, "we need not trouble him with it at all."

She met his solemn stare as long as she could, then gave him a subtle nod of gratitude. 'Twas diplomatic of him not to mention her father's feebleness. But while he waited expectantly for her reply, she grew uncomfortably warm beneath his steady gaze, wary of his sudden interest in her opinion.

"Very well. Then I *do* think the idea unworthy."

His eyes flattened slightly in displeasure, but he kept the disapproval from his voice. "Why?"

"The excavation itself would leave the castle vulnerable."

"Only for a short time."

"Long enough for enemy sappers to undermine the wall."

He furrowed his brow. "True."

Deirdre was primed to argue her point, but his words took the wind from her sails. Had she heard him properly?

He slowly began to nod. "You may be right. 'Tis not worth the risk."

She blinked. His concession melted something inside her, softening her heart and leaving her speechless. She could only stare at him in wonder. There was genuine trust in his eyes now . . . eyes, she noted anew, that shone as beautiful and clear and deep as a summer loch . . . eyes capable of icing over in cold rage, but brimming now with gentle warmth.

Then she remembered Lucy.

She quickly diverted her focus, gazing at the distant towers, hardening her heart against Pagan. "There may be other ways to strengthen the walls," she said. "Ramparts. Butteries. Machicolations."

"Butteries?" He frowned.

"Buttresses. I meant buttresses."

"Come," he told her, his eyes alight. "I had a different idea. Let me show you."

He dragged her off again at a lope, back through the gates and across the courtyard, scattering a flock of chickens in his wake.

She couldn't stay angry with him, not when he strolled hand-in-hand with her around the grassy perimeter of the keep, sharing his plans for a new wall to surround it, an idea that enthused him so much that he raved on about it like a lad with a new wooden sword. Despite Deirdre's usually skeptical nature and resistance to change, she couldn't help but be swept up in his exuberance.

"'Twould be roughly concentric to the keep," he explained, patting the stone of the south tower, "forming an additional barrier between the outer wall and the keep itself. But the inner gate would be offset."

She realized the significance at once. "With the gates out of alignment, an army would have difficulty breaching both."

"Precisely."

Deirdre smiled. She was wed to a resourceful man indeed. "Brilliant."

He grinned and impulsively lifted her hand, still clasped in his, to place a kiss upon her knuckles. To her consternation, a flush of pleasure rose in her cheeks.

"Naturally," he said, too preoccupied to notice, "archers could man both walls in the event of attack. And the additional towers could be used for storage of provender against siege. Best of all, the castle would remain secure during construction."

Deirdre let her gaze drift up the side of the tower. She

was understandably impressed. Pagan had clearly given Rivenloch's defenses a great deal of thought. His plan was ingenious.

There was only one problem.

"Listen," she said, gently extracting her hand from his. "There's something you should know. Rivenloch's coffers are . . ." she said under her breath, "modest. I fear my father's love of . . . of wagering has depleted our wealth." She met his eyes sternly. "Understand, I will not forbid him his play. 'Tis one of the few pleasures left to him. But his losses have left us short of coin."

"You needn't fret," he said with a droll grin. "I didn't come with an entirely empty purse."

"Perchance not. But I doubt you brought enough silver for such an undertaking."

"True." A glimmer of devilry stole into his eyes as he gazed thoughtfully across the sun-splashed courtyard. "Which is why we'll need to have a tournament soon."

Deirdre's heart skipped a beat. Surely she'd heard wrong. "What?" She blinked. "What did you say?"

"After harvest time, do you think?"

"A tournament? Are you serious?" Rivenloch hadn't sponsored a real tournament in a half dozen years. Once competitors learned that Deirdre and Helena were allowed to take part, fewer and fewer accepted invitations to joust at Rivenloch for fear of losing to a woman.

"Mayhap another in the spring."

"You *are* serious."

"Of course I am," he said, chuckling. "Men will travel far for the honor of fighting the Knights of Cameliard. We could win a sizable purse."

Was it possible? Could Pagan bring tournaments back to Rivenloch? Deirdre's pulse pumped wildly now at the possibility. From the time she could sit a destrier, she'd loved tournaments more than anything . . . the clash of steel on steel, the smell of horseflesh, the amazing feats of swordsmanship, the honor and chivalry and ritual . . .

But she dared not let false hope make her foolish. For years, the Warrior Maids had tried to reinstate tournaments at Rivenloch . . . and failed.

She tempered her voice to indifference. "Well, 'tis all very interesting, but what if you lose these tournaments?"

A predictable cocky smile brightened his face. "The Knights of Cameliard never lose."

With that audacious boast, he gave her a salute of farewell and swaggered off, leaving her to stare after him in amazement.

The rest of the day, despite her intentions to look at things with a cynical eye, tournament plans whirled among her thoughts. Visions of colorful pennons and pavilions from far-off lands, mysterious knights-errant with strange beasts on their shields, and magnificent warhorses adorned with silver and jewels stirred her blood. She could almost hear the crack of lances and the clang of blades as champions battled, could almost smell the savory meat pasties and perfumed ladies and damp horses.

If Pagan could carry it off, if he could restore twice yearly tournaments at Rivenloch, Deirdre might do more than simply respect him. Forsooth, she might feel a measure of genuine appreciation for her husband, enough to almost make her forgive him for Lucy and the buttery . . . almost.

*   *   *

Why Boniface saw fit to sing a roundelay with two dozen verses in her honor after supper, Deirdre didn't know. But when the unwieldy song finally ended, she was surprised to find Pagan missing from the hall.

An unexpected twinge of loss pinched her heart, for she'd just passed a remarkably pleasant supper with him, discussing some of her favorite subjects—castle defense and upcoming tournaments, Welsh archers and Spanish steel. Pagan had been gallant and diplomatic when her father momentarily forgot him, speaking kindly and patiently until he remembered. He'd sung praises to the knights of Rivenloch for their progress in the lists. He'd even managed to befriend Sung Li by speaking a few words in the old woman's tongue. For a while, as Deirdre and Pagan sat together, knee to knee, chatting away contentedly, 'twas almost possible to imagine growing old with him.

But now that he'd deserted her, misgivings crept in among her thoughts, and her defenses rose to protect her. No doubt, she thought peevishly, gulping down the last of her perry, he'd had a pressing appointment with Lucy in the pantry. Forsooth, he'd probably entreated Boniface to perform that tiresome song in her honor to keep her occupied while he trysted with the wench under her nose.

He'd not bothered to solicit his kiss from her today. She supposed he'd forgotten. But she didn't intend to be cheated out of her practice time on the morrow. If she happened to be in bed and asleep when he came to collect payment . . . well, she couldn't be blamed. 'Twould still count.

So, thanking Boniface for the wretched song and

blinking the sting of disappointment from her eyes, Deirdre headed upstairs.

At first, when Deirdre pushed open her door and glanced within, she thought she'd come to the wrong bedchamber. She frowned warily, her hand going instinctively to her sword, which she unfortunately wasn't wearing.

The room glowed with candlelight. Candles were perched on the sill, stuck onto stands beside the bed, and placed in a ring about a wooden tub in the midst of the room, a tub from which wraiths of fragrant steam arose. Fire crackled on the hearth, lending a smoky note to the bath's flowery scent. Jasmine. Or rose. She wasn't certain, for she never bothered to put flower petals in her bath.

Absorbed by the unfamiliar ambience of her chamber, she almost failed to notice that Pagan hadn't gone to meet Lucy after all. Forsooth, he stood in the far corner of the room, silhouetted in candlelight and looking as handsome as the Devil.

Chapter 21

"AH, WELCOME, MY LADY," he invited with a half bow.

In the golden light, his tawny hair gleamed, and his eyes sparkled like softly twinkling stars. He was now clad in a robe of dark blue velvet that draped his powerful shoulders and was tied at his hip. She suspected he wore naught beneath.

Deirdre tensed, and her defenses engaged at once. What was the knave up to? Suddenly the chamber reeked of more than flowers. It smelled suspiciously of seduction. Aye, they'd passed a pleasant supper, forsooth a pleasant day. But did he think her convictions so weak they could be swayed by a few candles and a flowery bath?

On the other hand, perchance his gesture was sincere. He *had* begun to exhibit signs of almost husbandly devotion of late.

Her breathing hastened as she hesitated in the doorway. Her thoughts reeled around and around among all the variations of Pagan—honorable bridegroom, wretched philanderer, patient teacher, loyal defender, smug seducer. Which one was he tonight?

Standing there, she felt as if she lingered between two worlds, one of familiar comforts and one of fascinating dangers. She could step back outside, shut the door, and her life would go on as it had, calmly, predictably. Or she could face this new challenge and risk leaving herself vulnerable to whomever Pagan was this eve.

The corner of his mouth lifted into a mocking smile. "You're not afraid, are you, damsel?"

That made up her mind, as he no doubt knew 'twould. Raising her chin, she entered and closed the door behind her. She did, however, leave her hand upon the latch.

"What is this?" she asked, her throat tight.

"This . . . is a bath," he said with an easy grin. "I'm almost certain you've seen one before."

"For me?" She looked at the steamy, inviting water. 'Twould feel heavenly upon her aching muscles. But part of her was more reluctant to step in than a cat at the edge of a puddle.

"Well, 'tisn't for the castle hounds," he assured her, moving toward the bed where several squares of linen were stacked. "Though the dogs could use a good scrubbing. I'll have a couple of the lads take them to the river on the morrow, if you like."

Deirdre didn't know what to say. The way Pagan bounced back and forth today between the roles of attentive husband and capable steward of the castle dizzied her. "Fine."

He unfolded the linens, then swept his fingers across the surface of the water, testing the temperature. "Did you like the roundelay?"

"What?" How could he make casual conversation

when her chamber was arranged like a bloody shrine to Venus?

"Boniface's roundelay."

"Oh. Aye." Forsooth, she couldn't remember much of the song. It had gone on so long, her mind had wandered to other things.

He reached for a vial of something and poured a few drops into the water, then swirled it around. "I hope you like lavender." Returning the bottle to the table, he said without lifting his eyes, "Do you need help undressing?"

She hesitated so long that he finally looked up at her. She gulped. "Nay. I can manage."

Drawing a fortifying breath, she set about the task as unceremoniously as possible. After all, she'd never been coy about nakedness. But somehow, stripping in front of Pagan made her feel utterly vulnerable.

Pagan turned to add a log to the fire, prodding at the coals and humming under his breath as sparks showered the hearth. Perchance if she hurried, Deirdre could slip surreptitiously into the tub before he was finished toying with the flames.

So eager was she to get the ordeal over with that she slipped as she stepped into the tub and fell in with an enormous splash that startled Pagan and slopped water over the edge, extinguishing several candles.

He chuckled, tossing a few of the linens onto the floor to soak up the mess. "Are you all right?"

She tried not to blush, but was unsuccessful.

"How's the water? Too hot? Too cold?"

"Fine." Forsooth, 'twas perfect. Accustomed to bathing in a cold pond or a bath that was tepid at best, she found the warm water a welcome pleasure. She had to confess, 'twould be easy to get used to Norman indulgences. Already she felt her sore muscles relaxing as they absorbed the heat, felt her inhibitions easing and her cares drifting away as the fragrant waves lapped gently at her flesh.

"Give me your hand," he murmured.

She glanced at him warily, but he lifted his brows, all innocence.

Reluctantly, she gave him her hand. To her surprise, he only placed a chunk of Saracen soap into her palm.

When he turned away again, she began to soap herself with deliberate languor, enjoying the silkiness against her skin, working some of the cardamom-scented bar into her hair as well. He returned with a pitcher of clean water, and she tilted her head for the rinse.

She would normally bathe in haste and get out, knowing her sisters and a servant or two might make further use of the bath. But tonight 'twas all hers, and the water was still warm and pleasant. 'Twas a shame to waste it. She closed her eyes and settled back against the rim of the tub, relishing the sensual heaven of lavender and candlelight.

Once, she stole a glance beneath her lashes to see what Pagan was up to, and what she glimpsed left her breathless. He sat by the fire, his hands steepled before his chin, idly rubbing a finger across his lips as he stared at her. There was raw desire in his gaze, almost painful desire, and yet 'twas carefully leashed. His restraint moved her, but she also saw how fragile his hold was. Precious little stood between them now. Only her will and his honor.

She lowered her eyelids again, trying to forget the forbearance in his face and the debt of consummation she owed him. Anon the soft crackle of the fire and the warmth of the water began to ease her anxieties, lulling her into a dreamy languor. For a while, she was wafted on a fragrant sea of repose, edging nearer and nearer to slumber's shore.

'Twas Pagan's amused whisper that ultimately roused her. "By the Saints, your fingers are beginning to shrivel, damsel. Anon they'll look like rotten apples."

She opened one eye. Her fingers weren't wrinkled in the least. The varlet only teased her. She scolded him with a halfhearted glare. To her relief, his knavish smile had returned, as if the expression of torment from before had belonged to another man.

He came toward her with a large linen square. She arose from the bath, wincing as her thigh muscles pulled, and before she could begin to chill, he wrapped the linen about her. With but one thin layer of fabric between them, she could feel the warm pressure of his fingertips as they brushed across her back, blotting the moisture from her body. He stood close to perform the task, so close she could smell the spicy scent of his own freshly washed skin, so close she shivered as his breath blew across the droplets of water upon her shoulder, so close that she wickedly wished he would lower his mouth the last few inches to lap them up. But even as an errant rush of desire dizzied her, he retreated with an evasive smile, leaving her to dry herself off, then turning to add a couple of logs to the fire.

His back to her, he said, "Your legs yet pain you."

"'Tis naught," she lied. Her muscles strained as she lowered herself, bundled in linen, onto the edge of the pallet.

"'Twill be worse on the morrow if you let the muscles stiffen." He finished at the hearth, dusted off his hands, and faced her, his gaze deceptively virtuous. "Shall I rub them for you?"

Despite the tempting proposition, she narrowed suspicious eyes. He was definitely trying to seduce her now. Rub her legs indeed. She started to refuse his offer.

"Or if you'd prefer," he added with a shrug, "I could call for my squire. He's deft at rubbing down the horses. I'm sure he would—"

"I am *not* a horse."

The twinkle in his eyes gave him away. He jested with her.

What was wrong with these Normans anyway? The Scots simply gritted their teeth and endured pain. They didn't coddle their bodies with lavender-scented baths and sensual massages. Such things were a luxury that the busy steward of a castle could ill afford. Aye, they were pleasant enough . . . and soothing . . . even, forsooth, divine, but . . .

"I'd hate to see you lose a day of practice." He clucked his tongue.

'Twas a tantalizing prospect. She well remembered how skilled his fingers were, how soothing his touch. Still, leaving herself literally in his hands, particularly when she was feeling so pliant . . . and warm . . . and receptive . . .

"Fine," she blurted before too much thought could convince her to decline.

He nodded, picking up the vial of lavender oil. He poured a small pool into his palm and knelt by her bedside. Peeling the linen carefully back from her left leg, he spilled the oil onto her knee, then began to gently knead upward along her thigh.

She stiffened defensively.

"Too hard?"

She shook her head, suddenly all too aware of the intimacy of their position. She felt his breath upon her thigh, and with each stroke, his fingers pushed ever closer to that damp place betwixt her legs that had known his touch before.

He pressed his thumbs forward again, and she braced her leg, clenching the coverlet in anxious fists.

"Yield, my lady. I'll be gentle."

She swallowed hard. How could she yield? 'Twas not in her nature, not on the battlefield, not in the bedchamber. Already she felt her control slipping, which served to heighten her defenses.

After several tense moments, he stopped abruptly, drawing her glance. He regarded her with an arched brow and a perceptive smile. "You're afraid."

"Nay."

"You're wound as tight as a crossbow. If 'tisn't fear . . ."

" 'Tisn't."

He stared at her, obviously amused. "Then lie back. Relax."

She couldn't.

"Don't you trust me?"

She trusted him. She didn't trust herself.

Finally, with a soft chuckle, he placed three fingers on her forehead and pushed her backward onto the bed.

She closed her eyes, and it didn't take long before the magic of his fingers began to work on her willpower. Softened by the warm bath and the sweet-scented oil, her muscles seemed to melt beneath his touch. Her pain diminished with each pass of his hands, replaced by a pleasant tingling that increased until it felt as if her blood fairly sang through her veins. Yet every time his thumbs approached the juncture of her thighs, then abandoned her, the unrequited ache of desire throbbed sharply in her womb. Each unfinished brush of his fingers honed her sensual frustration to a keen point. Anon she was filled with the most perverse longing to seize his hand and place it . . . there!

"Does that feel good?" he murmured.

Oh, aye, it felt sinfully wonderful, but she dared not confess it. Instead, she shrugged.

"Ungrateful vixen," he chided, guessing her lie, grabbing her wrists, and hauling her upright.

Pagan was unprepared for the naked desire glazing Deirdre's eyes. Jesu, 'twas almost his undoing.

This was undoubtedly the most challenging deception he'd ever undertaken, pretending nonchalance while his bride disrobed before him, lounged naked in a steaming bath, let him caress her bare thighs, and currently sat before him in naught but damp linen. His loins throbbed painfully, and every instinct told him to seize the day. But he'd not make that mistake again.

Deirdre was like an unbroken mare. Aggression only reinforced her resistance. If he circled his quarry carefully, patiently, eventually she'd come to him of her own free will. And if he was clever, she'd even believe 'twas her idea. But, sweet Mary, 'twas not an easy task. Not when she looked at him with those smoldering blue eyes.

He trained his voice to indifference as he let her go and retrieved the lavender oil. "You know what I think?"

"Mm?"

He thought he'd never seen a woman more beautiful, more arousing, more desirable. Before he spouted out something he'd regret, he rose and ambled across the room, depositing the vial of oil on the table. "I think you have a mortal fear of men."

"What?"

He turned toward her, smiling confidently. "I think you fear men."

Now the passion deserted her eyes. Indignation took its place. "What!"

He crossed his arms over his chest, daring her to disprove him.

"How can you think that?" she countered. "I fight men all the time. I've *killed* men. You of all people should—"

"Oh, I don't mean in battle," he said, chuckling.

"Then what *do* you mean?" Lord, she was beautiful even when her eyes flashed silver with anger.

"You're afraid of men in your *bed*."

Her blush betrayed her. "Pah! 'Tis not fear. 'Tis—"

"Oh, aye," he assured her. "'Tis fear. 'Tis quite apparent. Your hands clench, you avert your eyes . . ."

She defiantly released the coverlet and lifted her gaze. He smiled and sauntered toward her, brushing her cheek with the back of his finger. She flinched.

"You fear my touch." He bent forward until he was near enough to whisper in her ear. "And you're absolutely dreading my kiss this eve." He nuzzled her hair. "Are you not?"

She answered with an uncertain, "Nay."

"Shivering in your bones."

"I am not afraid of you," she insisted, her voice growing stronger.

"Then prove it."

*   *   *

Deirdre sensed she was being manipulated, but she couldn't quite figure out how. Her emotions and reason, anger and desire, logic and longing, whirled about her like battling currents, pulling her this way and that as she fought to keep her head above the engulfing waves.

She knew she should, as Pagan maintained, choose her battles wisely. This was one from which she should definitely walk away. But he'd issued a challenge she couldn't resist. Her courage had been called into question. Her pride had been insulted. She must answer his charges.

Before caution could squelch instinct, before her conscience could make of her a coward, she pushed him away and blurted out, "Do your worst then. Touch me anywhere. Kiss me anywhere. I care not. I am *not* afraid of you."

On some level, she realized what her bravado invited, what her words inferred. But she was no half-wit. While surrender might be delayed, she recognized 'twas inevitable. One day she *would* have to submit to Pagan. She was, after all, his wife, and 'twas her duty to make heirs for Rivenloch.

At this moment, however, she was in control of that surrender. 'Twas *her* challenge, *her* charge. He might vanquish her this night, aye, and inflict upon her that most demeaning of acts, but by God, 'twould be at her own bidding.

"Is that your will then?" he asked.

She hesitated, then leveled her gaze at him. "Aye."

To her wonder, Pagan's eyes gentled as he returned her gaze, and though his lip curved up, 'twas not in the cocky grin she expected. Instead, his smile seemed one of almost . . . relief.

Perchance, she imagined, 'twould not be so terrible. Perchance she could retain some dignity in the face of this degradation.

Pagan loosened the tie of his robe and let it slip from his shoulders, leaving his splendid body bare. He was unquestionably aroused now, she noted. His cock jutted from its dark nest like a dagger, waiting . . .

Waiting to stab her.

She swallowed down her foolish trepidation. Let him do his worst. 'Twas not in her nature to abstain from battle for fear of a wound. She braced herself for his attack.

But to her surprise, he didn't reach out to violently strip the linen from her. He didn't smother her with kisses. He didn't dive forward to flatten her upon the pallet. There was no pawing or groping or clutching. Instead, he stepped near and sat calmly beside her on the bed as an equal, so close she felt the heat coming off of his skin.

"I *know* why you fear me," he murmured.

"I don't fe—"

"You fear me because you think I'm your enemy."

He was half right. She *did* still consider him a foreigner, an invader, a threat.

"You know the first rule of warfare, don't you?"

When she did not reply, he gave her the answer.

"Know your enemy."

With that revelation, he stretched out upon the pallet, flat on his back. Then he spread his arms wide, palms up, in a gesture of absolute surrender.

"Come," he bid her. "Know your enemy."

Deirdre gulped. She would have preferred to crawl under the coverlet. Still, she realized the value of Pagan's offering. Aye, she'd already implied consent to lie with him, but now 'twas clear 'twould be on her terms. She need not feel subjugated or shamed, for he'd let her come to him of her own volition. She would be in control. 'Twas a precious gift he proffered.

However, knowing that wouldn't make the task any easier. She was as ignorant as a novice knight about to don chain mail for the first time.

She bolstered herself with a deep breath, then twisted where she sat to look down at him, considering how to begin.

Her gaze lit upon his left hand, to the long scar bisecting his palm. She wondered how he'd gotten it. With trembling fingers, she reached out to trace the mark.

"Used my hand as a shield when I was ten and six," he softly volunteered.

She winced at the thought, then followed the scar to another farther along the inside of his forearm. She looked at him in question.

"Slip of the knife, cutting captives free." Then he added meaningfully, "*Scots* captives."

Next she turned her attention to a jagged white line high above his left breast. She brushed it with a fingertip.

"My first melee," he said.

She smiled in memory. Lifting the hair off her neck, she showed him the nick from her father's sword. "*My* first melee."

Their eyes met. He grinned, and Deirdre felt a sudden and curious kinship with him. Every scar had a story, and theirs weren't so different. Forsooth, with each passing moment, Pagan seemed less Norman and more fellow warrior, less enemy and more husband.

Emboldened, she ran her thumb along his jaw, over

the scar she'd noticed when she'd first seen him. His chin was recently shaved, and 'twas smooth to the touch. She could see the pulsing of his throat, strong and steady, beating almost as rapidly as her own.

"Almost lost my head in battle," he confided.

She gasped.

He smiled. "'Twas Colin who saved me."

High on his brow, near the hairline, was another faint mark in the shape of a triangle.

"And this one?" she prompted.

"A jealous falcon."

She glanced into his eyes. They shimmered with humor.

"He didn't like me kissing his lady falconer."

Jealousy pricked Deirdre for an instant as she envisioned Pagan kissing another woman. But she shrugged it off, letting her gaze wander to his right shoulder. She ran her fingers over the flesh there. 'Twas unblemished. Then, as she traced down to the underside of his arm, toward his elbow, he twitched.

She frowned at him and stroked again.

"Ah!" he gasped, flinching.

"Does that hurt?" she asked in concern, sliding her fingers along his flesh again with less pressure.

"Cease, wench!" His arm slammed down, trapping her hand against his ribs.

"What's wrong?"

"Naught."

She narrowed her eyes. He was lying. She repeated, "What's wrong?"

"Naught, I said. Just do not . . ."

"Are you wounded?"

"Nay."

"Deformed?"

"Nay!"

"Crippled?"

"Nay, naught!"

She moved her squeezed fingers gently between his arm and chest, searching along his ribs for a flaw. "Have you—"

"Nay, you prying wench!" He clenched his arm even tighter.

"Then what—"

"It tickles, damn you!"

Chapter 22

EVEN THE FIRE ON THE HEARTH silenced at his revelation. Deirdre blinked in astonishment.

"Are you content now?" he grumbled, his brow furrowed in irritation, his swarthy cheeks actually pink with shame. "It . . . tickles."

For a moment she didn't know what to say. Then a smile tugged at her lips, and a devil whispered in her ear. She wiggled her trapped fingers.

"Ah!" he cried. "Stop!"

Naturally, his pleas only inspired her to further mischief.

"God's hooks, I cannot seem to get my hand free," she lied, wriggling her fingers even more enthusiastically between his ribs.

"Bloody wench!" he growled, even as laughter spilled from his mouth.

Highly entertained by his helplessness, Deirdre moved to kneel above him and began to use both hands, tickling him with even more zeal. She fluttered her fingers along his twitching belly, the inside bend of his elbows, the hollows of his hips as he made ineffectual grabs for her mischievous hands.

"I think I've found my enemy's weakness," she crowed as his giggles and curses warmed the air.

Exactly when the linen wrap slipped away, she didn't know. She was too preoccupied with her fortuitous discovery to notice. But her advantage didn't last long. After several moments of tormenting her captive, he finally found purchase. Seizing her wrists, he used his weight to bowl her over, and when he rose in triumph above her, pinning her naughty hands to the bed, their bodies met, skin to skin.

Deirdre scarcely noticed at first. Loving naught as well as a good fight, she grinned. Breathless, he, too, laughed down at her, his teeth gleaming, his eyes bright with emerald mirth. Lord, he was comely, as wickedly beautiful as a fallen angel. She wondered how his laughter would feel, spilling into her mouth.

As they stared at each other, their breath coming rapidly and their hearts hammering in counterpoint, the humor of the moment gradually faded. Pagan's gaze drifted over her features as if seeing them for the first time, and his smile softened as he eased his grip on her wrists.

She felt his tender regard like an ice-encrusted pine must feel the summer sun. But Pagan's eyes did more than thaw her. She grew hot, simmering, beneath his stare, and now she became aware of the dearth of cloth between them. His flesh burned against hers like a broadaxe still warm from the forge. His weight fit her as comfortably as a well-made coat of chain mail. And pulsing low on her belly, like an uninvited invader, his cock seemed to pound at the gates of her innermost keep.

Yet she was not afraid. Forsooth, her body thrummed the way it did when she was about to spar with an unknown fighter, with anticipation and excitement.

"Ah, wife," Pagan breathed, "may I take my kiss now?"

She wanted naught more. "If you wish."

She closed her eyes, expecting to feel his mouth upon hers. Instead, he slid slowly down her body, his flesh smoothing hers the way a hot stone smoothed cloth. Mayhap, she thought hazily, he'd kiss her throat, where her pulse surged in her veins. But nay, he slipped further, taking her Thor's hammer between his teeth and moving it aside. Perchance he'd kiss her breast again. She drew in a cool breath, anticipating the exquisite sensation. But he didn't stop there. His hair tickled her belly as he moved lower still.

His hands yet encompassed her wrists, so the instant she realized his destination and gasped in mortified panic, he tightened his grasp to still her ensuing struggles.

"Nay!" she hissed as his breath stirred the delicate curls guarding her womb.

"Hush, my lady," he whispered. "'Tis the place of my choosing."

Deirdre felt her face go hot. Oh, surely he couldn't mean to kiss her . . . there. She twisted her wrists in his grip.

"You've promised me this," he murmured, the heat of his breath seeming to sear her, "of your own free will."

She shivered. 'Twas true. She'd said it herself. Touch

me anywhere. Kiss me anywhere. But she'd never imagined he might do it.

And now she must comply. 'Twas a matter of honor. As difficult as 'twas, she fought her nature, forcing her body to yield. She relaxed her arms and ceased fighting him. Stifling a moan of frustration and horror, she shut her eyes tight and waited.

When he released her hands, her fists immediately clutched at the coverlet beneath her. His palms slid along her waist and settled upon the bones of her hips, stroking her with gentle assurance. His thumbs grazed the place low on her belly where the hair began, edging nearer and nearer her most secret spot. To her amazement, her body began to quiver with anticipation, to swell with need, as if it somehow wanted this. The suspense was excruciating.

His hands glided lower. A sob caught in her throat as his thumbs tenderly parted the petals betwixt her thighs, forcing them to blossom, leaving her distressfully exposed.

And then his mouth closed with searing heat over her flesh. She'd felt his touch here before, the warm slip of his wet fingertips. But this . . .

Sparks of radiant fire shot through her body, incinerating any thought of vulgarity or guilt or disgrace. 'Twas beyond shame and care and even thought, this glorious sensation, and it robbed her of the last shred of her resistance. The moist pressure of his lips, the molten ecstasy of his tongue, drove her to such mindless madness that she could not help but cry out and arch up to eagerly receive his kiss.

She'd thought 'twas heaven enough. But when he began to bathe her, lapping and circling and suckling in a rhythm of primitive hunger, her body jerked to life as if struck by lightning. Though she knew not the music, yet she answered his cadence, rocking, twisting, sobbing with yearning. 'Twas as if the world danced on that one sweet point called desire.

Higher and higher her passion wound, like the tightening spring of a crossbow, until at last she could rise no higher. Yet, impossibly, a part of her *did* rise. Some piece of her soul soared, transcending the worldly realm to send her shuddering across the sky like a spent arrow shot at the sun.

Crying out in the throes of bliss and awe, she bowed upward, and in that instant of beatific turmoil, Pagan moved swiftly to join with her. There was a brief, sharp sting, no worse than the shallow graze of a dagger, and then an incredible fullness as he plunged within. So deeply did he impale her, she feared at first he dealt her a mortal blow. Yet the pain vanished as quickly as it came, and she was left with only a strange sense of invasion and possession as he abided within her womb, waiting for her tremors to subside.

Pagan shivered above her, letting the waves of her climax flow over him, delaying his own satisfaction until she fully accepted his intrusion. Sweet Saints, 'twas nigh impossible, for he wanted her more than he'd ever wanted any woman.

God, she was beautiful. She'd surrendered to him, aye, but there was still the look of a conqueror about her. Her skin was slick with clean sweat, her brow creased with exertion, and the pure womanly strength with which she'd answered his seduction had nearly made him crest before his time.

At last she calmed, though her breath still came in half-gasps, half-moans that gave voice to his own silent longings.

He wished to take his time with her. He wished to make love to her slowly, patiently, the way she deserved. But the nights of unrequited lust would not allow such leisure. He'd be gentle with her, aye, but his need was great. And imminent. He wouldn't last long. Not with the way her womb enveloped him. And not with the way her eyes fluttered open at that moment, revealing in their indigo depths both satisfaction and desire.

Trying to keep the intensity of his craving contained, he held himself up on his elbows and cupped the sides of her head, stroking her velvety cheek with his thumb.

"I didn't wish to hurt you," he whispered.

Her eyes glittered, not with tears, but with courage.

"The pain will pass," he said, "I vow."

His gaze fell upon her irresistible mouth, so full, so pink, and he lowered his head to taste her. Her lips were warm and soft and accepting. Gradually she answered his kiss and initiated her own, tilting her head and lapping timidly at his mouth. He wondered if she liked the salty-sweet taste of her sex upon him.

Slowly, carefully, he withdrew from her, tensing his jaw against the exquisite friction, then pressed inside again. She gasped in wonder, echoing his awe. 'Twas wholly divine, the way her body embraced him. He retreated briefly, then plunged forward once more.

This time she groaned, a low sound of pleasure that drove him to new heights of passion. Unable to resist the natural rhythm of desire, he eased back and advanced more urgently now, savoring her sultry moans almost as much as the sheer euphoria of her flesh caressing his.

His blood pumped too fast. His lust rose too quickly. Too soon he felt his loins tighten, eager to spill their seed. And then, by some miracle, Deirdre was gasping in tandem, catching up with him on her own steed of desire. When she threw her legs about him, squeezing his buttocks in ardent demand, her body lurching with release, 'twas his utter undoing.

Like a pinecone exploding upon the fire, his body seemed to burst into a hundred bright sparks. The heat was excruciating, unbearable. Yet he craved its purifying fire. Where they joined, it felt they fused. Every spasm of ecstasy they shared, like two riders on one beast. He cried out in joy and terror, for never had he joined so completely with another. His loins reveled at the sweet relief, aye, but his rapture ran far deeper.

Deirdre was his. At last. He'd fought hard for her and won. She trembled beneath him like a conquered rival fallen to the earth, breathless, beaten, subdued.

And yet his triumph was a two-edged sword. Even as he loomed over her in victory, shuddering with the vestiges of passion, he became ruefully aware that his beautiful warrior, his magnificent bride, now possessed him as well.

The first fiery spear of sunlight pierced the misty morn, igniting the needles of pine and fir, and lodging in the moss-mottled wall of the stable.

Deirdre took note of the dawn, absently sweeping her sword through the air, then returned to her restless pacing before the tiltyard gate.

He was late.

'Twas bad enough that she felt uneasy about addressing Pagan today after the unsettling intimacies they'd shared last even. But for him to delay that confrontation made her even more anxious and led her to dangerous introspection.

What if their relationship had changed?

She swung her sword along the ground, decapitating a dandelion.

What if he deemed her surrender in bed proof of his dominance?

She bit her lip.

What if he faced her today with the smug condescension of a conquering foe?

She wheeled about so violently that she stumbled over her own feet, catching herself against the gate. She immediately pushed off in irritation, glancing furtively about for witnesses.

What troubled her most, what quickened her pulse and made her fists work like a maid's at milking, was the realization that their relationship *had* forsooth changed, but in ways she'd never foreseen. As incredible as it seemed, when she'd awakened this morn to the wreckage of their tryst—the cool bath, the lumps of melted candle wax, the rumpled bedlinens—the rush of memory that washed over her had been anything but regrettable.

Indeed, those recollections had been most pleasurable as she gazed upon Pagan, slumbering in deceptive innocence beside her. Her heart fluttering, she'd feasted on the sight of his tousled hair, his sensual mouth, his stubbled jaw, his open hand. Her bare thigh had brushed his and, like metal upon flint, sparked a tingling heat that swept through her whole body quicker than wildfire. Aye, she knew her enemy now, thoroughly. Knew him . . . and desired him.

'Twas an awful coil, one that left her recklessly vulnerable. For Pagan knew her weakness was *him*. And if he realized how easily she could be vanquished, how readily she could be controlled . . .

She let out a shuddering sigh. She mustn't let him find out. She must appear to be unaffected by what had transpired last night. She must act as if they'd never kissed or touched or, God help her, shared their bodies.

She sliced a sunbeam in half with her blade, spun, and lunged a few times, trying to focus on anything but the magnificent Norman who'd kissed her so sinfully and filled her with his seed. And his power. And his love. Whisked her to heaven in his arms . . .

"You're early."

Deirdre gasped, nearly tripping over her sword. There stood the man himself, dressed in a blue surcoat and braies, handsome and golden, as resplendent as the dawn. By the Rood, her memory hadn't done him justice. Had she truly surrendered to this Adonis last night? Had she lain, mouth to mouth, breast to chest, flesh to naked flesh, with that splendid body?

Feeling the blood rush to her face, she forced her gaze away, examining the hilt of her blade as if she'd never seen it before. "You're late," she managed to choke out.

He chuckled softly, a sound that curled seductively around her ears. "I indulged in a very potent sleeping draught last even."

Her glance was drawn upward, catching his suggestive smile. Her cheeks grew hot, and her heart raced. Lord, he was irresistible. His sleepy grin was enchanting. The ribald flicker in his eyes beguiled her. Even the careless riot of his hair caused a thrill of lusty memory to course through her veins. Sweet Jesu, how would she ever manage to conceal her attraction to him?

Distraction, she decided. Anything to take her mind off of him. And the best distraction was sparring.

There was just one problem. He obviously hadn't come to fight. "You've no armor."

He shrugged. "No time. But 'tis no matter. I can defend myself well enough to spar." Then he narrowed his eyes at her with feigned reservation. "Unless you intend to strike to kill."

Smiling weakly, she shook her head. She was only lightly armed herself, wearing but a mail hauberk over her gambeson. She sliced a challenge in the air between them. "Shall we?"

Unsheathing his weapon, he opened the gate to the tiltyard for her, murmuring as she passed, "Are you sore today?"

Blood rushed to her cheeks. He was a knave to ask such a thing. Aye, there was a faint ache betwixt her legs, but . . .

"Did the massage help?"

She blinked. Her muscles. Of course. He meant her muscles. Instantly contrite, she mumbled, "Aye. Thank you."

Lord, 'twas going to be a challenge to keep her mind focused.

Contrary to her expectations, rather than distracting her from wayward thoughts, battling with Pagan brought them into sharper relief. Never had she realized how like the act of mating sword fighting was—advancing, retreating, withdrawing, thrusting. Pagan fought much as he coupled, with passion and skill and patience. He moved with easy grace, and yet wasted no motion. Every grunt, every lunge, every thrust reminded her of their tumultuous joining. Anon, despite the residual ache between her thighs, despite the wrongness of place and time, despite her determination otherwise, her desire warmed as quickly as her blood.

Chapter 23

RAVAGING HIM WAS NOT a conscious decision on her part.

Forsooth, it started innocently enough.

The tip of her sword caught on his sleeveless surcoat and slashed the shoulder through, leaving the garment sagging.

"Pah!" He threw his hands up in mock displeasure. "'Tis my best surcoat, damsel," he growled. But despite the vexed shake of his head, there was amusement in his eyes as he engaged her again.

Her heart racing at the impulsiveness that suddenly seemed to possess her, she attacked him again, this time ripping the opposite shoulder. With only his leather belt to hold it up, the surcoat drooped from his chest, exposing the linen shirt beneath.

"What!" he exploded in surprise, reeling backward. "My lady, what do you—"

Before he could finish, she slipped her sword betwixt the laces of his undershirt and sliced them open.

The shirt slid from his shoulders, catching below his elbows. Then, while he stood in open-mouthed awe, she swept his sword away with her blade, sending it clattering against the fence.

Breathless with her own aberrant daring, she rested the point of her blade against his chest, his magnificent chest, and prodded him back one step, two.

He frowned warily. "Damsel, what is it you—"

"Go," she said, her voice strangely hoarse. "Into the stable."

Hampered by what was left of his shirt, he nonetheless raised his hands in a gesture of concession, reminding her all too vividly of his surrender to her explorations last night. Step by step, her heart cantering in her throat, she backed him through the stable doorway, all the while questioning her own sanity.

The sweet scent of fresh hay and the shadows of the stable interior welcomed and inspired her. Her heart began to pound against her ribs, and the womanly core of her seemed to throb in synchronous anticipation.

He must have read her intentions in her eyes, for he let out a shudder that was half groan, half sigh as she backed him against the stable wall.

Her breath coming feverishly, she pinned him with her sword in one hand and used the other to reach for his belt buckle. He clenched his jaw as a flick of her wrist unbuckled the leather. His surcoat fell away, but his undershirt yet bound his arms. She cast her sword aside, and the blade clattered against the stall, eliciting a soft whicker from one of the horses. Then she seized the linen of his shirt in both fists and tore it in two.

"Ah, wife," he sighed, his eyes growing liquid.

But her mood was far from tender. The fighting had

stirred her blood. 'Twas impossible to tame the wild currents raging inside of her.

"On your back," she gasped, pushing at his chest with the flat of her palm.

He staggered, collapsing onto a mound of straw. Then, rising up on his elbows, his clothing in shreds, his chest heaving, he riveted her with a stare of raw lust.

All the breath deserted her, and the air quivered with tension. Acting on pure instinct, she knelt before him, scrabbling at his braies, tearing them away to free the handsome beast within.

Her own garments thwarted her. She couldn't remove her hauberk quickly enough. With a cry of frustration, she struggled to loosen her swordbelt, but her desperate fingers fumbled at the task.

His hands took over, and he tossed the belt aside. Then she tried to work her arms out of the hauberk.

"Never mind," he bid her. "Just lift it up."

She gathered the chain mail in her arms, hefting its considerable weight, and Pagan reached beneath and swiftly rent her linen trews, the last barrier between the two of them.

Deirdre could wait no longer. Her blood was afire. Her skin craved his touch. Her loins ached with need. She straddled him and lunged forward, impaling herself on him.

"Ah!" he cried out, arching his head back as if she'd mortally stabbed him.

Her mouth fell open in wonder. There were no words to describe the rapture of their union, the heady triumph of command as she held him there, then her unfettered bliss as she initiated the motion of coupling, rocking to a current as old as the sea.

The links of her chain mail jangled with every thrust, like a timbrel accompanying their tempestuous dance. Her blood, already warm from battle, simmered now like lava in her veins. The exquisite friction of his flesh within hers made her swell with insurmountable yearning. A strange buzzing began in her ears, rising in volume and power, encircling her in sensual music, a portent of euphoria to come.

He braced his palms on her shoulders as she sat astride him, trying to slow her. "I can't . . . wait . . ." he gasped.

Why he wished to wait, she didn't know. She wanted him *now*. She seized his wrists and forced his arms back, plunging forward and trapping his hands in the straw beside his head.

This seemed to upset him more. "Ah, God, wench!" His eyes darkened with helpless lust. "Ah, God!"

But she didn't care. This was *her* tryst. Today she'd have delicious vengeance. Today she was his master.

Her chain mail pooled upon his chest now, undulating in waves of increasing speed. He squeezed his eyes shut and turned his head aside. His jaw clenched, as if he tried to stem the inevitable tide. Deirdre, however, kept her eyes open. She wanted to witness his defeat, his surrender, his humbling.

A drop of sweat dripped from the tip of her nose onto his cheek, and suddenly his body froze. Beneath her hands, his fists tightened, and a grimace of intense agony twisted his face. The sweet sight catapulted her own passions beyond redeeming. And as he arched and thrust and bellowed with his release, she followed him victoriously into the violent melee.

Moments later, spent, Deirdre sprawled atop him, listening to his slowing heartbeat, awash in feelings she scarcely understood. Aye, she felt powerful. And dominant. And smug. But she hadn't won vengeance, and she never would, for she discovered the triumph of lovemaking was not hers alone. 'Twas a triumph they shared, like two well-matched opponents whose every battle was destined to end in victory for both. 'Twas a curious thing.

"You've slain me, my lady," he murmured in exhaustion.

She smiled. "Nay. I can yet hear your heart beat."

"Aye, my heart beats for you. But I assure you, the rest of me is dead."

Her smile broadened. "I know a way to bring the dead to life." She ran mischievous fingers up along his ribs.

He snatched her hand at once, groaning. "Oh, nay. Mercy, I beseech you."

She took pity on him, nestling harmlessly once more against his chest. His arms circled about her, and for a peaceful moment, they drifted together.

"Do you know how amazing you are?" he whispered against her hair.

His words flustered her. She didn't know how to answer him.

But before she was compelled to reply, he clasped the back of her neck in one gentle hand. "I am truly pleased 'tis you I chose to wed."

She lifted her head and frowned at him. "You did not choose me," she corrected. "I chose you."

"Forsooth?" His eyes sparkled coyly, enigmatically.

"Aye," she assured him.

He raised rueful brows. "I suspect 'twas more of a . . . sacrifice than a choice."

She traced the scar upon his chest. "I am not . . . unhappy with my sacrifice."

"Not unhappy." His chuckle made her words sound weak, inadequate. He added wryly, "I am glad to hear it."

She settled back down to listen to his heart. 'Twas a comforting sound, strong and steady and soothing.

He stroked her hair. "You know, I was thinking . . ."

"Aye?" she said sleepily.

He furrowed thoughtful brows. "Mayhap *one* sparring drill a day is not enough to—"

She rose up and gave him a playful swat on the arm. "Greedy varlet. You would—"

His hand abruptly moved up to cover her mouth. He'd heard something. She stilled instantly.

Pagan was grateful for Deirdre's warrior instincts. She'd sensed danger as well. She knew when to be quiet.

Muffled voices came from the tiltyard. Men's voices. He strained to hear. Then he recognized them. His own knights, Rauve and Adric.

He removed his hand from Deirdre's mouth, leaving a finger upon her lips to silence her while he listened.

"Come on, be a good lad," Rauve coaxed. "I'll pay you back in a fortnight's time. You know I will."

"I can't believe I'm doing this," Adric grumbled.

There was a sound of clinking coins.

"'Tisn't my fault, you know," Rauve said. "That thief in the wood sneaked up on me like a, like a . . ."

"Like a shadow? That's what they call him, you know. The Shadow. What were you doing, ranging around the wood anyway?"

"Nothing."

"Nothing," Adric echoed. "You weren't alone, *were* you? Was it the milkmaid or the serving girl?"

"Mouthy knave, 'fwasn't either of them. That's why I can't figure out how he stole up on me."

"Well, you deserved to be robbed," Adric said, "after that sweet Lady Miriel made such a kind request for us to return our winnings, and you *kept* yours."

"That's the cruelty of it. I swear, I was so deep in my cups, I don't even *remember* winning. When that robber found the silver in my pouch, I had no idea where it came from."

"Until Lady Miriel reminded you."

"Nay, until the little damsel I took in the wood reminded me. She saw me win it."

"I knew it!" Adric crowed. "You *did* tryst in the wood."

Their voices grew louder, and Deirdre started fidgeting. Pagan knew if his knights walked in, there would be no way of hiding the truth of what had transpired here. After all, clothing was strewn everywhere, Deirdre's hair was festooned with straw, and Pagan couldn't wipe the self-satisfied grin off of his face. 'Twas useless to jump up in panic and try to hide.

But, of course, that would be Deirdre's intention, and 'twas pointless to try to stop her. She scrambled up to her feet and retrieved her sword from the floor. Then, to his surprise, she turned to face the intruders, placing herself between them and him as if she might protect his honor. Forsooth, 'twas touching, albeit unnecessary.

"You wouldn't believe it," Rauve said as his shadow fell across the stable entrance. "All black like Lucifer he was. Moved as fast as the Devil, too, whist-whist-whist, leaping, kicking. Still, I could've caught the bastard if I hadn't been protecting my lady love."

"The Scots say he can't be caught," Adric said. "They say he's not of this world."

"Well, if he's not of this world, then what does he need my silver for?"

Rauve filled the doorway then and, like a trusty Knight of Cameliard, as soon as he laid eyes on Deirdre, drew his blade.

She began concocting a tale at once. "Go! Get Sir Pagan some clothing. His . . . his horse has attacked him and . . . and he's torn his surcoat."

Pagan didn't know what was more amusing, Deirdre's pathetic attempt at lying or Rauve's expression of disbelief, given that his horse stood placidly munching hay in the adjoining stall. But Pagan burst out in a peal of laughter that threatened to shake the dust from the rafters.

The scowl Deirdre turned on him could have melted steel.

"My lord?" Rauve asked, clearly confused.

Pagan grinned, grabbing a handful of straw to shield his nakedness as he sat up. "Prithee fetch me new garments. And braies for Lady Deirdre. And both of you, not a word about this or I'll have your heads."

Deirdre turned a most adorable shade of pink.

"Aye, my lord." Rauve's face was a mask of decorum

as he sheathed his sword, having doubtless been in many such awkward situations himself.

As for Adric le Gris, that knowing smirk would cost him extra duties in the armory later, Pagan vowed.

Eventually, Deirdre's dignity was restored, and despite her suspicions that the entire castle would soon learn of their perfidy, Rauve and Adric were true to their word. There was no snickering among the servants, no whispering in the armory. And if Pagan was a bit saddened by the likelihood that she'd never make the mistake of ravaging him in the stables again, he took comfort in the fact that she didn't seem to mind molesting him everywhere else.

Thoroughly.

Repeatedly.

Exhaustively.

The days were spent in relative harmony now, with only scattered disagreements.

Pagan remained firm in matters of castle defense. There were reports now of a few rogue English lords who'd joined forces, forming a veritable army that was attacking castles along the Border. So Pagan set teams of fletchers to making arrows day and night, and the armorer's forge was seldom cool.

But he bowed willingly to Deirdre's expertise regarding the Scots' curious system of justice. He didn't question her when she praised a lass who'd blackened a boy's eye, nor did he raise a brow when she forced two constantly quibbling Norman maids to share a single stool for a day.

As peaceful as the days were for the two of them, however, the nights were filled with conflict. They battled over who would lie on top in their bed, disagreed about whether to make love before or after supper, fought for the coverlet when they somehow wound up on the floor. 'Twas the kind of sweet discord Pagan gladly endured. And over several nights, he grew convinced he was the most fortunate knight in the world, for how many men could say their favorite sparring partner was also their wife?

Chapter 24

FROM HIGH ATOP THE BATTLEMENTS of the curtain wall, Deirdre wrapped her cloak more snugly against the misty afternoon and happily surveyed the commotion in the courtyard below. Pagan's improvements to Rivenloch over the past several days were impressive. New planks replaced rotting timbers in the outbuildings. Masons repaired the crumbling rock around the well and towers. Stones were cut and carried in preparation for creating the second wall about the keep. Pagan had men hammering at all hours of the day and children mixing daub and fetching tools. Meanwhile, Deirdre and Miriel kept up the everyday operations of the castle and made certain there was an ongoing supply of oatcakes and ale to feed the workers.

She smiled. Even Norman-hating Helena would be impressed.

She turned then to gaze toward the forest and the faraway copse of cedars where she knew the old crofter's cottage stood, the place she suspected Helena had taken Colin.

Forsooth, she was surprised they hadn't yet returned. Surely with Helena's voracious appetite, she must be running out of food by now. But Deirdre wasn't worried. Helena was self-sufficient. She'd be secure enough in the secluded cottage, and, according to Pagan, safe enough with his man.

Beyond the woods, over the distant hills, ominous columns of ashen thunderheads rose. She scowled at them, hoping the rains would wait until the thatch on the new dovecot was finished.

Wiping the mist from her brow, she returned to observing the courtyard. As she'd expected, 'twas only a matter of time before Pagan crossed the sward, in the thick of the activity. He strode with confidence, carrying a bundle under one arm, waving at Kenneth as he passed, stopping to talk to his master builder. Deirdre sighed, wondering if her heart would ever be still while Pagan was in her sight.

Her entire understanding of marriage had been transformed over the last few days; she realized now the bond between husband and wife could be potent. 'Twas not only that the physical intimacy she and Pagan shared proved more of a pleasurable adventure than she'd foreseen, but their union created a strength of spirit exceeding their individual power. As on the battlefield, two warriors could fend off more foes when they fought back to back.

Their union had created something else as well, at least if Sung Li's prophecies could be believed. The old woman could be damnably cryptic at times, but her omens were seldom wrong, and she'd informed Deirdre only this morn that a new heir of Rivenloch had arrived.

Deirdre rested a palm low on her belly, marveling at the possibility.

Passing the well, Pagan caught sight of her and stopped in his tracks. For a moment he only stood, staring up at her. God's eyes, his gaze, even at this distance, warmed her to her core. 'Twas difficult to imagine having an intelligent conversation with him any time soon.

But she knew she must. Turning toward the stairs, she prepared to go down to meet him, not to tell him of the babe, for 'twas too soon to rouse his hopes, but to discuss her father and what must be done about him.

Sadly, amidst the chaos of construction—the demolishing and rebuilding and altering of walls and outbuildings— the Lord of Rivenloch's wits had grown progressively more feeble. Now not only did he grieve for his wife, but for the very world dying before his eyes. Rivenloch, his solid fortress, was no longer familiar to him. And to a man as lost as her father, that change was crippling.

She couldn't ask Pagan to stop the improvements. They were essential. There was but one thing to do, something the three sisters had put off as long as they could, and that was to remove Lord Gellir from power. Forsooth, 'twould not change things visibly. The lord held little sway as 'twas. But once power was officially transferred, once Pagan's designation was no longer steward, but lord, 'twould be irreversible. And if Lord Gellir, in a moment of clarity, perceived that transfer as disloyalty . . .

Deirdre shivered. As much as it pained her, she

couldn't risk Rivenloch's safety for the sake of her father's feelings.

She meant to confront Pagan at once. But when she saw the expression in his eyes as he met her on the spiraling steps, the one that said he was up to mischief, her mood couldn't remain sober for long. And as he hummed a merry tune, making her cares melt away, she decided perchance the matter of her father could wait one more day.

"I have something for you," he purred.

She grinned back. "Is it the same something I glimpsed this morn beneath the bedclothes?"

"Saucy wench. Is that all you think of?"

She would have continued their sly repartee, but she noticed the bundle he carried was swathed in expensive velvet. "Ah, what have you here?" She made a grab for it.

He snatched it out of her reach. "Take care!"

"Is that for me?"

He arched a brow. "Mayhap."

"What is it?"

"How greedy you are," he teased. "And on your birthday, too."

Startled, she blinked. While she reeled in surprise, he swept past her up the stairs.

"What do you mean, my birthday?" she asked, charging after him. She frowned. Was it her birthday?

He stopped suddenly at the top of the stairs, and she almost collided with him. Then he wheeled about. "You didn't know?"

"You *did*?"

"Sung Li told me." His brow clouded with misgiving. "'Tis true, is it not? A fortnight after Midsummer Eve?"

"I . . . I guess so." She no longer paid mind to such things.

They emerged upon the wall walk, and he dropped to one knee before her. "Then here, my lady, is your birthday gift." He smiled, offering the velvet bundle in both hands.

Deirdre didn't know what to say. She hadn't received a birthday gift in years. A father who couldn't remember her name certainly couldn't remember her birthday. And the three sisters, with typical Scots pragmatism and thrift, purchased little that wasn't essential. Her fingers trembled as she reached out to touch the soft fabric.

"Open it," he softly urged.

Carefully, she folded back the edges of the cloth, gasping in awe as she saw what lay within. Nestled in the dark blue was a bright blade of polished steel. She quickly uncovered the rest. 'Twas a sword, a magnificent sword. And there, engraved upon the hilt, were the figures of the Unicorn of Cameliard and the Dragon of Rivenloch, inseparably entwined. She ran a thumb along the pommel, over the inscription. *Amor Vincit Omnia*, it said. Love Conquers All.

"Do you like it?" he asked, knowing full well she did.

A lump in her throat made her choke on the words. "'Tis the most . . . the most beautiful thing I've ever seen."

"Try it."

She took the hilt in shaky hands and lifted it, sighting along the blade. 'Twas flawless, as true as any she'd ever held. She whisked it through the air, and it whistled sweetly. "Oh."

He grinned. "Oh?"

Turning aside, she slashed left and right and thrust

forward. The sword was like a weightless extension of her own hand. Such a blade could increase her speed and agility until she fairly flew at her opponents. "God's teeth."

"Nay. Only Toledo steel."

She was too fascinated to appreciate Pagan's quip. While he retreated to a safe haven of the wall walk, she tested the weapon, spinning and lunging and whirling it over her head.

"This is . . ." she said, at a loss for words, "'tis amazing."

He chuckled. "Oh, aye."

"The balance. The grip. Everything is . . ."

"Perfect?"

She nodded.

"I'm having my armorer make them for all the Rivenloch knights."

She spun and locked gazes with him. "Forsooth?"

"He has a half dozen made already."

Such joy coursed through her now that she had to express it. As calmly as she could, she replaced the precious blade across its velvet wrap. Then she strode directly up to Pagan, wrapped her arms about him, and hugged him thoroughly.

"Thank you," she whispered.

He returned her embrace. "My pleasure."

But as he held her, she noticed a subtle change in his grasp, a wary stiffening. Without looking, she sensed that his attention was no longer focused on her, but on the far horizon.

"What is it?" she breathed.

"Well, by Lucifer's ballocks, 'tis high time."

Chapter 25

'TWAS JUST LIKE HELENA to evade a sound scolding from Deirdre by charging through the front gates, bringing new drama to distract from the old. But this time, Deirdre discovered, 'twas no ploy on her sister's part. The urgency in Hel's eyes as she confronted Pagan was sincere. Trouble was coming. She and Colin had seen a huge company of English knights, marching toward Rivenloch.

Kidnapper and hostage had apparently come to a truce of sorts, for they'd limped across the hill together, Helena helping to support Colin, who'd been the victim of some mysterious injury he insisted was but a scratch. Deirdre wondered at the truth of that, but there was no time for questions.

"Ian!" Deirdre barked. "Sound the alarm. Round up the crofters. Gib and Nele, gather the herds."

"Rauve!" Pagan tossed him the key to the weapons chest. "Gather the men in the armory. And Adric, make sure the horses are stabled."

Not to be outdone, Colin shouted, "Helena! Take Miriel and find shelter with the other women inside the keep."

But to his surprise, his command was greeted with stony silence. Hel's glare could have burned holes in him. "Do not order me about, you pompous—"

"*Now*, wench!" he said. "'Tis no time to be playing games."

She tossed her head. "Have you learned naught, sirrah? Who took you hostage at knife point? Who defended you from outlaws? Who saved your worthless—"

"Cease, the two of you!" Pagan held up his hands. "We've no time for this. Helena, can you prepare the archers?"

"Of course," she sneered for Colin's benefit, then added under her breath, "if I can find them in the mess you've made of my keep."

"Then do so."

Colin laid a palm on Pagan's chest. "Wait! You cannot mean to let her stand atop the battlements. She's . . . she's . . . a woman."

Pagan smiled ruefully at his friend, clapping him on the shoulder. "She's perfectly capable. Trust her."

"Are you mad?" Colin scowled, perplexed. "You can't let her—"

But Helena was already halfway up the stairs.

Pagan squeezed Colin's shoulder. "She'll be fine. Anyone who can singlehandedly abduct Colin du Lac . . ."

The usually cheery Colin looked miserable as he reluctantly nodded, gazing at the spot where Helena had disappeared. Forsooth, if Deirdre didn't know better, she'd say the poor man was . . . smitten with his kidnapper.

"Can you walk well enough to find my father?" she asked him.

Colin, glad to be of use, obliged at once, hobbling toward the stairs.

Meanwhile, Miriel led the women and children with calm efficiency, escorting them safely into the keep. When all were accounted for, she took refuge there as well.

Ian drove the last of the cattle into the courtyard. In the chaos, no one noticed the small shadowy figure slipping out the gates. Angus closed them and dropped the portcullis, sealing Rivenloch to the outside world. Only then did Deirdre breathe a sigh of relief.

"Well, my lady," Pagan said to her after the knights were assembled and armed, "shall we see what we're facing?"

They ventured up to the walk of the outer wall together, and Deirdre was pleased to see that Helena's archers were in place, their bows at the ready. As the sentries scoured the distant hills, one of them cried out, "There they are!"

Only the tops of their fluttering pennons could be seen as the foreign army crested the rise, but 'twas enough to strike fear into Deirdre's heart.

She gulped. "There are . . . so many."

"Aye," Pagan said, his lips curving into a scornful smile, "but they're English."

English or not, Deirdre counted at least four dozen mounted knights and an equal number afoot. This had to be the alliance of rogue lords that had been terrorizing the Borders.

"No one fights the Knights of Cameliard willingly," Pagan reassured her. "Once they know who they're dealing with, they'll lay siege rather than face our swords."

Deirdre hoped he was right. Pagan seemed to stake a lot on the reputation of his knights.

He studied the approaching soldiers. "Still, 'twould be useful to make them believe they're outnumbered."

"A show of force from the battlements?"

"Aye."

Deirdre thought for a moment. Then inspiration struck. "We'll use everyone. Grooms, cooks, maids. Tell them to hide their faces." She nodded toward the army. "At this distance, none can tell knight from servant, man from woman."

Pagan stared at her, stunned. Then his face dissolved into a proud grin. "Brilliant."

But as she grinned back, her cheeks warmed by his praise, a Rivenloch archer cried out, "What the Devil . . ."

Pagan's head whipped about to see what afflicted the archer, and his face sobered as he followed the man's gaze toward the invading army. "Bloody hell."

Deirdre stared after him, at the gray horizon where the darkening clouds seemed to travel with the enemy, like the shade of death on the march. Silhouetted against the sinister sky, an enormous wooden structure, pulled by two pairs of oxen, slowly rolled over the top of the hill. It looked like a giant tower or the mainmast of a ship. "What is it?"

Pagan's voice was flat. "They've got a trebuchet."

She blinked, then narrowed her eyes. "What's a tre-buchet?"

He was too distracted to answer her; he began barking orders at once. "Archers! If they set up that machine, fire at those who wield it. Do *not* let them use it."

He lunged past her then, and she had to run to keep up with him as he charged down the steps.

"Do you have more bows?" he asked her as he hurried across the great hall.

"Crossbows."

"We'll need everything you have. What about sulphur for Greek fire?"

She frowned. She'd never heard of Greek fire.

"No sulphur," he murmured. "Rags we can soak in oil?"

"Aye."

"'Twill have to do. And fetch candles, lots of candles."

As much as she wanted to ask him what the bloody hell he was up to, she sensed his urgency, and she trusted his judgment. As she left to find rags and candles, she heard him command the knights to the western battlements, bidding every free man to arm himself with a crossbow and bolts. And again and again, among the men of Cameliard, she heard dire whispers of "trebuchet."

As he paced behind the archers, Pagan cast an uneasy glance at the sky. Storm clouds bruised the heavens now. 'Twas only a matter of time before they loosed their store of tears. He restlessly fingered the pommel of his sword as he watched the enemy make camp.

There was naught more thrilling to Pagan than battling a foe with sword in hand. Aye, he recognized the merits of other weapons—the axe, the dagger, the quarterstaff, the crossbow. But they lacked the spirit of a fine length of Toledo steel in the hands of a trained knight.

To a warrior like Pagan, the trebuchet was an abomination, a machine of war that relied upon brute force rather than finesse. 'Twas a machine for cowards and barbarians too dim-witted to employ strategy. Using such devices was loathsome, unchivalrous.

And so when Pagan laid eyes on the monstrosity rolling over the hill, a quiet rage began to simmer within him. For the English to resort to using such a weapon, a beast of destruction that devoured everything in its path, leaving behind only shattered wood and broken rock, meant that they intended no siege, no negotiations, no compromise, and likely no prisoners. Forsooth, they probably meant to make quick work of the keep, to claim it before the sun set and before help could be summoned.

But what exasperated Pagan the most, what made guilt ride deep upon his shoulders, was the fact that because he'd been so eager to start construction on his inner wall, the sward surrounding Rivenloch was littered with great chunks of quarried rock—perfect, deadly missiles for the springing arm of the trebuchet.

The Scots had apparently never seen such a machine. With any luck, Pagan thought, tightening his grip on his useless sword, they'd never see it in action. But he had to get rags and oil to the archers quickly so they could fire a barrage of flaming arrows at the thing. 'Twas the only way to cripple it.

Deirdre emerged upon the battlements, her arms full of candles, a half dozen lads following with rags and oil. He thanked God she wasn't one of those whimpering wenches who might distract him from the task at hand, but a true helpmate. Her face was etched with concern, but the dark fire in her eyes told him she was as fearless and determined as any of his knights. Pride swelled his chest as he gazed upon her, pride and awe and . . . aye . . . love. He loved his stubborn Scots wife.

He wished there was time to tell her how much. When this was over, he silently vowed, he'd weary her ears with pledges of his love. But for now, they had a castle to defend, *their* castle.

Deirdre studied the wooden tower, trying to puzzle out its workings. " 'Tis like a catapult."

"Aye, only far more powerful," he said. "A trebuchet can breach a castle wall with a single . . ."

Deirdre paled. Pagan could have kicked himself for his careless words. Deirdre might be a capable steward and a valiant warrior, but she'd never had to face such absolute menace to her stronghold. Forsooth, the worst threat imposed upon her up till now had likely been the King's appointment of a Norman as her husband.

He gripped her by the shoulders and gazed forcefully into her eyes. "Listen, Deirdre." Then he made her an oath, one he prayed to God he could keep. "I won't let Rivenloch fall."

For a moment, doubt lingered stubbornly in her eyes. But he persisted, willing her to believe in him. Finally she nodded.

"You had *better* not," she warned him, her gaze harsh, reminding him that beneath her soft flesh lay bones of rigid steel. Then her eyes glittered mysteriously. "I would leave our babe more than a pile of rubble."

He blinked. While they stared at each other, her words sank in, and he frowned in confusion. What did she mean, "our babe"? Was she . . . Nay, it couldn't be. 'Twas too soon to tell.

Nonetheless, the possibility sent a thrill of secret wonder surging through his veins, leaving a strange turmoil in his heart.

He would have questioned her further, but already she was leaving his embrace to make herself useful, distributing candles to the archers.

He, too, had other matters to attend to if he was going to keep his promise. "Soak the rags well in oil and affix them to the points," he instructed the knights. "Ignite them, and make sure they're burning well before you fire."

Helena poked her head above the stairwell. "I've stationed sentries around the perimeter," she told him, "in the event they try to undermine the wall elsewhere."

He nodded his approval. Deirdre's sister might be impulsive, but she was admirably efficient and capable. As dire as their situation was, as unprepared as the people of Rivenloch were for war, as outnumbered as the knights were, Pagan began to believe they might have a chance against the English, if they could cripple the trebuchet.

Then the first raindrop fell on his cheek.

"Jesu," he said under his breath.

Any other day rain would be welcome, for bad weather was the bane of besiegers. But today, 'twould be England's ally, dousing the fire of Rivenloch's arrows.

Deirdre and Sir Rauve came to his side, glowering up at the rain.

"Shite," Deirdre muttered. "We have to fire *now*."

Rauve shook his head. "The thing is out of range."

Pagan rubbed his jaw, weighing the circumstances as the rain began to pelt the sod like the hooves of a charger. "We can't afford to wait. If we don't disable it soon . . ."

She squinted toward a break in the clouds near the horizon. "How long will it take them to set up the device?"

Rauve followed her gaze. "Not long enough."

"Ballocks."

"Let's see what the archers can do," Pagan decided.

Rauve turned out to be right. The trebuchet was out of bow range, even for Cameliard's best archers. The fiery shafts shot across the silver sky, only to plunge into the damp sod, several yards in front of the front line, then sputter out.

The enemy seemed impervious to the rain. They continued their work, edging the trebuchet forward, protecting it with an array of shields that formed what looked like an enormous breastplate of scale armor. Though they drew in range of the archers, no shaft could penetrate the steel mantle. Even those arrows that happened to lodge fortuitously in the upper beams of the trebuchet were soon doused beneath the raging downpour.

Glaring up at the cruel sky, Pagan began to wonder if God might be English.

Deep within a storeroom of the keep, Miriel hushed the children and their mothers, ever vigilant for the sound of a battering ram. As long as the outer walls were secure, she knew, they would be safe. And if Sung Li had successfully slipped out the front gates, help would arrive within a day.

Meanwhile, she would do as Sung Li had advised and listen for sounds of invasion, for if the siege turned into a full-scale attack, if Rivenloch's security was breached, she might be forced to disclose one of the castle's most closely guarded secrets.

Failing that, Miriel had one other option. She eyed the small cache of weapons she'd stowed in the corner of the storeroom—her sais, tonfas, kamas, and nunchakus. If the need arose for close combat, she wouldn't hesitate to use them. She'd have a lot of explaining to do later, but at least she'd be alive to do it.

High atop the curtain wall in full armor now, Helena loped past the archers she'd stationed at vantage points along the eastern perimeter. So far, she thought, the English were focused on only the west side of the castle, but that could change at any time. 'Twas essential that the archers watch for small bands of sappers.

She smiled in grim satisfaction as she gazed down the long row of attentive sentries. At least *these* men didn't gainsay her every command, unlike the bullheaded Norman she'd held captive for the last several days.

She bit her lip, wondering what had become of Colin. She hoped, after all the pains she'd gone to caring for him, defending him, helping him limp back to Rivenloch, that he wouldn't do something foolish and get himself killed.

He had a lot of audacity, thinking he could order her into the keep along with the other helpless females. Hadn't he discovered anything from their escapades? Didn't he realize she wasn't an ordinary wench, but a

Maid of Rivenloch? Couldn't he accept that she was just as worthy a warrior as his own fellows?

Colin du Lac had much to learn about Helena of Rivenloch. That was certain. She only hoped he'd live long enough to be taught.

Colin winced as pain shot through his thigh. Sweat dampened his brow as he ascended the steps of the western tower of the outer wall, leaning heavily against the rough stone. He still hadn't found Helena's father, but at the slug's pace he was forced to, the old man likely outdistanced him at every turn. Colin was clearly not the man for this task, not with his half-healed leg. But at the moment he was glad of the distraction, for all he could think about was Helena and her stubborn insistence on participating in the battle.

God, she was a wayward wench. Once she put her mind to something, it seemed neither common sense nor wild chargers could sway her from her course. It had been so with abducting him. No matter how he reasoned with her, assuring her that her sister wouldn't suffer at Pagan's hands, warning her that Pagan's justice would be harsh if she insisted on ransoming him, persuading her that all would be forgiven if they returned safely, she wouldn't listen.

Of course, her tenacity had also saved his life. She'd been uncommonly brave in the face of grave peril. Forsooth, he might have bled to death were it not for her determination to keep her hostage alive.

But this . . . this was different. There was an entire army out there, and no matter how invincible she believed she was, her flesh was still mortal. Mortal and vulnerable and . . . and as smooth as fine silk.

He furrowed his brow, cursing the lusty memories that haunted his every waking thought. He didn't *love* the wench, he told himself, no matter what had happened last eve. She was amusing, aye, and attractive. Desirable. And fascinating. But she was trouble. Besides, if she continued living so dangerously, with no care for her own safety, she'd not last out the siege.

He staggered against the wall as another pain streaked through him. This one, however, pierced not his leg, but his heart.

Directly above Colin, at the top of the outermost tower of the castle wall, the Lord of Rivenloch listened to his beloved Edwina. She was calling him, calling for help. A sob clotted in his throat, and tears rolled down his cheeks, for no matter where he wandered, he couldn't seem to find her.

"Edwina, my love," he called, his voice grating with despair.

She wept softly, and the sound seemed to envelop him, coming from everywhere and nowhere. He spun slowly round and round, gazing upon naught but empty gray stone. He felt helpless, so helpless. He pulled at his hair in frustration, straining to hear, but now it seemed only the rain murmuring upon the stone sill.

He plodded to the window and peered through the arrow slit. Upon the knoll before the castle, an army had gathered. They were not Rivenloch's soldiers, nor were they the knights belonging to the Norman. He gazed at the strange company with a sense of detachment, as if he watched preparations for a Christmas play. They had some wooden thing, he saw, that looked like a giant child's toy. He absently scratched his head as they blocked the wheels into place and fussed with the various ropes and protrusions. Then several men hefted a great chunk of rock onto the platform at the back.

As if from Thor's hand, a hail of fiery arrows suddenly descended from the heavens. But the flames instantly sputtered out, drowned by the downpour.

Then, like a loosed crossbow, the toy sprang with such violence and speed that he barely glimpsed the missile catapulting toward him. The rock hit the tower, impacting with a deep thud, then an ominous crack, shuddering the stones beneath him, dropping him to his knees.

Like a bone-jarring roll of thunder, the rock around him rumbled and quaked loose with an unholy roar. Before his eyes, the western half of the tower crumbled away, and he could do no more than huddle on his hands and knees, cling to the oak planking of the floor, and watch the walls disintegrate. Wet wind suddenly whipped his hair and stung his face, and he squinted against the abrupt brilliance of the open sky.

He must have displeased the gods, he decided as the rain pelted him like angry tears. The devastation around him was clearly the work of Thor's hammer.

Deirdre's hand tightened on the wet stone of the parapet as she watched the far west tower collapse, along with the section of the wall walk connecting it. Her heart stopped, and she could suck no air into her lungs. She'd beheld the arm of the trebuchet as it flung its burden with incredible force, but she'd never imagined the powerful blow 'twould deal—the earthshaking impact of the rock and the deep, gaping wound 'twould leave.

All around her, the Rivenloch men stood in mute

awe, clutching their bows with white knuckles, though such weapons now seemed as useless as a feather against a sword.

For the first time in her life, fear and doubt made sweat trickle at the back of her neck. These were no mere mortals with blades they battled, but a monster fashioned upon Lucifer's forge. How could they hope to triumph against such a machine?

Despair lurked over her shoulder like a carrion crow, eager for the spoils of war, threatening to consume her before she was even defeated.

Then she glanced over at Pagan, who gazed out at the enemy with a fierce glare and a clenched jaw. He was not vanquished. Far from it. Pagan of Cameliard would not surrender. He would *never* surrender. Even if that damned trebuchet flung a rock straight at his belly, he'd die facing the English with a raised fist and a defiant sneer.

How could she be any less brave?

Inspired by him, Deirdre of Rivenloch straightened her spine and steeled her nerves, loosening her grip on the wall and clenching a fist instead around the pommel of her new sword. "Hold your fire!" she shouted to the archers, surprised at the steadiness of her voice.

The walls were still crumbling, sending up white plumes of dust and rubble, as the English prepared to strike again. The soldiers held their ground. They didn't need to advance on foot, not when they wielded such a formidable weapon. She studied their position, the trajectory of the trebuchet.

"Will they aim for the same tower?" she asked over the drumming of the rain.

Rauve nodded. "Aye, to make a point of entry."

"Good. A single point is easy to defend. We'll move the men-at-arms there."

"'Twill be easy," Pagan agreed gravely, "unless they move the trebuchet."

She lowered grim brows. "Then let's kill them while we can."

Chapter 26

PAGAN FROWNED. He didn't intend to allow Deirdre into the thick of battle, no matter how much she insisted, no matter how much he respected her skills, no matter how much she begged him. 'Twould be too distracting for him to worry about her safety while he engaged the enemy.

Besides, if 'twas true that she was with child . . .

He'd not meet her eyes. "I need you to command the archers from here."

"But the archers are useless."

"The rain may let up."

"Then they will know enough to fire."

He sighed. "I want you up here, Deirdre."

She was silent long enough for him to realize she knew the truth, that he didn't intend to let her fight. "Oh, aye," she said bitterly, "while you're down there risking your neck, I'll be dancing upon the parapet, waiting for the sun to appear." She spat on the stones. "This is my castle, and I'll be damned if I'll let a Norman—"

"Jesu!" one of the archers cried. "'Tis the lord!"

Pagan followed the man's gaze along the west wall to the distant tower. Through the white haze of rising dust, he saw a figure crawling across the splintered floor at the top of the ruin. 'Twas Lord Gellir. "Bloody hell."

Beside him, Deirdre drew in a ragged gasp.

"Bloody *hell*," he repeated.

As he watched in dread, the lord crept closer and closer to the ledge, where the rock yet trickled away. Whatever drove him, Pagan knew he'd never reach the lord in time. The wall walk between them was damaged. The only passage to the tower was through the courtyard.

"Look!" Rauve shouted.

Another figure emerged upon the tower floor. At this distance, covered in mortar, bowed in fatigue, limping across the planks, he was barely recognizable. But Pagan knew his man like he knew his own scars. "Colin."

The parapets silenced as everyone watched, breathless with hope. Slowly, Colin advanced across the ruined chamber. He appeared to converse with the lord, for the old man turned and listened for a bit. But eventually the lord resumed his course, heading inexorably for the precipice, and Colin hesitated to follow.

"What is Colin doing?" Deirdre demanded in a whisper. "Why does he stop?"

"Their combined weight might collapse the tower."

"But . . . can he not . . . my father . . ."

Pagan shared Deirdre's frustration, as well as a heavy measure of guilt. He should have seen to the lord's safety himself before he faced the enemy.

Everyone watched as the lord inched toward the ledge. Colin's hands were cupped about his mouth now as he shouted over the storm, likely trying to convince the lord to come back, mayhap attempting to override the voices the haunted man heard in his mind.

For a moment, as the lord stopped at the outer rim of the precipice, Pagan thought he might have at last awakened to reason, that he would now retreat. But nay, the lord climbed to his feet there and held his arms high, as if beckoning lightning to strike and the heavens to claim him.

With the English already reloading the trebuchet, Colin could stand idle no longer. Casting aside caution, he dove forward, catching the lord about the ankles. But instead of tripping him, the excess weight caused the planks to slip, and the entire floor listed forward.

"Nay!" Deirdre screamed, the sound like a slash across Pagan's heart.

The lord slid over the edge, head first, saved from plummeting to the earth only by Colin's firm grasp upon his ankles. But Colin could not hold him long. A ledge of rock was all that braced him against descent, and that leverage slipped with every spray of pebbles that sifted loose.

"Stay here!" Pagan barked at Deirdre. He grabbed Sir Rauve by the front of his surcoat and hauled him aside, riveting him with an iron glare and biting out the words he didn't want Deirdre to hear. "No matter what happens, you hold this keep. Do not negotiate for hostages. Not me. Not Colin. Not Lord Gellir. Your loyalty is to the King."

Satisfied by Rauve's grim nod, he released him. Then he bolted down the stairs three at a time, banging his elbows on the narrow walls. He slipped once on the wet grass of the courtyard, but charged forward, sending up sprays of sod with each desperate stride. As he passed the armorer's shed, he snatched a coil of rope from the wall and slung it over his shoulder.

The west tower stairs were clogged with rubble. His lungs heaving, he hauled rock out of the way, clawing at stone and choking on dust, until he could clamber through the wreckage to the next floor, certain the trebuchet would fire at any moment. His fingers bleeding, he scrabbled at the mortar and grit, climbing higher and higher until he felt the welcome kiss of raindrops upon his head. He scrambled up the last few steps, surfacing upon the skewed, rain-slick planks.

Thank God, Colin was still there, grasping the lord with a grip as rigid and bloodless as the Reaper's.

"Hold on!" he shouted.

But in the next instant, a bolt like thunder pounded the earth, rattling the stones of the tower as if they were dice. The ground beneath him trembled. An ungodly shrieking of timber and rock echoed from the depths. And the world turned on its edge.

Deirdre screamed. Though the impact happened in an instant, the tragedy played out with torturous sloth in her mind's eye.

The trebuchet arm slowly shot forward, loosing its heavy burden. The chunk of rock tumbled gracefully through the air, obliterating the raindrops as easily as swatting gnats, arcing with dark purpose toward the curtain wall of Rivenloch. After an interminable flight, it found its target, kissing the gray stone, then sinking deep with a reverberant thud, opening another mortal wound in the tower at the second floor. A hollow, ominous silence followed. Then the already damaged tower lazily collapsed in a waterfall of rock and rubble and ruin.

Everything happened in a terrifying rush after that, and from Deirdre's perspective, the men looked like chess pieces flung by an angry child. Pagan, flattened by the impact, slid across the tilting planks, his fingers scrabbling for purchase. Momentum cast him over the edge. He was saved only by catching hold of a splintered beam protruding from the wreckage.

Colin was thrown hard onto his back, striking his head on a rock before he, too, slipped across the floor. When he finally came to rest, he lay silent, his body in an unnatural sprawl. One knee snagged by chance on a chunk of stonework, or he might have fallen to his death. If he wasn't dead already.

Meanwhile, in a macabre imitation of the sledding Deirdre used to do on snowy slopes, her father skidded down the steep side of the disintegrating tower, turning and twisting as he rode atop the shifting rocks.

God must have watched over him the way He did drunks and fools. At the end of his jarring ride, though the old man lay helpless atop the rubble at the base of the destroyed tower, he yet flailed with life.

Still, he was on the enemy side of the curtain wall. 'Twas only a matter of moments before the English would intercept him. And once they discovered what a valuable hostage they held, she'd lose all leverage.

She couldn't let that happen.

Snapping to attention, she shouted, "Archers! Watch my back! Rauve, take my command!"

With those orders, she fled down the stairs, scraping her heel on the bottom step, then hobbled across the courtyard toward the remains of the tower. Helena, having left her post on the eastern wall to investigate the deafening sound, met her halfway.

"What the Devil are those bastards using?" she asked, unsheathing as she trotted beside Deirdre. "Thor's hammer?" When she looked up and saw how little was left of the west tower, she skidded to a halt. "Ballocks," she said in awe.

"Come on!" Deirdre urged. "We have to save Father."

"Father? What—"

"Hurry!" Deirdre caught Hel's arm and pulled her along.

Though the second impact had demolished the flooring of the tower and collapsed a good portion of the exterior wall, by sheer luck, it had also exposed what remained of the stairs, allowing them access to the top. They scrambled heedlessly over the rubble, gouging their hands on the sharp rocks and coughing on mortar dust.

Helena gaped at the wreckage, incredulous. "Holy angel of . . . Was father . . . ? Is he . . . ?"

"He's unhurt," Deirdre called over her shoulder as they climbed. "Colin climbed the steps and managed to—"

"Colin? Colin was here?"

"Aye, but—"

"Bloody hell!"

Hel shoved past her then, as if demons snapped at her heels, ascending the winding stairs at breakneck speed. She burst through a pile of debris blocking the passageway and emerged first from the stairwell. Before Deirdre could shout a warning about the shifting floor, Helena gave a shrill cry, then hurtled forward to fall upon her knees beside Colin's unmoving form. Luckily, the planks held.

But Colin was not Deirdre's foremost concern. She frowned, eyeing the splintered beam protruding from the ledge that had saved Pagan's life. It still jutted from the rubble like the sturdy root of a tree, but no hand clasped it. Her heart pummeling at her ribs, she charged forward with no thought for her own safety, for once as impulsive as her sister.

She slipped on the slick planks, sliding down the sloping floor, and would have followed her father's course to the bottom of the tower, but for that same beam. She quickly thrust out her left arm to catch it, and a pang of agony tore through her shoulder as all of her weight wrenched against it. Somehow she managed to grapple her way back up to the ledge, and once there, breathless with exertion, she peered down over the edge, clutching her damaged arm.

Already the sun was sinking below the horizon, behind the thickening clouds, for 'twas becoming difficult to see in the fading light. But she discerned that to one side below her, secured around the stone frame of what had been an arrow slit, a rope hung taut with its burden.

Pagan.

He'd lowered himself to the ground. She watched with halted breath as he rushed over to her father, who appeared groggy and battered, but none the worse for his dramatic landslide. A wave of relief dizzied her. Bless Pagan's brave heart, he was rescuing her father.

Not far away, however, she could see the dim figures of the enemy approaching at a cautious lope. Rivenloch's walls were still not easily scalable, so 'twas not likely their intent to make a full-scale attack upon the castle yet. But the English surely recognized from Pagan's heroic maneuvers that the man who'd fallen from the tower might be a valuable hostage.

"They're coming!" she shouted down to him.

He looked up at her and nodded. Then, hauling the lord up with rough haste, he secured the rope around the old man's waist. "Can you pull him up?"

She wasn't certain. She scrambled down to where the rope was secured, but there was little leverage there. She was strong, aye, but her father was no small man, and her injured shoulder throbbed with pain. "Helena! Help!"

Hel came to the edge almost at once. She seemed distraught, her cheek wet with more than rain. But she immediately assessed the situation, glancing at Pagan, the advancing army, and the gap closing between them. Slithering down to where Deirdre waited, she lent her hands to the task. Together they hauled their father up, straining against the frame, their palms slipping on the wet rope.

Meanwhile, Rivenloch arrows arced across the rain-peppered air toward the approaching enemy, felling a few. But their numbers were too great, and the day was growing too dim for accuracy. By the time she and Helena deposited the lord safely atop the wall and loosed the rope from around him, a dozen English knights had reached the base of the outer tower.

Deirdre stared down in despair. The rope she'd planned to toss back down to Pagan coiled uselessly at her feet. She was too late. The enemy had already captured him.

"Hold your fire!" she screamed to her archers, praying they could hear her. "Hold your fire!"

Pagan didn't fight his captors. He was a valiant soul, but he was wise enough to know when he was outnumbered. Deirdre felt tears of frustration well in her eyes, watching in helpless horror as they hauled him roughly to his feet.

'Twas not fair, she thought. 'Twas a travesty of justice. She wiped angrily at her tears. Curse Lucifer! She'd not allow it. Not when Pagan had made such a noble sacrifice, saving her father at the peril of his own body.

"Nay!" she cried. "Let him go, you bastards!"

He pulled back once then, wrenching his head around to answer her. "Do not surrender the keep, no matter what! One man is a small sacrifice. Do not let Rivenloch fa—"

His words were cut off as a knight cuffed him into silence and he slumped forward. She flinched, feeling the blow as if it bruised her own body. Then they dragged him, senseless and vulnerable, away from Rivenloch, into the shadowy twilight and the camp of the enemy.

"Pagan!"

Her cry was lost to the wind, buried beneath the thunder cracking the sky. She longed to rage like the storm, scream at the heavens, rain vile insults upon the enemy, curse the English and the Devil and God Himself for such an injustice. But 'twould do no good. No words could express such grievous fury. And so she hung her head, inconsolable. Tears rolled unabashedly down her cheeks, dropping onto the ruins below. She clenched her hands together so tightly that the crest from Pagan's ring left its mark upon her palm.

Never had she experienced such impotence. Never had she known such despair. Never had she imagined she could be brought to such depths of sorrow over a Norman.

Pagan was awakened by a sharp kick to the ribs. He jerked reflexively, but could move little, for his arms and legs were bound. Blinking, he tried to orient himself. He lay upon a damp carpet within a striped pavilion. Shadowy tongues of candlelight licked at the sides of the tent. Night had fallen.

'Twas good. The English would not attempt to storm Rivenloch by night, which would give his men time to better prepare for her defense.

Surrounding him, mangy brutes, wet and ragged and reeking from too many days on the road, crouched and narrowed their eyes, as if they studied some strange new beast.

"Pagan," someone grunted.

Pagan raised his eyes. This must be one of the rogue English lords. The black-bearded man's gap-toothed grin looked like the hideous grimace of a gargoyle.

"That's what the Warrior Maid called ye," the man said smugly. "Not too many by that name. I'm thinkin' ye're Cameliard."

The rest of the savages eagerly drew close, like men playing at dice, wagering on his response.

"Never heard of him," Pagan said.

"Is that so?" a second man asked, stroking the rust-colored stubble of his jaw. "Then I suppose ye're just some hapless wretch dropped down to retrieve the old sot who fell from the tower?"

"That's right."

The first man's eyes narrowed to reptilian slits, and he

kicked Pagan again, this time in the belly. Pagan groaned in pain.

"Ye're lyin'," he sneered. He bent close then, close enough that Pagan could smell the stench of his unwashed body and his rotting teeth. "Ye're him, all right. And ye've been discourteous, puttin' a coil in our plans like this."

No doubt he *had* ruined their plans, Pagan thought. The Englishman had probably assumed the castle was defended by three Scots maids and a handful of feeble knights.

"But mind ye . . ." A third man rolled raven black eyes at him. "'Tis only a *bit* of a coil. Forsooth, I wager ye might be worth ransomin'."

"You're wasting your time," Pagan muttered. "My men do not barter with English swine."

The first man snagged Pagan by the throat. "If not yer men," he said slyly, "then mayhap yer mistress. The way that lusty Scots whore was squallin' after—"

Violent rage erupted in Pagan. He spat in the man's leering face.

Revenge was swift as the English guards came to their lord's defense. Fists and boots pummeled him from all sides. Again and again the soldiers pounded at him until his blood flecked their hands and his body throbbed with bruises.

"Enough!" the man finally shouted.

Pagan wheezed through battered ribs. The sweat of nausea beaded his brow. He'd already conceded to forfeit his life, if need be, for the security of Rivenloch. Not only was it his duty as a soldier of the King, but his desire as Deirdre's husband. He'd risked his life to save her father, because he couldn't bear to see her hurt. He'd realized the moment he scaled down the tower wall that the odds were against him.

But knowing how much Deirdre doted upon the lord, knowing that she'd surrender Rivenloch before she'd let them torture her father, Pagan made what he considered a reasonable sacrifice. 'Twould be far easier for Deirdre to turn a blind eye to the sufferings of her new husband than those of her beloved father.

And it appeared those sufferings would resume on the morrow.

The English were no fools. While they were capable of demolishing the castle with the trebuchet, 'twould not be wise, for once they won Rivenloch, they'd need to guard their prize in turn against other invaders. Damaging the castle walls would only weaken their own capacity for defense. The trebuchet, for all its effectiveness, was essentially a double-edged sword.

The marauders had clearly thought Rivenloch an easy conquest, a remote, unguarded castle governed by a feeble lord, and so they'd not planned much beyond frightening the Scots into submission. But now that they saw 'twould not be so, 'twas more prudent to seize the castle by cunning or negotiation.

The English imagined they had a valuable hostage in Pagan. They were wrong, of course. Pagan's men had been trained to follow his orders strictly. He'd commanded Rauve to hold Rivenloch, no matter what happened. Pagan had faith he would do so.

"But there *has* to be something we can do!" Deirdre snapped at Sir Rauve, who sniffed and scowled darkly into his ale.

The rest of the knights assembled in the great hall

grew quiet at their heated exchange. Lord Gellir, only vaguely aware of what transpired, sat beside the fire with Lucy and a warm cup of mulled wine. Miriel comforted a pair of sniffling children in a corner of the keep. But Helena, chewing her nails over Colin, who lay unconscious near the hearth on a makeshift bed of straw, listened intently.

Deirdre smoldered with barely contained rage. "He's your captain. You can't just let him—" Her throat closed on the word.

But to her amazement, as she scanned the room, looking into the faces of Pagan's men, she saw the same stubborn refusal in all their averted eyes.

With a cry of fury, she knocked the cup from Rauve's hand, spattering wine across the floor. The dark liquid seeped into the rushes like spilled blood.

Without a word, he straightened to his full height, towering over her. The rest of the Knights of Cameliard followed suit. Tension bristled in the air.

Hel shot suddenly to her feet. "What is wrong with you Normans? Are you a bunch of sniveling cowards, afraid of the dark?"

A muscle in Rauve's cheek twitched, and Deirdre saw his hand tighten on the pommel of his sword.

"Pah! The Scots are no cowards," she gloated, elbowing her way through the knights of Rivenloch, thumping some of them on the chest, jostling the shoulders of others. "We'll take on the English, won't we, lads? Without the help of these miserable, cowering—"

"You will not leave this keep." Rauve's voice was as grim as his face.

Hel's jaw dropped.

Deirdre shoved the insolent knight in the chest. "And you will not issue orders in my castle."

Though his gaze darkened, he made no move to fight back. "They are not my orders, my lady. They are Pagan's."

"What?"

"What?" Hel echoed.

"Before he left to rescue your father, he charged me to hold Rivenloch at all costs."

Deirdre narrowed her eyes. "That was before they took him hostage."

"He knew they might. 'Tis why he gave me distinct orders."

"What orders?"

"Orders not to negotiate."

"Who said anything about negotiating?" Hel chimed in. "I say we go out there and fight the bloody bastards. Right, lads?" She lifted her arms, raising a cheer of accord from the Rivenloch knights.

"Nay!" Rauve bellowed. "The first man to step out the front gates will be shot by Cameliard archers for treason."

Helena's eyes widened.

The Norman knights moved carefully away from the Rivenloch men then, creating a clear separation, their hands hovering over their weapons. The Scots froze, their eyes shifting about warily. The air grew as taut as a drawn bow.

"You can't be serious," Deirdre whispered.

Rauve's lips thinned, and Deirdre saw at once that Pagan's man was just as displeased with his orders as she was. But he was a loyal soldier, and he'd given his oath to Pagan.

"'Tis at the King's behest that we hold Rivenloch. That directive outweighs the life of any one man."

He choked over the last words, and Deirdre suddenly realized she'd judged Rauve too harshly. He, too, probably longed for any excuse to storm from the castle, lop off a dozen English heads, and bring his captain back alive, his royal allegiance be damned.

"If we take them unawares," Deirdre insisted in desperation, "catch them with their trews down . . ."

Rauve shook his head. "They've posted guards around the castle wall."

"We could take them," Helena muttered, pouting. "I know we could."

Helena's boast was groundless, of course. They were outnumbered three to one, and that was only if every fighter available left the keep unguarded to attack in full force, which was irresponsible. Besides, the English had the trebuchet.

Deirdre resisted the urge to scream in frustration. More now than ever, Pagan needed her cool head. And for all their sake, her men needed her to ally with the Normans before a fight broke out here in the great hall. "What would Pagan expect us to do?"

Rauve spit into the rushes. "At daybreak, they'll demand his ransom."

Deirdre's throat thickened with pain. Her eyes brimmed with tears of despair, but she refused to shed them. "And?"

"And we'll refuse."

"Splendid!" Helena crossed her arms impatiently over her breasts. "And they'll just load up that bloody giant sling and smash Rivenloch to bits."

"They're more likely to lay siege," Rauve said, "try to

starve us out." Then he added bitterly, "They won't want to damage their prize."

Deirdre's thoughts raced ahead. If the English intended to lay siege, they wouldn't hesitate to use Pagan as leverage, hoping to hasten Rivenloch's surrender. They might do anything—break every bone in his body, cut off his fingers, string him up as carrion for the crows. She swayed as a wave of nausea enveloped her.

Through a dizzying haze, she heard Helena grumbling, "I still say we should storm their camp," then Rauve replying, "No one leaves. Defy Sir Pagan's orders and the orders of the King, and I'll have no choice but to take action against you."

At Helena's snort of contempt, the knights began to disperse, making ready for a restless night. But Deirdre, lost in thought, remained where she stood.

As the men milled about, Miriel came up beside her, bending down to retrieve Rauve's cup. She murmured timidly, "What if . . . if there was another way?"

Deirdre sighed. Miriel, of course, disapproved of anything that involved fighting. She probably hoped they could somehow befriend the English and live happily ever after, sharing the castle. But Deirdre knew better.

"Are the women and children safe?" she asked, scanning the great hall, where trestle tables were being propped on their sides to serve as makeshift bulwarks in the event the enemy reached the keep.

Miriel tugged insistently at her sleeve. "Listen, Deirdre."

Deirdre was perhaps less tolerant than she should have been. "Miriel, I don't have time for this." She wiped a shaking hand across her brow. "I know how you feel about warfare, but—"

"Nay! You don't understand."

"Sometimes," she choked out, "we have to make sacrifices that we—"

"Aye! But sometimes we *don't* have to. If you would just—"

"What?" Deirdre snapped, losing patience, wheeling on her. "What is it, damn you? I told you, I don't have—"

In an uncharacteristic show of mettle, diminutive Miriel reached up to seize Deirdre's jaw, using her fingers and thumb like a vise, riveting her with an unflinching stare. Deirdre was shocked into silence. "Look, you swell-headed, overgrown tyrant of a sister," she bit out with a boldness Deirdre had never heard in her before. "I have something to show you."

Chapter 27

WHEN THE HOUR FOR ACTION CAME, the keep was dark and silent but for the snores of Pagan's knights, who were accustomed to grabbing sleep when and where they could. As for Deirdre, she hadn't slept a wink.

Miriel had presented her an astounding alternative, and she planned to take it. If all went well, by dawn tomorrow, the English would awake to find their hostage gone.

Only she and Miriel knew of the daring plan, for 'twas a task for stealth, not force. 'Twas also counter to Pagan's orders. Her lips curved into a grim smile. Thank God she had no qualms about disobeying Pagan's orders.

Miriel met her at her chamber door with a rushlight. "Are you sure you want to do this alone?"

Deirdre nodded. Then she frowned. "Where is Sung Li?" She hadn't seen the old woman all day.

"She left when the English first arrived."

"Left?"

"To fetch Lachanburn."

"What?" Miriel might just as well have said she'd gone to visit the moon. "Why would she—"

"She said 'twas her destiny," Miriel interrupted. "Are you ready?"

"Aye." Deirdre wanted to know more about Sung Li's self-imposed mission, but she knew better than to risk Miriel's newfound temper when so much was at stake.

"Then follow me."

Deirdre trailed Miriel along the hallway and down the stairs, into a storeroom deep beneath the castle. Deirdre's brows lifted as the rushlight illuminated the room. 'Twas filled with neatly organized casks of ale, wheels of cheese, sacks of grain, smoked meats, and jars of spices, as well as a small desk with a three-legged stool and an accounting ledger. Deirdre hadn't come to this room, which was Miriel's domain, in years. But now she had an appreciation for the meticulous care with which her little sister managed the supplies.

What Miriel showed her next added a deeper dimension to that appreciation, making her regard her sister with new respect.

At the back of the storeroom was a heavy oak chest, which Miriel slid away from the wall with Deirdre's help. And behind that chest was a small square hole at the base of the wall through which Deirdre felt a cool draft.

"Sweet Mary," Deirdre breathed. "And where does it lead?"

"Once you're on the other side of the wall, there's a tunnel tall enough to crouch in. It curves slightly to the left and continues for a hundred yards or more, then emerges in the wood, within the stump of a dead tree. It should bring you within two hundred yards of the pavilions."

Deirdre nodded.

"Listen." Miriel gripped her shoulder with surprising strength. "If you don't return in an hour, I'll send the knights of Rivenloch through the passage after you."

She shook her head. "'Tis too great a risk. If I don't return . . ."

She left the sentence unfinished, ignoring Miriel's frown, and checked her weapons again. A dagger was slipped into each boot, and her new sword of Toledo steel hung against her thigh. *Amor vincit omnia*, the blade read, *love conquers all*. She hoped to God 'twas true.

But Miriel handed her another weapon, a star-shaped disk of steel from her collection. "'Tis for throwing," she said. "Aim for the throat."

Deirdre looked one last time at Miriel, who was full of surprises tonight. A dozen questions flitted through her brain, but Deirdre had no time to ask them. Besides, part of Deirdre's barter with Miriel for access to the secret passage had been that she not question Miriel further about it. She tucked the star into her hauberk, then clasped Miriel's forearm. "I'll be back for breakfast."

Miriel gave her a rueful smile, the smile of someone who'd just given away the key to Pandora's chest. Then Deirdre ducked into the passageway.

When she emerged from the rotting tree trunk near the edge of the wood, the rain had stopped, and stars pricked the cloudless night like tiny moth holes in a black cloak. The scent of moss and mushrooms and leaf fall hung heavily in the damp air, tainted by the acrid stench of English fires, banked and smoldering along the edge of the forest.

She'd seen the pavilion where they'd dragged Pagan. She only hoped he hadn't been moved. Stealing silently through the wood, she approached the striped tent from the rear, staying close to the ground. She'd have to cut through one of the serge sides to gain entrance, and she'd have to guess at the best place so as to not disturb the guards.

Finally choosing a spot, she slipped the point of her dagger into the heavy fabric, wincing at the rasp it made as she slowly dragged the blade down the length of the serge stripe. When the slit was long enough, she drew in a déep breath and carefully pulled back the edges.

She couldn't have made a worse choice. A large candle in a tall stand illuminated the pavilion, and by its light, Deirdre spied Pagan, slumped against the furthest wall. For an instant, she was paralyzed by the sight of him, for though he was wide awake and alert, he was gagged, his cheek was caked with blood, and one of his eyes was swollen nearly shut. Worse, as he stared at her, his face darkened with burning fury, and for a moment, she wondered if *he* would kill her before the English could.

From the corner of her eye, she glimpsed movement, a guard waiting beyond the gash she'd just cut, leering at her like a drooling wolf ready to feast on her flesh.

Mayhap if Deirdre had had a few more feminine wiles in her arsenal, she'd have been able to convince him she'd come for a tussle in the hay. But her first instinct was always to fight. She didn't hesitate, switching her dagger to her left hand and thrusting through the slit to smash the hilt into the man's face, breaking his nose and leaving him squirming in pain on the ground.

But his mewling awakened the rest of the denizens of the tent, and she barely had time to squeeze through the breach and draw her sword before she faced at least a dozen savage foes.

"What have we here?" one of them asked.

Another chortled. "Oho, it's the Rivenloch wench."

The first clutched suggestively at the front of his trews. "Did ye come for a bit o' English blade then?"

Pagan jerked his head violently at her, commanding she retreat. But she stood firm, shaking her head nay, and blowing out a focused stream of air to steady her nerves for the fight ahead.

Pagan scowled pointedly at her, wiggling his fingers against his bonds, indicating she should cut him free first. But already the knights advanced on her like a pack of wolves. Instead, she reversed her dagger and fired it in his direction. It landed a good yard from him, and she silently cursed her injured left arm's faulty aim. Nonetheless, he immediately began to edge toward the weapon, straining to reach it before someone else did.

Deirdre swept her sword in a swift, wide arc before her, leaving no question as to her intent, giving the advancing knights pause and dimming their lewd smiles. She slashed left, then right, and the men leaped back, their laughter more nervous than amused.

She glanced toward Pagan. His bound hands were still several inches from the dagger. Frustration seemed to boil off of him in waves.

She made two more quick slices through the air, nicking one man's hand. Now the men's grins vanished altogether, and a few of them drew knives. She had to delay them, long enough for Pagan to cut himself free. But how?

Hel would have used her sharp tongue. By taunting her foes, she oft managed to distract them enough to seize the advantage. 'Twas a perilous gamble. But 'twas a perilous situation.

Deirdre tossed her head in imitation of her sister. "What are you afraid of?" she goaded the men. "Come on! Scots *bairns* brawl with more courage."

The ruse worked. Two of the guards, angered by her insult, came at her ill-prepared and suffered wounds to their sword arms because of it.

"Is that all you have?" she sneered.

Another man swung his dagger in a wide arc at her belly, and she shrunk back as the blade whistled past. Catching him off balance, she shoved him into a pair of his companions, bowling them over.

Inevitably, the knights discovered the merits of attacking all at once. When they charged, Deirdre drew the second dagger from her boot. Her sword in one hand, the dagger in the other, she sliced left and right, feinting and lunging, blocking what blows she could, doling out as many injuries as possible.

"Pah! 'Tis child's play!" she crowed.

She sunk her dagger into a man's thigh, and he screamed, then limped away, unfortunately taking the weapon with him. Brandishing her sword in both hands, she managed to distance her attackers momentarily, but could gain no ground. Her advantage was slipping fast as more soldiers took up arms.

She hazarded one last hopeful glance at Pagan. His fingers, strained to the limit, were now a mere inch from the dagger. But a guard, following her gaze, saw what he intended and dove for the weapon himself.

God's blood! If she hadn't lost her second dagger . . .

Suddenly she remembered the throwing star tucked into her hauberk.

She'd never used such a thing before. She didn't even know how to use it properly.

The guard's fingers closed around her dagger. 'Twas no time for misgivings.

She surreptitiously slipped a hand inside her hauberk, grasped the star between her thumb and fingers, and with a subtle flick of her wrist propelled it across the pavilion.

God must have guided her hand. Just as the guard raised his prize in triumph, the star lodged in his throat, widening his eyes and rendering him incapable of screaming. He collapsed silently forward onto Pagan's lap.

Deirdre cried out to distract the others. "Ha, you half-witted sluggards!" She swept her sword low, forcing the guards to dance back out of the way.

From the corner of her eye, she saw Pagan pull the bloody star free and push its victim off his lap. As she jabbed randomly forward at the swarming English, he began using the weapon's finely honed edge to cut through his bonds.

But in the next moment, a brazen guard swatted her blade aside and plunged forward with his sword. She scarcely managed to recoil in time, but as she leaped back, her foot tangled in a heap of blankets, and she fell hard on her hindquarters against the wall of the pavilion.

She managed to hang on to her sword, but when she whipped it up to defend herself, a half dozen blades already threatened her throat.

"Drop it," her attacker said.

Cursing silently, she flattened her eyes to cold, hard slits and slowly lowered her weapon.

"That's it," he purred, "nice and slow."

Even before her blade met the ground, one of the guards wrenched it from her grip. As soon as she was disarmed, the rest of the men began to swagger with renewed arrogance.

"Not so high-and-mighty now, are ye?"

"Has the kitten lost her claws?"

"Now the giglet's right where she belongs."

The leader prodded her with the point of his weapon, lascivious heat in his eyes. "Be a good lass and lie back, and mayhap I won't run you through. At least not with my sword."

The others snickered.

She met his fire with ice. She longed to spit in his face. But if she pretended to be docile, stalled him long enough, mayhap Pagan could get loose. She hoped so, for 'twould not be long until the whole camp was roused. And then they wouldn't have a prayer.

"Be still," the leader said, caressing her throat with the tip of his sword, forcing her back upon her elbows, "and maybe I'll let you live."

'Twas almost impossible to resist checking on Pagan's progress, but she dared not divert the men's attention.

"That's it, wench," he crooned, tossing aside his sword. "You be nice to me, and I'll be nice to you."

Mistaking her silence for assent, the guards lowered their weapons and began interjecting their own ribald advice.

Taking even, measured breaths and making fists of her hands, Deirdre watched as the man untied his trews and jerked them down, spurring whistles of glee from the others.

Then, beyond the man's shoulder, rising slowly like a deadly thundercloud, Deirdre glimpsed a most welcome figure. Pagan. She clenched her jaw and tensed her muscles to spring.

The moment her attacker came into range, she drew back her leg, then catapulted it forward as forcefully as any trebuchet, kicking him hard between the legs. Before he could sink in pain, Pagan lunged forward with Deirdre's dagger. He wrenched the man around to pierce his heart, putting him instantly out of his misery.

"Run!" Pagan bellowed at her.

He had to be jesting. She wasn't about to desert him. In the ensuing pandemonium, she scrambled for her sword, and Pagan seized the dead man's blade. Back to back, they rose to confront the remaining knights.

"I left orders," he muttered angrily. "You were to stay in the keep."

She smiled grimly. "No one gives me orders."

The guards surrounded them, wolves closing in for the kill.

"You shouldn't have come," he hissed.

"You're welcome."

There were still ten Englishmen to subdue, and eight

of them were only lightly injured. 'Twas a challenge, but possible, now that Pagan was able to help.

But just as she drew breath to begin the desperate fight, the air outside the pavilion exploded with roars.

"Shite," she hissed.

The rest of the English had been alerted. Her heart sank. They were doomed.

Chapter 28

THE SIDES OF THE PAVILION sagged inward as multiple steel blades sliced through the serge. The men wielding the swords followed, tearing their way through the resulting gaps. But to Deirdre's amazement, the invaders were not more English soldiers. They were her own men.

Miriel had disobeyed her command and sent the knights of Rivenloch.

Chaos erupted at once. The candle stand was knocked over in the melee, and flame began lapping hungrily at the damp shreds of the pavilion. At Pagan's back, Deirdre fought relentlessly, but soon smoke and shadows obscured her vision as the din of clashing steel and screams rose around her. 'Twas a reckless fight, a hopeless fight, for though the Scots might dispatch the guards in the immediate quarters, their arrival would rouse the entire camp. Soon a horde of Englishmen would descend upon them.

But Deirdre had never shied away from a fight. She'd be damned if she'd do so now. With her dying breath she'd defend those whom she loved. And, God help her, she loved Pagan.

So she battled as if the fate of her soul depended upon it, pairing with her husband to rout the soldiers within the pavilion, then following him out into the night to take on as many as she could of the English army.

The Rivenloch knights set fire to the rest of the pavilions, one by one, and the enemy spilled out of their blazing tents like rats fleeing a flood. But like rats, there seemed to be an endless supply of them.

"You know we cannot win," Pagan muttered, dispatching an attacker with his dagger.

"I know." Deirdre dodged a sword slash.

"You should have let me die," Pagan said, clubbing someone in the face with the butt of his sword.

"Never." She swallowed the lump rising in her throat. "I . . . I love you too much."

"If you love me," he snarled, hurling a man into the bushes, "then get out of here. Run. Flee. Before they find you."

"I won't do that." She punched a soldier in the nose, then shook her bruised knuckles.

"Rivenloch will fall."

"Not without a fight, it won't."

She straightened to her full height, blew out a forceful breath, and stood fast—where she knew she belonged now—shoulder to shoulder with her beloved husband. She would fight beside him until she had no more strength to raise her blade.

Until she could no longer draw breath.

Until her lovesick heart ceased beating.

And when the time came for her to die, she would do

so bravely, defending the man she loved, knowing she'd done everything in her power to save him.

From high atop Rivenloch's battlements, Sir Rauve d'Honore squinted into the darkness. Swords clanged in the enemy camp, and the distant screams and shouts of men suddenly punctured the heavy silence. "What the Devil . . .?"

"See?" Shivering on the parapet beside him, Miriel noted with satisfaction that the Rivenloch knights had begun to sow turmoil in the English camp, setting fire to their tents and wreaking general havoc. "'Tis the men of Rivenloch. *Now* will you send reinforcements?"

But Rauve was confounded by the fact that the Scots had somehow slipped beneath his guard. "Impossible! The gates are closed, and I have men posted all along the wall. How could they have—"

She stamped her foot. "Never mind! We have to hurry." She hoped Sung Li was right, that Lachanburn and his men would arrive anon. But mostly she hoped she could convince the stubborn giant beside her to lend a hand. Loyalty was a fine quality. Blind loyalty was not. She tugged on his hauberk sleeve. "Pagan is there. Deirdre is there."

Rauve's eyes narrowed as he stared sternly toward the hillside. "Nay. I have my orders." But his voice was colored by frustration as he added, "They were fools to disobey. Fools." And while his brow was furrowed in bullheaded refusal, his jaw worked in indecision. 'Twas obvious he'd be glad of almost any excuse to join the battle.

Miriel chewed thoughtfully at her lip. As Sung Li always said, there was more than one way to move a mountain.

There was no time for subtlety. Taking a deep breath, she suddenly burst into tears.

Sir Rauve almost jumped out of his armor.

She let out a loud, mournful wail, and several of the archers along the wall walk turned to gape.

"Shh!" he bid her, casting an uneasy glance toward the archers. "Hush, my lady."

"How could you?" she wailed, burying her face against his shoulder and pounding ineffectually at his chest. "How *could* you?"

Disconcerted by her outburst, he awkwardly patted her back. "Ah, prithee don't cry, my lady."

"How could you leave my sister to die?"

She felt his shoulders sink. "But 'tis not my fault," he said bleakly. "I follow my captain's orders. Your sister . . . your sister should have heeded them as well."

Miriel froze, intrigued by something he said. "Wait. Your *captain's* orders?"

"Aye."

She sniffled. "But Pagan is not lord here. My *father* is lord. *He* commands Rivenloch's army."

Rauve cleared his throat. "Well, aye, but . . ." He was obviously uncomfortable discussing her father's feeble state of mind.

"*And* the Knights of Cameliard."

"I . . . suppose."

"And if he were . . ." she said, angling her head to look pointedly up at him, her eyes conspicuously dry, "awake . . ."

Rauve returned her gaze. A spark of understanding passed between them, and he cursed under his breath as he realized her ploy. He shook his head in self-mockery. "What would he do, your father . . . *if* he were awake?"

Mischief glittered in her eyes. There was no time to waste. She caught his hand and tugged him toward the stairwell. "I'm certain he would command the Knights of Cameliard to lend a hand."

Deirdre knocked another enemy blade away from Pagan's head. She could see his wounds exhausted him. Her own strength flagged as she battled foe after foe and suffered untold cuts and bruises.

"Away!" she yelled, lashing out at one of the half dozen knights surrounding them.

Suddenly, as if by magic, two of her attackers were yanked backward, and she wheeled to find Sir Rauve, grinning malevolently, his battleaxe in one hand and a squirming English knight in the other.

"Rauve, you son of a . . ." Pagan growled in disapproval, his words punctuated by hacks of his sword. "Does . . . no one . . . heed my . . . commands?" His opponent finally slipped on the grass, and Pagan bested him.

Rauve used his wriggling captive to block a charging attacker. The two collided with a dull thud, slumping to the ground. "We came at Lord Gellir's comman—will."

If Deirdre detected something evasive in Rauve's manner, she held her tongue. All that mattered was that her knights no longer battled alone. With reinforcements, their hopes would be restored, and they'd fight with new determination.

"For Rivenloch!" she cried.

"For Rivenloch!" Rauve replied.

"For God's sake," Pagan grumbled, "I hope you left *someone* guarding the keep."

"Oh, aye." Rauve caught an attacker square in the nose with his elbow. "Colin. And Helena."

Deirdre would have smiled at that, but she was preoccupied, ducking under an English blade.

Forsooth, so focused was she upon fending off the advance of a soldier wielding a particularly lethal mace, she never noticed the column of rushlights cresting the northern hills. 'Twas not until she disarmed her attacker, clubbing him with his own weapon, that she heard the loud hue and cry rising from the slope above the encampment.

She narrowed her eyes at the parade of torchbearers.

"God's wounds!" Pagan spat in weary aggravation. "More English?"

Deirdre's heart wavered uncertainly as she studied the procession between blows. Then she smiled in recognition. "Nay."

'Twas the Lachanburn clan, armed to the teeth. And strutting proudly at their fore, as if she herself commanded the army, was Sung Li.

"More allies," Deirdre told him, watching the advancing Scots in wonder.

Rivenloch had always had an uneasy alliance with Lachanburn. For years, they had stolen each other's cattle and swived one another's women, yet when winters were fierce, they'd always shared their hearth if a clansman was caught in the storm. Still, she'd never expected *this*.

Chiefly cow herders, the Lachanburns were crude fighters at best, but there were dozens of the red-haired lads. With naught to do but raid cattle, the prospect of waging a real war against the English must have proved too tempting. And Sung Li, bless her imperious nature, had somehow managed to wrench them from their beds to take part. Now the battle would be more fairly fought.

Their faith renewed, the knights of Rivenloch warred even more valiantly. Injuries were suffered, but by God's grace and thanks to Pagan's elite warriors, few casualties. Over the next crucial moments of battle, 'twas mostly English blood now that spilled and stained the soil of Rivenloch.

After routing a pair of enemy men-at-arms, Deirdre stopped to catch her breath, surveying the progress of the fighting around her. She wiped her brow with the back of her bloody arm and happened to glance toward the giant trebuchet, silhouetted against the night sky. Like a soundly sleeping dragon, it had lay silent while the war waged all around. But now it suddenly roused, lifting its head.

Her fingers tensed about her sword.

"Nay," she breathed in horror, belatedly noticing the English soldiers swarming about the machine. "Nay."

They'd decided to damage their prize after all.

Time seemed to grind to a snail's pace as she swung her head toward Rivenloch. With so many knights outside the keep, battling the enemy, the castle was practically defenseless. Only Colin, Helena, and a handful of knights and archers remained within the walls. And huddled in the keep, trusting to their protection, were Lord Gellir, Miriel, and the women and children of Rivenloch.

"Nay!" she bellowed. But her voice was lost in the clamor of war.

Desperate, she started toward the great beast. As if

she moved in a dream, every step felt like she slogged through honey.

Above her on the hill, four Englishmen hefted a great slab of rock from the sward. A missile for the trebuchet.

She'd never make it in time. Her lungs burned as she struggled up the slope, fighting her way through the masses of battling soldiers.

The enemy began to lug the slab toward the sling.

Bloody hell! The trebuchet was fifty yards away. It might as well have been a mile.

Still she persevered, barreling forward, cursing her leaden feet and the muddy ground and the relentless distance.

And then the unthinkable . . .

She slipped on a mossy stone. With a sharp cry, she stumbled to the ground, landing hard on her hands and knees, wrenching anew her injured shoulder. Tears of frustration welled in her eyes as she watched the horrifying spectacle continuing above her.

They dropped the slab of rock into the sling.

'Twas too late. Rivenloch was lost.

But then, whether 'twas a trick of her watering eyes or the shifting firelight, she thought she saw the shadow of something clambering up the side of the wooden structure.

She blinked. 'Twas not possible. No one could cling to a vertical wall that way.

But when she narrowed her gaze, she saw what looked like a human, moving like an acrobat over the crossbars of the trebuchet, a slight figure clad all in black.

The Shadow.

Nay, it couldn't be. She wiped her blurry eyes with

the heels of her hands. By the time she returned her gaze to the trebuchet, the figure had disappeared. But where The Shadow had passed shone a curious point of light, and as she watched, it began to spark like a steel sword on a grinding wheel.

In the midst of the killing, over the shouts and screams of attacker and victim, Pagan heard Deirdre's faint cry of dismay.

His heart seized.

Forcing his current opponent away with a violent shove, he whipped his head around, seeking her.

There she was—thank God, alive—struggling up the hill towards . . .

The trebuchet.

Bloody hell.

'Twas loaded and ready to fire.

While his knights had been busy fighting hand to hand, the damned English had armed their monster.

Whatever Deirdre intended, she would be too late. Even as he watched her, she lost her footing, slipping on the slope and going down hard.

He bit out a foul oath and bolted up the hill, but as he drew near, his gaze caught on a curious flame near the top of the trebuchet. By its light, he spied a dark creature scrambling over the structure. As he watched, perplexed, all at once the figure made a daring leap, appearing to vanish into the night.

Then the flame began to spark.

And Pagan knew.

"God's blood!"

He lunged forward with renewed purpose.

The sky flashed suddenly white, as if the sun had

burst through night's cloak, and he dove atop Deirdre, shielding her with his body.

A deafening explosion rocked the earth, flattening them to the ground. He covered his head, certain the world had been cleaved asunder. Gasps and shouts of astonishment rose around him as splinters of the trebuchet pierced the night and trickled down like demon rain.

"Ballocks!" Deirdre squirmed impatiently beneath him for a better view. "What was that?"

"That," he told her in breathless disbelief, "was salvation."

"Holy . . ." She was left speechless, gazing at the grim remains of the beast.

He eased some of his weight off of her. "Bloody Saints, are you all right?"

"Aye." She twisted onto her back so she could look up at him. "You?"

Gazing down at his precious warrior maid, he was filled with warring emotions. He'd never felt more grateful to be alive. And he'd never been more furious at her disobedience. He'd never experienced such sweet relief. Nor such burning rage. He was bloody and battered, his body a battlefield of cuts that would sting and bruises that would ache once the skirmish was over, but just looking into Deirdre's adoring eyes seemed to heal his hurts and melt his anger. "I'll mend."

"Do we have a chance now?"

He scanned the crowd of cheering knights further down the slope. "I think we may."

"Then let's finish this."

Forsooth, Pagan didn't want to move. He'd much prefer lying atop his beautiful wife, holding her safe in his arms till dawn. But she was right. They had to make an end to the battle. Anon the English would regroup and launch another attack. The war was not yet over.

But if obliterating their trebuchet didn't completely destroy the morale of the English, the thundering herd of red-haired savages charging over the hill like wild cattle sealed their fate. Even before the stars began to wink out in deference to the impending dawn, the enemy, their lords slain, exhausted and finally outnumbered, recovered their dead and fled.

As the last panicked English soldier retreated over the hill to the sound of Norman taunts and rattling Scots blades, Pagan sheathed his sword, grabbed his wife, and gave her a deep kiss of sweet victory they would remember for the rest of their lives.

Triumphant cheers echoed along the starlit hills and glens of Rivenloch as Helena threw the castle gates wide in welcome. Forsooth, the keep had never known a gathering of such magnitude. The great hall swarmed with the clan of Lachanburn, the Knights of Cameliard, and the crofters and craftsmen and maidservants of Rivenloch. Ale flowed freely, and while winsome lasses tenderly cared for their wounded heroes, tales and exaggerations of tales already sprang from the seeds that would turn them into legends.

Already, men speculated upon the trebuchet's destruction. Some said a freak bolt of lightning, hurled by God's avenging hand, had struck down the machine. Some claimed 'twas the work of the Devil.

Still, unless her eyes had deceived her, Deirdre suspected 'twas neither divine intervention nor demonic mischief, but the hand of their resident outlaw that had saved Rivenloch.

As the revelers celebrated and boasted and drank to their triumph, Deirdre, bone-weary but sublimely content, sat upon a bench, casually surveying the great hall and letting Boniface tend to her injuries.

"I've already got the first lines," Boniface confided, dabbing at a scrape on her arm. He cleared his throat and sang softly, "More fierce than Ariadne when she slew the Minotaur; More bold than brave Athena when she led her men to war." His voice swelled with exaggerated zeal as he placed a mawkish hand over his heart. "More valiant than Nemesis with her avenging sword, Was Deirdre, Maid of Rivenloch, the night she—"

Deirdre seized him about the throat, choking off his song. "You sing that, lad," she warned him with a dangerous smile, "and I'll see you get no supper for a sennight." Helena might enjoy such lofty praise, but 'twas an embarrassment to Deirdre.

She released him, and Boniface scowled in disappointment and returned to cleaning her cuts.

Athena indeed. Deirdre had fought well, but 'twas not her hand that had turned the tide of battle. That honor belonged to The Shadow. Whoever he was.

She took a swallow of ale and glanced in speculation about the hall. In one corner, Miriel and Sung Li conversed with Lachanburn and two of his flame-haired sons. Deirdre studied the boys. The mysterious figure climbing on the trebuchet had appeared with the arrival of the Lachanburn clan. Mayhap one of the mischief-making lads, unbeknownst to his father, had a criminal avocation.

Deirdre smiled, then drank from her ale. If so, then far be it from her to disclose his identity, in light of the good he'd done earlier that morn.

In another corner of the hall, Helena and Colin, who was fully awake now, argued vehemently, even as she carefully tended to a cut on his cheek. Deirdre shook her head. One day, if the two of them ever ceased quarreling, mayhap she'd hear the story of their adventures in the woods.

Beside the fire, the Lord of Lachanburn and her father drank together, nodding sagely and exchanging words of comfort only old widowed warriors could understand. Perchance this battle had been a blessing. Their alliance and their renewed friendship might serve to mend the wounds both men had suffered.

And there, across the hall, by the flickering candle-light, Pagan, her magnificent Pagan, bruised and bloody and beautiful, leaned against the buttery wall, sipping from a cup of ale and merrily chatting with . . .

Lucy Campbell.

Deirdre arched a brow, muttering, "Don't even think of it."

"My lady?" Boniface looked up.

She hadn't battled fierce English soldiers away from her husband all night just to have a conniving Scots kitchen maid mince up and lay claim to him.

She banged down her cup of ale and rose from the bench.

Boniface sputtered in protest. "But my lady, I'm not f—"

"Later." She straightened to her full height and strode across the hall, her fingers resting idly on her dagger hilt and an even direr threat in her eyes.

When she reached the buttery, she swept up between the two of them with a deceptively sweet, "Pagan, my love," looping her arm possessively through his. But the glare she gave Lucy was pointed as she asked him, "Will you come upstairs with me?"

Lucy pouted, her plans foiled. Deirdre made a mental note to assign the wench to emptying chamberpots on the morrow.

But one glance at Pagan's face, and Deirdre knew he'd intended no mischief with the maid. Adoration shone in his eyes as he smiled at her, adoration and a bond that no amount of dallying with a kitchen wench could unmake.

Not that she'd allow him to test her . . .

She took the cup of ale from him and handed it off to Lucy, dismissing the thwarted maid. Then with a waggish smile, she led Pagan through the cheering crowd.

Somehow, despite the revelers who insisted on delaying them with congratulations and hearty salutes, they managed to finally climb the stairs to their bedchamber.

Deirdre paused before the door. There was one thing still nagging at her brain, one thing she had to ask. "Pagan, just before the trebuchet exploded . . . did you see . . . ?"

"What?"

"Anything?"

He grinned. "I saw you. Only you." His eyes glowed with worship as he lifted a lock of her hair and kissed it.

Lord, the lust in his eyes almost made her forget her question. She gulped, then furrowed her brow. "I meant . . . *on* the trebuchet."

His gaze drifted down to her lips, and she could almost feel his desire for a kiss. "Aye," he said dreamily.

"You did?"

"Mm."

Then she hadn't imagined it. "A dark figure?"

"I suppose so."

"'Twas The Shadow then. It had to be," she said. "But he just . . . disappeared."

Pagan shrugged, his gaze lingering on her mouth. Clearly his mind was on other things. "Your outlaw seems to prefer obscurity."

Her heart fluttered as she fought to concentrate on the issue at hand. "Then let's not disclose his secret."

"Done," he said, lifting her hand and placing a gentle kiss upon her fingers. "As long as I am steward of Rivenloch—"

"Lord of Rivenloch," she corrected. After the battle, Lord Gellir had, of his own free will, officially ceded authority to Pagan.

"As long as I am Lord," he amended, laying his hand across his heart as a pledge, "no one shall ever lay a hand upon The Shadow. Whoever he is." Then he gave her a sly grin. "As for you, however . . ."

She returned his smile. Already her blood warmed in anticipation. "To the victors," she whispered as she opened the door.

His grin widened. "Go the spoils."

And, ah, what spoils they shared . . .

Within moments, they were nestled beneath the thick furs, their naked bodies entwining in a tender embrace.

"'Twas a terrible risk you took," Pagan chided her, reaching up to caress her jaw, "coming to rescue—"

She sucked a quick breath between her teeth as he touched a tender spot, and he withdrew his hand.

"I caught an English fist," she explained with a sheepish smile. "And your rescue? 'Twas a risk worth taking." She tucked a lock of his hair behind his ear.

He winced.

She lifted a questioning brow.

"Dagger nick," he said. Then he shook his head. "Oh, wife," he sighed, "when I first saw you tearing your way into that pavilion . . ." He clasped her hand in his.

She gasped.

He let go.

"Caught an English *face*," she said, flexing her sore knuckles. Sighing, she ran a palm experimentally over his bare shoulder. "I couldn't bear to leave you there with those miserable bas—" He tried not to flinch, but she could tell it pained him.

"Mace bruise," he admitted.

"Ooh." She cringed in sympathy. "Is there anywhere you're *not* . . ."

He thought for a moment. Then one side of his mouth curved up into a wolfish grin.

Battle-weary and bone-bruised, they made love slowly, *carefully*, murmuring endearments against each other's lips. And as they merged in blissful union, Deirdre perceived that *this,* more than anything, represented the truth of their bond.

Before, she'd envisioned their marriage as a battle waged between the two of them, where one triumphed and one surrendered, a contest for control and power.

But marriage, she now knew, was not war at all. Marriage was man and wife, side by side as they were now, sharing life's adventures and battling its challenges . . . together. 'Twas an alliance forged of the finest steel, tempered in the fires of adversity, and thus blessed by unrivaled strength.

Anon their limbs and murmurs and hearts tangled in the lovely disarray of trysting, and Deirdre grew less and less capable of clear thought. Instead, she found herself enveloped in a mindless mist of sensual pleasure and sweet relief. And finally, as one, they culminated their passion, holding one another, heart to heart, crying out their soft ecstasy, just as sunlight poured over the horizon on a new day.

Pagan had never felt such contentment, gazing upon his fair Scots bride. Her adoring eyes shone as pure and clean as the cloudless sky, and the golden hue of her hair rivaled that of the sunlight spilling through the half-shuttered window. He stroked her silken locks while her breathing slowed and her eyes drifted closed.

But there was much more to her beauty than her blonde Viking tresses and clear crystal eyes and sensual curves, he realized. Deirdre possessed a beauty of spirit. She'd shown him faith and loyalty. Strength and honor and, aye, love.

He smiled. It had taken them bloody long enough to admit to that love. But now that they had, he wouldn't ever let her forget it. Forsooth, he wondered how long 'twould take for Colin and Helena to realize that they, too, belonged together.

Deirdre sighed happily, and he pressed a gentle kiss to her brow. From the moment he'd glimpsed her ripping through the English pavilion, sword in hand, come to rescue him, he'd realized she was as courageous as any of the Knights of Cameliard, and as headstrong. Now he supposed there was no getting that ale back into the keg. But he'd gladly fight beside his brave Warrior Maid any time, for together, they could conquer the world.

Amor vincit omnia.

Together, they'd fortify Rivenloch's walls.

Together they'd build an army of peerless renown.

Together, he thought with a devilish smile, they would raise the next generation of Knights of Cameliard and Warrior Maids of Rivenloch.

All at once he remembered her words on the parapets about their babe . . .

He swept the back of his scarred knuckles lightly over the soft flesh of her still flat belly. "Deirdre," he whispered.

But she was already asleep, a pleased smile curving her lips, probably dreaming even now of their brood of children and their future together.

He smiled in response. He'd let her dream and ask her later. After all, they had years of bliss ahead of them. He could wait a few more hours.

About the Author

Born in Paradise, California, Sarah McKerrigan has embraced her inner Gemini by leading an eclectic life. As a teen, she danced with the Sacramento Ballet, worked in her father's graphic arts studio, and composed music for award-winning science films. She sang arias in college, graduating with a degree in Music, then toured with an all-girl rock band on CBS Records. She once played drums for a Tom Jones video and is currently a voiceover actress with credits including "Star Wars" audio adventures, JumpStart educational CDs, Diablo and Starcraft video games, and the MTV animated series, "The Maxx." She now indulges her lifelong love of towering castles, trusty swords, and knights (and damsels) in shining armor by writing historical romances featuring kick-butt heroines. She is married to a rock star, is the proud guardian of two nerdy kids and a pug named Worf, and lives in a part of Los Angeles where nobody thinks she's weird.

She's reckless,
insatiable for adventure,
and will go where even her
warrior sister would not dare . . .

Please turn the page for a chapter
from Helena of Rivenloch's story—
the sequel to LADY DANGER,

Captive Heart

Available October 2006.

Chapter 1

The Borders
Spring 1136

Helena was drunk. Drunker than she'd ever been in her life. Which was why, no matter how she struggled against the cursed brute of a Norman oaf wrestling her down the castle stairs, she couldn't break his hold on her.

"Cease, wench!" her captor hissed, stumbling on a step in the dark. "Bloody hell, you'll get us both killed."

She would have grappled even harder then, but her right knee suddenly turned to custard. Forsooth, if the Norman hadn't caught her against his broad chest, she'd have tumbled headlong down the stone steps.

"Ballocks," he muttered against her ear, his massive arms tightening around her like a vise.

She rolled her eyes as a wave of dizziness washed over her. If only her muscles would cooperate, she thought, she could wrench loose and push the bloody bastard down the stairs.

But she was well and truly drunk.

She'd not realized just *how* drunk until she'd found herself in the bedchamber of her sister's bridegroom, Pagan Cameliard, dagger in hand, ready to kill him.

If she hadn't been drunk, if she hadn't tripped in the dark over Pagan's man, slumbering at the foot of the bed like some cursed faithful hound, she might have succeeded.

Jesu, 'twas a sobering thought. Helena, the daughter of a lord and an honorable Warrior Maid of Rivenloch, had almost slain a man quite *dis*honorably in his sleep.

'Twas not entirely her fault, she decided. She'd been up until the wee hours, commiserating over a cup, indeed *several* cups, with her older sister, Deirdre, lamenting the fate of Miriel, their poor little sister, betrothed against her will to a foreigner. And under the influence of excessive wine, they'd sworn to murder the man if he so much as laid a hand on her.

It had seemed such a noble idea at the time. But how Helena had gone from making that drunken vow to actually skulking about the bridegroom's chamber with a knife, she couldn't fathom.

Indeed, she'd been shocked to discover the dagger in her hand, though not half as shocked as Sir Colin du Lac, the brawny varlet over whom she'd tripped, the man who currently half-shoved, half-carried her down the stairs.

Once more, Helena had become a victim of her own impulsiveness. Deirdre frequently scolded Helena for her tendency to act first and ask questions later. Still, Helena's quick reflexes had saved her more than once from malefactors and murderers and men who mistook her for a helpless maid. While Deirdre might waste time weighing the consequences of punishing a man for insult, Helena wouldn't hesitate to draw her sword and mark his cheek with a scar he'd wear to his grave. Her message was clear. No one tangled with the Warrior Maids of Rivenloch.

But this time, she feared she'd gone too far.

Pagan's man grunted as he lifted her bodily over the last step. Damn the knave—despite his inferior Norman blood, he proved as strong and determined as a bull. With a final heave, he deposited her at the threshold of the great hall.

The chamber seemed cavernous by the dim glow of the banked fire, its high ceiling obscured by shadow, its walls disappearing into the darkness. By day 'twas a lofty hall decked with the tattered banners of defeated enemies. But by night the frayed pennons hung in the air like lost spirits.

A cat hissed and darted past the hearth, its elongated shadow streaking wraithlike along one wall. In the corner, a hound stirred briefly at the disturbance, chuffed once, then lowered his head to his paws again. But the other denizens of the great hall, dozens of snoring servants, huddled upon mounds of rushes and propped against the walls, slumbered on in oblivion.

Helena struggled anew, hoping to wake one of them. They were *her* servants, after all. Anyone seeing the lady of the castle being abducted by a Norman would send up an alarm.

But 'twas impossible to make a noise with the wad of the fur coverlet that was stuffed into her mouth. Even if she managed, she doubted anyone would rouse. The castle folk were exhausted from making hasty preparations for the travesty of a wedding on the morrow.

"Cease, wench," Sir Colin bit out, giving her ribs a jerk of warning, "or I'll string you up *now*."

She hiccoughed involuntarily.

Surely 'twas an idle threat on his part. This Norman couldn't hang her. Not in her own castle. Not when her only crime had been protecting her sister. Besides, she hadn't killed Pagan. She'd only *attempted* to kill him.

Still, she swallowed back the bitter taste of doubt.

These Normans *were* vassals of the King of Scotland, and the King *had* commanded that Pagan wed one of the daughters of Rivenloch. If Helena had succeeded in slaying the King's man . . . 'twould have been high treason, punishable by hanging.

The thought made her sway uneasily in Colin's arms.

"Whoa. Steady, Hel-fire." His whisper against her ear sent an unwelcome shiver along her spine. "Do not faint away on me."

She frowned and hiccoughed again. Hel-fire! He didn't know the half of it. And how dared he suggest she might faint? Warrior maids didn't faint. 'Twas only her feet tangling in the coverlet as they shuffled through the rushes in the great hall.

Then, as they lurched across the flagstones toward the cellar stairs, a different, all too familiar sensation brought her instantly alert.

Sweet Mary, she was going to be sick.

Her stomach seized once. Twice. Her eyes grew wide with horror.

*   *   *

One look at the damsel's beaded brow and ashen pallor told Colin why she'd stopped in her tracks.

"Shite!" he hissed.

Her body heaved again, and he snatched the wad of fur coverlet from her mouth, bending her forward over one arm, away from him, just in time.

Fortunately, no one was sleeping there.

Holding the back of her head while she lost her supper, he couldn't help but feel sorry for the miserable little murderess. She obviously wouldn't have tried to slay Pagan in his sleep if she hadn't been as drunk as an alewife.

And he certainly didn't intend to have the maid hung for treason, no matter what he led her to believe. Executing the sister of Pagan's bride would destroy the alliance they'd come to form with the Scots. She'd obviously done what she'd done to protect her little sister. Besides, who could drop a noose around a neck as fair and lovely as hers?

Still, he couldn't allow the maid to think she could attack a King's man without consequence.

What Colin couldn't fathom was why the three sisters of Rivenloch so loathed his commander. Sir Pagan Cameliard was a fierce warrior, aye, a man who led an unparalleled fighting force. But he was kind and gentle with ladies. Indeed, wenches often swooned over the captain's handsome countenance and fine form. Any woman with half a brain would be ecstatic to have Pagan for a husband. Colin would have expected the sisters, sequestered so long in the barren wilds of Scotland, to vie eagerly for the privilege of wedding an illustrious nobleman like Pagan Cameliard.

Instead, they quarreled over who would be burdened with him. 'Twas perplexing.

Poor Helena had ceased heaving, and now the pretty, pitiful maid quivered feebly, like a storm-tossed kitten locked out of the barn. But Colin dared not let compassion override caution. This kitten had shown him her claws. He let her up, then instantly drew his dagger, placing it alongside her neck.

"I'll spare you the gag now, damsel," he told her in a stern whisper, "but I warn you, do not cry out, or I'll be forced to slit your throat."

Of course, if she'd known Colin better, she would have laughed in his face. 'Twas true, he could kill a man without a moment's hesitation and dispatch an enemy knight with a single expert blow. He was strong and swift with a blade, and he had an uncanny instinct for discerning the point of greatest vulnerability in an opponent. But when it came to beautiful women, Colin du Lac was about as savage as an unweaned pup.

Happily, the damsel believed his threat. Or perchance she was simply too weak to fight. Either way, she staggered against him, shuddering as he wrapped the fur coverlet tighter about her shoulders and guided her forward.

Beside the entrance to the buttery was a basin and a ewer for washing. He steered her there, propping her against the wall so she wouldn't fall. Her drooping eyes still smoldered with silent rage as she glared at him, but her pathetic hiccoughs entirely ruined the effect. And fortunately, she hadn't the strength to lend action to her anger.

"Open your mouth," he murmured, using his free hand to pick up the ewer of water.

She compressed her lips, as contrary as a child. Even now, with fire in her eyes and her mouth tight with mutiny, she was truly the most exquisite creature he'd ever beheld. Her tresses cascaded over her shoulders like the tumbling froth of a highland waterfall, and her curves were more seductive than the sinuous silhouette of a wine-filled goblet.

She eyed him doubtfully, as if she suspected he might use the water to drown her on the spot.

He supposed she had a right to doubt him. Only moments ago, in Pagan's chamber, he'd threatened to, what was it? Take her where no one could hear her scream and break her of her wild ways at the crack of a whip? He winced, recalling his rash words.

"Listen," he confided, lowering the ewer. "I said I wouldn't punish you until the marriage is accomplished. I'm a man of my word. As long as you don't force my hand, I'll do you no harm this eve."

Slowly, reluctantly, she parted her lips. He carefully poured a small amount of water into her mouth. As she swished the liquid around, he got the distinct impression she longed to spew it back into his face. But with his blade still at her throat, she didn't dare. Leaning forward, she spit into the rushes.

"Good. Come."

Yesterday, Pagan's betrothed had given them a tour of the Scots castle that would be their new home. Rivenloch was an impressive holding, probably magnificent in its day, a little worn, but reparable. The outer wall enclosed an enormous garden, an orchard, stables, kennels, mews, and a dovecot. A small stone chapel sat in the midst of the courtyard, and a dozen or more workshops slouched against the inner walls. A grand tiltyard and practice field stood at the far end of the property, and the imposing square keep at the heart of the holding was comprised of the great hall, numerous bedchambers, garderobes, a buttery, a pantry, and several cellars. 'Twas to one of the storage rooms beneath the keep that he now conveyed his captive.

Placing Helena before him, he descended the rough stone steps by the light of a candle set in the stairwell's sconce. Below them, small creatures scuttled about in the dark on their midnight rounds. Colin felt a brief twinge of remorse, wondering if the cellars were infested with mice, if 'twas cruel to lock Helena in there, if she was afraid of the creatures. Just as quickly, he decided that a knife-wielding wench prowling about in a man's chamber, prepared to stab him in his sleep, was likely afraid of very little.

They'd almost reached the bottom of the stairs when the damsel made a faint moan and, as if her bones had melted away, abruptly withered in his arms.

Knocked off balance by the sudden weight against his chest, he slammed into the stone wall with one shoulder, cinching his arm around her waist so she wouldn't fall. To prevent a nasty accident, he cast his knife away, and it clattered down the steps.

Then she slumped forward, and he was pulled along with her. Only by sheer strength was he able to keep them from pitching headlong onto the cold, hard flagstones below. Even so, as he struggled down the last few steps, the fur coverlet snagged on his heel and slipped sideways on her body. He lost his grip upon her waist and made another desperate grab for her as her knees buckled.

His hand closed on something soft and yielding as he

slid off the last step and finally found his footing at the bottom of the stairs.

Colin had fondled enough breasts to recognize the soft flesh pressed sweetly against his palm. But he dared not let go for fear she'd drop to the ground.

In the next instant, she roused again, drawing in a huge gasp of outrage, and Colin knew he was in trouble. Luckily, since he'd received his share of slaps for much of that past fondling, he was prepared.

As her arm came around, not with a chiding open palm, but a fist of potent fury, he released her and ducked back out of range. Her swing was so forceful that when it swished through empty air, it spun her halfway around.

"Holy . . ." he breathed. Had the maid not been drunk, the punch would have certainly flattened him.

"Y' son of a . . ." she slurred. She blinked, trying to focus on him, her fists clenched in front of her as she planned her next strike. "Get yer hands off me. I'll kick yer bloody Norm'n arse. Swear I will. S-"

Her hands began to droop, and her eyes dimmed as she swayed left, then right, staggering back a step. Then whatever fight she had left in her fizzled out like the last wheezing draw on a wineskin. He rushed up, catching her just before she collapsed.

Cradled against his flank, all the fury and fight gone out of her, she looked less like a warrior maid and more like the guileless maid he'd first spied bathing in Rivenloch's pond, the delectable Siren with sun-kissed skin and riotous tawny hair, the woman who'd splashed seductively through his dreams all night.

Had it been only yesterday? So much had transpired in the last few weeks.

A fortnight ago, Sir Pagan had received orders from King David of Scotland to venture north to Rivenloch to claim one of Lord Gellir's daughters. At the time, the King's purpose had been a mystery. But now 'twas clear what he intended.

King Henry's death had left England in turmoil, with Stephen and Matilda grappling for control of the throne. That turmoil had fomented lawlessness along the Borders, where land-hungry English barons felt at liberty to seize unguarded Scots castles.

King David had granted Pagan a bride and thus the stewardship of Rivenloch in the hopes of guarding the valuable keep against English marauders.

Despite the King's sanction, Pagan had proceeded with caution. He'd traveled with Colin in advance of his knights to ascertain the demeanor of the Rivenloch clan. The Normans might be allies of the Scots, but he doubted they'd receive a hearty reception if they arrived in full force, like a conquering army, to claim the lord's daughter.

As it turned out, he was right to be wary. Their reception, at least by the daughters, had been far less than hearty. But by God's grace, by midday on the morrow, after the alliance was sealed by marriage, peace would reign. And the Scots, once they were made merry with drink and celebration, would surely welcome the full complement of the Knights of Cameliard to Rivenloch.

Helena gave a snort in her sleep, and Colin smiled ruefully down at her. *She'd* offer him no word of welcome. Indeed, she'd likely prefer to slit his throat.

He bent to slip one forearm behind her knees and hefted her easily into his arms.

One of the small storerooms looked seldom used. It held little more than broken furnishings and tools, piles of rags, and various empty containers. It had a bolt on the outside and a narrow space under the door for air, which meant it had likely been employed at one time for just this purpose, as a gaol of sorts. Indeed, Ætwas an ideal place to store a wayward wench for the night.

He spread the fur coverlet atop an improvised pallet of rags to make a bed for her. She might be an assassin, but she was also a woman. She deserved at least a small measure of comfort.

After he tucked the coverlet about her shoulders, he couldn't resist combing back a stray tendril of her lush golden-brown hair to place a smug kiss upon her forehead. "Sleep well, little Hel-hound."

Taking his post as guard, he closed and bolted the door behind him, then sat back against it, crossing his arms over his chest and closing his eyes. Perchance he could steal one last hour of sleep before morn.

If all went well, by afternoon the deed would be done, and the rest of the Cameliard company would arrive. Once Pagan was decisively wed, 'twould be safe to release Helena.

He marveled again over the curious Scots maid. She was unlike any woman he'd ever met—bold and cocksure, yet undeniably feminine. At supper, she'd boasted of being an expert swordswoman, a claim none of her fellow Scots had disputed. And she'd regaled him with a tale of the local outlaw, trying to shock him with gruesome details that would have unnerved a lesser woman. She'd exhibited the most unbridled temper when her father announced Miriel's marriage, cursing and slamming her fist on the table, her outburst checked only by the chiding of her older sister. And her appetite . . . He chuckled as he remembered watching her smack the grease from her fingers. The damsel had eaten enough to satisfy two grown men.

And yet she inhabited the most womanly form. His loins swelled with the memory of her naked in the pond—the flicker of her curved buttocks as she dove under the waves, the gentle bounce of her full breasts as she splashed her sisters, her sleek thighs, narrow waist, flashing teeth, the carefree toss of her sun-streaked hair as she cavorted in the water like a playful colt . . .

He sighed. There was no use getting his trews in a wad over a damsel who currently slumbered in drunken oblivion on the other side of the door.

Still, he couldn't stop thinking about her. Helena was unique. Intriguing. Vibrant. He'd never met a woman so headstrong, so untamed. As fresh and wild as Scotland itself. And as unpredictable.

Indeed, 'twas fortunate Pagan had chosen quiet, sweet, docile Miriel for a bride, and not Helena. *This* wench would have been a handful.

More than a handful, he considered with a wicked grin, recalling the accidental caress he'd enjoyed moments ago.

Earlier, when he'd foiled her assassination plans, imprisoned her in his arms, and, in the flush of anger, threatened to break her, she'd skewered him with a green glare as raging hot as an iron poker. But she'd been besotted and desperate and not in her right mind.

By the time she awoke on the morrow and recognized what she'd done in a drunken furor, she'd likely blush with shame and weep with regret. And when, by the light of day, she realized the mercy this Norman had shown her—his patience, his kindness, his compassion—she might feel more agreeable to his advances. Indeed, he decided, his mouth curving up in a contented smile as he drifted off to sleep, mayhap then she'd *welcome* his caress.

Sugar, spice and everything nice
Doesn't make a perfect romance heroine.
Where's the spirit, the sass, the fire?
There's a new kind of lady on the block
and she's a live wire.

Now join **Annie Solomon**
(author of BLACKOUT)
and **Sarah McKerrigan**
(author of LADY OF DANGER)
as they discuss what makes this modern heroine tick.

Sarah: I love the new trend in romance toward tough-as-nails heroines. What do you think is their appeal?

Annie: In real life, women are vulnerable. Many of us earn less, work harder in the home, and are more fearful for our safety than men. So a woman who can handle herself in any situation is fascinating. In my newest romantic suspense, BLACKOUT, Margo can't remember the last month of her life. Everyone close to her has vanished. But though she doesn't know why, she can go *mano a mano* with anyone. I mean, no one is going to sneak up on this woman in a blind alley at midnight. Myself, I wouldn't go near a blind alley at midnight. But if I can't do it—hey, my heroine can do it for me. How about you? How does your heroine fulfill your fantasies?

Sarah: Deirdre in LADY DANGER is a kick-ass Scots warrior wench, a damsel in shining armor. She'll do anything to protect her lands and family, whether it's crossing swords with an outlaw or marrying a fierce Norman warrior to save her sister. I think sharing in the adventures of a smart-talking, sword-wielding heroine is great fun when done from the safety of a less action-packed world. At least *my* world is less action-packed. What about yours? Are you a kung fu expert?

Annie: Only in my dreams. Which is probably why I don't sleep much. But I could never do what Margo does. I go weak-kneed when someone looks at me the wrong way. How about you? Do you have anything in common with your heroine?

Sarah: I can hold my own in a battle of wits, but Deirdre has me beat when it comes to physical combat. She never backs down from a threat, even when it's a war-seasoned husband intent on taming her. But her self-confidence is seductive, and Pagan finds himself swept away by his bride's courageous spirit. Those are the stories I find most satisfying, where the hero and heroine are evenly matched. I'm also a huge fan of rollicking swordfights a la *The Three Musketeers*, *Pirates of the Caribbean*, and *Lord of the Rings*, and my favorite swordswomen on film are Marian in *Robin Hood*, Sorsha in *Willow*, and Callista in *Xena*. What inspires *you*?

Annie: I've always been drawn to stories with lots of action, high stakes, and vibrant characters. Like Zoe in the movie *Serenity* and Aeryn in the TV show *Farscape*. Of course, ya gotta have a good love story, too, which is why I like strong heroes. In BLACKOUT, Jake is hunting a killer. He isn't sure if Margo's an assassin or a pawn, but he knows how to get under her skin. Which is a real pain, and also painfully necessary. Especially if, like Margo, you don't know who you are, what you've done, or why you can't remember. What about your hero? What's he like?

Sarah: Pagan's a pretty cocky warrior. He's not intimidated by Deirdre's strength. But in this battle of wills, he has to use brains, not brawn. And Deirdre has to learn to fight a new kind of enemy, one who turns her resistance into desire. Ultimately Pagan recognizes and claims the soft heart beneath her tough exterior, and Deirdre learns that love is not a matter of conquering and being conquered, but of mutual triumph and mutual surrender. And that's what romance is all about, isn't it? A man, a woman, some rousing swordplay, and a happy ending.

Annie: Well, I like a happy ending myself. But things in Margo's world are rarely black and white. Uncovering who you really are and what you've done can be a difficult, dangerous journey. And when it's over, you may not like what you've found. So happy ending? Of course. I don't believe in anything else. But for Margo, it's not the hearts and flowers kind.

Annie and Sarah would love to hear what you think of kick-ass heroines. Drop them a line at their Web sites: Annie at www.anniesolomon.com and Sarah at www.sarahmckerrigan.com

*Want to know more about romances at
Warner Books and Warner Forever?
Get the scoop online!*

WARNER'S ROMANCE HOMEPAGE

Visit us at www.warnerforever.com for all the
latest news, reviews, and chapter excerpts!

NEW AND UPCOMING TITLES

Each month we feature our new titles
and reader favorites.

CONTESTS AND GIVEAWAYS

We give away galleys, autographed copies,
and all kinds of fun stuff.

AUTHOR INFO

You'll find bios, articles, and links to personal
Web sites for all your favorite authors—and
so much more!

THE BUZZ

Sign up for our monthly romance newsletter,
and be the first to read all about it!